GUARDING GRACE

ERIN SWANN

This book is a work of fiction. The names, characters, businesses, and events portrayed in this book are fictitious. Any similarity to real persons, living or dead, businesses, or events is coincidental and not intended by the author.

Copyright © 2025 by Swann Publications

All rights reserved.

No part of this book may be reproduced, stored in a retrieval system, or transmitted in any form or by any means, electronic, mechanical, photocopying, recording, or otherwise, without the express written permission of the publisher. Reasonable portions may be quoted for review purposes.

The author acknowledges the trademarked status and trademark owners of various products referenced in this work of fiction, which have been used without permission. The publication/use of these trademarks is not authorized, associated with, or sponsored by the trademark owners.

ISBN: 9798284632925

Edited by Jessica Royer Ocken

Proofreaders: Jen Boles, Victoria Straw, Your Fairy Proofmother

The following story is intended for mature readers. It contains mature themes, strong language, and sexual situations. All characters are 18+ years of age, and all sexual acts are consensual.

CHAPTER 1

GRACE

ON THE FAR SIDE OF THE ROOM, TERRY GOODWIN STEPPED AWAY FROM THE group he was talking with, looked my way, and nodded toward the corner again. It was unfair that a man with such a black personality looked so gorgeous in a tux.

Rolling my eyes, I gave him another subtle headshake and looked away. This distance was perfect for me. I wouldn't get another whiff of the sexy cologne he'd worn tonight.

Where did that thought come from?

Terry's last name was laughable because, as far as I was concerned, there was nothing good about that Goodwin. His sister, Deb, however, was a sweet friend. It was a shame she couldn't make it because her flight back from London had been canceled.

As a reminder of Terry's nature, I had his words to me when I'd arrived at this shindig. They'd been cutting as always. *"Maybe I'll call you when I need my sock drawer organized."* How was it possible he and Deb came from the same gene pool?

Ugh. He knew I'd built SpaceMasters, the premier organizational design firm in town. We provided elegant solutions for organizing everything from home closets to business spaces. Yet he still took every opportunity to cut me down.

It hurt to have my baby, the project I'd poured blood, sweat, and tears into, belittled at every turn by Terry the Tyrant. It raised my blood pressure every time I thought about it.

Then he'd added, *"Nice claws, Kitty."*

He'd called me Kitty instead of Hellcat, Wildcat or worse, but only because we were in polite company. I couldn't remember the last time he'd said something nice to me—not that it mattered.

A few minutes later, when I looked back in Terry's direction, Janice, one of Serena's coworkers at the EPA, was chatting him up. As I watched, Janice slipped him her card and stroked her fingers down his chest. *Terry had no idea who he was dealing with.*

Janice was a tall blonde, with incredible boobs and a waist I'd die for, on the hunt for her next husband and not bashful about it. According to Serena, Janice figured she'd need to sleep with thirty-four men to find the right one. It was some math she'd read about that nobody understood. Serena noticed the interaction as well. "It looks like somebody is getting lucky tonight."

I turned away. "She better be up to date on vaccinations."

"He's not like that," she countered.

I used to wonder what it would be like to be a, Janice, a girl with incredible boobs, who got her pick of the men around. It no longer mattered, now that I had zero time for a man. But if I did, I'd be smart enough to avoid someone with as rotten a disposition as Terry, even if he was the most intensely male man in the vicinity. Such a waste of hotness.

We were at Cardinelli's, which offered the best Italian food in town by my estimation. My best friend, Serena Benson, had arranged this party to publicly thank the team at Hawk Security that had rescued her from a fate worse than death *and* uncovered a hazardous-chemical-dumping scheme that threatened our local drinking water.

Lucas Hawk himself was here, looking as deadly as ever. My brother had once told me that Lucas could kill a man with a single finger, and damn if he didn't look scary, even in a suit.

Hanging around Serena, I'd met all the Hawk team.

After dinner, Serena had given a gracious speech thanking the Hawk team, and she'd even brought the director of the EPA himself to award medals to all of them, which included Terry.

I'd even clapped for the Tyrant.

Thinking of the hell Serena had been through reminded me of the last time Terry had been civil to me—a few months ago at Disneyland, when Serena had needed my help. I'd joined her and pretended to be Terry's girlfriend for an outing to the park. It was all a show so Terry could be an inconspicuous part of her security team. She'd been hunted by a pair of madmen intent on sex-trafficking her.

Disneyland had been a surprisingly pleasant day with Terry. I'd seen a different side of him than I'd witnessed before. For a day, I'd even come to think of him as likable. No, more than that—desirable even. But then the day ended and he reverted to form, becoming the nemesis I was used to.

Luckily, tonight Serena had seated me at a different table than Terry. Now that we were in the stand-and-chat portion of the evening, I only had to keep my distance for maybe another half hour.

"I'm really glad you came," Serena told me, smiling as she slid an arm behind her fiancé, Duke Hawk. Until recently he'd been her hot former SEAL bodyguard, and he remained a founding member of Hawk Security.

"I wouldn't miss my best friend's big night," I assured her.

Serena cocked a brow, and I inwardly cringed, afraid I'd given up the surprise Duke had arranged for her.

"You look stunning this evening," Duke said before Serena could ask any questions.

"It's thanks to your lovely fiancée." I smoothed my hands down the exquisite Valentino gown. "She loaned me this dress."

Winston Evers, a former FBI Special Agent and now a member of Hawk Security, wandered over, and the conversation thankfully pivoted. When I looked back, Terry scowled at me and tried his come-hither head nod again. I settled for sticking my tongue out at him behind a raised hand. Not as classy as I should be at an event like this, but Terry deserved it after all the aggravation he'd given me over the years.

Turning, I noticed Nick Butcher, another of Serena's coworkers, eyeing me. I pulled in a deep breath, which made my boobs almost pop out of this tight dress. Serena saw him as well and whispered, "You could get lucky too."

"I don't have time for a man." That had been my life ever since starting my company, and it needed to stay that way until the company was on a more solid footing.

"He's a fun guy."

"Pass."

"Do you have time to join us after?" Serena asked. "The Hawk guys are going over to Tito's to shoot some pool."

I liked Tito's, and I'd played darts there often, but I shook my head. "Sorry, I have an early morning tomorrow." It wasn't a lie, but mostly I didn't want to chance that Terry might be there. Better to end things on a high note.

Despite Terry's presence, I was grateful to be here this evening, and I knew how lucky I was to have my best friend still alive. Besides a car-bomb attack, a sex trafficker had kidnapped Serena—twice. But she'd survived the ordeal and had come out the other side to get to her happy place, engaged to a wonderful man.

I shivered, thinking about how terrifying those days must have been for her, then couldn't help sighing over how lucky she was to have found a man as wonderful as Duke. I'd never had that kind of luck in my dating life.

I excused myself to use the ladies' room. When I returned, Nick Butcher had joined the group of Hawk brothers, Duke, Lucas, and Jordy. Unfortunately, Terry was also with them. *So much for talking to Nick.*

Checking my watch, I decided it was too early to bug out and go home to work on the Sanderson design that I needed to review, so I searched out Serena.

She was now talking with some EPA folks and Winston, another Hawk employee.

On the way to her, my phone vibrated in my clutch. I pulled the device out but clicked the screen off after seeing the name—*Tyrant*, the moniker I'd given Terry years ago. It vibrated in my hand again, and I gave in, moving to the messaging app.

> TYRANT: I need to talk to you.
> TYRANT: It's important

I had no problem crafting a reply.

> ME: No way

"You know," said Remy Laurent, Serena's new boss at the EPA, "wedding planning takes a long time."

He should know. He was planning his own wedding.

"Yeah," Serena said wearily.

"Have you decided on a venue?" Jacques, Remy's fiancé, asked.

Serena shook her head. "Not yet."

Winston looked disinterested, as most guys did when a discussion turned to wedding planning.

"And you need a dress," Remy added. "That can take a while. And your maid of honor and bridesmaids. And flowers, and—"

Serena held up a hand. "We have to set a date first."

Remy looked heartbroken that this topic was closed. He and Jacques shared a look.

I turned away, and half a minute later, my phone vibrated again.

Ready to kill Terry for the constant interruptions, I answered hurriedly, "I don't have time for you."

Only the creepy voice wasn't Terry's.

"We have your cousin Elliot. Do exactly as I say, or he dies."

My blood froze as I sought privacy behind a tall ficus tree. "Please don't hurt him." I kept my voice low, trying not to cry.

"You will bring your phone and ATM card. Meet me in the parking lot of the Starbucks on Langley. Come alone. Do you understand?"

I shivered. Wasn't kidnapping for ransom supposed to happen to rich people? "I understand, but—"

"Be there," the creepy voice demanded.

"Just don't hurt him."

I didn't have big bucks, and obviously, they didn't think Eliot was worth much. My withdrawal limit was twenty-five hundred, and when it ticked over past midnight, I guessed they could double that.

"Come alone. Bring anyone, tell anyone, or call the cops, and we'll know. Then Elliot dies."

I shivered. "Langley and where? I don't know all the Starbucks."

"Look it up. There's only one."

"But that's a long way. I can't make it in a half hour."

The line was silent.

"Hello?... Hello?"

I checked the screen. *Unknown number*. And the call was over.

Serena appeared, her face concerned as she reached for my shoulder. "What's going on?"

I held back the tears. "Nothing." I couldn't tell her or anyone.

"Who was that?" She blocked my way when I tried to leave.

"You have to let me go," I implored her.

"Grace, what's wrong? Talk to me."

I sniffled. "They have Elliot."

"Who's Elliot?"

I'd made a big mistake even mentioning his name. "I need to go."

"Who's Elliot?" she repeated.

"Uh..." I struggled for anything that wasn't the truth. "My newest cat, Elliot Ness. I have to go."

"Did he get loose or something?"

Seeing an opening, I nodded. "I've gotta go."

The clock was ticking down on my half hour.

"Do you need help?"

"No, no. You stay and enjoy yourself."

With that, I escaped the room.

∼

TERRY

I ANSWERED THE PHONE. "WHAT NOW?"

"*Do you know where Grace is?*"

Elliot Boyle, her loser cousin, had called to ask me this question a half hour ago.

It paid to read between the lines in this career, and my assessment had been that he needed Grace's help for something. This was not the first time.

When I'd told him she was in the same room as I was—at an awards function, he'd promptly hung up—like the little snot he was.

I'd motioned for her to come over and talk, but she'd only stuck her tongue out in response. Since I had no tolerance tonight for any more of Grace's snarky attitude, I'd texted her from across the room, asking for a moment of her time. I'd been polite about it.

She hadn't responded in kind, and that had ended my need to follow up on Elliot's call. He could damned well call her himself.

Sure, she looked good from a distance—bright-red hair and curves for miles, with pale-blue eyes that pulled you in if you got close. I had to admit, she was a total smokeshow. Problem was, whenever I got close enough to talk to her, she was about as cuddly as a porcupine.

Her prickly attitude helped keep my mind off those curves. After all, I'd promised my best friend, her brother Pete, I'd take care of her. She'd be perfect for some guy, so long as that guy wasn't me. Our code didn't allow that.

Nope, not going there.

I opened my phone and read the message again—the one that had led to the oddest phone call before this party.

> CAROL HAWK: Please call me. I need to talk to you privately.

Why the hell did my boss's mother want to talk to me? No, the message said *need* to talk to me, which only made it weirder.

I'd squeezed in the return phone call shortly before this dinner, and it had been an odd exchange. All she'd said was, "*Perhaps later, dear. I'm tied up at the moment."* She had never referred to me as *dear* before. Something was up, and it required secrecy.

Scanning the room again, I found her standing with my boss, Lucas, and her husband, the family patriarch, Henry Hawk.

I tried to catch her eye, but the one time I did, she pretended she hadn't seen me. Message received: *not here, not now*. My curiosity would have to wait.

Glancing to the side, I noticed there were still a few unclaimed pieces of chocolate cheesecake on the dessert tray near me. One large piece in particular called my name. So, being the concerned citizen that I was, I quickly liberated that piece from the table in order to minimize the garbage footprint of this party.

"I saw that," Winston said as he cruised up and snagged one as well. "Good idea. These shouldn't go to waste."

We munched a moment, but then Winston wandered away when a striking redhead caught his eye. Janice, who'd given up on me, was currently latched onto Zane.

The evening had been excellent, as these things went, with good food and a comfortable setting. When I'd been with LAPD SWAT, awards had usually been given out while we sat on folding chairs in the sun, roasting in our dress uniforms and listening to some self-important politician drone on for an hour about nothing of any interest to us cops.

Tonight was much better, but our real reward was knowing we'd saved our buddy's girl, Serena, from the certainty of being sex trafficked by those Spinelli asswipes. The world was safer now that both Spinelli brothers were locked away in San Quentin.

My phone rang again with Elliot's name on the screen. "What, Elliot?" I answered.

"You gotta watch out for Grace," he said. "You gotta protect her. She's in a shit ton of trouble."

I scanned the room for Grace but came up empty. "What's going on?"

"Man, they're after her. These guys don't fuckin' mess around."
"Slow down, Elliot. Who?"
"I don't suck until you pay up," a woman said in the background.
"Keep her safe," Elliot said.
"Who's after her?"
"No money, no action," the annoyed woman said.
"Fuck, I gotta go."
"Shit, Elliot, tell me who is after her."
The line went silent. The little snot was too busy getting a blow job.

He'd hung up without telling me what I needed to know. God, I hated that guy.

I scanned from the far left to the right—still no Grace in sight. Elliot hung out with the wrong crowd and wasn't the sharpest tool in the shed, but running with them had probably tuned his survival instinct. The fear in his voice was not a good sign.

It took me only seconds to run to my Hawk Security team—the three Hawk brothers, Lucas, Jordy, and Duke, as well as Winston and Zane March, our latest addition. "Have you seen Grace?" I panted.

"Which one? Kitty, Wildcat, Bobcat, or Cat Woman?" Duke joked.

I shook my head. I didn't have time for this shit. "Fuck, I've gotta find her."

Lucas grabbed my arm. "What's wrong?"

"I just got a call saying she's in danger."

Lucas's eyes narrowed. "In danger from whom?"

I shrugged. "No idea. First her cousin called asking if I knew where she was, and then he called back and told me to look out for her because she was in danger. The little twerp was scared shitless."

"Last I saw, she was talking with Serena," Zane said, pointing to the far side of the room.

I reached Serena quickly. "Where's Grace?"

Serena startled at my shout. "She got a call. She seemed rattled and took off to meet somebody who had her cat, Elliot. It didn't make any sense."

"When?"

"Just now. What's going on?"

I sprinted for the door.

Grace didn't have a cat named Elliot. The calls instantly clicked. Somebody claiming to have Elliot had lured her out to a meeting. I had to get to her first. Grace excelled at being a royal pain in my ass, but I'd promised Pete I'd take care of her. He hadn't returned from his deployment. I could not fucking fail on that promise.

Outside, I looked both ways but didn't see her. I accosted the closest of the two valets. "I'm looking for a girl who just came out—green dress, bright-red hair. Which way did she go?"

He pulled an earbud out of his ear and held out his hand. "Ticket?"

I repeated myself.

The guy shrugged. "No idea."

I grabbed him by the lapels, and his eyes went wide. "Time to concentrate." I checked his nametag. "Will."

CHAPTER 2

Grace

I hadn't wanted to spend the money for the valet, and the only available parking tonight had been on side streets, so I'd turned left out of the restaurant when I exited and hurried toward my car. I moved as fast as I could in these heels, retrieving my car keys from my purse as I went.

What kind of idiot would kidnap my cousin Elliot? Nobody cared whether he lived or died except me. Life was certainly cheap to these people. If they knew anything about me, they would have asked for the necklace Mom gave me. It was worth more than I had in my bank account.

The lighting and traffic had both dimmed considerably when I turned the corner onto the side street where I'd parked. I got the prickle at the back of my neck that any woman walking alone in the dark sometimes got.

Halfway down the block, a shadow detached from a building ahead of me. On any other night, I would have turned around and returned to the bright lights behind me, but Elliot needed me. I crossed to the other side of the street and palmed my key between my fingers as a weapon like Terry had taught me years ago.

Terry was a former SWAT officer with the LAPD, and as terrible as his personality was, he knew a shitload more than I did about self-defense.

Passing between the parked cars on the opposite side of the street, I lost sight of the guy. I assumed it was a man. Dread crept up my spine as I hurried along.

Then he came out from between two cars. "There you are."

Heart pounding, I turned and ran.

A few steps later, he grabbed my hair and yanked.

I cried out. *Fuck, that hurt.* My scalp burned from the pain.

Beefy arms wound around me and lifted me off the ground.

"Where is fucking Spider?"

The brute slammed me against a car and spun me, pinning my arms. His breath was heavy with garlic.

Spider was Elliot's nickname among the dangerous crowd he hung out with on account of the gold chain he wore with a stupid spider pendant.

A second skinny dude came out of the shadows. "Yeah, where is he?"

"I don't know."

Why ask about Elliot? Restrained like this, I couldn't bring my hand up to slash him like I'd been taught.

Skinny Dude yanked my purse away and rummaged through it.

"I got the phone. We can find him."

"Maybe." The big one scowled, shaking me. "Where is he hiding?"

"I told you, I don't know." I spat at him.

He wiped his cheek. "Not good enough." The big guy punched me in the face.

My head snapped back against the car window. Pain flashed across my cheek, and my vision blurred. I brought up the hand he'd released and slashed him across the face with my key.

He howled but didn't release his grip.

"Bitch."

He pulled back to hit me again.

My eyes had partially acclimated to the dim light. When his grip loosened, I tried to knee him, but my dress was too tight.

The brute retaliated with another punch.

My nose erupted in pain, and I tasted blood. *My God, why does he have to hit so hard?*

"Yeah, fuck her up good," Skinny Dude urged.

"Tell us where Spider—" The brute's question was cut short when a fist from nowhere landed on the side of his head.

"Get off her," Terry roared.

The big man stumbled to the side, releasing me, then regained his footing.

"Grace?"

"I'm okay," I lied. Why did he, of all people, have to see me like this?

Everything depended on me getting out of here in time to meet with the kidnapper.

"Who the fuck are you?" Skinny Dude yelled as he pulled a knife.

My heart stopped. The rules of the party tonight had been that the Hawk Security people would come unarmed, and this looked bad.

The big guy shook off the effect of Terry's punch and straightened. Things went from bad to worse when he pulled a knife as well and advanced.

"You guys don't want to do this," Terry warned.

The corny movie line got a laugh from Skinny Dude. "Fuck off. She's going to tell us where Spider is."

The brute kept coming. "We're going to fuck you up so—" He didn't have time to finish his threat before Terry launched a series of hits and kicks that made Jackie Chan in a karate movie seem like slow motion.

His knife hit the ground, and Terry kicked it under a car.

The brute crumpled, wheezing after a final throat punch from Terry.

Skinny Dude lunged.

Terry sidestepped and threw him against the wall. My phone clattered to the ground.

The guy bounced off the bricks, turned, and ran right into Terry's fist. His head snapped back with the sickening sound of crunching cartilage. He ended up motionless on the sidewalk.

Running footsteps approached. "Terry?" The voice was Zane's.

"Here," Terry answered, picking up Skinny Dude's knife.

Zane ran up. "What the fuck?"

"These two attacked Grace."

"I have to go," I announced.

Time was slipping away, and I had to meet the kidnapper.

Terry ignored me. "Call Constance—I think she just left—and take these two to our guest rooms at Hawk." Constance was the ex-Secret Service woman working at Hawk.

I'd been inside their building and seen the holding cells they referred to as *guest accommodations*. I moved away from the car.

Terry held up a hand to block my path. "Grace got hit in the head. I'll take her to get checked out."

Zane flipped on his phone's flashlight. "Who are they?"

I shouldn't have looked.

Skinny Dude was bleeding—a lot.

I got a sick feeling as the world went from dim to black.

∼

TERRY

. . .

I watched Grace's face go ashen and heard the long sigh but realized too late what was happening.

She went limp, fell to the ground beside the car, and hit her head before I could reach her.

"Fuckers," Zane spat.

Gently, I lifted Grace, cradling her head. "I've got to get her to the hospital."

"Go," Zane ordered as he picked up her cell phone. "Take this. I got these two dirtbags."

With her phone in my pocket, I took off for the restaurant at a jog, supporting Grace's limp body as best I could.

The valets gawked at me as I ran past.

"Call 9-1-1," I yelled as I made it back to the party. "Grace was attacked."

Gasps and a dozen questions rang out.

Lucas and Serena were the first to reach me. Duke was on the phone.

I laid Grace down on the settee along the wall, feet propped up. She had a bloody nose, but thankfully no cuts from the knives the guys had. "She got jumped by two goons on the way to her car."

Lucas's hands clenched into fists. "Are they still breathing?" Men abusing women was a hot-button issue with him. Once, he'd delayed a mission for two hours to visit a drug kingpin running a rape house. The bastard and four of his lieutenants had ended up buried under a pile of rubble.

"Barely. They hit Grace and came at me with a knife." I shrugged. "I had to incapacitate with extreme prejudice. Zane has them now. He's calling Constance for transport to guest accommodations."

Serena stroked Grace's hair. "Why would anyone beat her unconscious?"

"She fainted, and I didn't reach her in time. She hit her head on the pavement."

"Too much blood?" Serena guessed.

I nodded. "Theirs, not hers."

Duke got off the phone and urged the crowd to give us some room. "They're on the way."

Lucas smiled and pulled out his phone. "Zane, don't bother cleaning up our guests. I'll be over to see them shortly." Lucas's tone was scary cold. Those two guys were going to wish they hadn't gotten up today.

Grace's eyes blinked open, a bit unfocused. "What—"

"You fainted," Serena told her. "You haven't kept up your training, have you?"

She shook her head. "I forgot to tense… So much blood."

Serena and I had both seen this fainting before, most recently, when Grace cut her finger in the kitchen.

When she tried to sit up, I forced her shoulder down. "Stay still for a little longer."

"I have to get to—"

I sat on the edge of the settee next to her. "You have to go to the hospital for a CAT scan. You hit your head pretty hard."

"I have to go meet—"

"No. You're going for a scan, and that's final."

She crooked her finger, urging me closer. "They took Elliot," she whispered. "They said to meet them with my ATM card."

"No, they don't have Elliot. I just talked to him. He told me somebody was after you."

Her brow furrowed.

"Don't you see? That was a ruse to get you outside."

"Those guys wanted to know where Elliot was."

Just then, the paramedics rushed in.

I stood and waved them over. "Vasovagal syncope episode. She fell and hit her head hard. She needs a CAT scan."

The paramedic cast me aside with barely a look. "We've got it from here."

Lucas pulled me over to join the Hawk group while Serena stayed with Grace. "What's going on?"

I filled them in about the calls from Grace's cousin, the call Grace had gotten from some unknown party claiming to have Elliot, and that the guys on the street had demanded to know where her useless cousin was.

Duke shook his head. "ATM card? What a joke. Nobody demands a ransom small enough that you can get it out of an ATM."

"Her cousin has to be who they're after, and they only wanted her to get leverage over him," Jordy guessed.

I nodded. It made sense.

"If that's the case, she's in danger until we figure out who's after this Elliot character and get them to understand that Grace is under Hawk protection and is not to be threatened." Lucas patted me on the shoulder. "We've got your back on this. What's his last name?"

"Boyle. Elliot Boyle."

Lucas turned to his brother. "Jordy—"

"A full workup pronto, I know," our resident hacker, make that tech specialist, replied. He was also a damned excellent investigator, following faint trails through the digital landscape. "Who's got her phone? I'll copy it and try to trace where that call came from."

I nodded and pulled her phone from my pocket. "Get it back to me at the hospital."

I would do everything I could to help Grace, but having the Hawk Security team in on it was a huge boost. Our firm had a serious reputation, and even vicious bad guys like the Russians knew not to mess with us. Men who underestimated Lucas Hawk and this outfit quickly regretted it.

The paramedics got a complaining Grace strapped on the gurney and rolled her out. I followed. "Which hospital are we going to?"

"UCLA," one of them answered.

I hurried to the passenger side of the ambulance and climbed into the front seat. Better to assume I could ride along than ask permission.

After the back door slammed shut, the paramedic I'd spoken to climbed up into the driver's seat. "Are you family?" he asked.

"No."

"Then out." He pointed at the door.

"I'm her bodyguard. You take her, you take me."

"I don't know—"

"LAPD orders. Take it up with Lieutenant Wellbourne if you want."

Marcus Wellbourne was our ace in the hole with the LAPD. Lucas had rescued his wife from a kidnapper and dispatched the asshole in the process.

"Let's just go," came from the paramedic in back.

The driver shrugged and started the engine.

CHAPTER 3

GRACE

HOSPITALS WERE THE WORST. I CRANKED UP THE BACK OF THE BED WHILE I waited for the ER doctor to return with my CT results. They would be negative. I knew because I'd been through this before, and I felt fine. Okay, not *fine*, but relatively good, considering I'd been attacked on the street and beaten up.

"You've done your duty," I told Terry over the incessant beeping of the heart monitor attached to my chest.

The tyrant stood at the foot of my bed in the little curtained-off section of the emergency room, looking all broody.

"I'll be fine," I assured him. "You can leave now."

He shook his head. "I'll believe that when I hear it from a doctor."

"Really? Don't you have a date with that blonde? Janice?"

"No. Besides, I'm driving you home, if they let you out."

"You don't have to. Just go give Janice a call. I saw her slip you her number." This was my best play to get rid of him. Janice was pretty, with a nice body—actually a killer body—and willing.

Terry didn't move. "Not interested."

As I stewed, I replayed the events of tonight in my head and came to an awful realization. I hadn't thanked Terry for saving me, and that made me a terrible human being. *Despicable* was more like it. "Terry." I sucked in a deep breath. "Thank you for being there for me tonight."

He merely nodded.

"I mean that. You saved me."

His eyes softened. "You're very welcome, Grace."

It hurt to realize this was our first noncombative exchange in forever. Plus, he'd called me by my name instead of Hellcat or the like.

My head still hurt from being banged against the stupid car window. Feeling the back of my skull, I found the bump I expected. My hair would hide that, but I didn't need a mirror to know it would take heavy-duty makeup tomorrow to deal with my face.

Terry moved closer and lowered his voice. "I know they lured you out with a fake ransom call, and I heard them ask where Elliot was. Why?"

"I don't know." In the moment, I'd thought they'd been a pair of asshole muggers, but now everything fell together—the ransom call that didn't make sense and the guys staked out by my car. They wanted me in order to get to Elliot.

Terry stared at me, waiting for more.

"Really, I don't know."

Dr. Nelson breezed in. "Let's see if radiology has given us an update." He tapped on the computer terminal, scanned the screen, and turned to me. "The report says your scan is clean."

I knew it would be. "I need to get home," I said as I sat up.

The doctor placed a hand on my arm. "Not so fast, Ms. Brennan. Being as you are a repeat customer, you know we're not done yet."

Terry's brows drew together.

I knew what was coming. "Where would you like to start?"

"Symptoms. Headache?"

I nodded. "Yes, but that's because when the guy hit me, he slammed my head against the car window."

The doctor shook his head. "Nausea?"

"No."

"Balance issues?"

"None."

"Loss of consciousness?"

With Terry here, I couldn't fake this one. "Yes, but not from hitting my head. I fainted."

"And then hit her head pretty hard on the concrete," Terry added.

"Vision issues?"

"None." It seemed we were going to go through the entire concussion test.

After finishing with the list of symptoms and confirming my age, when and where I was born, and today's date, he asked for the months in reverse order.

"December…" I'd had to do this several times, so I knew the drill. I went through them quickly and ended with, "February, January."

"You skipped August," the doctor informed me.

Before I could argue, Terry agreed. "You did."

The doctor didn't look pleased. "I'm going to categorize this as a minor concussion." He checked his computer screen again. "You're in luck. Dr. Chen is on the floor tonight. You've seen him before."

I nodded. "Yes." He was the neurologist I'd seen after my last fainting spell.

Terry was silent as we waited for Dr. Chen, who arrived about ten minutes later.

"Ah, Grace. I hear you've been a naughty girl again and hit your head." He shook my hand.

I shrugged. "I couldn't avoid it."

He turned to Terry and offered his hand.

"Terry Goodwin, concerned friend."

I couldn't remember Terry referring to himself as my friend before.

"So tell me what happened," Dr. Chen said.

"I was mugged," I explained. "There was a lot of blood, and I forgot my tension exercise."

"And?" he prodded.

"I forgot to close my eyes."

"What about your desensitization exercises?"

I felt like curling into a ball of shame. "I didn't get to them."

Not having time was an excuse. In reality, I was afraid of them.

"Well, young lady, I suggest you get serious about the desensitization kit. You do understand that the effects of these concussive incidents can be cumulative. At your current rate, you run the risk of serious damage."

Terry's face showed true concern. "Will the desensitization stop the fainting?"

I had the same question. Last time the doc had only said, *"You should do this."* And I'd responded the same way I did to most demands—I rebelled. Not such a good idea in retrospect.

The doctor nodded. "The best approach would be to come to my office for sessions, but failing that, she can do sessions at home, and I believe they will help."

"She'll do them," Terry said, like it was in order.

Vintage Terry to insist on making decisions for me—again.

His eyes shifted my way. "Won't you?"

Trapped. "Sure. If it will help."

"Do you still have the kit?"

I nodded. I hadn't even opened it.

Dr. Chen typed on the keyboard. "I am also prescribing that you not be alone for the next twenty-four hours."

I nodded. That was pretty standard after a concussion.

"I'll be with her," Terry confirmed.

Gritting my teeth, I decided against creating a scene.

TERRY

I'D KNOWN GRACE FAINTED AT THE SIGHT OF BLOOD, BUT UNTIL TODAY, I'D never realized how dangerous that could be.

My insides had been tied in knots since the moment I saw her head hit the concrete. She could have been badly hurt and not known it. I'd seen car-accident cases where the victim suffered a hit to the head, declined a trip to the hospital, and dropped dead within a week from an undetected brain bleed.

It was an immense relief to have the CAT scan come back clean.

When Jordy arrived, I joined him in the lobby.

"The call came from a burner," Jordy said, handing me back her phone. "I'll watch to see if it turns on again, but the odds aren't great. How is she?"

I shrugged. "Okay, considering. A concussion, and the CAT scan was clear. But she shouldn't have put herself in that position in the first place. She should have told me about the call. I would have gone with her."

Jordy laughed. "The way you treat her, I think she'd drink sewer water before she'd ask you for help." He pulled a bag from his pocket. "Jelly Belly?" The guy was hooked on jelly beans.

When he left, I returned to her exam space, and had to face the fact that he might be right. Had my efforts to keep her at a distance contributed to tonight by making her hate me that bad?

It took another hour after Dr. Chen's desensitization lecture for the release paperwork to come through. I stepped out of the curtained area as Grace redressed. I rubbed the back of my neck. This episode was over, and I was damned relieved that she hadn't been hurt.

I'd promised her brother and my best friend, Pete, I'd keep her safe.

Safe from bad guys like what had happened tonight had been half his meaning.

The other half had been that he wouldn't let her date anyone with a dangerous profession, not after what had happened with their aunt and uncle. That responsibility fell to me while he was deployed and I could be very persuasive.

Grace didn't need to know that the young firefighter she'd taken a liking to only ghosted her after a threatening visit from her brother. Nor did she need to know that I'd chased off the cop from Glendale in the time since Pete had been gone.

After going missing on a mission four years ago, Pete was declared KIA based on the claims of the terrorist group that captured him, but that didn't relieve me of the obligation to follow through on my promise to him to keep his sister safe. It also put me in charge of Grace's finances, since Pete had put his life insurance into a trust that I was tasked with managing for her. Those first months had been hard.

Then, Lucas informed me that through his Omega contacts, he was told that Pete was still being held, alive somewhere despite what the DOD said. When Lucas passed this along, he warned me that only six people in the country knew this and with me it was seven.

Not only couldn't Grace know because the circle couldn't grow to eight, but after seeing her destroyed once, I couldn't give her hope and then crush it a second time.

Now, all I could do was wait for Omega to get a window to extract him. It sucked to be helplessly silent, but that was the nature of a hostage rescue operation.

Our code meant I had the added task of keeping Grace safe from me and my desires.

Grace was goodness and light. She needed to be shielded from the darkness I carried around with me, from the monster I hid from the world.

"I'm decent," she announced.

When I reentered the curtain, she had turned away, gathering up her papers. But that killer gown of hers showed me an acre of bare back—almost to her ass—and my cock instantly noticed. This was why I tried not to be in the same room as her when I could help it.

She turned around. "I'm ready to go home."

"You're coming to my place," I insisted. I never sugarcoated things with her. Expectations needed to be clear. It was the way of the world. "Doctor's orders—you can't be alone."

Her pale-blue eyes flared.

I could get lost in those eyes for days, which is why I made such an effort to avoid her.

"Stop being a jerk and ordering me around." There was her argumentative side again. "I want to go home."

"Wildcat, have you forgotten what happened tonight? I'm sure they know where you live. Going back to your apartment is the stupidest thing we could do."

Her face contorted into the angry Grace I knew too well. "Now you're calling me stupid."

"I'm telling you what we're going to do and explaining why."

"You're not the boss of me. Those days are over."

Her acting like a ten-year-old changed nothing. "There are guys that carry guns and knives after you, and you're my responsibility."

"*Who* carry guns and knives," she corrected.

"Whatever," I snarled. "My place, not yours."

"That's right, you tell her," a guy on the other side of the curtain said.

"You keep out of this," Grace snapped, slapping at the curtain.

"You sure got a wild one there," the guy continued.

I grabbed her arm as she went for the curtain, probably to pull it back and tell the guy off to his face. "We're leaving, and you're staying by my side."

"You're impossible," she said, stomping out of the little exam area.

As she swept past out of the space, I caught a whiff of her lemony scent. Carrying her, seeing her bare back, touching her, now smelling her, it was all going to drive me insane. I followed her wordlessly because the nurses at the station down the hall were all looking our way. Our argument would play out better in the car than here in public. "You're limping," I observed as I followed her.

"Sore hip from the fall."

"No aspirin for you," I noted.

"Thank you, Captain Obvious. I know that. This isn't my first…" Her words trailed off.

"There she is," Serena said as we pushed through the doors to the waiting area. "They said one person max, and they wouldn't let us back to see you."

Duke was with her.

Serena engulfed Grace in a big hug. "My God, you look like you lost a fight with a bulldozer."

When the girls parted, I instinctively moved next to Grace.

"The guy was big," Grace admitted. "But Terry here took care of him like he was a ten-year-old." She made two punching moves with her fists. "Pow, pow, and he was down."

Duke nodded with a smile.

"Mild concussion," Grace explained to Serena. "They don't want me to be alone for twenty-four hours, soooo…" She drew out the word. "Could I spend the night with you guys?"

"Sure." Serena squealed. "Sleepover time. We'll keep an eye on you, right, honey?"

"Of course," Duke agreed.

I rolled my eyes. The minx had just outmaneuvered me. "I'll pick you up in the morning to go to work," I told her.

"Whatever." Grace didn't even look my way.

I pulled her phone from my pocket. "I think this is yours."

She snatched it with a smile and a nod. "Thank you. I need that."

All the way to my car, I berated myself. Sure, I needed to protect Grace, but could I have been more diplomatic about it? Sure. Would it have made a difference to her? Given her disposition, probably not. But I was also suddenly envious of Serena and Duke.

BACK HOME, I CLIMBED OUT OF THE RENTAL TUX, NOTING THE BLOODSTAINS. I hoped it could be cleaned. But if I'd been a minute later, Grace would have been hurt even worse, and that would be a stain on my soul that nothing could clean.

Our boss, Lucas Hawk, was as tough as they came, a former member of both Delta Force and Omega Section. His connections in the spec ops and the intel communities ran deep. His reputation was legendary. Men who underestimated him could be found in graveyards around the globe.

I needed a quick shower to rinse the blood spray from my hair, and also the stink of near failure from my body. I turned on the water and waited for it to heat.

At Duke and Serena's tonight, Grace would be safe and secure. Duke would see to that. Plus, I wouldn't be tempted to check on her in the middle of the night. That thought had me hard, so I turned the water to lukewarm. It didn't help that my mind returned to her in that damned sex-goddess dress tonight. What would I have said if she was awake when I opened her bedroom door to check on her?

Grabbing my cock, I stroked and closed my eyes, imagining the scene. It got more erotic when I imagined her stroking herself and murmuring my name. I sped up the pace. What if I joined her in bed? After a few more brutal strokes, an electric jolt ran down my spine and I came, spurting ropes onto the wall.

Leaning against the tile for support, I opened my eyes, panting heavily. I was going to drive myself insane thinking about the impossible. I used the shower wand to rinse off the wall, and the fantasy disappeared, just like my cum down the drain. I'd never get closer to Grace than this.

You never fucked your best friend's little sister—unless you were a complete douchebag. No, I wasn't going there.

After drying off, I found a message on my phone.

> WILDCAT: Thank you for tonight.

For once, I was honest with her.

> ME: I've been thinking of you.

Why had I written that? When I reread it, it was even worse the second time. What in the fucking hell had possessed me to write that? Yeah, I'd jerked off thinking entirely inappropriate things about her, but acknowledging that I'd thought anything at all about her wasn't a direction I wanted to take this conversation.

> ME: I meant I've been worried about you, and I hope you're OK. I'm sorry I didn't arrive sooner. I hate that you got hurt.
> WILDCAT: I owe you. I mean it. Anything you want.

I paused. I didn't dare ask for any of the things I really wanted but couldn't have—a kiss, to feel her pressed up against me, or more. The out-of-control lust-demon in my head was not helping.

> ME: How about a pleasant cup of coffee?

I'd settle for a cup of coffee without any of her usual snark.

> WILDCAT: Deal. I've been thinking about you too.
> ME: Sleep well.

That was not at all my style, but after what she'd been through, she deserved some kindness tonight instead of my usual cutting sarcasm.

I got out of the messages app and called Zane. "Anything out of our two guests yet?"

"Just names from their IDs. The big guy is Marco Vitelli, and the skinny dude's name is Rocco Esposito. Ring a bell?"

"Nah." I had a pretty good idea, but I asked anyway. "What did they want with Grace?"

"Don't know yet. I'll get that out of them before too long."

"Thanks. I'll check back in the morning."

CHAPTER 4

Grace

I woke the next morning in Serena and Duke's guest bedroom to sounds outside the bedroom door—breakfast preparations, no doubt. A quick swipe of my hand revealed a bump at the site of the ache at the back of my skull. Nonetheless, it was time to get moving. I had a business to run and a life to live.

Getting out of bed, I realized my head wasn't the only area of soreness. After shedding the nightgown I'd borrowed from Serena, I took a quick turn in front of the mirror, revealing bruises on my face and back. Now I knew why I hurt so much.

My phone mocked me from the nightstand. Did I dare?

I gave in and reread the message string with Terry from last night. Heat surged in my core as I read again that he'd been thinking of me.

Watching him destroy those two thugs had been hot as hell. After his texts, in spite of my aches, I'd brought myself to a towering climax as I imagined him stroking his enormous cock and thinking about me. Big, strong, badass Terry. I didn't know if when he said he'd been thinking of me he meant it sexually, but a girl could dream.

Also, I didn't actually know he had a large cock. But everything else about him was big and strong, so it made sense. After hundreds of dreams of him holding me, it totally sucked that I'd finally been in his arms last night, and unconscious the whole time.

Terry had always been the ultimate contradiction for me. Although my brother swore Terry was a good guy, around me he was mean as a snake and always riled me. My body though never understood what my brain did. If I saw him with another girl, petty jealousy roiled my stomach. I wanted to know what it would be like to be her, to be in Terry's arms, to have his lips on mine, to have all his attention on me, in spite of his rotten personality.

Was that me lusting after the bad boy merely to be rebellious?

Swiping aside thoughts of Terry, I put my hair up and made do with a quick rinse under the shower. Toweling off, I glanced at the phone again, but instead of giving in, I faced the reality of my situation. I had to get to work.

Since Duke had vetoed a stop at my apartment last night, all I had with me was my phone, a clutch with almost nothing in it, a backless evening gown, fabulous shoes that would kill me if I had to wear them all day, and day-old underwear. My shawl had gotten lost along the way.

Serena had a gorgeous wardrobe, but we weren't the same size, so I'd have to go by my place before work. Still with a towel wrapped around me, another message arrived. This one made me want to puke.

MRS. MONTEFINO: I'd like to see you.

Fat chance of that happening. With my hand shaking, it took two tries to delete the message. No way was I revisiting that period of my life. I leaned against the counter and practiced my deep breathing until the tremors in my hand stopped. Slipping into the bathrobe I found on a hook, I ventured out.

"How are you feeling?" Serena asked when I entered the kitchen.

I touched the tender spot on the back of my head. "Like I got run over by a train."

She offered me a steaming mug. "Coffee?"

"Love it." I blew over the surface before chancing a sip. "Thank you. Where's Duke?" I asked just before hearing the clank of metal on metal.

Serena nodded to the left. "In the gym." She checked her watch. "He'll be at it for a little longer." She handed me a plate with scrambled eggs and toast. "We already ate."

I sat at the counter and started on the eggs.

"Bacon or sausage? I didn't know what you liked, so I made both."

"Either. It doesn't matter to me."

She shook her head. "I'm going to tell you what Duke is always telling me. Life is about making choices."

"Sausage, please."

She brought the sausage over and pointed to the corner of the counter. "I have a tracksuit you can wear to your place, since I'm guessing you don't want to go out this morning in last night's dress."

"You're a lifesaver, you know that?"

She shrugged. "It's what friends do."

The plate was larger than my usual, but I quickly finished the breakfast. Maybe danger increased one's appetite.

"When's Terry coming by to pick you up?"

Her question reminded me that Terry wanted to dictate every move I made. *Don't do this. Don't do that.* I'd had enough of that treatment to last me a dozen lifetimes.

Checking the time, I rose quickly. "Real soon. I better get changed." I gave Serena a hug. "Thanks for everything."

"I'll call later," she promised as I headed to change.

Back in the guest room, my phone buzzed.

ELLIOT: I need to see you

I called him immediately.

"Gracie, are you okay?" he asked hurriedly. "I heard you had a little trouble."

"No, Elliot. I'm not okay. I got beat up and almost worse." After a breath, the questions spilled out of me rapid fire. "What the hell's going on? They wanted to know where you were. Who's after you? And why? What did you do?"

"It's complicated," he said after a pause.

It always was with him.

"What are you involved in?" I demanded. "I deserve to know, now that you've dragged me into your shit."

"You're not at home."

Of course, he couldn't give me a straight answer.

"No, I spent the night at a friend's house."

"I need the key to the warehouse."

Once again, not even a please. I shook my head. "Why?"

"I gotta hide out for a while."

I'd figured that part out. I owned a tiny section of a larger warehouse. "Why? What kind of shit are you into?"

"Meet me at that first burger place I worked at. You know the one."

There'd been a string of them, since he hadn't been a model employee. "You mean the one on—"

"Don't say it. They might be listening. You know, the one with the mean boss."

He'd considered all of his early bosses mean, but I knew the one he meant. When I'd gone to bat for Elliot and explained that he'd been late to work because of a power outage, Fat Fred, his manager, had crudely suggested that he'd give Elliot another chance if he could *"give me a spin."*

I'd spat on him after telling him what I thought of that. "You mean Fred?"

"That's the one. I'll explain."

I didn't get the chance to argue because the call disconnected.

A few minutes later, I sneaked out to the street, out of sight of Serena's windows, and waited for the Uber I'd called.

Elliot needed me. He was my only remaining family, and I couldn't let him down. There was no way Terry would let me go meet Elliot without him tagging along, and that would be a recipe for disaster.

Terry and Elliot were like oil and water, or maybe gasoline and a match was a more appropriate analogy.

A minute later, a little Prius pulled to the curb to collect me.

THE ENTIRE DRIVE HOME, MY PHONE FELT LIKE A HOT POTATO IN MY HAND as I dreaded the *where-are-you* call from the tyrant. I silenced it, just in case.

When we stopped in front of my building, I climbed out and thanked my driver. Since she had been nice enough to not comment on my bruising, I gave her a five-star review and a nice tip.

The journey up the stairs to the third floor went slower than normal, on account of my sore hip and the fact that I was stuck in these heels from last night. Yes, a tracksuit and sky-high heels. High fashion.

As soon as I left the stairwell, I could see the door before mine was open again. I kept telling Mrs. Finn she should keep it closed for safety, but she refused, instead complaining about her apartment being stuffy. With the door open, she got a slight puff of air from her window anytime the door to the stairwell opened.

I walked the length of the hallway, composing my safety speech.

She raised her knitting needle to stop me before I got a single word out. "I don't want to hear it. I need the fresh air. Everybody here knows my son is a judge, and nobody wants to mess with a judge's family."

"Millie, I was going to ask how you are this morning," I lied.

She lowered her glasses to look over them. "My goodness, girl. I'm doing a damned sight better than you. What happened?"

I shrugged and improvised. "I don't have anybody important in my family... And some guys wanted to take my phone."

"Did they catch them?"

"Sadly, no."

"If they do, you let me know. I'll make sure my Leonard sends them up to the big house. He even knows some guys who'll teach 'em some manners." She giggled to herself.

I moved to my door. The idea of a judge who had links to criminals in prison wasn't so funny to me.

When I tried my key, it only turned halfway. The deadbolt was already unlocked. I froze. Had I left it unlocked? Or had Val, my cleaning lady? Yesterday was my day on her schedule, and I hadn't seen her before I left to prepare the venue for last night's party.

"Millie, have you seen anybody go into my apartment?"

She looked up over her glasses again. "Why no, dear."

I gulped when a whoosh of air hit me as I cracked the door.

I definitely knew better than to leave a window open.

TERRY

ON MY TERRACE, I FINISHED MY BREAKFAST AND SQUINTED AT MY PHONE screen. I'd hoped for a message from Grace, but no such luck.

I called Zane. "Did you find out what our two guests wanted with Grace?"

"They were sent to get Grace to call or text her cousin Elliot. Apparently, he's the one they're after, and they thought he would respond to her and crawl out from wherever he's hiding."

"Why do they want him?" Understanding the motive would be the key to protecting Grace.

"These guys said they didn't know. I believe them."

"Anything else?"

"That's all I had time for before a relative showed up to get them," Zane said. "Seems at least one of them had a tracker on him."

"Probably the watch," I guessed.

"A guy named Victor Russo showed up, and he came with muscle. Four guys backing him, all armed."

"Victor Russo?"

"Yeah. I called Lucas, and he told me to hand them over. That's all I know."

"Probably a good call. Tall Tony Russo is the head of the local Italian mob, and Victor is his son. They're not the kind of guys you want to have a fight with on their terms."

"Good to know." Zane was new on the team, and he didn't know all the players in town.

Having the Russo family interested in Grace was not a good turn of events. The Italians were not as big here in LA as they were on the East Coast, and they had given way in some areas to the Russians, but they were still dangerous and ruthless.

I thanked Zane and called Serena to tell her I was on the way.

She didn't answer, so I left a message and grabbed my keys.

While driving, I tried again—still no answer. Maybe she'd slept in.

NOT WANTING TO PUT DOWN THE FOUR COFFEES I'D GOTTEN ON THE WAY, I pushed the buzzer to Duke's place with my elbow.

Serena answered the door. "Oh goodie, just what we needed. You should stop over more often." She opened the door wide. "Grace," she yelled. "Terry's here."

"Which one's mine?" Duke asked, appearing with a towel over his shoulders. He'd been working out.

"Two black on my left, and two mochas on the other side." I wasn't sure, but I'd bet that Serena was a mocha girl like Grace.

"She should be down any minute," Serena said as she plucked a mocha from the carrier.

While we waited, I filled Duke in on what Zane had said.

Serena eventually went up to retrieve Grace. "I don't understand what's taking her so long."

Duke rolled his eyes after Serena left. "Probably makeup. Her face is going to need it."

Serena came back empty-handed. "I'm sorry, Terry. She's not here."

"What the fuck?" I yelled.

Serena rubbed the back of her neck. "Sorry, Terry. I didn't think she'd give me the slip."

"What the hell is she thinking?" I swore. "She can't go out alone. She was supposed to wait for me."

I pointed a finger at Duke. "You should have kept an eye on her."

"You said keep her safe, and we fucking did." His fists clenched, a sign

I'd gone too far. "If you thought she might try to slip out, you should have warned us to keep a leash on her."

"Sorry, man," I said, raising my hands. "I didn't expect her to pull a stunt like this either."

Duke relaxed. We were going to be okay.

"Serena, I'm sorry I yelled," I told her.

She giggled. "It's cute that you care."

My stomach tied itself in a knot as I headed back to the door. I called Grace's number, and it went to voicemail again. "Grace, call me."

She was out there somewhere, alone, refusing to answer the phone, with Russo's thugs looking for her.

On the jog to my car, I dialed Jordy.

He picked up before I even heard it ring. "What can I do you for?" Jordy was our company guru for all things tech.

I bleeped the lock on the door to my Porsche Cayenne Turbo GT and slid in. "Do you still have a back door into those ride-sharing apps?"

"Suggesting I might not is an insult. You know that, right?"

I started the engine. "Grace left Duke's place, and since she doesn't have her car, I'm guessing she called a rideshare. I need to know where she went."

"Hold on." Keys clacked in the background. "Got it. She went to four forty-five Woodmist."

That was the address of her apartment building.

"Thanks, Jordy." I checked my mirror and burned rubber, leaving the curb. Damn her. Her apartment would be the first place Russo's people would stake out looking for her.

"If you like the service, I accept payment in Amazon gift cards," Jordy joked.

"Right." I hung up and punched the gas after the next turn. The big twin-turbo V-8 roared.

I had to get to her in time.

CHAPTER 5

GRACE

AFTER PUSHING MY APARTMENT DOOR OPEN, MY HEART SLOWED, AND I breathed easier when I spotted the trash bag.

Val always left it for me to take down to the dumpster.

"Everything okay?" Millie called.

"Peachy," I replied before closing the door and latching the deadbolt.

Clyde, my American shorthair, ran over to brush against my leg, while Bonnie, my Persian, watched from her perch on the back of the couch.

Picking up Clyde, I crossed the distance and closed the window. Good thing it was only cracked open, not wide enough for a cat.

Things were off. I cataloged the discrepancies. Two drawers in the kitchen were partially open, and my tiny desk wasn't as orderly as I'd left it.

Val was more careful than this. My blood chilled as I held my warm cat closer. Somebody had been in my space, looking for something.

Setting Clyde down, I pulled the treat bag from the cupboard.

The crinkle of the plastic bag motivated Bonnie to jump down and hustle over. They each got two treats before I toured the rest of my space.

I seethed when I went into the bathroom and found the toilet seat up. That was my answer. Only three people had ever had a key to my apartment—Serena, Val, and Elliot, because I'd taken him in last summer when his girlfriend dumped him.

He promised he'd given me back his only copy when he'd moved out, but obviously not.

After checking my watch, I rushed to my nightstand and retrieved the extra copy of the warehouse key from the small wooden box at the back of the second drawer. I certainly wasn't giving him the one from my keychain.

Elliot was a shitty cousin with a very loose relationship with the truth. But he was blood. I owed it to him to help, no matter what. Family or not, that didn't mean I wouldn't give him a piece of my mind when I saw him, though, the little shit.

With no time to spare, I swapped last night's heels for a pair of Nikes and pulled out my phone. I typed the location into the rideshare app and left. I'd have to come back afterward to change for work and do my makeup. Swapping the useless clutch for my oversized handbag, I headed out.

∼

Terry

I was almost at Grace's address when the call came in.

"What's up, Jordy?"

"You need to divert. She's not there anymore. She caught another Uber."

"Work?"

"No. A Burger King on Weatherby. Me? I prefer the Waffle Palace for breakfast." He read off the address for me.

"How far behind am I?"

"I'm not tracking the ride, but she got picked up ten minutes ago."

"Thanks, man." Clicking off the call, I took the next left at speed.

It didn't add up... I clenched the wheel harder and let the V-8 roar. I'd just passed a Burger King close to her building. If she was hungry, why go all the way to Weatherby?

∼

Grace

. . .

I pointed when my driver approached the Burger King. "In the parking lot will be fine." After she pulled in, I exited, looking around for Elliot. The parking lot only held a few cars and a van. When I didn't see him, I started for the door.

"Gracie."

I turned to find him standing behind a parked SUV in the far corner of the lot. "What the hell, Elliot. What's going on?"

He waved me over.

"You broke into my place."

He held up a key. "I didn't break in."

"You're not supposed to have that."

"I made a copy just in case."

I rolled my eyes. As I'd suspected, Elliot felt he was entitled to everything. As my only remaining relative, and one who'd had a shit upbringing, in the past I had always cut him slack, but that would not include him moving back in with me again. Last summer had been a disaster. The cats had gotten out twice.

"Came in handy, cuz." He pulled a breakfast sandwich out of a bag.

I walked over and held out my hand to solve this before I forgot. "I can't trust you. Hand it over."

He laid the key on the hood of the SUV and unwrapped his sandwich. "Did you bring the warehouse key? I didn't find it, and I need to lie low for a while—at least until I get this shit sorted out."

"What shit? What are you mixed up in?"

"Nothin'. I just gotta…lay low."

Still not an answer.

"Not good enough. Why are people after you? And more to the point, why are people beating up on me to find you?"

"You don't look that bad," he said around the food in his mouth as he looked past the SUV toward the street.

I felt the painful lump on the back of my head. "I don't like being a punching bag. So, no explanation, no key."

His eyes shifted the way they did when he was about to lie, which was pretty often. "I had a delivery go bad."

He'd told me he'd gotten a job with a courier service, which sounded like a big step up from the fast food job he'd had at Burger Castle. "What's that mean?"

"I got ripped off, and my boss is pissed."

I shook my head. "Man up for once and go explain the situation to him."

"No way. He'll kill me."

"I'm done. You sort it out like a big boy for a change." I turned.

He lunged and grabbed my elbow. He shook his head, his eyes crazy. "You don't get it. He'll literally kill me." He sliced a finger across his neck.

I yanked my arm free. "You can't be serious."

He blinked rapidly. "These guys don't mess around." He checked the street again. "Oh, shit." He crouched behind the SUV. "Duck."

"What?" His change of mood alarmed me.

"They're here." He dropped his food and peeked through the windows.

"Who?" I asked.

"My boss's guys. They must have followed you."

Of course, in the world according to Elliot, this was my fault.

I raised up to peek. Two tattooed bruisers, one taller than the other, got out of a Suburban on the street, then closed the door. They were not the kind of guys you'd like to meet in a dark alley.

I ducked down as their heads turned in our direction.

"Shit, shit, shit..." Elliot's voice grew shrill. "You let them follow you. Now I'm screwed."

After another peek, I confirmed they had started into the parking lot. "Stay down," I urged him.

I couldn't have waited for Terry this morning, but it sure would have been good to have him here right now.

"We can't stay here," Elliot whimpered.

"And how are we going to get by both of them?"

I glanced again.

The taller, bald one turned toward the door to the restaurant. The other went between two cars to check behind them.

I watched. "This is going to be our chance. The bald one is going inside. If we just wait until the other guy goes behind that van, we can make a run for it." As soon as I looked back, I realized I'd spoken too late.

Elliot had already scurried away along the wall behind the cars.

"Got ya now," yelled the bruiser still in the parking lot as he spotted Elliot and gave chase.

Looked like he had Elliot cornered. I darted around the SUV to race toward the street. He couldn't go after both of us. "Hey, fatso," I yelled.

It wasn't my best insult, but it shifted his attention to me for a second.

"Yeah, you," I added as I ran along the building.

It worked. With Short Stuff distracted for a second, Elliot sprinted past.

My legs burned as I gave it my all and poured on speed to make it to the street before Baldy joined us from inside. At least my running shoes gave me an edge.

Short Stuff decided to follow Elliot, but he wasn't as fast as my cousin.

When I reached the sidewalk, I turned right. My distraction had given Elliot the seconds he needed, and we could now both outrun this goon in opposite directions.

"Oh, no you don't, bitch," sounded from behind me. Baldy had joined the chase.

Then, the awful pain started, and my muscles seized up as I fell to the ground and rolled.

Baldy trotted up, sneering. The Taser he held continued to click as he held down the trigger.

With every terrible electric jolt, pain shot through my body. I tried and failed to make my arms and legs respond. I tried to yell, but it was useless.

"Not so fast, are ya now, bitch?" He yanked me up and heaved me over his shoulder. "Now you and me are gonna have some fun."

I heard the bleep as he unlocked the Suburban they'd driven up in, but I still couldn't get my body to obey. Slung over Baldy's shoulder like a sack of potatoes, with my limbs shaking, I couldn't move. I couldn't kick or hit. This was true helplessness, and I hated it.

"Good. You got her." Short Stuff wheezed as he jogged back to us.

"Where's the kid?" Baldy asked.

"He got away."

I looked over at the window of the restaurant. Everybody was facing the other way, enjoying their meals. So much for a Good Samaritan rescue.

Baldy shifted me on his shoulder. "You had one job to do, Gio. One job and you fucked it up."

Fighting through the numbing tingles, I finally got a few fingers to move on one hand. Maybe I could scratch Baldy's eyes out, if I could lift my arm.

"Fuck you, Mario. He's a fast little shit." Gio yanked my hair to lift my head. "She's a looker. I call dibs."

Nausea rolled through me, and I spat at him.

"That's gonna cost you, stupid bitch." He used his sleeve to wipe his cheek, then punched me in the face.

It stung something wicked. It should be illegal to hit a woman this hard, especially when she couldn't move. "Gio," I croaked through the pain. "My boyfriend's going to wipe the sidewalk with you." I didn't have a boyfriend, but I'd pulled the line out of a romance novel, and it sounded good.

"Enough fucking around," Mario said as he opened the car door. "We gotta get her to Victor."

It was now or never to get away from these guys before they got me inside the car. I used all my willpower to lift my arms and fight.

It wasn't enough. They hung down like useless, limp fish.

CHAPTER 6

Grace

Screeching tires signaled a car almost hitting the Suburban as they maneuvered me toward the back seat.

"Put her down." Terry's yell came a second later.

I'd never heard a more welcome voice. I pulled in a relieved breath as he came into view.

"Stay the fuck out of this," Gio countered.

Terry moved lightning fast, landing three punches in succession, the last one sending Gio against the side of the SUV.

"Asshole," Mario sputtered as he dropped me in a heap on the sidewalk.

I landed hard enough to know I'd just collected another set of bruises, but at least my head faced the action.

"You were warned." Mario pulled a gun. Before he could aim, Terry's foot collided with the asshole's hand, and the gun skittered under the car. Mario lunged at him.

Terry dodged.

Mario turned like an enraged bull.

As soon as the goon started forward, Terry landed two swift hits and a kick that sent the guy back against the restaurant window. Surprisingly, it didn't break.

Terry swiveled and rushed to me. "What happened?" he asked, kneeling down.

"Taser."

Mario stumbled to his feet and hobbled to Gio.

"He's getting away," I croaked.

"Not my priority. You are."

I melted a little bit inside and lifted my hand as much as I could.

Terry knelt beside me and took my hand. "I've got you, Grace." This made it two times now that he hadn't called me some derogatory cat name.

Mario pulled Gio to his feet, and the pair stumbled down the street.

It seemed too obvious, but I had to say it. "You saved me. Thank you."

He squeezed my hand. "It's my duty. I promised Pete."

I'd hoped for a better reason.

"You were supposed to stay put with Serena and Duke," he added after a moment.

There it was, the recrimination I'd expected. It was always my fault. "I couldn't. I had to…help Elliot."

"Yeah, right." Derision coated his words. "And where is the little pussy now?"

A man came out of the Burger King. "Hey, you all right? Want me to call 9-1-1?"

"I've got her, thanks," Terry responded as he took my hands. "I'm going to help you up. Okay?"

Some muscle control had returned, so I nodded. "I'll try." My back, my ass, my head, every damned thing hurt like a thousand bee stings.

After helping me up, Terry turned us toward his Porsche. When I stumbled, he caught me and helped me to the car, opening the back door instead of the front. "Lie down on your stomach in here."

"You're kidding."

"I have to get the barbs out right away. Do you want me pulling your pants down in public?"

I grumbled, but did as he said and folded my knees so he could close the door.

He came around to the other side after retrieving a first aid kit from the back. "He got you in the back and the ass."

"Thanks for the news flash. They're starting to hurt."

He placed a hand on my lower back. "When the barbs come out, it will just be a little prick. On three. One…two—"

"Shit," I screamed. "What happened to three?" He'd yanked it out without warning. "You did that on purpose."

"Yeah."

"You said little." It felt like he'd pulled off a pound of flesh.

He huffed and tore open an antiseptic pad. "Stop being a baby." He lifted my top and rubbed antiseptic on the spot.

That stung, but after the baby comment, I wasn't telling him so. "Is it going to heal?"

"You'll be fine. It came out clean. See?" He held the barb attachment in front of my face. It didn't have the flesh hanging from it I'd expected, so that was good. After another swipe of the antiseptic pad, he tore open a bandage and applied it.

"The other one hurts more."

"Hang on."

I felt his hand on my ass and then a very slight tug.

"Crap."

I didn't like the sound of that. "What's wrong?"

"The tip broke off."

"What does that mean?"

He laid a hand on my shoulder. "It'll have to be dug out."

I was sure he meant his touch to be reassuring, but the warmth of his hand on me was more exciting than soothing. It took me a second to register that he meant cutting into me. That did not sound fun. I tried to get up.

He held me down. "Hold on, Tiger. Lie still. It's like a fishhook. Movement will make it go deeper."

"This day just keeps getting better." I shook my head, but refused to cry. "Get me to the hospital."

"It will be better if I take you to my place and take care of it there."

I cocked my head. He was insane. "And have you cut into me?"

"Trust me. I know what I'm doing."

"Hold on. I'll go with the professionals on this."

He pulled his hand away and laughed. "It's your choice: trust me to get the barb out or take your chances with the cops."

Instantly, I missed the contact of his hand. "What do you mean cops?"

"We can go to the hospital, if you want, and then they'll report to the cops that you got Tasered because it's a rule. They have to. Then the cops start asking you how this happened, and you have to tell them about Elliot. Is that a talk you want to have?"

I trembled.

Terry brushed my hair behind my ear. "Or you let me handle it." His gentle touch soothed me.

My phone rang.

Terry jerked his hand away and pulled the device from my purse, handing it to me.

Talking to my assistant was not something I had time for right now. With a sigh, I answered. "Peyton, I'm busy. I'll have to—"

"Where are you?" she asked frantically. "We're lucky Mrs. Eclestone called to say she's running late, but she won't be long. Tell me you're only a block away."

This was bad. I'd completely forgotten about her appointment this morning. Mrs. Eclestone was on the board of directors of her country club and a half dozen charities. Her recommendation for working with us would be big in her upscale community.

"Sorry. I got held up. Car trouble." That was at least partially true, because I didn't have my car. "Have Paul handle the design with her. I'll be in as soon as I can." Paul's mother had actually gotten us the introduction.

"Paul? He hasn't flown solo before."

"Then have Marci join in and help him out. And don't let him push black enamel and chrome. And…make sure he gargles first."

That pulled a laugh out of Peyton. "I'll do my best, but hurry."

I felt silly as hell as I lay on my stomach in the back of Terry's car having this conversation. I ended the call. "Shit. Shit. Shit." The hospital was definitely out.

"What's wrong?" Terry asked.

"Change of plans. I don't have time for the hospital. Take me to my place. Do whatever you need to get this sucker out of me, but I need to change and go to work."

"Wherever you go, I'm coming along, and that's nonnegotiable."

I sighed. Now that he'd saved me twice, my normal tendency to fight him was gone. "Prepare to be bored out of your mind."

After the first pothole, I had to ask. "Do I really have to stay on my stomach like this?"

"It's entirely your choice. Feel free to sit up if you want the barb to dig its way farther into you. It's designed to dig into your skin and not let go, even if you're running."

It only took him a minute to criticize me again. "This only happened because you didn't wait for me."

∽

Terry

. . .

I answered Lucas's call as I drove. "Hi, boss."

"What's the status?" he asked.

Grace surprised me by speaking up from the backseat. "My cousin is in deep trouble and needs my help is what the status is."

"She got ambushed because she went to meet Elliot on her own. Two guys, a black Suburban partial plate eight mike echo lima. Her cousin took off."

"I'll have Jordy run the plate. Grace that wasn't very smart."

"So I've been told," she responded, like a smart ass.

"Were these the same guys as last night?"

"No," she answered.

"Stay with her, Terry."

I was way ahead of him on that score. "Roger that."

"He's right," I told her after ending the call.

"You're mad at me," she said as we neared her building.

"Damned straight. You almost got yourself killed."

"What was I supposed to do?"

"First, you should have waited for me like you were supposed to. Second, you should have known better than to meet Elliot by yourself, and third, you should carry some protection, like a Taser."

"That's dangerous," she objected.

"You're obviously in a dangerous situation, so yes, carry something dangerous—pepper spray if you don't like a Taser. I can provide whichever one you want."

"I've got my darts in my purse."

"What are you going to do? Wave them and give him a pinprick? You need more than that."

I'd known that Grace was a dedicated dart player and carried her set around with her, but those wouldn't stop guys with the kind of weapons she'd been up against last night or today.

Shaking her head, she ignored my logic. "I said no."

Typical Grace, she'd rather fight me than accept my help.

"I'll bring you a Taser later."

"I won't use it."

"Goddamnit, woman. You have to fight back. Do not go quietly. Fight with whatever you have. The heel of your shoe, even a pencil can be a weapon. A Taser is just a tool. It's not inherently dangerous."

She didn't acknowledge me one way or the other and was quiet on the rest of the drive to her building.

I parked as near to her door as I could manage. After exiting, I grabbed needle-nosed pliers and my small first aid pack from the back before opening her door to get her out.

"I want to walk," she complained as I pulled her from the car and picked her up.

I kicked the car door closed with my foot. "Remember about movement making it dig in deeper?"

She sighed. "I'm not a child. I feel stupid being carried."

"Now you're acting like a child."

She looked away. "You're always putting me down."

"Do you have any idea who those guys were?"

"Elliot said they worked for his boss."

That gave me one piece of the puzzle. Elliot worked for Tall Tony Russo.

"They work for Tony Russo, the local Italian mob boss. You get on the wrong side of those guys in New York and they give you cement shoes and dump you in the East River." I pulled open the door to her building and scooted in sideways so as not to bump her head.

"Oh."

"Out here," I explained, "they don't bother with the cement. They just take you out on a boat, cut you a few times to make you bleed, and throw you overboard for the sharks."

She cringed.

I carried her up the stairs of her building, and damn if she didn't feel right in my arms as she laid her head against my chest and closed her eyes.

She pulled in a deep breath. "Thank you. Did I say thank you? What can I do to repay you? Anything. Just name it. And before you say it, yes, I'll ask for help next time."

I chuckled as we started down her hallway. "Those are dangerous words with a man like me."

A come-hither smile appeared on her lips. "Anything. I mean it." She had no idea how tempting her offer was.

"Dinner," I said like the good man I aspired to be and definitely wasn't. "Home-cooked," I added to make it clearer.

"All you want is dinner, in addition to coffee I already owe you?"

"I did specify home-cooked. I have simple tastes."

"Somehow, I doubt that."

I managed a smile. *Not a date. She's your best friend's little sister, you fuckwad.*

CHAPTER 7

Grace

Dinner with Terry? That sounded good.

I laid my head against his chest as he carried me.

Of course, I'd always found Terry attractive. What woman with a pulse wouldn't? It had only been his less-than-winning personality that had kept me from angling for a date with the man.

My brother Pete had always claimed Terry was a great guy.

Maybe that was why I'd had a recurring dream that Terry would hit his head or something, change into charming Terry and ask me out. And here I was, in his arms. It felt right.

He reached my floor and strode to my door.

"What's going on?" Millie demanded. Of course, her door was still open to the hall.

Terry turned so I could see her.

"I took a fall, and he's helping me," I assured her. No way was I telling her Terry was about to take a knife to my ass cheek.

"Terry Goodwin, ma'am, ex-LAPD and a friend of her brother."

I noticed he didn't claim to be my friend.

Millie looked over her glasses at us. "I can call an ambulance, if you need one."

"No need. I just need to rest a bit."

"Key?" Terry asked.

I pulled it out, and we probably looked hilarious as he leaned over so I could reach the lock.

"Nice to meet you," he said as we slid inside. He kicked the door closed.

Clyde ran up to us.

"Trip me and you'll regret it, cat," Terry warned.

Clyde took the hint and bolted for the bedroom.

At my pathetic excuse for a couch, Terry set me on my feet, which caused Bonnie to jump down and run to join Clyde under the bed.

Terry pointed to the cushions. "Pull your pants down and lie on your stomach."

"Yes, sir." I saluted. "Are you sure you don't want me completely naked?"

A sly grin took over his face. "Want, yes. Need, no. Strip down as far as you feel like."

Normally callous Terry had somehow morphed into joking Terry. After coming to my rescue twice in twenty-four hours, insisting on taking care of me, and now joking about wanting me naked, it seemed the surprisingly nice Disneyland side of him had resurfaced.

"Really?" I shimmied my pants down a few inches, adding a wide smile, a genuine one because I liked this side of him. Disneyland had been a wonderful day.

"Don't be a tease. Lie down."

Had it been a joke or not that he wanted to see me naked? Facing him, I impulsively pushed them down a few more inches. "Or what?"

His jaw clenched, and his eyes flared. Had I just waved a red flag in front of the bull? Yes, and I'd gotten to him.

"A nice girl like you shouldn't want to find out," he growled.

He'd never before referred to me as *nice*. He turned away. Yes, the nice Disneyland Terry was back. There was an actual gentleman hidden in there somewhere.

"Do you have any super glue?" he asked, still turned away.

I waited a few seconds to see if he'd turn back for the view he'd said he wanted. I found his question odd. "Sure. Top drawer to the right of the fridge." *Come on, turn around. Show me you're human, dammit.*

He cast a quick glance my way. "You best get on the couch now."

Feeling I'd won this round, I flopped down on the couch, getting a few cat hairs in my mouth in the process. I wiped them away.

He strode into the kitchen. "I'll also need alcohol, antiseptic ointment, Band-Aids, and a razor."

"You won't need the razor. I don't have a hairy butt."

He didn't laugh.

"Okay. Razors are in the top left drawer in the bathroom. First aid stuff is one drawer lower, and isopropyl is under the sink."

When he returned, I added, "Knives are two drawers to the left of the fridge." My own words made me cringe. The idea of getting intentionally cut made me want to puke. At least this would be happening behind me, and I wouldn't be able to see the blood. Just thinking the word *blood* made my vision constrict for a moment.

Terry returned and, with a snap, broke the head off the razor. "A razor blade is sharper and will hurt less." He pulled needle-nose pliers from his pocket and settled on the couch by my knees.

I shifted to the side, feeling suddenly self-conscious about my naked butt. Was I really going to let him slice me with a razor blade? "Maybe I really should go to the hospital for this…"

"I have three words for you: cops and Elliot."

That was no choice at all. "Okay. You promise it won't hurt?" Elliot was *so* going to pay for this.

"I said less. Now hold still. The alcohol may sting a bit."

I braced, and when he dabbed it on, I felt only a tiny twinge. So far, so good. "You're sure you know what you're doing?"

"Cops and Elliot."

"Okay. Let's do this thing."

"I'm going to use a little local anesthetic." Then he pinched my ass.

I felt a bigger sting and two more pricks.

"Now we wait for it to take effect."

"Not long, I hope." I certainly wouldn't make it as a stripper, feeling this vulnerable with only my bare butt hanging out. "How's it look?"

He laughed. "*Everything* looks pretty good from here."

Vulnerability shifted to a tingle of excitement as I read meaning into his words. How had I gone from hating being around him to being excited that he enjoyed looking at my bare ass? My heart pounded in my ears as time slipped by quietly.

"That should be long enough," he finally said. "Does this hurt?"

I felt only slight pressure and shook my head.

"Okay then. Hold still, and I promise you my best work."

I clamped my eyes shut when he picked up the razor blade. After some pressure, I felt a tug. "Are we done yet?"

"Got it. Wanna see?"

I dared to open my eyes. "No thanks." When I started to move, he held me down again.

"Hold still. It'll only take a minute to finish up. I'm going to close the wound with super glue, and you'll be as good as new in no time, as long as you don't scratch at it."

I laughed. "Got it. No ass scratching." Yes, I had changed. Last week, suggesting that I scratched my ass would have earned him a slap instead of a laugh.

I stayed silent, feeling surprising tingles as his hands worked on me and I imagined them sliding beyond the Taser site. I'd spent many a night imagining his hands on me, but never like this.

"All done." He gave me a light pat on the backside, and my fantasy evaporated.

"That was fast." I felt him lift off the couch.

"You can pull up your pants now."

When I rolled over and stood, I felt somewhat lightheaded.

He turned away to give me privacy.

As I pulled up the bottoms of the tracksuit, the bloody gauze and razor blade caught my eye. My traitorous brain imagined the blade cutting into me—big mistake. Darkness pushed in from the fringes of my vision.

∼

TERRY

I HEARD THE SAME LONG SIGH AS LAST NIGHT. DREAD FILLED ME AS I SPUN. This time I was fast enough and got to her just as she wobbled.

She went limp in my arms.

With a sigh, I supported her head, relieved that I'd been quick enough to catch her. We were standing next to her coffee table, which had a very unforgiving marble top. If she'd hit her head on the edge of that, it might have been catastrophic. I kissed her hair and tried to remember how long last night's episode had lasted. Long enough that holding her upright like this wasn't a good solution, I decided.

A phone rang behind me—her cell phone.

I ignored it and twisted to settle slowly back down on the couch. I landed with her on top of me. The weight of her head on my chest made the rapid beat of my heart obvious. Yes, she'd scared the shit out of me again.

Then, my mind wandered to her breasts pressed against me, a reminder that I'd failed at my vow to keep distance between us and avoid the temptation of touching her. Should I have laid her on the couch rather than cradled her on top of me? Maybe.

I'd promised to take care of her, but was so far failing at my responsibility. I hadn't protected her from the attack outside the restaurant last night, even though I'd been warned she was in danger. And I'd let her get away from me this morning to see her dipshit cousin and almost lost her again.

"I've got you, Grace." I kissed her hair. "You're safe with me."

She didn't stir, still a limp weight on top of me.

I draped an arm around her. Having Grace pressed against me felt even more right than I'd imagined it would. Fate had intervened, and now staying close was the only way to keep her safe.

She stirred and lifted her head, her eyes blinking up at me. "What—"

"You fainted again," I answered.

She sighed heavily. "I'm not going back to the hospital."

"No need. I caught you this time."

She closed her eyes and snuggled into me. "Thank you." Then her eyes popped open. Seeming to realize her position, she lifted up somewhat. "How long have I been like this?"

"Not long." I removed my arm.

"I'm scared."

"Don't worry. Nobody's getting to you. I'll do anything and everything to keep you safe."

She brushed a finger down my nose and settled back against me. "Why? Because I'm Pete's little sister?"

"That's part of it." I settled my arm back around her.

"What's the rest of it?" she asked.

"Nothing much," I hedged.

"You promised to always tell me the truth." She stroked her hand over my chest. "What's the rest of it?"

Long ago, I had promised to always tell her the truth, a promise I now regretted. "And I want to keep this curvy little body intact."

"But you don't even like me."

"I don't dislike you."

That was my most dangerous truth, the one I'd always kept hidden. I was no saint. Like all men, I had the occasional secret desire to reach for the forbidden fruit, the fantasy I only indulged in the dark of the night— she was that fantasy for me.

"Bullshit. Except for the day we spent at Disneyland, you've never acted like it. Remember that day?"

Of course I remembered it. It had been the one day I'd had a cover story to enjoy being with her and ditch my asshole persona. After that, it had been right back to being Mr. Crabby to keep her away. "I remember."

"Well then, Terrence, why have you always treated me so shitty? Tell me, what have I done to deserve it?"

I hated anyone using my full legal name. It seemed too pretentious.

She'd only used it three times that I remembered, and at none of those times had she allowed me to escape the conversation without a full explanation. The first time had been when I wouldn't let her spend any of her trust money to buy a car. The others had been similar. I was trying to keep her from making irresponsible decisions so her money would last.

My strategy had paid off when she had enough money to realize her dream and start her organizing business after college.

"Let's hear it, Terrence," she insisted. "Tell me why you're so mean to me. Tell me what I did to you. I couldn't have kicked your dog because you've never had one. Did I call you an evil name and forget it?"

Being accused of being mean hurt, though it was pretty easy to see how she'd feel that's the way I treated her. "We need to go." I started to lift her off me.

She fought. "Stop it. I'm not going anywhere until you explain it to me." She poked me in the chest.

I relented and settled back.

Her eyes held fire. "And the truth this time."

I was trapped, physically and emotionally. Her leg rubbed against my crotch, and my cock took notice. "I need to keep some distance between us. You're my best friend's little sister."

"And why does that make you mean to me?" She rubbed against me again, on purpose no doubt.

I finished the explanation. "Don't you get it? You're off limits."

Her head lifted, and her eyes went wide. "Because I'm Pete's sister? That's stupid." I could feel her temper reaching the boiling point. "Off limits, so you act like you hate me so I'll hate you back?"

Just asking that question meant she didn't understand.

"That's the way it is," I told her.

She climbed me until we were eye to eye, nose to nose. "I'm a grown woman, and you don't get to decide what's right for me." A second later, her mouth was on mine.

It was just as I knew it would be, irresistible, the entire reason I'd kept my distance for so long. She was temptation personified. I knew I was going to hell as I opened my mouth and joined her in the kiss, battling for control.

She slid her hand down to rub me through my jeans, and my cock went instantly hard.

I rolled us to the side and cupped her breast, toying with her nipple through the fabric of the tracksuit. She wasn't wearing a bra. Quickly, I deepened the kiss, and she gave it back to me in full measure.

She tasted like pure temptation, and the intensity of her kiss was off the charts as each of us maneuvered for dominance. Yes, she wanted this just as much as I had on many lonely nights.

I had no idea how we'd gone from zero to Mach One as fast as we had, but I'll be damned, I was in no mood to slow us down.

Her phone rang again, with the opening bars of Beethoven's Fifth Symphony, and she broke the kiss. "I have to take that. It's my evil assistant."

Breathless, I helped her get up off the couch.

"Hold that thought," she said, pointing at me before she rummaged through her purse for the insistent phone.

I scratched the back of my neck and gathered my senses.

As my big brain battled my little brain for control, I realized how bad this was. What the hell was I doing? She was still Pete's sister, and he'd kill me. Rationalizing this by second-guessing whether he would make it back to us alive was tantamount to giving up on him. That was a place I couldn't go. This had happened so quickly… I was lucky her call had interrupted us before the situation got more confusing. I adjusted my aching cock, which had almost gotten me into deep shit.

*

GRACE

WHEN I LOCATED MY PHONE, I PUNCHED THE GREEN BUTTON. "HI, PEYTON." I kept my voice light.

"Where are you?" She sounded frantic.

"I got held up." I didn't mean it as a pun.

"Mrs. Eclestone won't accept working with Paul," she said. "She insisted it's you or nobody, and I know how important you said her account is, so I convinced her to reschedule for later. But she'll only talk with you."

"I'll be heading in shortly." I glanced at the gorgeous hunk of man in the room and really wished I could have said I'd be there in an hour or two.

"Hurry. She's due back now, and I won't be able to stall her again. I'm good, but I'm not a miracle worker."

"And so modest. I'm on the way."

She laughed, and we ended the call. I didn't know what I would do without her.

Terry approached with a glass of water and an open hand. "For the pain."

I shook my head. "No thanks." I tried to avoid painkillers after what I'd seen them do to my sophomore-year roommate, Denil, in college, and he knew that.

He shoved them at me. "It's just Advil, and I'm not taking no for an answer. Promise to take them for two days and then stop if you want."

"okay." I took the tablets and swallowed them, finishing off the glass of water. "Thanks."

He moved behind me and kneaded my shoulders. "You need to slow down. You've been attacked twice in twenty-four hours, and you need to give me and the team some time to figure out what's going on."

"I can slow down later. You've heard of parallel tasking, right? You guys do whatever investigating it is you do, but right now, I have to get to work before we lose a big opportunity."

Terry took a deep breath, clearly disappointed. "I'm coming with you, and you can tell me what the hell Elliot is into on the drive."

"Fine, but only if you sit in the corner and don't distract my employees."

I knew that was too much to expect. He would draw all the female eyeballs around, and the gossip about us would be immediate.

Rushing to change, I marveled that I had kissed Terry Goodwin, and he'd kissed me back with a passion I wasn't used to. The kiss had been better than in my dreams, and feeling his hard cock through his jeans said one thing very clearly. We were on the same page about wanting each other.

If Mrs. Eclestone hadn't represented my biggest opportunity in a while, I would have blown her off and focused on straddling Terry right now. I couldn't remember being this turned on in forever.

Tonight, I was going to indulge in all the naughty fantasies I'd pictured for Terry and me. The literal pain in my ass told me not all the positions could be on tonight's menu, but certainly we'd find enough to keep us busy all night long.

Me and Terry Goodwin? Yesterday, I never would have believed it. Well, at least before I got attacked. His saving me had changed things.

Now it seemed like fate demanded we explore the chemistry our kiss had revealed.

Changing quickly, I didn't bother with either makeup or my hair, opting for a natural look. As jazzed as I was, I probably would have messed it up anyway.

CHAPTER 8

Grace

We hustled downstairs and into Terry's Porsche, where I expected to get a chance to take a breath. *Wrong.* When he pulled away from the curb, the beast of an engine roared, and its power threw me back against the seat.

"Speed won't do me any good," I squeaked, "if I don't get there in one piece." It didn't hurt much, but because of the cut in my ass, I sat crooked in the seat.

"Trust me, Kitten. I'll get you there safely."

Kitten. I liked the sound of that much better than his other names for me. Still, it took a minute of white-knuckling the door handle and pressing my feet against the floorboards before I relaxed.

Eventually, I realized Terry knew how to drive fast. His hands were sure on the wheel, and he methodically scanned the mirrors and traffic ahead as we darted between lanes and rounded corners. Maybe it was the adrenaline from that kiss that had my motor revved, but I soon found watching him drive at hyperspeed to be sexy.

"Why were you meeting with Elliot?" he asked as he sped by another car.

I braced as he hit the brakes to slow for a delivery truck. "He called. He needed my help, and I had to go because he's—"

"I get it. So what did he say? What's going on with him?"

There wasn't much, but I tried to recall it exactly. "I don't know details, but it sounds like he's a courier for some criminal. He said his boss sent the guys at the restaurant."

Terry nodded. "That would be Tall Tony Russo, head of the Italian mob in town. He's bad news. Fuck, they all are. How did the little snot get on the wrong side of them?"

"He said a delivery went wrong."

"It figures he wouldn't know better than to work with those whack jobs." He huffed. "What kind of delivery? Drugs?"

Dammit, Elliot was my cousin, but Terry was right that he made bad choices. "He didn't say."

"What else?"

"That's all he told me before the goon squad arrived." I shivered, remembering those few minutes.

"If that's it, why meet with you?"

"He wanted the key to my warehouse space."

"And you gave it to him?" he asked incredulously.

I looked out the window and sighed. "I had to. He needed my help." Was I enabling more bad choices?

"Kitten, I'm not judging. Where is this warehouse?"

Kitten made me smile. I gave him the address. "Elliot said he needed to lie low."

Terry considered things silently as we took the next corner fast. "Okay. We'll look into it. Hopefully that's where he went."

"Thank you." I rested my hand on his shoulder. "I mean that."

He nodded. "I promise I'll do what I can to help him. For you, not for him."

As we drove on, I replayed what had happened upstairs in my apartment between me and this honorable man I'd always referred to as Tyrant.

Oh, my God. I'd kissed Terry Goodwin, the one-time bane of my existence, and it had been breath-stealing. He'd blown my mind by admitting to wanting me. Instead of our day at Disneyland being an aberration, it had revealed the truth of how things could be for us—playful banter hiding attraction. His crude meanness was the inconsistency, the falsehood. And all for some stupid sense of obligation to my brother who'd died years ago. I loved my brother and missed him terribly, but he wasn't here and shouldn't be a factor anymore.

The first time Pete had gone on a deployment, it had been a hard talk. He'd sat me down to talk about the possibility that he wouldn't make it back.

I'd cried a gallon of tears that day.

He'd insisted that if the worst happened, I should go on and live my life, relying on his best friend, Terry, and a few others. He'd made me promise to stop mourning him after a month if he didn't come back.

It had to have been the toughest thing a teenager had ever agreed to.

But Pete did return from that deployment, and several others.

Then, four years ago, had come the awful news that he'd been captured overseas by the worst people on the planet. That information had allowed me to both worry and hope. Then, a month later, I'd opened my door on a Saturday morning to the sight of an officer in dress blues and two others. It was the visit I'd dreaded.

Pete had been declared KIA based on claims by the terrorists and a video that I thankfully didn't watch.

I closed my eyes, recalling how I'd cried and cried, trying to adhere to Pete's one-month limit. I failed, but eventually I'd pulled up my big-girl panties and gotten on with life. I'd finished college and after that started SpaceMasters with the money from Pete's life insurance.

A smile overtook me as I remembered the day I'd landed my first customer with a business I wouldn't have been able to get off the ground without the money Terry had forced me to save. I'd wanted to spend it on the car I'd coveted—a sweet little blue BMW that I'd thought would heal the hurt I felt from Pete's loss.

"We're here," Terry announced. "Safe and sound as promised."

I opened my eyes as we pulled into a space in the building's underground parking.

Terry took my hand as we rushed to the elevator.

I pulled it back. "This is my place of work, and I need to be professional. No PDA—none, get it?"

"Yes, ma'am. I'm only Grace's guard."

"And don't ma'am me either."

"Sure thing, Kitten."

I slapped his arm. "You're impossible."

Upstairs, I breezed out of the elevator and down the hall to SpaceMasters with the sense of pride I got every time I saw our name on the door. We were quickly becoming the premier organizational design firm in town. It didn't matter if you had a walk-in closet or the backroom storage space of a large hardware store that needed to be organized and optimized. We could provide space-saving solutions from functional to tastefully elegant.

The tingle at the small of my back as Terry guided me through the door reminded me that having him here was not going to be so simple. I'd never been able to ignore Terry's presence, but since that kiss, I now had to consciously fight the urge to turn around and admire him.

Down girl, I reminded myself. The kiss had lit my fuse, but the explosion would have to wait until we were alone.

We bumped into Marci, one of my designers, just inside the door. "Peyton's looking for you," she said.

"Thanks."

"You made it," Peyton exclaimed as she rushed up. "Mrs. Eclestone just returned, and she's in demo room one. She's still not very happy about you being late." Then she paused to look at my face. "What happened to you?"

"I was mugged last night." I didn't have time to elaborate on this morning as well.

"That's terrible. Can I—"

I shook my head. "Not now. Mrs. Eclestone first."

Terry stepped up beside me.

Peyton startled as her gaze shifted to my bodyguard. "Oh." She gave him a quick once-over and an appreciative smile.

"Ignore Rambo. He's shadowing me today."

"Rambo?" squeaked my usually cool-headed assistant. "I could show him around for you."

He extended his hand. "Terry Goodwin. You must be Peyton?"

"Guilty… Wait…*the* Terry Goodwin?"

Terry smiled. "Has Grace mentioned me before?"

Turning red, I admitted, "I may have." I scanned the office. As I suspected, women around the space were attempting to be discreet while getting a look at my bodyguard. Maybe it had been the Rambo mention.

Terry chuckled. "Nothing good, I'll bet."

Peyton's smile gave it away.

"The truth can sometimes be ugly," I added. "Best not to ask." I turned back to Peyton. "Anything I need to know before I meet her?"

She tore her eyes away from Terry and held out a folder. "I've loaded up the layout and pictures she brought, so everything is set, but…" She raised a finger to her temple. "Your face."

"Maybe later." I turned to Terry. "You can wait in my office. Peyton will show you the way."

Peyton's face lit up. I'd always known Terry was attractive, but seeing his effect on my pretty assistant twisted my stomach in an uncomfortable way.

"No." Terry's tone was unyielding. "As your bodyguard, I go where you go."

I nodded. "Okay, but only because I don't have the time to argue with you." I didn't do these customer sessions with onlookers, but I was out of time.

Peyton led the way and whispered, "Bodyguard?"

"Temporary," I whispered back, then fell in behind her.

With Terry beside me, my stomach calmed. I hated needing to have him here, but I liked that he wanted to be with me. I took a breath before we followed Peyton into the demo room.

Mrs. Eclestone was everything I'd been told to expect—clear skin, impeccable makeup, and nicely styled hair, longer than normal for a woman of her age, and without a speck of gray.

Her perfection made me question my decision against makeup.

One of our materials brochures sat in front of her, alongside Gucci glasses. Yes, she was a woman who kept up her appearance and would expect elegance in her house as well.

"Mrs. Eclestone, this is Grace Brennan, our visionary and the owner of SpaceMasters."

I rounded the table and gave the woman my best smile and handshake.

She looked up and squinted at Peyton. "Thank you, dear. You may leave us."

I took the seat opposite her, careful to sit upright on the edge and not put pressure on my butt where I'd been hit by that stupid Taser.

She waited until Peyton had closed the door to lift her Gucci glasses to her lip and pause. "Young lady, I was told excellent things about you, but frankly I'm very disappointed to find that this is the way you run your business."

I pasted on a smile and steeled myself for more. "I'm sorry to hear that." She was the customer, and the customer always came first, even if she was a pretentious bitch.

"How can I have confidence that you'll be on time with my project if you're late to a simple meeting? We'll be in Europe for only a short time, so I have a very tight window to have the work completed."

"She was mugged last night," Terry interjected. "Then Tasered and almost kidnapped this morning."

I put a hand up at Terry. "That's not important." I didn't need him defending me at my business meeting.

Mrs. Eclestone dropped her precious glasses.

Terry didn't stop. "She should've gone to the hospital, but she prioritized this meeting with you over herself, so I think you should cut her a little slack."

"Enough," I growled.

Mrs. Eclestone's jaw went slack as her gaze zeroed in on my face. "Oh, my dear, I had no idea," she exclaimed. "That must've been horrible."

"It's over now," I lied. If we didn't focus on her design, I could lose this sale and the potential of others to all her upscale friends. "I think we should get started on your project."

She ignored me. "And who might you be?" she asked Terry.

I shifted my weight to my thighs, hoping for a more comfortable position. "Mr. Goodwin is my bodyguard." I wished I could use another, more personal term.

Mrs. Eclestone's brows creased. "Perhaps you should trade him for a better one."

I held back my gasp at her insult.

Terry tensed.

"Without him, I wouldn't be here right now." I sucked in a short breath. "He saved me both times, fighting off multiple men with guns and knives." I paused. "Now, about your project—"

"That can wait." She turned. "Mr. Goodwin, is it? May I get your card? If you're that good, I know some people who might wish to use your services."

Terry spoke up before I could complain. "Have them call Lucas at Hawk Security."

The old lady's brows rose. "My goodness. Would that be the Lucas Hawk who saved Amy Wienhausen a few years ago?"

Terry nodded. "The same."

With eyes as big as saucers, she turned to me. "You should keep this one."

I nodded and turned my smile on Terry. "I intend to, Mrs. Eclestone." *And as more than just my bodyguard.*

"Please call me Gina, dear." Turning back to Terry, she asked, "Is it true that you—"

"I don't discuss client engagements, not ever," Terry said, cutting her off. He stood and slid a card across the table. "Perhaps you should go over your project with Grace before she gets called into another meeting?"

"Why, of course," Gina spluttered. "You're right."

After Terry stepped back, we shifted gears and she explained her desires. Then, I brought out the VR headsets.

"If you put this on, Gina, we'll be able to take a look at options for your closet." I rose and helped her fit the headset in place before putting mine on.

"My goodness, this is amazing," she exclaimed.

Staying on my feet, I changed out wood finishes and adjusted item placements.

She only got more excited as I helped her envision different options. This virtual reality tool for evaluating placement and options was a selling point that put us above all the other alternatives.

"Could we put an island in the middle?" she asked.

"You might think it a bit crowded, but here's what it would look like." I selected the narrowest island option and made it a warm cherry with a marble top and drawers only on one side. "This doesn't give you very much room to maneuver."

"I see what you mean."

I deleted the island. "There's another option that would be narrower and leave you more space." I selected a short padded bench and placed it in the center at the far end of the closet. "This would give you a place to sit as you pulled up stockings or put on shoes."

"Much better."

With the headset on, I didn't see him, but I felt Terry's touch on my shoulder.

"I have to make a call," he whispered. "I'll be right outside."

Nodding, I quickly grabbed his hand, turned my head, and kissed it, a gesture that didn't show up in the VR headsets.

The room felt oddly colder after the door opened and closed.

TERRY

THE TEXT I'D GOTTEN HADN'T BEEN URGENT, BUT I DIDN'T WANT TO WASTE ANY time chasing down Grace's dweeb cousin since he was clearly the cause of all this.

LUCAS: We traced the car.

I dialed. The partial plate had been enough for Jordy to do his thing with traffic cameras.

"Where are you?" Lucas asked when he answered.

"At her work. She's secure."

"How's she doing?"

"Remarkably well. A little shaken, and she won't be sitting comfortably for a day or two. She got Tasered in the ass."

"Ouch. I texted because Jordy tracked that plate to a company owned by the Russo family."

I nodded. "That makes sense. Her cousin, Elliot, said he was working for Tall Tony and messed up some delivery or other. That looks like what started all this."

"Delivery of what?"

"No idea. He didn't tell Grace, and maybe he didn't even know. They lock the cases and don't give the couriers the combination." We knew this from surveillance on a previous case.

Lucas blew out a breath. "The idiot's lucky he didn't get blown up."

"It's true then?" The rumor was that ever since getting ripped off two years ago, his shipments were wired with explosives that only the guy at the destination with the correct combination could open without getting blown to bits.

"It sure is. One of his couriers found out the hard way."

I silently agreed that Elliot was an idiot for taking on a job like that.

"I'd like to warn Russo off, but it would help to know where the cousin is first."

"Grace gave him a key to some warehouse space her company has."

"Why'd she do that? It only gets her in deeper— Never mind. It doesn't matter at this point." Clearly Lucas had the same thoughts as I did about Elliot.

I read off the address for him.

"That's close," he said. "Hold fast while I have Winston check it out."

I liked that idea. Winston Evers was ex-FBI and a solid guy who could easily corral a slippery dude like Elliot if he was there.

"How will she take it if we move her to the Fontana safe house tonight?" Lucas asked.

I'd already considered that and made up my mind that there was only one option for keeping Grace safe. "She'll hate it. I'll have her stay at my place until this is over." Pete deserved to have my full attention on keeping his little sister safe. This was the best and only way.

"Is she on board with that?" Lucas asked after a second of silence. He'd seen some of our previous frosty interactions.

"She will be." Another call interrupted us, one I had to take. "I've got a call coming in from my sister," I told him.

"Later." He disconnected.

I switched to the incoming call. "Hi, Deb. We missed you last night." Her flight back from London yesterday had been canceled.

"Just got in," she said. "A day late, but I made it. That is one long-ass flight, but better than changing planes in Chicago. How was the party?"

"Boring." That was true about the event itself, and I left it at that. My sister didn't understand my job and would go off the deep end if I tried to explain what happened after.

"How can that be? You got a medal from the damned EPA."

I valued my Purple Heart from the Marines way more than the medal I'd gotten last night. "They probably hand them out like candy."

"Bullshit." That was Deb's favorite word. "Hey, let's get together. I'm super proud of you, and I'm itching to see it."

"I can't tell my work schedule right now, but I'll try."

"Did you meet any nice EPA girls at the party?"

Now we were getting to the real reason for her call.

"None that stood out." Janice was pretty, with a killer bod, but that didn't matter. I couldn't have the only one at the party who'd attracted me.

"Serena mentioned a Janice somebody was hot and going to be there and available."

I wished there was a way I could shut down the matchmaker pipeline between Serena and my sister. "Really?"

"I worry about you, big brother. You need to socialize a little. A girlfriend would be good for you."

I knew one way to get her off the phone. "I don't need a girlfriend to get a nice hot fuck when I feel like it."

"Now you're just being crass." Deb yawned. "I'm going to nap for a while so I can stay up until tonight. Love you."

"Back at ya, sis."

CHAPTER 9

Terry

I picked up Lucas's call on the first ring. "Yes?"

"Duke is checking with his LAPD contact to get a current location on Russo. Then, as soon as we assemble the team, I want to pay the guy a visit and let him know Grace is off-limits."

We all knew Lucas's preference when visiting one of the crime groups in town, and that could be summarized as *overwhelming force.* When it came to close-quarters combat or gunplay, the local bad guys didn't stand a chance against the former spec-ops guys I worked with. But sometimes, the criminals were too egotistical to understand that.

To avoid drawing weapons, it was safer for us to have the numerical advantage and keep the dumbshits from wanting to start anything.

"I want to go along on that visit." Knowing he wouldn't like the idea, I added, "I want to look the fucker in the eyes and deliver that message."

I could almost hear Lucas's teeth grinding. "Okay. I'll send Zane over to relieve you."

"Yes, sir. Hold fast."

Zane was our newest addition, and so far he seemed a little cavalier to me—as if things outside of combat couldn't turn dangerous in a hurry. That was a lesson I'd learned more than once. But he'd get there. More important than him being a former SEAL was the fact that Duke had personally vouched for him.

"How can I help you?" Grace's assistant, Peyton, asked when I found her.

"I need to hang out and wait for an associate. Would it be okay to use Grace's office?" I knew better than to make an enemy of the assistant by not asking her permission.

"Sure." She pointed. "Right behind you. Who are you expecting?"

"Zane March is his name, but I don't know his timing."

She winked at me. "Got ya covered."

The call came a half hour later. "Zane is on the way," Lucas informed me. "Let me know when he arrives, and I'll send you rendezvous coordinates."

"Are we kitting up?" I had no idea how firm a statement Lucas wanted to make.

"No vests, handguns only. This is a friendly visit and discussion only."

"Copy that. What about the warehouse?"

"Empty, but Jordy set up cameras to monitor for activity from here. One more word of caution..."

"Yeah?" His tone made it sound ominous.

"Serena is on the way. Don't let her get in the middle of anything there."

"Copy that." *Great.* Duke's woman and Grace's best friend, Serena Benson, could be a handful at times, and now I was going to be responsible for two hard-headed women.

Duke and our team had rescued Serena when she had been in trouble with some truly bad dudes—situations she hadn't helped with some of the decisions she'd made. The last thing I needed was to have Grace get bad advice from Serena.

Zane arrived not long after the call, and before Serena. "Duke's woman, Serena, is going to be here soon," I warned him.

"You say that like it's a bad thing. I think she's cute."

Zane clearly needed a mouth filter installed. If Duke overheard a comment like that, Zane would need emergency dental work.

I shook my head. "It's a storm warning, sailor. She might want to take charge of things. Don't let her. Also, you're now responsible for two women instead of one. If those Russo pricks come looking for trouble and hurt Serena, then Duke—"

Zane raised a hand. "I get it. If anything happens to his woman, I pay the price."

"No." I poked him in the chest. "If anything happens to either of them, you pay the price."

He smirked. "I thought you wanted to throw Grace off a bridge last week."

"Protection is the job. My personal feelings are irrelevant. Understand?" I had acted terribly toward her last week, which had been normal for us. But since the attacks on her—not to mention our lip-lock moments—things had shifted.

"Understood." He put his hands in his pockets. "Does she like Italian food?"

"No." Of course Grace loved Italian food. "Concentrate on the job. The threat can come from anywhere."

"Understood."

"Don't let her leave the office," I warned Zane. Grace's last two ventures out onto the street had not gone well. "Let's go." I brought Zane with me into the demo room.

When she heard the door open, Grace excused herself and removed her headset. "We're almost done."

"Sorry, but I have to run an errand. You know Zane, here."

Grace nodded and waved at Zane. She'd met him at the dinner last night.

"He'll be with you until I get back."

She'd always been happy to see me leave in the past, but today her smile faltered. Things really had shifted between us.

"I'll stay out of your way," Zane assured her.

She shooed us out of the room with a hand motion.

Back in the front room, Peyton was meeting with two new customers who'd arrived.

As I walked past, I heard her tell them they could squeeze in a meeting with Grace after her current one finished.

Downstairs, when I drove out of the parking lot for the meeting with Russo, an odd sense of foreboding passed through me. I couldn't put my finger on it, but something didn't feel right.

GRACE

SERENA WAS WAITING BY MY OFFICE DOOR WHEN I escorted GINA ECLESTONE out of the demo room, I smiled and gave Serena a nod. "We'll be back in touch to schedule a time to bring the samples to you."

Serena, to her credit, knew enough to not interrupt me, even though her expression told me she was irritated to put it mildly.

Gina smiled. "Thank you so much. I'm looking forward to it."

This had gone better than expected, and the installation would be one to be proud of. I noticed a man I didn't recognize on our reception couch. Zane was at an empty desk near my office, facing the man.

"As soon as you're done," Peyton murmured as I got close, "your next is waiting in demo two, and she needs a minute." She motioned toward my upset friend.

I nodded, although I didn't recall that we'd booked anyone before the Morgenthous this afternoon.

"It's been wonderful meeting you, Grace," Gina said as she grasped my hands. "I can't wait to get started, and also to tell all the ladies about you. Seeing how these changes will look in my house with that system was simply marvelous."

"Call Peyton here when you know your husband will be out of the house and we have a window to bring the sample materials over." She'd said she planned to have the installation done during their upcoming Europe trip and surprise him upon his return.

The next step in our process was to bring samples of the materials that would be used so the customer could touch them, feel them, and appreciate—or not—the colors and textures involved. We couldn't allow pictures alone to suffice. And we had to take exact measurements, of course.

Her face lit up. "I will. This is going to be so exciting."

We said our goodbyes, and Marci escorted her to the door. I turned to Peyton after Serena left. "Who's in demo two?"

"She called this morning and couldn't wait. Her name's…" She consulted her notepad. "Maria Torelli." She shifted her eyes toward the reception couch. "He's her driver."

"Torelli? I don't recognize the name." But a personal driver spelled money in this town.

"And your friend—"

"Gracie…" Serena came barreling down the hall from the restrooms. "I'm here to rescue you."

I opened my arms to her and the predictable bear hug.

"I heard what happened," she said. "Tell me you're okay."

I nodded. "I'm good." Opening my arm toward my office, I suggested, "Let's step in here a moment?"

Not wanting to rehash this morning's events in front of my employees, I closed the door after us. Instead of sitting, I leaned against the desk.

"Duke said you got attacked again after you snuck out this morning."

"Yeah," I admitted, looking down.

"Are you really okay? Maybe you want to take a day off and talk." Having been kidnapped herself, Serena was probably the only person I could talk to who understood the terror.

"No. My kids here need me. This business doesn't run itself." I slipped up using the word *kids*, but didn't correct myself. Peyton had accused me of being motherhenish with my employees, and rightly so. My people deserved a boss who would look out for them in the way that I hadn't been.

She folded her arms. "You can't help them if you put yourself in danger, girl."

"I've already had that lecture. You're supposed to be on my side."

"And he was right." She stepped forward and took my hands. Hers were warm. "Look, I was stubborn and I acted out like you did, ignoring some of Duke's advice. It was a bad idea. Instead, you should stop hating him and let him help you. He cares."

" You know, Terry was beyond pissed at Duke for letting you get away."

Hearing that tugged at my heart. I shrugged. "I had to. Elliot needed me."

"And," she added, "I got in trouble for not watching you closer."

"Sorry. I couldn't take the chance that you'd try to stop me."

"And I would have, as soon as you mentioned Elliot." She leaned against the chair back. "That guy needs to grow up, and you need to stop enabling him."

"Maybe," I allowed.

"You can't bail him out of every situation."

I'd gotten this same lecture from Terry a dozen times. "You're right." Agreeing with her was easier than trying to explain my need to be there for Elliot when nobody else would. I was his only relative, the only one who cared, the only one who would help him.

"Lucas has everybody looking for the little dipshit as if he caused this."

"He did," I admitted. Then I explained the encounter at Burger King, including what Elliot had told me and getting Tasered before Terry arrived to save me...again.

"Tasered? No shit? Duke got Tasered saving me." She shivered. "He shook it off as nothing, like the macho badass he is, but I could tell it really hurt."

"Yeah. He got me in the back and..." I patted my butt. "Lower."

She laughed. "Ouch. I'd hate that."

"It's like a piranha latched on to your ass and won't let go. I don't recommend it. I still can't sit right." I omitted the part that had required me to pull down my pants for Terry.

"You really should have waited for Terry."

"Not you too." I raised a hand. "Don't you think the Tyrant himself already told me that roughly a hundred times? Including when he was…"

"Was what?"

I smiled, remembering our kiss and the gentle way Terry had treated me not long ago.

Serena's brows creased. "What?"

I shifted to my other foot. One of our rules from our group therapy was that we never lied to each other. "I don't hate him." My cheeks felt warm.

She let go of my hands and waved a finger at me. "I know you, Grace Ellen Brennan. What are you keeping from me?"

I sucked in a quick breath. "I… We sort of kissed."

"Sort of? Like a peck?"

I gave in. "Like a real kiss. A really hot kiss."

Serena's eyes went wide. She leaped forward and gave me a quick hug. "Good for you, girl. You really need to get laid."

I pulled away. "Not so fast."

"Duke swears he's a good guy, and I've seen the way he looks at you. Live a little. Have a fling. Like I told you, life is about making choices. You decide. Either the company is your entire life forever, like it has been, or devote a sliver of your time to living. You know my vote." Her hands went to her hips and her head cocked as she waited for a response.

Her words hit home, but it wasn't as simple as she made out. I had allowed the company to dominate my life, but my employees and their families depended on me. "I love that you came to check on me, but I have a customer waiting."

Her face took on a disappointed look. "See, company, company, company. When are you going to take care of yourself?"

She stared at me, a silent demand that I agree with her.

Checking my watch, I decided it was time for my next pain pills. Opening the bottle on the desk, I popped two and chased them down with a slug of water.

Serena continued her death stare. "Why can't you admit I'm right?"

"Okay already." I sighed dramatically. "Terry was right. You're right. It would have been better if I'd waited. Satisfied?"

I even said the words without my fingers crossed behind my back.

"I meant about you're giving yourself permission to live."

"I'll try."

Her smile returned. "Now that wasn't so hard, was it? So, Terry?"

So what if my first instinct for years had been to fight with Terry? I didn't think her question merited anything more than silence.

"I saw Zane outside," she said. "But I didn't see Sir Galahad."

A smile came naturally. Sir Galahad was a cute nickname for Terry, one I never would have considered before. "He said he had to run an errand, and he called Zane in to watch over me until he gets back."

"When can we get out of here? I've got a blender at home just itching to make us margaritas."

I pushed away from the desk. "Not right now. I've got a full day here. Maybe after work."

"I know how Terry grates on you, and Duke is on another assignment right now, but I can have Duke talk to Lucas and switch things around so you can get some distance from Terry and spend some time with me and Duke. We can do another sleepover. How's that sound?"

I hid my smirk. After our kiss, no way was I putting intentional distance between me and Terry until I figured out this thing between us, whatever it was. "No thanks. I don't want to rock the boat. I'll stick with Terry and sleep in my own bed tonight. Bonnie and Clyde need me too."

She eyed me warily. "Are you sure? I mean, it won't be any trouble to get Duke—"

I cut her off with a hand. "I'll stick with Terry." The memory of him carrying me this morning warmed me.

She cocked her head. "You're smiling."

I laughed. "I'm just so happy that I've got as good a friend as you looking out for me." I started for the door. "Now, I have customers waiting for me."

She sighed and followed. "The offer is open, if you need it." Reaching the door, she gave me a quick hug. "Remember, I'm only a phone call away."

"I know," I said.

As Serena left, Peyton gave me the quick rundown on the new prospects. "She's in demo two. They have a three-hundred-and-forty-lot subdivision going up in Thousand Oaks, and they want us to do the master closets and pantries. She said they have nine styles, but it's only three sizes of closet and pantry. She was insistent that she had to see you today or go with somebody else for the project."

This was exciting stuff. Three-hundred and forty homes would be a monster order for us.

Zane stood to follow me when I turned toward demo room two.

"I've got this." I didn't need him spooking a potentially big client.

He nodded and sat back down.

In demo two, Peyton repeated my intro as visionary and owner of SpaceMasters before leaving us alone.

After a quick handshake, I gingerly took a seat. Having my ass sliced open sure put a crimp in my movements. "Maria, I understand you have a large project you wish us to bid on."

"I do need your help." She held her phone up for me to see and flipped between pictures of Peyton and Marci out in the office. "This is important. If you make a sound, my associate outside will kill one of these women. Do you understand?"

My blood froze. This couldn't be happening. Shakily, I nodded. I had no way to warn Zane.

"Good. I want you to listen very carefully, because Lorenzo won't hesitate to kill more of them if they scream. He hates women who scream. Nod if you understand."

I nodded again. Lorenzo and this lady were both first-rate assholes. I'd disliked people before, but this lady and Lorenzo had just moved to the top of my shit list.

A knock sounded at the door, and Peyton opened it. "Would you like coffee, water, or a soda?"

"No thank you, Peyton," Maria replied with a smile.

I didn't turn around and merely shook my head. "Not me either." I had to keep her away from this monster.

Peyton closed the door, and we were alone again.

I wanted to rip that smile off her face and make her eat it. "What do you want?"

"My employer wants to talk to your cousin, Elliot, but he seems to be avoiding us."

"What does that have to do with me?"

"You're his only relative. He has no friends he can trust. He sought you out this morning because he has nobody else to turn to. If you tell me where he is, I'll see that he goes to see my boss in one piece. My boss's other employees who are out looking for him won't be so gentle."

"I don't have any idea where he is."

She stared at me. "I don't believe you."

"Believe what you want. I can't lead you to him, because I don't know where he is."

She held up her phone again. "Eeny, meeny, miny, moe." She flicked back and forth between the pictures. "Which one of them dies to save your cousin?"

"I," I half yelled before lowering my voice, "don't fucking know." My hand started trembling. Why was it always my right hand?

"You should be quieter. If your assistant gets suspicious, Lorenzo will have no choice but to act. To make it easier on you, I could flip a coin. Would you like that?"

I sucked in a breath. "Look, you can threaten me all you want, but that doesn't change the fact that I don't know where he went after this morning. You leave my people alone."

"Their fate is in your hands. Where is your cousin?"

This was the first time I'd felt like I was in the presence of pure evil, the kind of person my brother had been sent overseas to dispatch from this earth. "I don't fucking know."

She appraised me for several silent seconds. "Let's say I believe you."

I let out the breath I'd been holding. She had to believe me. I couldn't betray Elliot to someone as evil as her, I couldn't let her harm my people, and the truth was, I didn't know where Elliot was right now.

"Then the equation changes." She slid me a business card across the table. "Take this."

Gingerly, I did. It had only her name and a phone number on it.

"If he contacts you again and you don't call me, it will be very bad for you." She pulled out a knife and slammed the tip into my pretty mahogany table. "Because Lorenzo will be forced to deal with you. It may not be the same day or the next, or even in the next month, but it will happen because he enjoys his work too much. And when he finds you, nobody will save you. Do you understand me?"

She left the knife stuck in the wood. My gut twisted.

"Grace, do you understand me?"

I nodded. What else could I do?

"That's right. I'm not a bad person. I don't want to see you get hurt. That's why you have that number. One call, and all of this ugliness goes away."

I nodded again. She had a screw loose. I needed Terry so badly. He'd know how to handle a psychopath like this. I almost puked when I glanced at the knife again, but refused to give this horrible woman the satisfaction.

"Good. Now we wait."

I narrowed my eyes, not sure I'd heard her. "Wait? If you think Elliot's just going to call out of the blue, you're nuts."

She merely smiled and put a finger to her lips. "We wait for instructions."

As the minutes of silence dragged on, I managed to calm my hand under the table, and my breathing, looking for a play. What would Terry tell me to do?

If she got distracted when her phone rang, maybe I could lunge for the knife. But then what? Even if I got control of her, how did I get the upper hand on Lorenzo outside? Maybe I could yell to Zane.

But that would alert Lorenzo to Zane and put a target on his chest. What if Zane didn't understand me and Lorenzo got the drop on him? Then everybody in the office would be at risk.

A half hour later, I jerked when her cell rang.

She laughed at my reaction, then answered without moving away from the knife stuck in the table. "Yes? I've got her with me."

It had to be her bad-guy boss on the other end, whoever that was.

"Come now? Okay." She hung up.

"Sorry you have to run," I joked. "I'd say it's been a pleasure, but I don't want to lie."

She stood, pulled the knife from the table, and waved it with a smile. "Very funny, Grace. You're coming with me."

My heart stopped. "Oh no, I'm not." This couldn't be happening again, not three times in less than a day. What the hell had Elliot gotten me into?

She swiped her phone and held up a picture of Peyton. "You're coming with me to see the boss. We can do this the easy way or the hard way. In the hard way, she dies. Which is it going to be, Grace? Do you want your assistant to pay the price for your stubbornness?"

The tremor in my hand started again. "I'll go with you. But you have to promise to leave my people alone." I picked up my purse, the one that didn't have a Taser or pepper spray in it because I'd been too combative with Terry, too pig-headed to accept the security professional's advice.

"Keep it nice and casual. You and I are going to waltz out of here to visit a location so you can take measurements. Peyton explained that as your process, right?"

I nodded.

"If anyone gets suspicious, then things get messy. And we don't want messy, do we?"

"No." I shook my head in agreement.

CHAPTER 10

Terry

The text message arrived on the drive to meet Lucas and the team. I glanced at it in case it was Grace—it wasn't.

> CAROL HAWK: Call me when you are alone.

The Hawk family had taken me in after my return from the Middle East. Carol and Henry Hawk had even invited me to their occasional family dinners.

With no siblings, and having lost my parents years ago, I hadn't ever expected to be a part of the kind of family dinner you saw on TV, but the Hawks had changed that. I was grateful.

This might be as alone as I was going to be all day, so I dialed her back using hands-free Bluetooth.

"Thank you for calling, Terry," Mrs. Hawk answered sweetly.

"I'm driving right now, so I have a few minutes. How can I help you?"

"I need somebody I trust will be discreet arranging something I need—something that has to be kept in complete confidence," she explained. "I know I can trust you."

"Of course," I answered. I had top-security clearance from my days in the military. Arranging a surprise birthday party or whatever should be a piece of cake.

"I need an investigation," she said.

My breath hitched. So *not* an innocuous surprise party.

My boss would not take violating the chain of command lightly. "I'm sure Lucas would be happy to help you."

She was silent for a few beats. "This is rather delicate," she said, with reluctance in her voice. "You can't mention anything about this to anybody, including Lucas. Not one thing, not even this phone call."

That got my attention, in a dangerous way. "I understand," I said. She wouldn't be asking me this if she didn't think it was extremely important. I had now agreed to deceive my boss, if need be. "What would you like me to look into?"

"Not what, but whom."

Holy shit. Lord help me, I'd better not have just agreed to get in the middle of a marital issue with my boss's parents. "Who is it?"

If she said her husband, I was going to puke. Lucas would have my balls.

"When can we meet? I don't want to discuss the particulars over the phone."

I was only two blocks from the meeting point for the Russo confrontation. "I'm very busy today. I'll get free as soon as my current assignment allows."

"Thank you, Terry. I'll look forward to hearing from you soon. I knew I could count on you."

"Of course. I'll be in touch. Bye." I ended the call and parked behind Winston's Cayenne, next to our little group.

It wasn't easy, but Grace's safety was on the line, so I exited the car one-hundred-percent focused on the Russo meeting and joined the team on the sidewalk.

"According to Winston's contact, the restaurant around the corner is the latest Russo headquarters," Lucas said. "Their intel is that Tall Tony might be out of town, so we could be meeting with one of his sons, which makes this unpredictable."

"Why?" Winston voiced the question we all had.

Lucas sighed. "Tony and I have a history. He won't be looking to cross us. But I haven't dealt with any of the sons, and they could be wild cards. Expect two guards at the door and two inside, probably one more in the back room with the guy in charge. We walk from here. Follow me, single file until we're inside. Nobody draws a weapon unless I do. I do all the talking. Understood?"

Around the circle, Duke, Winston, Constance, and I all nodded.

Lucas Hawk had a sixth sense about things. I half expected him to look at me and ask what was wrong. Instead he said, "Weapons check."

Relieved, I checked my SIG. Lying to the man was nowhere on my list for today.

The rest of the team did the same, and we holstered our weapons.

Lucas checked his ear. "Comms check, Jordy."

He was the only one of us wearing an earpiece.

Lucas nodded. "Jordy, you've got electronic overwatch. *Horseshit* is the word to call in the cavalry or if you hear things go kinetic." To the rest of us he explained, "Wellbourne is on standby with six officers, if we need them."

Lieutenant Wellbourne was our guardian angel at LAPD since Lucas had saved his wife during a kidnapping years ago. The problem was, if the LAPD group wasn't already here, they'd likely be too late to the party. But Lucas was calling the shots, so that was the plan we'd follow.

"Execute," Lucas said as he walked off.

My girl was the one in danger, so I bumped Duke aside to take the position directly behind Lucas.

Duke grunted and followed me with Constance and Winston behind him.

Rounding the corner, two goons on either side of the restaurant door came into view.

We marched on.

The guy on one side of the door saw us and surprised the hell out of me. He pulled open the door and held it for us as we approached. This was weird times ten.

Maybe Lucas had called ahead and forgotten to mention it.

Inside were two more guards.

"Mr. Hawk," the taller one said. "May I help you?"

"We're here to see your boss."

"All of you?"

"All of us," Lucas said seriously.

The shorter of the two smiled.

The taller one held his arm open toward a door at the back. "Very well. This way."

Yes, we had entered the *Twilight Zone* here. People like us, armed, were not just invited into the back room to see the head of a crime family.

I wiggled my fingers. Either Lucas had called ahead to arrange this, or we were walking into an ambush.

Duke looked on edge as well.

Constance had her hand close to her weapon.

Winston either didn't feel the tension or was putting on an act for the bad guys.

When we entered, the room smelled of cigar smoke. An unsmiling man with small, dark eyes sat behind a large wooden desk. As Lucas had predicted, there were two additional guards in the room. One with a bushy mustache had stationed himself in the corner behind the man at the desk. The other, bald, was off to our left with his arms crossed.

Lucas took position on the left, near Baldy, and I stood to his right, with Duke farther right. Candice and Winston flanked Tall and Short until they left the room, giving us the numerical advantage Lucas had predicted.

Mentally, I thanked Lucas for the spot he'd given me. If anything happened, Lucas would take care of the guy on the left, Duke the guy against the back wall, and I had the bossman behind the desk, whoever he was. He didn't match the picture of Tony Russo we'd been shown.

"Lucas Hawk, is it? I've been expecting you," the man behind the desk said, addressing me. Expecting us, but not knowing what Lucas looked like, was a rookie mistake. He motioned to the two chairs in front of the desk. "I'm Victor Russo."

Mustache Man behind him chuckled.

"I'm here to see Tony," Lucas announced.

Victor steepled his hands, shifting his gaze to Lucas. "He's busy. I'm handling this matter for my father."

"I understand you're looking for Elliot Boyle," Lucas said. "Why?"

"He took something that doesn't belong to him."

"What?" Lucas asked.

Victor shook his head dismissively. "That's not your concern."

Lucas shrugged. "You don't want to know where it is, then?"

Instantly interested, Victor sat up. "Where?"

"My investigators are top notch," Lucas replied. "I may be able to assist you."

Victor fidgeted and gave in. "He was supposed to make a delivery for us. He disappeared with the package. My customer is not happy."

"Send another."

"It can't be replaced, and my customer has already paid half."

"Tell him to wait while you find the guy. I'm sure he'll turn up sooner or later."

"These people are not the kind you say that to." Victor's face and his words telegraphed actual fear.

"How valuable?" Lucas asked.

"Not your concern."

"Do you want our help or not?"

Victor contemplated the offer. "Ten million."

I swallowed a laugh. Victor was an idiot to entrust Elliot with anything that valuable. "What does the package look like?"

"A metal briefcase."

"The exploding kind?" Lucas asked.

Baldy laughed.

Victor grinned. "Not your concern."

"What's in it?" Lucas asked.

"Still not your concern," he shot back.

"Then I should talk to your father," Lucas said.

"I'm in charge of this."

"Not if you don't even know what's in the case. I don't deal with underlings," Lucas said sternly.

Baldy pushed off the wall. "Don't you dare talk to him like that, asshole." Then he grabbed Lucas's arm. *Big mistake.*

Lucas grabbed his hand and with a practiced twist, forced a yowling Baldy's face down to the desk as his arm rose high behind him.

Mustache Guy reached for his gun.

Before he could get it out, Duke had his SIG aimed at the guy's head. "Don't even think about it."

I'd drawn on Victor, who hadn't moved, but his face showed the fear that Lucas brought out in anyone.

Mustache Guy slowly removed his hand from his jacket.

I noticed Victor move his hand below the desk. "Press that button and they'll be calling you One-Ear Victor." I shifted my aim slightly to one side.

He froze.

"Or maybe I can't shoot straight and they'll just call you dead."

He pulled his hand back and placed it on the desk. "You'll never get away with this. We'll squash you all like bugs."

"I came here to give you some friendly advice," Lucas said. "But you aren't being very friendly. Does your man here attack every guest and call him an asshole? I think an apology is in order."

Baldy squealed when Lucas applied a bit more pressure. "I'm sorry."

"I still think we should talk." Lucas released him.

Duke and I lowered our weapons.

I relaxed, as Lucas did.

"Grace Brennan is Terry's girl." Lucas tapped me on the shoulder. "And she is off-limits. She doesn't have anything of yours or know anything about it. Understand?"

"We have no interest in her. It's her cousin we need to talk to."

"Bullshit," I exploded. "Your guys tried to abduct her this morning." Lucas glared at me, and I shut up.

"A misunderstanding, I'm sure." Victor laughed. He was an asshole. "I want the package her cousin, Elliot, stole. She can choose to be part of the solution or part of the problem."

"Let me make myself clear," Lucas bit out. "She is not a part of this. If you come after her again, you go through us."

Victor let out a breath and leaned back. "You didn't need to bring all your friends with you for such a simple conversation."

Lucas shrugged. "I thought you might want to meet them before deciding to go after Grace again. My team is former special forces, FBI, and Secret Service. Constance is the only one who hasn't killed multiple people who messed with us."

"Hey," Constance complained. "I aimed to hit the guy in the crotch."

Victor and Mustache Guy winced. Baldy was busy massaging his sore shoulder.

"And my aim was true," she added. "He's singing soprano and won't ever be getting his equipment up again," she added.

Duke chuckled. "That's as good a being dead."

"But a lot less paperwork," she mused.

Victor didn't appreciate the humor. His beady eyes shifted to me and back to Lucas. "How long will it take you to locate Elliot?"

"Like I said," Lucas drawled. "I don't work with underlings. Have your father call me."

Victor's face distorted into a snarl as he picked up his phone and dialed. "Maria? Very good… Yes, now." A smirk crossed his face as he turned back to Lucas. "Since you won't help, I'll find Elliot with Miss Brennan's assistance."

I shook my head. "She doesn't want to talk to you."

"We'll see." He motioned to the door. "Show these gentlemen out."

Lucas touched his ear as we hit the street. "Jordy, relay to Wellbourne that we're clear and no blood was shed. He can release his people."

Outside, I finally had a chance to ask my question. "Are we really going to work with those assholes?"

Lucas shook his head. "We needed the intel."

"Who tipped them off to expect us?" Constance asked.

"Winston?" Lucas asked. "Who did you call to get this location?"

"My usual department source. I doubt it was him, but I'm sure he had to call someone else in the department to get the info."

"Or," I added, "it could have been one of the guys Wellbourne called for backup."

Victor, the little prick, had been too smug for my taste. I needed to get back to Grace and be ready for when the next shoe dropped.

Lucas nodded as we walked. "From now on, we don't talk to LAPD on this case."

∽

GRACE

"NO HEROICS," MARIA REMINDED ME AS I OPENED THE DOOR TO LEAVE demo two.

As soon as I cleared the door, I searched the room and spotted Zane. We would have to walk nearby to reach the door. Was there a way I could warn him nonverbally? My stomach dropped when I saw Lorenzo eyeing Peyton, who was in the open at her desk.

"Explain the trip normally," Maria whisper-warned me as we approached my assistant.

With each step, I got closer to vomiting and wishing Terry was here. I would have given anything to rewind this morning and decide to stay on the couch in Terry's arms. I could have told Mrs. Eclestone that we'd have to reschedule. How the hell could I get a message to any of them?

"The landlord needs a signature on some disclosures or other. I left it on your desk," Peyton noted.

"Sure." Scribbling on that could be my opportunity to get a message to them.

"But we're in a hurry," Maria said. "And legal documents can take so much time to review." Her demonic eyes conveyed very clearly that I didn't have a choice.

Lorenzo had his eyes on us all.

"Probably right," I agreed. "I'll get to it later."

Going into sales mode, Peyton asked Maria, "What did you think of our offerings?"

"I think my boss will be very interested in your proposal when it's finalized," Maria said. "But first we need to take some measurements, isn't that right, Grace?" She angled toward the door.

Message received. "Yeah. We'll do that right now."

"You look tired," Peyton said, picking up her phone. "Paul is up next. I'll get him."

"No," I said quickly and waved for her to put the phone down. "I'll do this one myself." I couldn't fail in getting Maria and her henchman out the door and away from my people. Without Terry here, it was the only way.

"But—"

"I said no," I repeated firmly as I started for the door. My people weren't safe until I got out of the office.

Peyton's face fell like I'd slapped her.

Ignoring her, I strode past, my eyes landing on Lorenzo's evil face before glancing away to Marci and then Zane.

The former Seal didn't even look up.

Fuck this. Nobody threatens my people and gets away with it.

Terry's words echoed in my head. *"Don't go quietly. Fight with whatever you have."*

By the desk Zane had chosen, my legs went wobbly, my head lolled to the side, and my eyes rolled back. Why was fainting my only gift?

"Grace," Peyton screamed as I fell to the floor.

CHAPTER 11

Grace

When I crumpled to the floor, I made sure to not hit my head this time.

Peyton screamed again.

Zane bounded up, rushed to me, and kneeled, cradling my head. "Grace?"

Through hooded eyes, just in case, I whispered, "Driver is armed, Tango."

Pete had drilled into me that military communications had to be short and simple.

It worked. Zane drew his weapon lightning fast, whirled, and trained it on Lorenzo. "Hands up, asshole."

Maria's eyes went wide as she froze in place.

I gritted my teeth and sat up. "I'm not going anywhere with you."

The woman snarled and bolted for the door.

"Fight with whatever you have. Even a pencil can be a weapon," Terry had said.

I pulled the pack of darts I always carried from my purse. "Stop right there, bitch."

Visualizing the bullseye I normally aimed at, I let one fly.

With an agonizing scream, she stumbled.

I'd gotten her square in the ass.

She got to her feet again.

I stood and let a second dart fly. "I said stop."

After another scream, she went down on her face, the second dart sticking out of her other ass cheek.

I ran to her and gave her a kick. "Take that, bitch. Nobody threatens my people." She deserved another dozen darts, maybe more.

She twisted on the floor and spat at me. "You'll pay for this."

I brandished my third and final dart. "Move and I'll jam this one into your ear. My brother tells me your death will be quick."

She cursed, but didn't try to get away.

Terry's advice to not go quietly had been spot on, and dammit, Pete would have been proud of me.

Peyton rushed toward me, while my other dozen employees kept their distance.

While I brandished my dart at Maria, Zane zip-tied Lorenzo and dragged him over to join us. "Damn, girl, that was a badass move. I like your aim with those things."

"Terry told me to not go quietly."

"I'll make you hurt," Maria snarled.

I waved my dart and kicked her again. "Shut up, you worthless piece of shit."

Zane grabbed my leg before I could kick her again. "That's enough, Xena."

I backed up. Xena Warrior Princess—I kinda liked that.

He pulled one dart out of Maria's ass, and then the second.

The woman squealed each time.

He handed them back. "Are these the poison-tipped ones?" he asked with a straight face.

Maria went pale.

I could see we made a good team. "Nope." I waved my third dart. "But this one is."

Zane smirked and shook a finger at Maria.. "Better not move."

The beet-red anger in her face drained away.

Peyton drew back. "I'll call the—"

"No," Zane barked. "Nobody…" He looked around the room. "Nobody calls anybody. Absolutely no calls until my team arrives." He pulled his phone out.

If Terry was Rambo, what was Zane? He'd labeled me Xena, like the TV show? Yes, I took in a deep breath. They could call me Xena the Dart Princess.

While Zane was on the phone, his eyes tracked Peyton.

I leaned over Maria. "If you come near me or my people again, you'll get a lot more than two darts in the ass."

As Zane spoke on the phone, he wandered closer to Peyton. *Interesting.*

∼

TERRY

AS I SAT AT THE STOPLIGHT ON THE WAY BACK TO GRACE'S FIRM, I contemplated what we'd learned, and it wasn't a lot.

Elliot had already told Grace this had to do with a delivery. If it fit in a briefcase, it couldn't be drugs, not at a value of ten-million dollars. So what the hell was Russo selling, and who was on the other end of the transaction that he and his family would be so afraid of?

Gold would be too heavy, and that much cash wouldn't fit in a briefcase, which probably left precious gems. I couldn't think of anything else that made sense.

According to Grace, Elliot said the delivery had gone bad. He hadn't said he'd been robbed or mugged, so how else would it go bad? The Russos weren't stupid enough to have Elliot exchange a case for five-million dollars, so it hadn't been a rip-off at the delivery point.

As the light turned green, I accelerated with a laugh. One thing was for sure, Elliot hadn't known what was in the case, or its value. Otherwise, he'd be long gone by now.

It still wasn't making sense to me when my phone rang through the car speakers. The display said Jordy.

I accepted the call just as a jerk cut in front of me. "Fuck."

"What's wrong?" Jordy asked.

"Nothing, just an idiot driver. What's up?"

"There's been an incident with Grace."

The hairs on the back of my neck stood at attention as I mashed down the throttle and swept around the asshole who'd just cut me off. "What happened? Is she okay? Where the hell was Zane?"

"Get a hold of yourself," Jordy insisted. "She's fine. Lucas is also on the line."

I pressed the gas harder to make the next light. "I'm on the way."

"No, you're going to get yourself killed driving like that," Jordy said. "I won't fill you in unless you slow down."

He tracked all our company cars, a fact I'd forgotten for a moment, and

I knew Lucas would back him up. I let off the gas. I wasn't fucking waiting to find out what had happened. "Tell me."

"A man and a woman came into the office pretending to be clients with a large business deal." It was Lucas's voice.

"Fuck." It had to have been that pair who'd been there when I left. "Tell me they didn't hurt Grace."

"They scared her, but she's fine," Lucas said. "She and Zane got the drop on them."

"How?"

"We don't have the details," Jordy said. "Zane is a little busy securing them. All he said was that Grace helped with something you taught her."

"You need to hustle," Lucas said, changing the subject. "And bring those two in for a stay in our hospitality suites. Before one of the employees calls the cops."

I sped up again. "Understood. Zane can transport. I should be guarding Grace."

"Zane was there for the takedown. He needs to stay in case one of the employees mentions a gun. Constance is on the way. She knows the evaluation script and will brief Zane. You transport the pair."

"Copy that." I didn't care for it, but his decision was logical.

"This time," Lucas said "we're not letting them go so quickly."

I made the next traffic light cleanly and was only three blocks away now. "Good thing. I'm going to have words with them."

"Words only," Lucas cautioned me. "But first, we need to get Grace somewhere safe."

I knew where I thought she was safest. "Copy that." I hung up and sprinted inside once I reached the building.

CHAPTER 12

Grace

Zane moved Maria and Lorenzo into the conference room at gunpoint.

I followed, brandishing my final dart like a micro-sword.

Then Zane bound their wrists and ankles with more zip ties and finished it off by securing them to the table legs. "They won't be bothering anybody."

Lorenzo grunted, his evil eyes trained on Zane.

"Don't worry, asshole. You'll get plenty of time to talk later," Zane assured him.

The woman shot daggers from her eyes at me. She was pissed, and I felt some pride in that. She deserved everything she'd gotten for threatening my people. If I hadn't needed to project class to my employees, I would have spit on her.

Leaving the conference room, Zane's eyes traveled to Peyton, who was on the phone at her desk.

"She's single," I said under my breath, answering the question in his eyes.

"I didn't ask."

I rolled my eyes. "I didn't say you did."

My employees were clearly shaken and mumbling between themselves.

Zane positioned himself at the door. "It's okay now," he told them. "The cavalry's on the way. Just hang out for a little while."

They didn't look convinced.

"Never a dull day," I joked. "But he's right. The excitement's all over." Still jittery from the adrenaline, I leaned against the wall like I had no cares at all and waited. I had to be strong for my people.

It wasn't long before Terry burst through the door with a yell. "Grace?"

I'd never been so happy to see anyone. I wasted no time running to him and planting a kiss on him.

He wrapped me in his powerful arms—and he broke the kiss far too early for my taste. "I shouldn't have gone," he lamented.

"It's okay. I'm safe. We all are."

"That's not the point. You're my responsibility. I'm the one who needs to be taking care of you."

"You did. You sent Zane, and he took care of business."

Zane watched us, a curious look on his face, then shifted his attention to Peyton again.

Peyton smiled at us, but she smiled a lot.

Looking up into the eyes of the man who'd saved me twice already, I smoothed a hand over his chest. "I'm fine, and Zane took down the asshole."

Terry released me. "Where are they?"

I pointed. "In the conference room. Zane trussed them up like two hogs."

Terry raised a hand to Zane. "Thanks, man. Keep the employees calm, and no calls."

It was only a split second, but I caught Zane try to hide how he looked at Peyton. Then the SEAL's face turned stoic and he nodded back at Terry. "Will do. That one's a wildcat." He inclined his head toward me.

"I know. My girl has claws." Terry pulled me toward the conference room.

That was the first time he'd ever called me *his girl*, and it warmed me inside.

"What's her story?" He pointed to Maria as we entered.

"She wanted me to go with her to meet a guy named Victor Russo."

"Victor, huh? He's the mafia dirtbag we just met with, the son of the guy who runs the Italian version of the mob here, a real piece of work."

"She introduced herself as Maria Torelli. I don't know if that's her real name or not."

"We'll check it out."

"She said the guy was her driver, called him Lorenzo. Anyway, once in the demo room, she threatened to have him start killing my people if I didn't tell her where Elliot was. I finally convinced her I didn't know, because I don't. Then she waited for a phone call, and when it came, she threatened to have him—" I nodded toward Lorenzo. "—kill one of my people if I didn't go with her quietly to meet this Victor guy." My hand tremor had started again.

"Dammit," he swore. "We were just leaving to see Victor when he made that call. The bastard must have told them to snatch you while we were with him." Anger at the situation, or maybe at himself, came off him in waves. "I—"

"It's not your fault."

Terry's anger ramped up. "I'm going to—"

"Stop it," I snapped. "Come with me." I led him to my office and closed the door. "Pete warned me a long time ago not to start something in anger. *Plan with a cool head,*' he said. You didn't do anything wrong. I'm okay."

Shaking his head, Terry disagreed. "The call was odd. I should have figured it out and called Zane to warn him. And as for going off half-cocked, I promise to make a careful plan before I go beat the shit out of him."

I laughed. "Still not your fault." I took his arm. Realizing this strong man had put all his energy, all his focus, into protecting me was a giddy feeling.

He blew out a breath, not arguing, but also not agreeing. "Go on. What happened next?"

"I thought it was too dangerous for my employees not to go along with her, but then I remembered what you said."

"Don't go quietly?" he prodded.

"Exactly, so I fainted right next to Zane. Of course he rushed to me."

He grabbed my shoulders. "You fainted? That was your plan?"

"No, silly. I faked fainting. I mean, I have so much practice I can pull it off pretty convincingly. And when Zane got to me, I whispered *driver armed tango.*"

Terry chuckled. "You know the lingo."

"What do you expect? My brother was spec ops. After that, Zane drew on the guy—caught him totally by surprise—and the woman made a run for the door, but I nailed her with two darts right in the ass."

Terry burst out laughing and hugged me. "You are truly something else, Kitten."

I hugged him back, still trembling a little from the adrenaline rush of it all, but warm and at ease in his arms. "You said to fight with whatever I had, and I'm a good shot with my darts. It'll be a week before she can sit. Or maybe she'll get an infection. I've never thought about sanitizing them."

"God, I lo... I like the way you think."

I pressed myself into him. He was all warm, hard muscle. Looking up, I only had one question. "When are you going to kiss me, big guy?"

He tightened his arms around me and chuckled. "I recall the boss lady saying something about no PDA at the office."

"The door is closed, so it's not public. It's just DA." I raised up on my toes and pressed my lips to his.

In seconds we were frantically pawing each other, and the level of passion was no less than it had been on my couch. His tongue invaded my mouth, and once again we dueled for control. He reached under my top and cupped my needy breast.

I drank in the taste of him, his hard muscles under my hands, the feel of his hair as I tangled fingers in it, and the sound he made when I cupped him through his pants. No, this was not the place to let it loose, but there was definitely a treat in there I wanted access to.

He growled into my mouth. "Be very careful what you do next, Kitten. Right now, I'm not capable of gentle, or quiet."

His phone rang, keeping me from having to make a decision. After a few seconds he untangled himself from me. "I have to get this. It's the boss."

Reluctantly, I disengaged. All I wanted to do was cling to this man and climb all over him.

"Yes?" he answered.

I couldn't do anything about my face or hair, but I smoothed my blouse and skirt just in case.

"She's here... Okay."

"Lucas wants to talk to both of us." He set the phone down and pressed the speaker button. "You're on speaker."

"How are you, Grace?" Lucas Hawk asked.

"It was harrowing for a while, but I'm recovered now, thanks to Zane."

"He said your quick thinking was key."

I bloomed with pride. "It was Terry's advice that made the difference."

"I'm calling to tell you we're going to put our full effort into protecting you and locating your cousin, Elliot, free of charge."

Everything had happened so quickly since last night—I hadn't even thought about the cost in manpower and time they'd invested in me and my stupid cousin already, but I didn't do charity. "No, that's—"

"Stop right there, Grace Brennan. You listen to me." Even over the phone, Lucas Hawk could be intimidating in the extreme. "Several of us worked with your brother, and Terry was the administrator of your trust. That makes you family in my book."

"I pay my own way," I insisted.

"You're family, young lady. We take care of family."

"While I appreciate the sentiment, don't you dare *young lady* me. I'm a grown woman. I do not accept charity from anybody, and that includes you, Lucas Hawk."

"Grace." I heard the exasperation in his voice. "That is not acceptable."

Pete and Terry had told me that *nobody* argued with Lucas Hawk, and now I understood what they meant.

"Lucas, the answer is still no."

"Very well. We'll do it your way. I'll submit a bill at the end of our engagement."

"Thank you." I'd gotten my way, but I don't know what I was thinking. I had just agreed to take on a financial responsibility I was certain I couldn't handle. *Damned pride.*

"You get the friends and family discount, of course."

That was a relief.

"Do you understand me?"

I was done arguing with him. "Yes, sir."

"Good. You can have either Terry or Zane as your primary bodyguard, your choice. Which would you like?"

Terry actually looked concerned that I might not choose him.

"Grace?" Lucas asked impatiently.

Zane would be the emotionally safe choice, but I had to go with the devil I knew, the one who'd just kissed me senseless, and the one I knew would create impossible arguments. Pete had trusted Terry, even if the man drove me crazy. "I would like it to be Terry." I detected a hint of a smile from Terry, although he tried to hide it.

"Very well. Remember, he's the security expert, so you need to do what he says. That's what's required to keep you safe, and I owe that to your brother."

His mention of Pete set me off balance for a second. "Sure, within reason," I quipped.

Lucas ignored my joke. "Terry, you and I should discuss the plan."

Terry took the phone off speaker and listened intently for a minute. "Yes, sir," he said, hanging up.

"Your apartment is not secure, so Lucas wants to put you in our Fontana safe house until we can get this sorted out."

"No," was my one-word answer, one it seemed I needed with every one of these testosterone-fueled security guys.

Terry's tone darkened. "I don't think you understand."

"I understand completely. The answer is no. I will take security advice from you guys because that is your expertise, not mine. I will allow a bodyguard nearby. But I will not abandon my life and the business I've built. If I abandon the business, then they've won. I have people who depend on me. Their families depend on me. I cannot and will not let them down."

"Maybe you didn't hear me. Your apartment is not safe and can't be made safe. You could easily be attacked there. We need to go to a safe place until we find Elliot and sort this out."

"With the traffic, Fontana might as well be Mars, as far as I'm concerned. You've got to come up with a better alternative than that."

He frowned. "I know a place in Marina del Rey. It's not an official safe house, but it'll do. Is that close enough?"

I didn't want to give in easily, but I had to admit it was. "Not ideal."

"We're shooting for safe, not ideal, so Marina del Rey it is. You're staying at my place. It's very secure."

"Wait a minute, your place? You said *a* place. You can't just decide how and where I'm going to live without my input. And I'm not moving in with you."

"Agreed," Terry said. "On bodyguard, your choice was Zane or me, and you chose me."

I relaxed.

"As for location, since your apartment is out of the question, I gave you the choice of Fontana or Marina del Rey, and you said Marina del Rey was close enough."

I could see now that I'd been maneuvered into this. "It's not fair. I need another choice."

"Life's not fair. At least you got a choice, and it's only temporary. And you won't be *moving in* with me. Your safety is the priority. If you really hate me that much, we can go to Fontana."

I waited, secretly hoping, and maybe if I was being honest, dreading a little, that he'd say he preferred I stay with him.

He didn't. "What'll it be, Kitty?"

I was stuck. "Staying with you will be acceptable, only if you have hot water and real food in the fridge."

"I have both," Terry announced. "And, this is only as long as you're in danger."

"You better not be lying." I was probably lying by omission here. The thing that scared me about staying with Terry was what had happened between us on the couch. The kiss had changed everything, but I had no idea how that was going to turn out, and it scared the bejesus out of me. Should I want him? Maybe not. But did I want him? Absolutely yes, underlined twice, and I was afraid of screwing it up.

"You know I don't lie."

I looked into his eyes and saw the conviction there. "I know."

"Grace, I have only ever wanted what was best for you."

That proclamation made me feel small. I'd just spent this conversation, and many years before that, battling the man who only wanted to keep me safe.

Terry was bossy to a fault and drove me up a wall sometimes. No, all the time, but his intentions were pure. He'd proven that. If only we could discuss things more calmly.

I had the sudden urge to jump into his arms and apologize for my bitchiness when a knock sounded at the door.

I backed away before Peyton stuck her head inside. "Are you ready for the next one?"

Terry smiled and coolly replied, "Grace will be calling it a day."

Peyton stepped into the room. "It's Mr. and Mrs. Morgenthou."

I sucked in a breath and gave Terry the bad news. "It's an important account. I can't miss this."

His face twisted. "More important than your life? You're not staying. I have to take those two to Hawk, and you have to come with me."

He'd moved from suggestion to command, and I wasn't having it. This was important. "I'm not going to shut down my business on account of those lowlifes. Zane can stay, and I'll bring him into the demo room with us. I won't be out of his sight, promise."

Terry grumbled. "No. You're coming with me."

Peyton watched us with rapt attention.

"Parallel work," I said. "Remember? I do my work while you do the security thing and take tweedle-dee and tweedle-dum to the dungeon or wherever."

"No."

"Listen here, Rambo. This is my business, and like I said, I'm staying to run it."

"What good does this place do anybody if you're abducted or dead? They know you're here, and those two idiots may not be the last. This is not a safe place for you." He pointed. "What just happened out there proves it."

"This is where I do my business, dammit. Now take your attitude and shove it. I'm staying. You guys figure out how to make it safe."

"Until we do, you come with me." His words were cold and unyielding.

"I'm staying here and working. Period." *Take that, Mr. Bossy.* I could and would be equally unyielding.

He thought for a moment. "I think we should set you up with a remote location, since most of your work is on the computer anyway."

I could feel myself close to blowing a gasket. "Why do you have to make this so hard? I have to meet with customers. That's the business."

"You're the one making this hard by not taking your safety seriously."

"Stop it." I threw up my hands. "I have a business to run, and I'm going to do it here. That's my job." I saw the crack in his determination. "Your job is to figure out how to provide security within that framework."

"I don't like it." That was at least an improvement from *hell no*.

"Grow up. Sometimes you have to do things you don't like. It's called life." I knew I was being too hard on him, but he wasn't listening to reason. "I said no, and that's final."

He set the folder down with fierce eyes locked on mine. "Okay, this time. Constance is on the way to handle the cops. Do exactly what they say, or else."

"Or else what? You going to spank me?"

"If I have to."

I nodded and moved close, enjoying that I could so easily rile him. "I'll behave, but only because you asked so nicely."

That surprised him. With a shake of his head, he strode quickly to the door. "I'll be back soon."

I returned the combination smile and sneer I'd practiced for him. "I'll be here."

After he stormed out, Peyton approached. "Tell me you're banging him."

CHAPTER 13

Terry

Down in the garage, I finally had the two prisoners properly zip-tied and strapped in so they couldn't get loose.

I didn't like transporting both of the Russo idiots in the back of my Cayenne without help, but I wasn't taking Zane off Grace's protection for a single second.

Gritting my teeth, I punched the car's start button hard and the engine rumbled to life. The tires squealed when I backed out too fast. Hitting the brakes, I stopped for a deep, calming breath. Damn, Grace could be infuriating.

Once on the street, I checked and rechecked for a tail, then dialed Jordy.

"Zane tells me you have two guests for us," he answered.

"Affirmative. A woman and a man, separate guest quarters for each." *Guest quarters* or *guest accommodations* was the terminology we used in public, but these two were essentially going to holding cells, and not very warm ones.

"Suites are already prepared," Jordy assured me. "And Winston will meet you in the garage. Do they need medical attention?"

"Not yet." I noticed Lorenzo, if that was his name, flinch.

After hanging up, I let them stew for a minute before asking, "Who do you work for?"

The woman stared out the window, mouth shut tight.

Lorenzo didn't follow suit. "Fuck you."

"Oh, I can see we're going to have some fun with you."

"You can't hold us," he spat.

"And who's gonna stop us?"

"Victor's going to pound you into the dirt," Lorenzo sneered.

"Shut up, you idiot," Maria hissed.

He clenched his teeth, but did as she'd commanded.

So she was higher ranking than him, and they worked for the Russo organization.

In the silence that followed, I replayed the conversation between Grace and the bossman. Grown men with brass balls didn't stand up to Lucas Hawk the way she had. The woman had backbone and conviction, I'd grant her that. I added compassion to the list, recalling her insistence on supporting her employees.

But I got hung up on our arguments about where to stay and her insistence on running the business like nothing at all had happened yesterday and today. I was trying to warn her about the dangers, and she was hell bent on arguing with me.

We'd shared two hot-as-hell make-out sessions, and then she had to go and yell at me, starting a fight. The woman was a walking contradiction.

Lucas had been right that it would be easier to protect her somewhere else, but with Grace as fired up as she was, we had to play it the way she wanted. He'd have to allow her business to continue unhindered while working the protection plan around that as best we could.

The only way to deal with that was to stick to her like glue. I'd spent years trying to keep Grace Brennan at a distance, but that was over. Needing to keep her safe—and also seeing her the way I did now, after those kisses, after having my hands on her—I couldn't go back to the way things had been between us.

Ever since Lucas had told me Pete might return, I'd treated each day as if he could walk through the door. I had to keep my confidence that things would turn out well for my best friend. And if Pete was unhappy about me and Grace when he returned, that was a battle I'd have to fight. We'd have to fight it together.

∼

At the garage, Jordy and Winston met me and took our guests.

Normally I would've stayed to interrogate one or both of them, but this time getting back to Grace was more important.

I drove the return trip only moderately fast. Zane would be keeping

Grace safe, and I didn't need the hassle of getting pulled over for speeding after all that had gone on today. I stopped for the red light.

I could still recall the feel of her curvy little body against mine. My God, it had been glorious—soft tits, luscious lips, and the taste of her. It was hard to fathom that I was getting hard remembering nothing more than a make-out session. I was acting like a damned teenager.

The car behind me honked. How long had the light been green? I drove the rest of the way verbally reading off license plate numbers to keep thoughts of Grace at bay.

GRACE

PEYTON STARED AT ME, CLEARLY EXPECTING ME TO CONFIRM THAT I WAS banging my bodyguard, my nemesis.

I scrunched up my brows in my most confused expression. "Absolutely not. You know our history." I'd mentioned more than enough tyrant episodes over lunches.

"The way he looks at you?" She fanned herself with the file she held. "You two fight like you're one second from ripping each other's clothes off."

I stomped around my desk. "I have no idea what you're talking about."

"Yes, you do. And Kitten? He even has a cute nickname for you."

I turned away from my harasser. "What time is the Morgenthaus' appointment?" I smiled, though.

"And…" Her voice went up an octave. "He wants to spank you."

I turned back. "The Morgenthaus?" I repeated. "And don't you have work to do?"

"You've got a half hour, and I'd let him spank me." She laughed. "But that's just me and my romance novels."

"TMI." I waved her away before she caught me smiling. "Shoo."

She crossed her arm, not listening any better than Terry. "He's got a point, and I don't understand why you're being so stubborn."

I matched her stance, crossing my arms too. "You're taking his side?"

"How often have you been together and not fought?"

I whisked a tendril of hair out of my face. "Pretty much never." I wouldn't admit to the day at Disneyland. "Except we didn't fight last night at the awards party."

"You were civil to him?"

"We didn't have the chance to talk."

"That doesn't count." She shook her head. "I get that he pushes your buttons, but you have got to stop perpetuating the cycle by pushing his as well. You're better than that."

The accusation stung. "He always starts it, not me." I searched my memory for good examples.

A smile grew on Peyton's face during my silence. "Good. You think about that for a while. I'll be outside." She moved to the door.

Marci was at the door when Peyton opened it. "Paul and some others really want to call the cops. I got them to hold off and said you'd explain everything after your meeting."

I nodded. "Thanks."

Peyton checked her elegant Rolex. "I have to run an errand. The file is already on your desk."

"Okay."

When the door closed, I was alone again, standing behind my desk, wishing I could sit in my chair and wondering how I was going to survive having all of Terry's attention on me. It had been too easy to fall back into being snarky with him. Did we only have a spark of attraction because we grated on each other? Were we steel and flint that couldn't coexist?

Spank me? My cheeks heated. If it weren't for the damned cut on my ass, I'd let him do that. Peyton thought we wanted to rip each other's clothes off. My panties almost burst into flames thinking about that.

I found the Morgenthau folder and opened it.

Work. I needed to concentrate on work, not the sexy-as-hell man who'd saved me from whatever ugliness Elliot had dragged me into.

The folder said the Morgenthau home had his and hers primary closets. Did they have separate bedrooms as well?

If I was married, I wouldn't want to sleep away from Terry.

I slapped the folder closed. Where the hell had that thought come from?

So what if I'd kissed him? That was all, a kiss—an off-the-charts-of-hotness kiss, but still just a kiss. Besides, he said he didn't dislike me, but that was a long way from where my mind had just wandered.

I'd wanted to be, and had become, a successful female businesswoman. That's who I was, and no man—least of all a Neanderthal Rambo wannabe—was going to boss me around and make me give up my dream.

Even if he was sexy as hell and had also saved me—twice now. Okay, three times if I counted that Zane had only been here because of Terry. The fact that he'd called me Kitten also didn't make up for him being an ass.

"Argh," I screamed. The man wasn't even here, and he was driving me crazy.

It was the adrenaline effect. That had to be it. I'd been through some pretty traumatic events, and because he'd been there, I'd attached totally inappropriate feelings to him.

Peyton burst in. "What's wrong?"

I breathed in deeply to calm myself. "Nothing. Sorry I yelled. I'm pissed that I can't sit down."

"What?"

I'd never allowed my personal life to interfere with the business, so I hadn't explained anything to my assistant, or anyone else. "This morning, I got attacked again."

"Again?"

"And Terry saved me, but not before I got Tasered in the ass."

She laughed. When I didn't laugh with her, she stopped. "You're serious?"

I shook my head at the absurdity of it. "Unfortunately, yes. And the tip of the barb thingie broke off, and Terry had to cut it out, so I can't sit comfortably for a day or two."

She smiled and started to laugh again. "Let me get this straight. Rambo the tyrant became your knight in shining armor, saving you last night and again this morning? Then you had to drop trou so Sir Galahad could perform field surgery on your naked ass? Wow, that's hot. No wonder you were looking at each other like I should leave so you could get naked on the desk."

"We were not," I complained, unsure now how much of a lie it was or wasn't.

"Did you ask him to kiss it and make it better?" She snickered.

"Get out of here. I would never." I added as much emphasis to the words as I could, while also wondering why I hadn't thought of that. "Especially not a man who thinks he can boss me around."

"Whatever you say, boss." She turned to go, shaking her head, then stopped before closing the door. "So, it's okay if I ask him out?"

"No." The word got past my filter before I could stop it. "Because he's my bodyguard."

She giggled. "Uh-huh."

"Shut up." I didn't appreciate the point she was making.

"I'll be outside."

When the door closed, my doubts surged forward.

My body had wanted Terry even before the kiss, but my brain had been more sensible about the absurdity of that. Now my damned urges had gotten the upper hand. Knowing what kissing him was like made it harder to tamp things down.

But nonetheless, my brain knew better. Tyrant was a name that fit Terry perfectly. He'd never missed a chance to tell me what to do, and one nice day at Disneyland, and a kiss, would change who he was.

The devil on my shoulder told me to give him a chance, that maybe he'd changed, or I could change him. Running a finger over my lips and remembering how it had felt to be in his strong arms made me almost want that chance.

Almost, but not quite, because Terry had just made it clear that he wanted to boss me around and interfere with my business. That was a nonstarter for me, more important than any stupid kiss. At the first opportunity, he'd reverted to telling me what I should do, like he always had.

I hadn't liked it then, and I didn't like it now. This was no different than ice cream. Knowing it was bad for me allowed me to resist grabbing a pint at the grocery store. Terry was bad for me, just like ice cream.

Walk past the frozen temptation, and a minute later I would forget about it. All I had to do was to ignore Terry and send him away to get past the temptation.

"Ice cream. Just like ice cream," I chanted.

I picked up the Morgenthou folder and opened my door.

Peyton's smirk mocked me.

No, this wasn't just like ice cream—it was harder, much harder.

CHAPTER 14

Terry

I RODE THE ELEVATOR BACK UP TO SpaceMasters, WISHING I DIDN'T HAVE TO stop at every single intervening floor, but today was not my lucky day.

Pushing through the doors into her offices, I didn't see Grace anywhere—or Peyton or Zane. I reminded myself that his job was to stay with her.

"Where is Grace?" I asked Marci when I reached her. I clenched and unclenched my fist to remind myself to slow down and take it easy.

Marci jerked her head up. The urgency of my words had startled her. I'd have to remember she was a skittish one. "Oh. In demo room one. And before you ask, yes, Zane is in there as well. He's pretty intense."

I nodded and started for the hallway.

"Hold on," Marci called.

I spun. "What?"

She rose from her chair and approached me. "This is an important client," she whispered.

The softness of her voice made me realize I'd raised mine.

"And the process of the VR session is delicate. She's safe, and I know she'd appreciate it if you didn't interrupt."

Two others in the cubicle area had raised their heads, watching our interaction, and it made me feel foolish. "Of course."

I followed her back to her desk. "If you sit here, you'll see her as soon as she's done." She gestured to the couch.

Feeling appropriately chastised, I sat. As the minutes clicked by, it seemed worse than an all-night stint in a sniper's blind, needing to stay absolutely still—no matter how many bugs buzzed around—until the mark arrived.

Marci leaned close. "What can you tell me about Zane?"

My cluelessness in social settings showed itself when it took me a solid three seconds to comprehend the question. "Zane is a good guy."

She raised her eyebrows, expecting more.

"He was in the teams before us." When I noticed her brows crease, I explained. "He was a SEAL. He and Duke, another member of our company, were on the same team, so he could tell you a lot more than I can. Duke swears by him, and that's all I need to trust the guy implicitly."

She whispered, "Is he single?"

Oh. I'd still missed her real question. "Yes."

A minute later, she casually applied lip gloss.

When the door to the demo room finally opened, Grace emerged, followed by an elderly couple—the customers, I guessed—and then Zane.

I smiled wide when her eyes found mine. I could finally see for myself that she hadn't been hurt.

Then Zane looked around. He focused on Peyton's empty desk.

I waited patiently for Grace to finish with her customers before I approached her. "I'm back."

"I see that." She nodded.

"Zane, the boss wants you back at home base to interrogate our guests."

"Copy that." After another glance toward Peyton's desk, he turned.

Marci watched him leave.

"How did it go?" I asked Grace. "Your customer meeting?"

"Rambo here wanted to barge in, but I tackled him," Marci interjected.

"Thank you." Grace wheeled on me. "My office, if you please."

She began as soon as the door closed. "I get that you want to build a wall around me, but we agreed I get to run my business. An interruption would have been terrible." She breathed in deeply. "I appreciate that you didn't barge in."

"Is that a thank you I hear?" "Don't let it go to your head." Then, she surprised me with a kiss.

I snaked one hand in her hair and backed her against the door. She might have meant for this to be quick, but I had a better idea.

She moaned into my mouth when I cupped her tit. Then, way too soon, she pushed away, breathless. "We can't… I have to talk to my people after what happened."

I backed away and sighed. "We can and we should."

Smiling, she brushed her hair, and straightened her clothes. "Later."

It felt good to have put that smile on her face. I followed her out of the office and through the cubicles.

She spent a few minutes with each of her employees, asking about their progress on this or that. Based on her questions, she clearly had an excellent memory and grasp of everybody's work. Several times, she was asked about the disturbance and why we didn't want to call the police.

I followed the training-exercise script we'd prepared for this kind of problem. "It was a training exercise, run by an outfit that rates the preparedness of security firms like ours," I explained. "The police don't generally approve of how realistic we are. Actually, they always tell us to do it in another city."

I went on to say that the scenario had to look and feel realistic to be valuable. No blood was spilled, and beyond what they'd witnessed, the fake assailants would also try to escape on their ride to our facilities.

That almost worked, until a fellow named Paul noted that Grace's bruises looked real.

"They are," she had to admit. "I was mugged last night. Terry and his company are looking after me until we catch the muggers."

After Paul, we had the explanation down pat, and each employee seemed genuinely relieved when Grace assured them that her issue would be resolved soon.

I hoped that was true.

As we continued through cubicle after cubicle, I liked that it seemed Grace had put our previous argument behind us. This was a chance for a fresh start.

Clearly, her employees loved her and the projects they were working on. She'd built a good work environment.

When she finished her rounds with the employees, I followed her back to her office.

"Do you have to hover all the time?" she asked. "Can't you maybe clear the space—isn't that the lingo?—and then guard the door?"

"Does the Secret Service operate that way, or do they go where the president goes?" I sat down in her office.

Two hours later, Zane returned and took me aside. "We're fucked. We've confirmed that the woman is Maria Torelli, and she is Tony Russo's niece."

"And we're still holding her, right?"

"Lucas says she's the leverage to get a meeting with Tony himself. High risk, if you ask me."

"Nobody asked you," I bit out. He was right about the risk. Holding the niece of a mafia don was a ballsy play, but that was Lucas's call to make.

Zane had been a SEAL and a tier-one operator, among the best of the best, and Duke had vouched for him. But on our team he was still the new guy, and it wasn't his place to be second-guessing Lucas on command decisions.

"I just meant—"

"If you have an issue with it, you take it straight to him and discuss it. But in the end, his decisions stand, and we follow them."

"Sorry. Forget I said anything."

Zane was apparently okay grumbling, but not ready to challenge Lucas Hawk one-on-one, which I would count as a smart move on his part.

"Okay." Zane raked his hand through his hair. "If direct is how we roll, then I have to say I don't think it's smart that you're the lead guarding Grace."

Suddenly I didn't like Zane using her first name. "Lucas made it her choice, and she chose me." I didn't need to justify anything to Zane. "Get over it." I crowded him.

He backed up. "Hold on, it's not that I wanted the gig." He held up his hands. "But I was told you were the executor of her trust."

"That's right."

"They may know that or find it out and find her through you."

His observation was a valid one, but this was no longer up for debate. "Grace made her choice," I snarled.

"I get it." The door handle turned, and Zane backed away.

"There you are," Grace said, breezing in and closing the door behind her. "I'm done for the day, and I really would like to lie down. This standing all day bit sucks."

Zane raised a brow.

"I got a Taser barb to the backside, and Terry had to dig the tip out," she explained. "I don't recommend the experience."

Zane cocked his head. "Understandable."

Grace addressed me. "I said I'd follow Lucas's security advice." She looked at me. "And stay at your place, but first we need to go by my apartment to pick up some things. And then I promised Serena I'd join her for a while after work."

"You shouldn't," Zane said quickly.

Grace frowned. "Shouldn't what?"

"The Russo people are likely to be watching your place," Zane continued.

That was the same advice I'd been about to give her. I shook my head. "We need to set up cameras and basic security here before you come back, so clothes can wait. Tomorrow you can wear whatever you'd like."

She went wide-eyed. "I have work to do tomorrow, just like today. I need my clothes, and I also have to get my cats. I can't leave them."

"Tell me they can't survive the night alone."

Sheepishly, she agreed. "Okay, but I have to pick them up after work tomorrow at the latest."

I could feel it coming on, another fight over simple security protocols. "You can come back here after we equip this building, but that takes a day. You can work remotely tomorrow, and we'll figure something out about the cats."

She stomped her foot. "And how does that look to my employees, not to mention my customers who are scheduled tomorrow? What do I tell my people?" She raised her arms. "Huh? I won't be here because it's too dangerous, but don't worry, it's safe enough for you guys?" She shook her head. "No way."

I pulled in a steadying breath to keep from yelling at this infuriating woman. "I don't like it."

"Figure it out." Zane aimed his comment at me. "I'm available as your backup here tomorrow while they do the security install and I can pick up her stuff and deliver it tonight. Between the two of us, we should be okay for a day."

Grace instantly calmed and nodded. "That works." "Give me your keys," Zane said, stretching out his hand. "I'll feed the cats, and I can get in and out without them knowing I'm picking up things for you. Less risk that way."

I clenched my fist at the vision of Zane picking through her underwear drawer, but I had to restrain myself. My job was to stay with Grace. It made sense for him to make the clothes run.

She swung her eyes to me.

I nodded. "We'll work it out."

"I didn't get lunch," Grace said as she walked to the door. "So you better have some food at your place."

"I have the basics." I kept my tone clipped and professional. She'd been argumentative on purpose, and I couldn't let it affect me.

Zane tapped Peyton's desk as we passed by. "I haven't seen your pretty assistant."

Zane wasn't the most subtle guy around. "Marci can help you if you need something," I noted.

He shook his head and held out his hand. "Keys?"

Grace handed them over. "She had an errand to run." She pulled open the door to the office, offering Zane a smile.

I followed them out.

CHAPTER 15

Grace

As Terry drove me toward his place, I squirmed in the seat next to him —partly because I couldn't get comfortable sitting on my wound, and partly because one half of my ice cream analogy was out the window. I wasn't going to be able to stay away from Terry, quite the opposite. Still intact was my growing desire for him, but also the doubt that we could be compatible. Our argument about whether I could work tomorrow still bothered me.

Zane had defused the situation, but I wondered if the multiple yelling matches with Terry today had caused a rift that couldn't be healed. Had I screwed up the budding attraction between us and take us back to our historical mutual anger with each other?

Suddenly, I remembered about Serena and Duke and margaritas. Pulling out my phone, I hastily dialed.

"Tell me you're finally on the way," Serena said when she answered.

I looked over at Terry. "I can't. Something came up. I'm headed to Terry's place to stay." Going into the Maria attack with Serena would result in an instant freak-out.

"To stay, huh?" she asked with a lilt to her voice. "And you're okay with that?"

"He's growing on me," I suggested.

Next to me, Terry's brows lifted. Realizing I found that cute, I had to admit I was falling for Mr. Grumpypants, Sir Galahad, ex-Tyrant.

"I hear that, Gracie. Is he there with you?"

I admired Terry's profile for a second. "Uh-huh."

"Tomorrow you better tell me what's going on, or I'm going to kidnap you myself."

"I hear you." I needed to get out of this. "Gotta go now, and Terry says hi."

"Tell him hi back, and don't forget—tomorrow no excuses."

"Tomorrow," I agreed and hung up. "Serena says hi."

Terry nodded. "She giving you the third degree?"

I looked out the window. "She's going to." Then I switched gears. "What did Zane get from those two, Maria and Lorenzo?"

His strong jaw ticked before he spoke. "We confirmed that Maria Torelli is her real name, and she's the niece of Tony Russo, head of the Russo crime family, which is odd."

"What's odd about it?"

"The crime family thrives by being a constant low-level nuisance. Generally, they're into extortion, drugs, and prostitution, state crimes where none of them individually are too serious. Only when you add them up is it a big deal. Kidnapping, though, is another level. It can quickly turn into a federal issue with a lot of attention."

I tensed. *Kidnapping* was an awful word to confront.

His phone rang, and he pressed a button to answer it. "Hi, boss. Grace and I are on the way to my place."

Lucas's voice came over the speakers. "According to chatter Jordy picked up, the buyer is most likely Aren Marku."

"Shit," Terry swore.

"What does that mean?" I asked.

"It means Elliot sure has dug himself a deep hole," Lucas said. "Marku is the head of the Albanian mob here. They make the Italians look like choirboys."

I shrank back in my seat.

"Does the chatter give us any idea what the package was?" Terry asked.

"Not directly," Lucas said. "In addition to the normal shit, the Albanians are heavily into human and arms trafficking. Word is that they sold some missile tech to the North Koreans last year, so maybe there's something similar in the case."

"With all the sanctions?" Terry asked. "How would the North Koreans get the money to buy military technology?"

"Drugs, counterfeiting, and cybercrimes. They were behind all of the big crypto heists." Lucas breathed heavily. "If they are the buyers and they get wind of Grace's connection, we could have another set of players to watch out for. I'll have Zane bring by the file on Marku."

Fucking great. Elliot, what the hell have you gotten me involved in?

"I'll keep her safe," Terry promised.

"If the Albanians are involved, Grace, we may have no choice but to move you to the safe house."

With Peyton's criticism fresh in my mind, instead of lashing out as I had before, I tried for something more conciliatory. "I have to run my business. We have a set of important clients coming up. People with families are depending on me," I said calmly. "If things change, we can discuss the options, and I hope you'll have something to offer me besides just locking me in a safe house and punishing my employees."

"I understand," Lucas said.

And I got the impression that he did understand. Why had Lucas gotten it so easily and Terry been so resistant so overprotective? It wasn't the reaction I would have expected from the man I used to call Tyrant who would have been glad to be rid of me.

After Terry ended the call, I asked, "How bad is this news? I mean, about the Albanians? And tell me the truth."

"They're bad players. Worse than the Italians."

Shivering, I wrapped my arms around myself.

Two blocks later, I got a bad feeling as I noticed Terry's eyes shifting repeatedly to the rearview mirror. "What's wrong?"

He turned left at the next intersection. "I think we're being followed."

I turned to look back.

"Don't look," he said sternly.

It was too late. "Which car?"

"The red one. I think it's a Maserati."

I gulped. "They turned."

"Hold on."

I settled back in my seat and didn't see anything except the door handle to hold on to. A few seconds later, with a set jaw, Terry made another turn and then floored the accelerator. A scream lodged in my throat as the engine roared and I was thrown back against the seat. This car was part rocket.

He checked the mirror again, cool as could be. "It's definitely a tail." He stabbed the dash, and a call connected.

"Hawk." It was Lucas's voice again.

"We picked up a tail leaving Grace's work. Red Maserati."

"Jordy will track you. I'm on the way." Lucas sounded like he was running. "Winston is to your south. Evade that direction."

The call disconnected as fear churned in my belly and we raced past parked cars and buildings. We were moving much faster than I considered safe. I braced my feet and gripped the door handle.

Terry took another turn fast and floored the car down a wide street, weaving through traffic before turning onto a side street. I hung onto the door handle as we screeched around the corner and came within inches of a parked truck. I'd never written a will.

As Terry cranked the car into another turn, I was thrown against the door. The tires screeched, but held. The red car was still behind us.

Terry looked completely at ease, stabbing the brake, whipping the wheel around, and then jamming down the accelerator.

My stomach revolted each time we rocketed out of a turn like a cat with its tail on fire.

"Bad news," he intoned.

"What?" It came out as a squeak.

"Only a few cars can keep up with us. He's got one of them."

I flinched at the sound of glass shattering.

"Get down," Terry ordered. "They're shooting."

With my heart lodged in my throat, I leaned down. Another bullet hit the rear glass, and then another.

"Glove box. Get my gun," Terry ordered.

As he took another corner, I pulled the Sig Sauer out, checked the clip, and racked the slide to load the first round in the chamber the way Pete had taught me. Then I undid my seatbelt, lowered the window, and swiveled out the side.

"What the hell?" Terry bellowed. "Stay down."

"Fuck that," I yelled angrily. I got off three rounds at the pursuing car before Terry yanked me back inside.

"Give me the gun," Terry yelled, then stretched out his hand. "You fucking do what I say, when I say."

"Stop yelling at me," I screamed. I gave the SIG over, then fastened my seatbelt again and raised the window as he accelerated down the narrow street.

"That was the stupidest thing you've ever done."

I shrank in my seat as he took the next corner at the same insane speed as the last.

"Damned stupidest," he repeated.

"Watch out," I screamed as a person emerged from between cars.

Terry hit the brakes hard and cranked the wheel.

We missed the man, but the car spun and skidded backward, hitting a parked car with a gigantic crunch of metal on metal.

The impact threw me into the seat. The side airbag went off next to my head, and all I could think was that we were helpless now against whoever was shooting at us.

Terry leapt out of his door. *Bang, bang.*

The red car swerved, went past us, and crashed straight into a light pole.

I tried my door, but it was jammed. Bile rose in my throat as I remembered all the movies where the car caught fire after a crash. I pushed harder. *I will not die in a fucking fire. That had almost happened to Serena.*

Terry rushed to the red car, gun in hand.

I almost yelled for him to come back before I realized that if he didn't deal with the gunman first, this could end very badly for us both.

I unbuckled and wiggled my way over the console and out his door. By the time I got out, Terry had a guy with a neck tattoo on the sidewalk with his hands zip-tied behind him.

The guy we'd almost hit ran away. *Way to help, guy.*

Neck Tat groaned as I ran up. Luckily he wasn't bleeding.

"Help me," came from the driver's side of the mangled car. "I'm stuck. I can't get out."

"Try to run and she'll shoot you," Terry said as he handed me the SIG, then ran around the car.

I leveled the gun at Neck Tat.

He curled into a ball. *Wise choice, asshole.* The way my day was going, one fewer dirtbag in the world would be a good thing.

The painful moans from the guy trapped in the car kept me from looking over at him. Fainting right now would be a very bad thing. *Don't look. Full body tense to keep blood pressure up. Don't look*, I mentally repeated.

Terry grunted and groaned as he pulled on the driver's door. It didn't budge.

A white Porsche Cayenne roared up, screeched to a halt, and Winston jumped out. Finally, some help.

"Give me a hand," Terry yelled.

Keeping my eyes focused on Neck Tat, I heard grunts and the sound of metal bending.

"That should do it," Winston said.

"I got him," Terry said. "Get his legs."

"Keep him behind me," I reminded Terry when I heard them shuffling around the back of the car.

"Right," Terry replied as a second Cayenne passed the wreck and pulled to the curb.

Lucas shot out of the car and ran to me. "Who are you?" he bellowed at my captive.

Neck Tat only whimpered.

"Who do you work for?" Lucas demanded.

Nothing but another groan.

Lucas patted me on the shoulder. "I can see Pete taught you well. You hold that weapon like a pro. Don't hesitate to shoot him if he moves."

Neck Tat froze, without even a whimper.

The compliment made me smile. My two-handed shooter's grip had become habit from the times Pete had taken me to the range.

He moved behind me to the second man. "Who hired you?"

"If I say, they kill me." True fear gave the man a trembling voice on top of his Asian accent.

"I hate cowards who shoot at women, so I might put you with your friend over there and flip a coin to see which one of you gets to live."

Several seconds of silence followed.

"Or, better yet, I think I'll introduce you to my Australian spider collection. They say that if one of those bites you, the pain is so intense you wish you were dead."

His words made me cringe, but neither of the men said anything.

"Winston, give Terry your keys and we'll take these two to our guest quarters," Lucas commanded. "Terry, get Grace out of here, now."

A moment later, Terry took my hand and led me the long way around the wrecked car to Winston's Porsche, shielding me from viewing the driver.

My pulse was still tripping a million beats a minute as we started off at a normal speed, which seemed so slow after that breakneck chase. My hand trembled uncontrollably.

"Are you okay?" Terry asked, a block away from the crash scene.

I nodded and put my hand under my thigh to hide the tremors. "Yeah, I guess," I said after a moment when I got myself settled enough to talk. "I'm scared," I admitted.

"Grace," he said, placing his large hand on my thigh, "you can count on me. I will always do anything and everything to keep you safe. I promise you that."

I nodded, feeling ashamed of my behavior with the gun. I thought it was good to help, but he didn't agree. Hell, I knew what I was doing with a gun, Pete had seen to that.

Now I could see our arguments in different light. He'd been doing everything he'd just promised—telling me what was the safest path forward and insisting on it in his dictatorial manner. His approach lacked subtlety, but his words, *"anything and everything to keep you safe,"* summarized it all.

I'd seen his yelling at me through the same lens of bossy, dictatorial, tyrannical Terry as always. But this situation was different. The queen of overreaction, that was me. I placed my icy hand over his warm one. "I'm sorry."

He squeezed my thigh in a reassuring way.

I added my other hand to hold his. I didn't want to let go of this big, strong, grumpy, annoying, opinionated, overprotective man.

"No more heroics. You're doing exactly what I say," he continued. "I'm done with your bitching. It doesn't matter how much you complain. I'll drag you by the fucking hair if I have to." There it was again, the same old sensitive, considerate, soft-spoken Terry.

I laughed. "Oh my, Rambo, you say the sweetest things." The big lug didn't know a different way to say he cared.

He tried to pull his hand away, but I didn't let him. Unwilling to admit just how scared I was after the conversation about the Albanians and being shot at, I held onto my rock, my anchor, my protector.

With every squeeze of his hand, I regretted more and more my earlier reaction to his protectiveness. How much of the angry and argumentative dynamic that we'd fallen into over the years had been my fault? Seemed like maybe a lot.

I looked at Terry in profile for the longest time. I'd always been attracted to the sexy man, but put off by his character. Why did it take being beaten up, almost kidnapped, Tasered, and shot at to see the admirable man beneath the gruff demeanor?

"What?" he demanded.

"Nothing. I'm just trying to see behind the mask to the nice guy underneath."

He puffed out a breath and shook his head. "Maybe I need to take you back to the ER for another CAT scan. You, of all people, should know there's nothing nice about me."

There it was again, the attempt to push me away. What was it he'd said earlier? *He didn't dislike me.*

The man who'd vowed to protect me no matter what, didn't hate me the way I'd always thought. So why had he always gone out of his way to anger me?

He slowed the car. We'd reached Marina del Rey. "I'm going to need my hand back to park."

"Of course." I released my grip, feeling a bit self-conscious about how clingy I'd been.

We were in front of an Ironman Fitness. He reached for the sun visor, pressed a clicker, and a garage door next to the gym opened.

"I've always known you worked out, but I never imagined you lived in a gym," I joked.

"Not in… Above," he clarified. "Lucas owns the building. He sold me a ten-percent interest, and with that I get the apartment above."

He pulled into the garage, parking alongside an old Mustang with its hood up and a huge motorcycle. Not being a gearhead, I couldn't tell much more than that. The door closed behind us, and the noise of the street receded. He led me upstairs where he opened a fancy electronic lock with a palm scan.

His home wowed me. It was light and spacious. No, spacious didn't do it justice. It was huge, with a view of the boat harbor and even a terrace. "This is gorgeous. How can you possibly call this sublime space an apartment? It's larger than a lot of homes in this town." It was no bungalow. This much space in Marina del Rey spelled money.

My entire unit would have fit in the kitchen off to one side. With simple furniture of black leather and oak, a monster television, and a minimalist feel, it screamed *a man lives here.*

He shrugged. "You only asked that it have running hot water, and it does."

I shook my head, feeling a bit in awe. "This place is a sweet deal."

"Lucas wouldn't let me say no to this."

"Does he own the gym as well?"

"No." He shook his head and walked toward the window. "The space is rented."

I followed him to the window, admiring his fine ass the whole way. When he stopped, I took in the harbor. This kind of view encouraged you to contemplate things. While he'd gone overboard in the protectiveness department, Terry was a good man. He didn't deserve the hassle I'd given him. One of us had to take the initiative and break the cycle of arguing.

As we silently admired the view together, I decided to take a chance. Wrapping my arms around him from behind, I leaned my face against his muscular back. "I'm sorry about arguing earlier and not following your advice."

"Orders," he corrected. He pulled my arms apart and walked out of my embrace. "Forget it. I told you I admire your passion."

"Thank you… I think" I bit my tongue and didn't tell him off about assuming he could order me around.

We'd gone from the best kiss of my life to arguing, and now to him walking away because I couldn't control my temper or my actions. I was even willing to admit it was my fault because I'd kept *pushing his buttons*, as Peyton put it, and wanting to shoot back. How could I blame the man who'd saved my life, who'd taken on armed criminals to protect me without accepting some of the blame myself?

As he walked away, the room suddenly turned cold and I felt empty.

∼

TERRY

I EXTRICATED MYSELF AND WALKED AWAY FROM THE INFURIATING WOMAN.

She was like a damned pendulum, swinging from amazingly sweet to intensely argumentative and back again. How the hell was I supposed to keep a woman safe who refused to listen?

She followed me. "Terry, why won't you talk to me?"

I needed to keep my distance from her. It had been a mistake earlier to forget that she was, before all else, Pete's little sister. It had taken Lucas's mention of Pete to remind me.

With a huff, I pulled open the refrigerator. "See? I've got apples, chicken, green onions, all kinds of things that qualify as real food." I was perfectly adept at being cold as I'd proven for years.

"I didn't mean that."

"Yes, you did. You even doubted I had hot water."

She stood with her hands on her hips, glaring at me. "I said I'm sorry. What more do you want from me?"

"Nothing." I opened the door wider. "What would you like for dinner, Hellcat?"

"I didn't mean it that way."

"That's not an answer, Wildcat. What would you like for dinner?"

She threw up her hands, turned, and walked away. "I don't care about dinner. Why won't you talk to me?"

"Octopus stew? Monkey brains? Chocolate-covered termites?"

"Very funny." With a dramatic sigh, she returned to the kitchen. "I'll settle for oatmeal. Do you have any?"

As expected, she was easy to anger. "Check the pantry." Like a pervert, I ogled her ass as she leaned over to view a lower shelf. As much as she aggravated me, I couldn't take my eyes off her. I couldn't help but lust after her.

"Who doesn't have oatmeal?" She looked like she was about to lose it.

With all that she'd been through, I couldn't keep this up. "Okay you want to talk? Let's talk." Mentally I crossed my fingers that she'd accept the olive branch. I didn't handle crying women well. "I almost lost you out there."

"I—"

I waved my arm and felt my face going red as I raised my voice. "What the hell were you thinking? It's not a goddamned movie where you hang out a window and shoot bad guys without them shooting back."

"I was helping," she argued with a hand on her hip. "And I know how to shoot."

"That's not the point. You put yourself in danger by not doing what I said."

"So what? They shoot me, one less problem in your life. You've hated me forever."

"I have not," I snapped. "Exactly the opposite." This woman drove me crazy, making me say things I didn't mean to let out.

Her eyes squinted and she cocked her head. "What did you say?"

I should never have started this conversation. "Oatmeal doesn't work for me."

"You're evading."

"I said you have to follow my instructions. It's important."

She nodded. "I heard you. But—"

"Good. We can do chicken marsala, if you're willing to help."

She shook her head in obvious frustration with me and opened the freezer compartment. "I don't see it."

"I mean from scratch."

"You can cook that?" Surprise laced her voice. She didn't believe me.

"You think all I can cook is chili straight out of a can, or maybe microwave a pizza?"

She closed the freezer. "I've never cooked that before—chicken marsala, I mean, not the pizza."

"Don't knock pizza. It has all the major food groups."

She half-heartedly opened the fridge. "Where's the beer?"

"Chicken marsala is the offer. Would you like it or not?"

"Sure."

"You need to help then."

She moved things around on the fridge shelf. "I don't see any beer in here."

"There's a bottle of Chardonnay in the door."

"A wine drinker and you cook? You surprise me, Mr. Goodwin." She rummaged around in the drawers next to the fridge. "I thought all you tough guys only drank beer."

"And scratched our crotches and opened the bottle caps with our teeth?" I suggested.

"I was going to say farted." She laughed.

"Insult me all you like. The corkscrew is one more drawer to the left." I joined her and pulled chicken from the fridge, followed by mushrooms and an onion. I was about to ask her if she hated all men or if it was only me, but my filter kicked in and I didn't.

"I don't hate you," she said, reading my mind. She uncorked the wine and poured two glasses, offering one to me. "Can we start again?" She raised her glass. "Pretty please?"

I nodded.

She raised her glass. "To being friends."

I didn't have it in me to say no, so I clinked my glass to hers. "Friends." I sipped.

"Put me to work, chef. I'd love to cook chicken marsala with you."

The pendulum had swung to teamwork, and I liked it. "First, we need a gallon-sized plastic bag and cassava flour. It's in the pantry."

"Cassava?"

"I make it gluten-free." I trimmed the chicken and pounded the pieces thin on the cutting board one at a time. Then she shook them in the plastic bag, coating them in the flour and spices.

"We'll need two-thirds of a cup of chicken broth—there's concentrate in the door of the fridge—and the same amount of yogurt and marsala wine."

She cocked her head. "I thought it was made with a cream sauce?"

As she turned away, I caught that profile view that always turned me on. "Yogurt is healthier."

"I didn't picture you as a health nut."

That was only one of a long list of things she didn't know about me.

I got my head back in the game in front of the stove. No thoughts of kissing or my hand on her tit while cooking—that had to be a rule. After adjusting the temperature and adding oil to the pan, I turned from the stove. "What's wrong with eating healthy?"

She worried her bottom lip. "Nothing. You've been in my life a long time, but I guess it shows how little I really know about you."

I added the first pieces of chicken to the pan and slid the splatter shield into place. Before, sharing personal things with her would have been counterproductive to my goal of keeping distance between us. Now, not so much.

While I seared the meat in the pan, she sliced the mushrooms, onion, and garlic.

After I'd flipped the meat to brown on the other side, she slid up behind me.

"What's next?" Her tit rubbed seductively against my arm as she leaned in to check the pan.

Two could play this game. Instead of pulling away, I shifted my arm back an inch and into her. "When the meat finishes, we'll put it aside and sauté the dry ingredients before adding the broth, wine, yogurt, and chicken." The feel of her softness against my arm made it difficult to get the words out without stumbling.

She added a hand on my hip. "How long does it need to simmer?"

My cock started to simmer as I enjoyed the warmth of the contact with her. "Long enough to reduce a little."

She pulled away to clean up the island.

My phone rang. Why did the phone always have to interrupt us? The screen showed Zane's name.

"What's up, Zane?" I answered.

"We have a problem."

I backed away from the stove. "Which is?"

"They had the apartment staked out all right, including some bozo in her hallway."

"So you couldn't go in?" I guessed.

"No. I got the clothes and things—"

"You shouldn't have. Now they've made you." That was a stupid move.

"No shit, Sherlock."

"Terry, where are the plates?" Grace asked.

"Cupboard on the far left," I responded.

"Playing house now?" Zane asked.

"Eating in is the safe alternative." *Fuck him.*

He knew I was right and didn't argue. "I took the whole load back to the office instead of bringing it to you. They already know Hawk is involved, so no harm, no foul. I'll bring the stuff over after they get tired of watching our building."

"Okay, see ya then."

When I hung up, Grace was at the stove sautéing the mushrooms, onions, and garlic. "When's he coming over?"

"Not for a while. They were watching your place, and they followed him, so it's not safe for him to bring your things here yet."

Her shoulders slumped. "Just great."

CHAPTER 16

GRACE

MEN. WHY DID THEY ALWAYS CLAM UP WHEN YOU WANTED TO TALK?

I stood in front of the stove, stirring while I replayed the few words Terry had said in my head—*exactly the opposite*. He said the words and then refused to talk about it.

Terry walked up behind me. "We'll get you your clothes when it's safe."

"And until then?" The mushrooms were cooking down. I felt like whacking the wooden spoon on the counter to let out some of my frustration, but caught myself before I broke down like the helpless woman he thought I was.

"I've got a T-shirt for you to wear tonight."

"Yeah, I'll go into work wearing a man's T-shirt. It's a great look for a professional woman."

He slowly turned me around, taking the spoon from my hand and setting it on the counter. "I said *to wear tonight*."

It felt so hopeless. "Not with my luck. So far I've been attacked, beaten up, almost kidnapped more than once, my employees almost killed, forced away from my apartment, and now shot at, and I don't even have any fucking clothes to wear tomorrow." I sniffled. "And I don't have my cats."

With one gentle finger, he lifted my chin and held my eyes with his. "You need to trust me. We're going to find your cousin and get this worked out. When you took down Tony's niece with your darts, we gained leverage."

I laughed, remembering how silly Maria had looked with my darts in her ass.

"When Tall Tony gets the message that you're protected by Hawk Security, he'll back down. He's not suicidal."

What I saw in Terry's eyes was a promise, a promise that things would be all right, and I couldn't resist the urge any longer. I stepped forward, wrapped my arms around Terry, and melted into him. I tried to hold back the tears that formed, tears of relief that this man was looking out for me—that he cared.

He stroked my back. "I'm not going to promise anything about your cats, but one way or another, you *will* be able to go to work tomorrow, looking marvelous as always."

For what seemed like an eternity, but was probably only a minute, I hung on to him.

"You'd better stir that pan so things don't burn," he said eventually. "There are more steps to this recipe."

I stepped away, wiping under my eyes, and turned back to the stove. "Yes, chef."

He started the pasta and set places for dinner at the bar behind the kitchen island, all the while calling out instructions to me. It struck me as thoughtful, since I couldn't sit comfortably.

Then my phone rang. I held it up. "Serena."

"Take the call. I'll finish up here." Once again, a simple statement that would have been out of character for him last week.

I walked into the next room. "Hi."

"My God," Serena's voice was agitated. "Duke tells me you guys got shot at."

A brief shiver went through me. "The story of my life this week," I said with as breezy a voice as I could manage. I moved further away from the kitchen.

"How are you holding up? I can come over."

"No. I'm fine," I insisted, without feeling like it was a lie. "Terry and I are cooking dinner."

Her voice took on a questioning tinge. "Together?"

I faced the window lowering my voice. "Yes."

"Hmm. Does that mean you're taking my advice about making time to have a life?"

"Sort of," I said softly, hoping that Terry and I were beyond the argument.

"What does that mean?" she asked. Serena's doggedness had been a strength in group therapy. She always eventually pulled out truth and laid it on the table to be dissected.

"It means I wanted to, but we fought."

"Over what?" This wasn't going to end until she was completely satisfied.

"I leaned out of the car and shot back at the bastards against his *orders*." I added particular disdain to that last word.

"Really? That's great."

"There was nothing great about it," I disagreed. "It was pretty heated."

"Duke was like that," she explained. "He still is. It just means Terry cares about you... A lot. It's a guy thing about being overprotective."

Heat bloomed in my chest as I absorbed the words. "He was pretty angry."

"Trust me. That's a good thing."

"Grace? Dinner's almost ready," Terry called from the kitchen.

"He's calling. I gotta go," I told Serena.

"Yeah, I heard. Be good now. Scratch that, be as naughty as you want."

I laughed. "Bye." And, I ended the call.

A few minutes later, I was standing next to Terry, with a glass of wine and the most delicious-looking home-cooked meal I'd ever had.

He lifted his wine glass, and we repeated my earlier toast. "Friends."

I hoped that word was only the beginning.

I could do a reasonable job on spaghetti and meatballs, and I made a decent macaroni and cheese and a killer meatloaf, but after two bites of this meal, it was clear Terry's cooking put me to shame. "Thank you. This is delicious," I mumbled through my food.

"Don't thank me. You did most of the work."

"I was just the minion. You're the chef," I insisted. I forked another mushroom and piece of chicken. "When you said the boss—the guy you called Tall Tony—wouldn't cross that line, what did you mean?"

Terry put down his fork. "Years ago, two idiots, the Barzon brothers, came after a Hawk woman, Lucas's wife."

That was news. "I didn't know he was married."

"He was, but she died."

My hand went to my mouth as my stomach revolted. "My God, that's terrible. I had no idea."

"We don't talk about it. That's a rule."

"Sorry."

"Anyway, it was kept out of the news, but it was a big deal in all the wrong circles that Lucas's wife had been targeted. We all knew the Barzon brothers were behind it."

"What happened?"

"A week later, the brothers were found dead. It wasn't pretty."

"Lucas?" I asked, unsure whether I wanted to know the answer.

Terry shook his head. "Couldn't have been. He was across the country at the time."

I breathed a sigh of relief. "Do you think—"

"It doesn't matter. The message the bad guys took from it was clear—you didn't ever mess with a Hawk woman. And that protection now applies to you."

I didn't know whether to be elated, or scared, or both. "I'm not…" I added air quotes. "A Hawk woman."

Terry twisted his fork in the pasta and lifted it. "Are you forgetting that Lucas said he considers you a part of the family? He also told Victor you were my woman."

I couldn't believe my ears. "I'm not yours or anybody's." After the words came out, I didn't know why I had said them, except as a gut reaction.

"True. I haven't claimed you," he said defensively. Then, he smiled wickedly. "Yet. When I claim you, you'll know it."

Damn him. Had he sensed that in the middle of our kiss this morning, I would have done anything to claim the title of Terry Goodwin's woman? But then the arguments had started again. Now it was all too confusing.

Terry smiled at me. "You're still a Hawk woman."

Before I could object again, he added, "You're mine to protect, and you have been ever since Pete left. You're under Hawk protection. That was Lucas's meaning."

Well, that explanation was certainly easier to swallow. "I guess I should say thank you. I mean, without you I would have been…" The words trailed off, too horrible to speak. "You and Zane."

His eyes narrowed at the mention of Zane. Then he cleared his throat, saving us both from an awkward moment. "I'd like to hear how your company uses the VR process."

Thankfully, I accepted the off-ramp from our conversation and started with the vision of interactive design that had been my inspiration to start SpaceMasters.

And so, we relaxed into pleasant conversation for a change. Our delicious food cooled as we had to fit in bites between explanations and insightful questions.

After dinner, I helped with the cleanup before Terry led me to the sectional facing his monster big screen.

Was it a bachelor requirement to have a TV so large you couldn't figure out how they got it in the door?

"You need to wind down and relax," Terry told me.

"I can't sit, remember?"

He sat at one end of the sectional, placing a throw pillow next to him. "I remember. You can lie down." He patted the pillow—an invitation.

I kicked off my shoes and settled on my side, my head on the pillow as he worked the clicker. At least I didn't have to put my head in his lap. That would have been awkward.

He placed a hand on my shoulder. "What would you like to watch?"

The warmth of his touch short-circuited my brain for a moment, and I was proud that I was able to hide my reaction. "You choose," I squeaked. Yeah, I wasn't keeping it as cool as I wanted.

"You're the guest."

I wasn't foolish enough to suggest a rom-com. Was it odd that I'd never had an inkling of his movie preferences? A guy like Terry probably went for sci-fi or action movies. All I had to go on was what Pete had liked, so I suggested my brother's favorite action movie. "Can we get *True Lies*?"

"Sure. It would be fitting since Pete is Omega."

"Yeah, Omega," I said, implying I knew more than I did. Pete had mentioned Omega on the phone a few times when he didn't know I was listening. I'd never asked him what it meant. "Personally, I think Schwarzenegger is hot in this one."

"Jamie Lee Curtis is the hot one."

"I can guess which part you like." It had to be the striptease scene in the hotel.

He didn't hide his smirk as he located the movie and started it. Before long, Arnold appeared, larger than life coming out of the icy water and then stripping off his diving suit to reveal an immaculate tux underneath. If that didn't out-class James Bond, I didn't know what did.

I enjoyed the lazy strokes of Terry's fingers on my arm as the movie continued. I'd spent way too many nights alone in my apartment with only Bonnie and Clyde as company.

I let my hand wander as well, stroking his thigh—it was a powerful thigh. Everything about Terry exuded power, but more than only muscles. It was in the way he carried himself, the way he spoke with others, the way I'd seen him make decisions. Terry was so—the best word for it was *male*.

As the movie went on, I caught him glancing at me, but only because I was also paying as much attention to him as I was Arnold and Jamie Lee.

He didn't merely glance at my cleavage, although I enjoyed that as well. No, his eyes traveled the length of me, like a gentle caress.

"It's so perfect," Terry said as the characters crossed the threshold into the secret offices with the Omega emblem set in the marble floor. *Omega Sector, The last line of defense*, it read.

"Yeah."

"Hiding in plain sight," he said with a laugh. "Any communication about Omega the news media overhears is like a joke about the movie. They have no idea we're real."

"That's what Pete thought," I lied. He'd never spoken with me about it. "He always made me proud."

"You should be." He gripped my shoulder. "Omega is the best. True ghosts."

Omega. The word rattled around in my head as I recalled the furtive conversations. I'd known Pete was in a black program he couldn't talk about, but I'd never connected the Omega mentions until this moment.

Terry's fingers started again.

It felt like a revelation to finally have a glimpse of my brother's world. I knew Pete's work had to be different than the movie, but how much different? It hurt to know I'd never be able to ask him, now that he was gone.

Terry's continued stroking brought me back to the present and the movie. I reveled in the way such a gentle touch conveyed so much. Soon I was yearning for more. I'd seen glimpses of it in his eyes.

He wanted me just as I wanted him. He just couldn't or wouldn't break out of the status quo. He was back to stubborn Terry.

During our kiss, he'd warned me that he wouldn't be able to stop, but now he had. Maybe it had been my fault for arguing with him too forcefully. "I can't thank you enough."

He gripped my shoulder. "I can't let anything happen to you."

I didn't need noble Terry, when I wanted the passionate man I'd tasted earlier, the man whose fingers and eyes caressed me this evening. "You know I like you."

He nodded while looking straight ahead at the screen. "Likewise."

That deflated my ego several notches, but if he'd changed his mind, I had to know. "When we kissed before…"

His eyes finally traveled to mine, with heat in them. "You deserve better than me."

Where the hell had that come from? "Don't put yourself down. I don't know a better man than you."

He chuckled. "That only shows you don't get out much." He hit the nail on the head with that one.

I'd poured all my time into my business, but a near-death experience made things much clearer now. I could work hard on my business while still making time for me. And, I knew what it was that I wanted first.

I TUGGED ON HIS ARM. "I KNOW ENOUGH PEOPLE TO KNOW YOU'RE THE ONE for me."

Slowly, he brought his mouth near mine. "Are you sure? Because this is a bell that can't be unrung."

I could tell the position was awkward for him, but I speared my fingers in his hair and pulled him down to meet my needy lips anyway. "I'm sure." I shifted down the sectional and soon our faces were upside down against each other, like in the Spiderman movie.

I couldn't reach his crotch like this, but I did pull his hand down to my breast. The feel of him kneading my flesh ignited the afterburner of my desire. He delved deeper, taking over the kiss, and soon there was no question who was in charge.

He pulled at the hem of my top and soon strong fingers slid into my bra, caressing me and tweaking my nipple. Moaning my pleasure, I reached up, but I could only barely reach the bulge of his erection with my fingertips.

Still, that was enough to pull a groan from him, followed by a quick yank on the hem of my skirt.

I moaned my agreement as his finger moved inside my panties and parted my soaked folds. I gasped as he teased my entrance and then slid that finger inside me. I couldn't control my moans as I bucked against his hand, still unable to do more than brush against the outline of his cock.

"Tell me if you want me to stop." His voice was rough with desire.

"No. I want this. I mean, I want more."

After today, I did need this. I needed him. I needed to leave the shitstorm of my life behind for a little while. This was the third time today our tongues had tangled, and arguments be damned, I couldn't get enough of him.

He pulled his hand away. "You better be sure," he warned.

"I'm sure. Please don't stop," I begged.

He sat up and shoved the coffee table away. "Kitten, I've been wanting to taste you all day long."

No man had ever talked that dirty to me. I wouldn't have guessed I would like it, but I did. The jolt of excitement went straight to my core. "Like I said, green light."

He pulled my legs off the sectional.

"Ouch."

"Sorry." He reached up to yank my panties down with determination—not too rough, but definitely not gentle. He was a man on a mission, a man in control.

On my back like this, my wound only hurt moderately. I steeled myself for what was to come, but the words escaped anyway. "I've never—"

He stopped, eyes wide. "Never? You're a—"

"No, no, no. I'm not a virgin, but I've not ever… I mean not like this." With flushed cheeks, I didn't know how to say I'd never had a man go down on me before. The closest I'd gotten had been Jeffrey in college who was going to, but I hadn't showered since the morning, and when his nose had wrinkled, I'd gotten cold feet. I also didn't mention that I hadn't showered since *this* morning.

Terry huffed. "Let me guess, the wimps you went out with wanted blow jobs but didn't reciprocate?"

I nodded. "And it's been a long time." My dry spell had been years now.

"Me too." His face softened. "But trust me, this is not something to be scared of."

I nodded again, hoping to God that it lived up to half the hype it received in my romance novels.

He dragged my panties down, throwing them across the room. "I'll bet you have no idea how beautiful you are."

I blushed. "Stop it." I was halfway there with just the way his eyes devoured me.

An instant later, his mouth was on me.

My brain froze.

He lifted my legs over his shoulders and began licking and sucking.

Grabbing handfuls of his hair, I cried out, "Terry." My sounds became unintelligible as he tortured my clit in the most delicious way. I squeezed his head with my thighs as he drove me higher with every skillful stroke.

Then he thrust two fingers inside me and the assault was almost too much to bear.

I rocked into him.

When he stroked that area inside me that I'd heard about, but never experienced, his eyes locked with mine. I was completely at his mercy, an instrument he played to perfection. He was too good at this, way too fucking good.

I clamped my thighs on his head and yanked at his hair, writhing against his mouth. It was all too much and not enough at the same time.

With another lick of his tongue, I exploded and screamed one last time. My body shook from the intense pleasure searing me from the inside out.

His wicked tongue teased me through the waves.

My shaking and spasms didn't stop for the longest time, and when they did, I went limp.

Finally, he pulled away with glistening lips and a very satisfied look on his face. "I told you it was nothing to be afraid of."

Breathlessly, I nodded. "That was—"

"Great?" he suggested.

"Great is a start…" I panted. "But I was going to go with out of this world."

He laughed and licked his fingers—oh, this man was sexy with a capital S. All these years, he'd been right in front of me, and all I'd seen was my tormentor.

Worn out, I held out my arms to him in invitation. "Lie with me." I wanted to return the pleasure, but would need a few minutes to recover first.

Repositioning us, he placed me on the side that didn't have a wound and lay on the sectional next to me. He tucked my hair behind my ear. "Kitten, you're something else."

"Something good, I hope." I ran my nails down his spine.

"You bet." After a short kiss, he snuggled me to him, cradling my breast.

I was certain he could feel the rapid beat of my heart. A few minutes later, I'd recharged enough to reach for the bulge of steel in his pants. "Your turn."

∽

TERRY

BEFORE I COULD REACT, GRACE RAISED UP TO HER KNEES AND ATTACKED MY belt. She pulled my zipper down. I cooperated by lifting myself as she pulled my pants off. There was nothing more beautiful than watching her face as she pulled my aching cock free. I was willingly crossing the Rubicon today. If Pete hated me when he got back, that would be the price I'd have to pay.

She stroked me from root to tip. "I always knew you'd be big, but my

God…" When she added her tongue and licked the bead of pre-cum from the tip, I didn't care if she was just stroking my ego or not.

I grunted. "Baby, you have no idea how beautiful you look right now." Yes, the view of her fisting me was intoxicating.

She dragged her hand up and down again. "I like this."

My cock grew impossibly harder under her touch. "Baby, he likes you too." I couldn't stifle my groans as she pulled hard and licked me again. "Are you gonna suck me or just torture me to death?"

"If that's what you want." Her tongue circled my crown before her lips took me in.

I hissed out a breath and arched up into her.

She met me and sucked me in deep before lifting off and releasing me with a pop.

"That's it, baby." I reached for her hair.

She batted my hand away and broke contact. "I'm in charge," she announced, and for once I didn't argue with her.

She fisted the base of my shaft and began a rhythmic slide of her lips up and down, taking me deep, sucking me hard. All the while, she maintained eye contact.

I couldn't look away. It was a vixen's mind-meld as she held me in her trance, watching my every reaction to her tongue, the way she hummed around my cock, the strength of her grip, every little thing.

When she cupped my balls with her other hand, I tensed, so close to blowing that I couldn't take it. I pulled her hair, lifting her off me. "Baby," I bit out hoarsely. "I'm not coming in your mouth the first time we do this."

"I said it's your turn. Let me finish you."

"No. I'm going to finish inside you, with your sweet pussy clamping down around me and you screaming my name so loud they hear it in Vegas. And you're going to come again and again for me, baby—all night long."

Her smile said she wasn't going to argue.

Then my phone rang. "Fuck." It was Lucas's ringtone.

"Just let it go," she pleaded as she stroked me again.

"I can't. It's Lucas." One of our inviolable rules was that you always picked up a call from the boss.

Rolling off the sectional, I answered, "Goodwin."

"How is Grace doing?"

I looked over at her. With the flush in her cheeks from what we'd been doing, she looked perfect to me. "Just fine, considering all she's been through today."

"Good. Tell her Constance is on her way with her things. She'll be there any minute."

"Copy that. What do we know about the two who shot at us?"

"They're not a part of Russo's crew. We established that much, but they're scared of whoever hired them and won't talk."

"Marku?" I asked.

"Could be. Or whoever the buyer of that shipment is. Jordy and Winston are still getting confirmation on that. This is turning into a real shitshow, so whatever was in that case had to be something special. You just keep our girl safe."

I looked at Grace and smiled. "Copy that."

Lucas ended the call.

Grace's phone dinged. I waited for her to get it, but she ignored it instead.

When she ignored it, I gave her the good news. "Lucas is sending Constance over now with your clothes."

She sighed a relieved breath. "Finally some good news. What about my cats?"

"He didn't say."

Her phone dinged again with the arrival of another message.

"You need to get that?" I asked.

Reluctantly, she nodded. "It has to be work." She struggled off the sectional. "How about a short timeout?"

I smiled. "To be continued." I pulled my pants back up and buckled my belt.

As I looked at her, I knew one thing for sure. I wasn't going back to the way we had been before. I wasn't going to push her away because she was Pete's little sister. Not anymore. If Pete had a problem with it, I'd have to deal with that later.

I'd gladly live with knowing I'd broken a trust between him and me if that was the cost. This beautiful, accomplished, and yes, annoying woman was going to be mine. I'd keep her safe and find a way to get past our disagreements.

She cursed as she searched her handbag for her phone. It was cute.

No, I was going all-in with Grace. The terror I'd felt almost losing her in the attacks today had made the feelings I held for her clear as day. I wasn't repressing them any longer.

She wanted me as much as I wanted her, and that made this the perfect decision, the only possible decision.

Holding up the phone triumphantly, she swiped at the screen. "Hi, Peyton. What's up?"

CHAPTER 17

Terry

Grace was still on the phone with her assistant when the sound of my exterior motion sensors startled me. I adjusted myself before checking the doorbell camera on my phone.

"Constance is here," I announced

"Huh?" Grace looked over.

"Constance is at the door. She brought your clothes."

Grace rushed to stand, and this time, I steadied her to avoid another pass out.

The doorbell rang.

When Grace seemed steady, I let go of her and answered through my phone. "Be right there."

Grace adjusted her top and smoothed her skirt as I strode for the door.

"Where did my panties go?" I heard her ask as she looked around.

I chuckled before descending the stairs. I unlocked and opened the heavy door. "Hey. Thanks for bringing her things," I told Constance. "I'll take them up."

Constance set down several garbage bags. "You take these. I'll get the rest." She retreated to her Porsche and returned juggling more plastic bags and two cat carriers. "Can't forget the important things."

"Uh-huh." I stepped aside to let her go first up the stairs.

"Special delivery," Constance called out at the top.

Grace put down her wine, squealed, and ran over. "Bonnie and Clyde."

"I thought you'd appreciate having them with you," Constance said. "They might not have survived with Zane."

I swallowed my chuckle. After a moment, Clyde left Grace's side and came over to rub against me. I kneeled down to scratch the little monster. "What's this button thing on his collar?"

Grace looked up from petting Bonnie. "That's a cat tracker, in case he gets out. I can find him with an app on my phone. Do you have any coin batteries? The one in his collar just died."

"Not here, but I'll get you one. Okay to take this with me?" When she nodded, I unsnapped his collar and pocketed it.

Constance lifted a bag. "Pardon the way everything is stuffed in plastic bags, but that's what you get when you send a man to pack."

They both giggled.

"You're a lifesaver," Grace said.

"They're so cute," Constance gushed as Bonnie disappeared under the sectional.

Grace picked up Clyde. "Thank you. I love them, but sometimes they drive me crazy."

Constance looked at me. "Where should I put her clothes?"

I pointed. "Guest room is the first door on the right."

Grace picked up a bag and followed her, and I brought the rest. As soon as unpacking morphed into discussing where to hang things and how to organize them, I left the room. Sorting blouses by color was not my thing.

"Hey, Constance, would you like anything?" I called from the kitchen.

"Just water, thanks," she called back. "Now this is cute," I heard her tell Grace.

Clyde appeared in the kitchen. Seems sorting wasn't his thing either.

A moment later, I heard Constance again. "You really are on a serious campaign against VPL."

"What do you mean?"

"You only have thongs here. My God, these are sexy. Where did you find these?"

I almost swallowed my tongue. I couldn't stop an image from forming in my head of Grace in a tiny red thong.

"No, that's not right," Grace said. "Most of my panties—"

"Cover more than these?"

"Of course."

Constance laughed. "This is what you get when a badass SEAL packs for you. He only includes what he wants you to wear."

I should have been the one going through Grace's underwear drawer, not Zane.

"Is there any way I can get my other underwear from my apartment?" Grace asked. "I mean, I'd rather not have to order more online. Terry's like a rabid guard dog. I doubt he'll let me go shopping. He doesn't even want me to go into work."

"He's just looking out for you," Constance said. "Would you rather have him be less serious about your safety?"

Right on. I pumped my fist at Constance's support.

"Maybe not, but a little less like my jailer would be good," Grace mumbled.

"I'll see if I can get your things, or I can go shopping for you."

"I'd like that." Grace's voice sounded lighter.

Less like her jailer—I'd have to remember that. Leaning against the counter, I imagined telling Constance to take a hike and going lingerie shopping for Grace myself. No, *with* Grace would be better. Now there was an idea that was less jailer-like.

I poured myself a glass of water while I waited.

Constance appeared a few minutes later. "She's scared," she said quietly. "What's the plan?"

"Keep her here at night and limited to her work building during the day until we get this sorted out. They don't know where this is yet, and I have a solid door downstairs, a good security system, and no ground-floor access, which makes this pretty defensible. What do you think?"

She started around the perimeter and stopped at the sliding glass door to the terrace. I followed her, and Clyde followed me.

She pointed down. "You should put a rod in the track. You don't want somebody climbing onto the terrace and picking this lock."

I nodded. "Will do."

She continued around, checking rooms, windows, and the angles of my hallway cameras. "Looks good to me." She returned to a corner of the living room and stopped.

My gaze followed her eyes to the floor. Grace's panties were in the corner.

"I'm not one to judge, but in the Secret Service, we would consider your level of…connection to the protectee to be disqualifying."

"It's not what it looks like," I lied with a straight face. It was totally what it looked like—or soon would be. And often, if I had anything to say about it.

She cocked her head with a sigh. "It never is." She lowered her voice. "Look, I don't give a damn what you do with your personal time, but getting involved with a protectee is reckless and puts her at risk. I know that, and—" She poked me in the chest. "—you know that. You can lose objectivity and make a mistake. Maybe you should have a chat with the boss about assigning somebody else."

"I've got this." Duke, Constance, and Winston had other commitments right now, which left Zane as the next choice for full-time protection, and I wasn't agreeing to that.

She shook her head, not ready to let this go. "You could take time off from other assignments and hang around or whatever, but not be the primary."

"I said I've got this," I assured her. Nobody would be better protection for Grace than me. Nobody else would be as invested.

"Last week, you were at each other's throats."

Here we go again. "That was then."

"Have you considered that she may be reacting to the events of the day? An attack, even unsuccessful, is emotionally jarring."

"I know that." Her implication was clear—what if Grace was only attracted to me because I'd been there for her during the attack?

"Then figure out how to cool it for a while," Constance insisted. "Objectivity wins over passion in this game."

"Sure," I agreed. But I hadn't thought through how I'd do that, given everything that had happened between me and Grace today.

Grace appeared around the corner. "Hi." Her voice held an obvious question.

"We were just discussing this as a defensible space," I explained as Constance and I moved away from the pair of panties in the corner.

"Because bad guys are after me?"

Constance raised a brow.

"Stressful day," I whispered.

"Grace, it's always better to be prepared," Constance said.

Grace sighed. "Constance, would you like to join me in a glass of wine?"

"No thanks. I've got to run." She picked up her purse and headed for the door.

I told Grace I'd be right back and escorted Constance downstairs.

"Cool head, professional and objective," she said, wagging a finger at me. "Given the way you've acted around her in the past, you might want to consider how these attacks are affecting you too." She walked out with that last statement hanging in the air.

"Got it." I locked the door after her and shook my head.

Damned straight the attacks had affected me. They'd made me question why I'd kept my distance from Grace all these years. I'd dreamed about her more times now than I could count.

Things were clearer than they had ever been. I was done pushing Grace away. She'd be mine, if I could convince her.

But it was time to get my head in the game, protection-wise. The sliding glass door upstairs needed to be secured. Searching the garage, I located a piece of wood that would fit in the track and found my hacksaw.

∼

GRACE

WHEN TERRY ESCORTED CONSTANCE DOWNSTAIRS, I STRETCHED OUT ON HIS sectional again, wondering how my life had taken such a turn.

Though I knew he was just downstairs with Constance, I missed him. How weird was that? It was truly the dawn of a new day for me.

Yes, I'd enjoyed my short bit of girl time with Constance as we unpacked the bags of clothes that Zane had thrown together, but I'd still been eager to have her leave.

After the take-my-breath-away orgasm Terry had laid on me, I was eager to officially bid farewell to my dry spell. Work had consumed my life for so long that I'd forgotten what letting go felt like.

After the attacks and now a near-death experience, I wasn't waiting any longer to live life to the fullest. Terry had admitted he'd spent years pushing me away, and I wasn't going to let him continue. Knowing now that he'd always been attracted to me changed everything.

Pete had once told me that Terry was the best man he knew, and after the events of these last two days, I understood what he'd meant. Now that I'd seen behind Terry's mask, I wanted to get to know the good man behind the gruff exterior and often nasty comments. I was determined to spend time with the Terry Pete had known, and to give us a chance.

Anticipation burned through me as I heard his footsteps coming up the stairs.

When he emerged, he was way more clothed than I wanted either of us to be. "Hi there," I said in my attempt at a sultry voice.

"Hi."

"Wanna join me, big guy?"

But he glanced away and strode over to the sliding glass door.

"What's wrong?" *What have I done wrong?* How did I take us back a step from intimacy to coldness?

"Nothing."

I clearly needed to watch more romantic movies. Was there such a thing as movie karaoke so I could get the sultry-voice thing down? Did I need to show more cleavage?

"I'm securing the perimeter," he added after a moment. "This is a recommendation Constance made."

That's when I noticed the piece of wood and the saw he carried. "Oh." Once again, this was the good man behind the mask, putting my safety first.

He turned to me with fire in his eyes. "Can you wait one minute, Kitten?"

∽

TERRY

LIKE A GOOD CARPENTER, I MEASURED THE LENGTH I WANTED TWICE BEFORE I cut the piece of wood. When I laid it in the track, it fit perfectly. Nobody was sliding this door open from the outside and getting to my woman.

"I'm getting cold," Grace said in a husky, Hollywood starlet voice.

I moved toward her. Okay, I almost jogged. "Do you remember what I said about you being mine?" I asked, letting my eyes linger on her lips as I knelt beside the sectional.

Her eyes narrowed. "Not really." *Liar, liar, pants on fire.*

"I said you would know when I'd claimed you, and that time has come, Grace."

She sucked in a breath. "But—"

I stopped her with a finger to her lips. "Kitten, hear me out before you argue. You're an amazing woman, and I know I've treated you poorly. I've wanted you forever, but I pushed you away because you were Pete's off-limits little sister. Well, that stops today. I'm not waiting any longer. You're mine."

"Come here, you big lug." She tugged on my shirt. "Are you telling me you want me as your girlfriend?"

My lips were inches from hers. "Isn't that what I just said?"

She pulled herself up to meet my lips, and once again, the chemistry ignited between us. She was insatiable, trying to establish dominance in our kiss.

But that's not how this was going to go. I stood. "You wet for me?"

She nodded breathlessly.

"Baby, I'm not fucking you for the first time on this couch."

A sly smile unfolded on her face.

"No, when I slide my cock into your slick pussy, it's going to be on a bed with plenty of room for all the ways I intend to fuck your brains out."

She looked away. "Promises, promises."

I shut her up with another kiss.

CHAPTER 18

Grace

I whimpered when Terry broke the kiss way earlier than I expected or wanted. When he said he wanted to fuck my brains out, I went sopping wet. No one had talked dirty to me like that before.

The professional businesswoman in me should have been repulsed, but the cavewoman was loose, and she liked that she brought out the animal in her man.

He leaned over and scooped me up in his arms—as if I wasn't five foot nine with curves. "You're coming to my bed."

His eyes were molten desire, and I couldn't help myself. "We could do it in the back seat of your sexy car."

"I was thinking of spreading you out on the hood," he joked.

"Okay." That naughty image sent a surge of tingles to my lady parts. What would it be like to be taken by this man that way?

But *wild* was not a word anybody used to describe me, and when he started down the stairs, fear reared its ugly head. "You were joking, right?"

He stopped. "Not that adventurous?"

He'd called my bluff. "With my cut, maybe a bed would be better."

"Okay." He turned us around and climbed back up the stairs. "But since you suggested it, the hood of the car is going on the list."

Goddamn, that thought was hot. I leaned into his strong warmth and closed my eyes. How had I not seen it before? This was where I belonged.

When we reached his bedroom, he set me on my feet.

After licking my lips, I stretched up and brushed my tongue over his mouth.

He groaned with me as our mouths crashed together. The kiss was feverish. We were all gas and no brake. His fingers bit into my ass, but he carefully avoided my injury.

I am not a weak damsel. The cavewoman was in charge and words I'd never said before came out hoarsely, as I pulled my top off. "I want you to fuck me now."

He reached behind me, unhooking my bra and tossing it aside. His gaze ignited as he looked down at my chest. "You have the greatest tits."

"You're talking too much," I answered as I cupped his erection.

"You asking me to sink my cock deep inside your pussy, baby?"

"God, yes…" I whimpered. I was putty in his hands. His words and the feel of his length eliminated any filter. "Take me. Fuck me like you mean it, like I'm yours."

"You are mine."

"Then take me. I'm yours," I mumbled into his mouth.

"Not yet…" He hissed when I went for his belt. Instead, he laid me on the bed and settled next to me, urging my legs apart.

I lifted a knee and turned toward him to take the pressure off my injured butt cheek. For the longest time, we lay there, facing each other, his fingers tracing my curves and circling my breasts, but not touching my nipples.

"Don't rush it," he said as I reached down again.

Somehow, he'd shifted from dirty-talking, going-to-fuck-my-brains-out Terry to slow and teasing Terry.

"As you command, sir." Following his lead, I ran my hands under his shirt and over the hard ridges of his chest and abs, stopping above his belt and feeling the warmth of his powerful body.

Leaning in, he whispered, "That's better," before nibbling my earlobe.

I shivered as he kissed his way down my neck and along my collarbone. "That tickles."

My complaint only resulted in him lavishing the same kisses on the other side of my neck and shoulder. He switched to a teasing figure-eight pattern over and around my chest.

My breasts felt so full and responsive, I wondered if I'd get a nipple-gasm when he finally reached the little buds. I'd never had a guy, correct that, a *man* treat me like this. I'd clearly only been with boys before.

"Tell me," he whispered in my ear.

I raked my fingers through his hair, briefly considering forcing his head down to my breasts. "What?"

"Are you wet for me?"

"As a fire hydrant." And that was no joke.

He nibbled my earlobe again. "Last chance to come to your senses. I warned you, I'm not a good man."

He'd actually said he wasn't good for me. There was a difference, a big one. But that only heightened my desire. "I'm all in."

"Hang on, baby." He cupped my breast and tweaked the nipple. "You have no idea how hard you make me." He pulled me against the rock-hard bulge in his pants. "Remember, you are mine." He ran his knuckles over my nipples. They responded by instantly hardening into even tighter buds. His head lowered to suck on one nipple while he caressed the other breast.

I closed my eyes and moaned, spearing my fingers into his hair.

He released my nipple with a pop. "I want you so much I'm not going to last long."

I pulled his head up so he could read the truth in my eyes. "Then fuck my brains out already." I yearned for the experience I'd read about but never had.

"You want it quick and hard, baby?"

Looking over the abyss, I jumped. "I want it all. Everything you've got." I'd had way too much quick action from guys, but I'd never had hard —and I'd also had a really shitty two days. I wanted the raw masculinity of this man, the passionate animal I brought out in him. I showed him by grabbing his erection through his pants and squeezing.

"I love your tits," he said as he leaned down to the other breast.

Though it felt amazing, with him hunched over me, I couldn't reach him the way I wanted. So I settled for pulling the hem of his shirt up and raking my nails over his back. That's when my fingers encountered a rough scar.

I knew he'd been injured overseas, but he'd never talked about it. I traced around and over it several times. "Do you want to talk about it?"

Releasing my nipple, he gave me the same answer Pete had given me the time he'd been wounded. "Classified."

Fuck, I hated that everything our bravest men did was top secret. "Mission went bad?"

He nodded. "Very. We lost one guy and…we almost lost more."

I tried again. "You got shot?"

"Mortar wound."

"I can't imagine how terrible that must have been." He was just like Pete had been, waving off the injury as part of the job.

He took a deep breath. I stayed quiet, hoping for more.

"The guy I was with died. I lost half a kidney and had to leave the Marines." His words carried pain.

"I'm sorry."

"Don't be." He shrugged. "I joined LAPD SWAT because one and a half kidneys were good enough for them, and that brought me here, to you. So in a way, it was the best thing that ever happened to me."

And there was the *good* in Terry Goodwin. He'd spent years putting his life on the line, doing the hard jobs so the rest of us could sleep safely, protecting others, and now me.

"You're talking too much," I reminded him.

In a quick move, he covered me with his hard, heavy body. I yelped in surprise, but relished the passion in spite of my wound. He pinned my wrists above my head and began a long kiss. I squirmed at first. Like all our interactions, this was partly a battle. That was our dynamic.

Knowing I'd lost, I gave in. But with him ravaging me like this, I'd actually won what I realized I'd secretly wanted for the longest time—the strength and passion of this man directed at me. "Is that all you got, big guy?" I teased when he broke the kiss.

He released my hands and sat up to pull off my skirt.

I raced to unzip the zipper before he ripped it. A second later I was bare to him since I hadn't found my panties from before.

"I bet you have no idea how gorgeous you are."

My blush came unbidden.

"If you want to torture me, wear a thong tomorrow. I'll be hard all the damned day knowing what's under your skirt."

"That can be arranged," I said with a lick of my lips—any way to get to him was a good way.

He yanked off his shirt and tossed it to the floor with my clothing.

When one of those clever fingers finally split my soaked folds, I moaned long and loud. Then a sharp gasp escaped me when it slowly entered me.

He followed that with a second finger. "Wet is right." As he slid in and out of me, his thumb found my clit.

I rocked into his hand. "Terry." I grabbed for his belt.

"No. You're going to come for me first. You're going to come on my hand before you get my cock." As he settled next to me, his other hand stroked my breast and teased my nipple.

I continued rocking into his hand, taking the pleasure he doled out.

"Or you can come on my hand and my cock," he added after a moment. His thumb didn't let up, nor did his breast play.

My hips kept bucking to the rhythm of his hand. Unstoppable moans escaped me as he tickled that secret spot inside my channel and strummed my clit. With incredible speed, the ecstasy built, and I felt the cliff approaching. "I'm gonna come." My hissed words matched the desperation I felt.

"That's it, baby. Come for me." He added pressure on my clit.

As much as I wanted this to go on forever, I couldn't hold off. My eyes clamped shut. He sucked on my nipple, and I came splintering apart into a million desperate shards, crying out his name. The waves rolled over me, my inner muscles convulsing on his fingers.

When the waves receded, the limpness arrived, and I opened my eyes again. His beautiful face came into focus, gigantic smile and all.

He brought his hand up and proceeded to lick and suck his fingers. "Baby, you taste so sweet."

Yes, we had arrived at a place I hadn't visited before—Dirtyville—and it excited me. I reached for his belt. "That was great. Now it's your turn, and we're not answering a phone this time."

Of course *great* was way too mild a word for the experience he'd given me.

He got off the bed and rummaged through one drawer and then another of his nightstand. "Gotcha." He held up a condom.

"Only one?" I teased.

He extracted the condom box from the drawer and rattled it. "I think this should do us for tonight."

Staying off my bad side, I leaned up on my elbow. "Sounds like a challenge."

He grinned as he undid his belt and lowered his pants. "I'm always up for a challenge." The bulge in his boxer briefs was huge.

My mouth dropped open as he shucked his underwear. "My God, I should have known you'd be big." It was always good to compliment a guy on his size, but with Terry, I didn't have to fib.

His cock was not only plenty long enough, but also impossibly thick and so hard it sprung up like a flagpole—a certified pussy destroyer. He fisted it and gave himself a stroke.

That cranked up my desire another notch.

Tearing open the condom packet with his teeth, he threw it to me. "Help me put this on."

Before, my boyfriends had always taken care of this, so tonight was one for challenges. I knelt on the bed as he came over, his cock bobbing as he moved. I could have watched it all day. Grabbing the beast, it was time for another first for me.

He moaned as I licked the drip of precum off his tip. The taste was salty.

"Faster, baby. I love your hands on me, but I can't wait to slide my cock inside your sweet pussy and fuck your brains out like you want." He grunted as I rolled the latex down. We were deep in the dirty-talk zone.

Seeing the effect my hands had on him, I took my time finishing the job.

∼

Terry

My cock was rock hard, and she tantalized me with her touch, rolling the rubber on inch by inch—sweet torture from my beautiful woman.

"Lie back," I told her when she'd finished.

Instead, she continued stroking me. "How do you get so hard?"

I was going to blow if she kept working me with her hands. "I can't help it. I see your luscious tits. I taste your sweet pussy. This is what you do to me. I want you so badly. Now lie back. I can't wait."

She did, but then said, "This isn't going to work. My butt still hurts."

"All fours then. I'll be gentle." That was a promise I knew would be difficult to keep. Her pussy was plenty wet, but also tight. "Tell me if I'm in too far."

She rolled over and, with her ass in the air, rested on her elbows. "I didn't ask for gentle," she said, looking back over her shoulder with a wicked grin.

I spread her knees a little farther, positioned my head at her entrance, and pushed in slowly. Proving that she didn't want slow and easy, she shoved back against me, impaling herself on my cock.

The sensation was otherworldly. "Baby, you feel perfect, slick and tight like you were made for me." Grabbing her hips, I started to thrust, careful to not go too deep. Some women couldn't handle my length in this position.

A few thrusts later, she surprised me again by pushing back hard. I ended up in her all the way to the hilt without a cry of pain. She was a tall girl, and big in the dimensions that mattered.

I always enjoyed sex, but the feel of my sweet Grace taking my cock was something else—a white-hot need to possess her in each and every way. Knowing now that I wouldn't hurt her, I pistoned into her hard and fast. Her little yelps of pleasure filled the room, the perfect music to go with the slaps of flesh on flesh as I gave her exactly what she'd asked for.

"Oh God, Terry, don't stop." Her voice was husky with need as she looked back over her shoulder again.

Stopping was impossible now.

"Fuck, I'm close…" She moaned as she continued to push back against me.

I brought a hand around her and found her clit. Pressing and stroking it was like hitting the ignition button on her.

"Terry…" She rocked harder, panting.

"Look at me, baby," I commanded.

She did. Our eyes locked. Her mouth opened and her body shuddered as her orgasm rolled over her. Her spasms gripped me like a fist and milked my own release out of me. I gave it one last plunge and held deep as my body locked up and the spurts began in a pattern that couldn't be controlled.

Panting hard, she leaned back against me. "That was something else."

"Yeah," I agreed as I pushed her forward to collapse on the bed. I settled to the side, with one leg and an arm over her. The continued tingling in my cock said *something else* didn't begin to describe it. I wasn't done with this intriguing, infuriating woman—not even close.

She turned her head toward me and pulled me close for a kiss.

After a few minutes, I got up to take care of the condom, and when I returned, I got my Kitten under the covers and snuggled behind her. I kissed her hair, finding the spooning position naturally comfortable.

She purred. "Why did we wait so long for this?"

"Because we spent all our time arguing over little shit."

She took in a deep breath. "I'll try to be better about that."

"Me too." It had all been my fault. The damned bro code was my excuse—an unwritten promise to Pete that I hadn't let go of until today. He might hate me for this, but I knew in my soul this was right where I should be.

After waiting forever to get to this point, Grace and I made up for lost time twice more in the middle of the night, and each time felt as good as the first. My little Kitten was a sex fiend, and I wasn't complaining one bit.

CHAPTER 19

Terry

I woke the next morning to hair tickling my chin and the faint lemony scent of Grace's hair. As I blinked away sleep, I was careful not to move my hand, which cupped her warm breast. Normally, I liked to sleep cold, but this morning I found the experience of her warmth against me supremely comfortable.

I'd doubted Duke when he'd told me that having Serena in his bed every morning provided a mood lift that had been new to him. Now I got it. There was a serenity to the start of the day with my woman in my arms, breathing slowly and steadily.

Grace shifted.

I stayed still.

She brought a hand up to cover mine and pressed me into her breast. Her ass shifted back against my morning wood. "Good morning," she mumbled groggily.

"Morning, Kitten." I pulled her closer.

Then she jerked. "What time is it?"

A cat bounded off the foot of the bed and scurried out.

Not letting go of her, I breathed in her scent. "Time for more sex."

She wiggled her ass against me. "I can tell. But really, what time is it?"

I released my hold on her. "The clock is on your side."

She raised up. "Shit." Twisting, she faced me, planting a quick kiss on my lips. "Rambo, we have to get up. I have to get into work and prepare."

"I thought I was Sir Galahad?"

"After the way I've seen you dispatch bad guys, I think Rambo is closer." She grasped my aching cock and gave me a tug.

"That's it, baby. Sir Galahad's sword."

"You do know that in mythology, Galahad was celibate."

I laughed as I pulled her down and rolled on top of her. "I'm certainly not planning on that."

She pushed on my shoulders. "That's good to know, but I seriously need to get up."

"I'm already up. Can't you tell?"

"What you are is incorrigible." She snaked a hand behind my neck and pulled me in for a kiss. "I have to shower."

When she slipped out of bed and stood, I was rewarded with an excellent view of my woman naked. God, she was gorgeous. Her boobs taunted me, just begging me to pull her back into bed. She turned for the bathroom, giving me a glimpse of an intriguing dragon tattoo on her lower back I'd never known about.

After taking a few minutes to get my cock under control, I used the bathroom. Of course I slowed down at the shower glass to take in my woman. Pulling myself away was a struggle I almost lost.

"You can join me if you promise to behave yourself," she called out just as I reached the door.

I turned back to look, but it was too much for me when she soaped her tits. "I can't make that promise." Instead, I left. I deserved some kind of medal for not joining her under the water and making her late to work.

As I listened to the shower run from the bedroom, Grace so consumed my thoughts that I almost fell over getting a pair of underwear on. *Screw it.* Pants were optional since this was my fucking house. I went to the kitchen, needing to get out of earshot or I'd totally cave and have her again against the marble of the shower.

Her two cats were lounging on the sectional, Bonnie on the back and Clyde on the cushions.

While the coffee machine did its thing, I surveyed the kitchen to find an appropriate place for a quickie. I was getting hard again, just hoping Grace would agree.

Then I heard footsteps coming up the stairs.

Shit. How had an intruder gotten past my lock?

Double shit. My weapon was in the bedroom, and I couldn't reach it without going by the stairwell.

Silently, I grabbed a knife from the block.

A woman's voice came around the corner. "Hey, big brother. Time to wake up." *Fuck me.* It was my sister, Deb.

"I'm awake." With my hard-on obvious, I swapped the knife for a dish towel to hide behind just as she rounded the corner. At least the sound of the shower had stopped.

She shrugged and strolled to the fridge. "We said we were going to get together, and I knew it would be next month if I waited for you to have a break in your schedule." She pulled open the fridge with a yawn.

I moved behind the island. "What are you doing up?" She hadn't ever been much of an early riser. "You could have called to warn me you were coming over so I could at least get dressed."

"Jet lag," she explained. "My sleep schedule is all screwed up. And I wasn't giving you a chance to sneak off and avoid me. No way." She glanced my way. "We used to take baths together, so it's nothing I haven't seen before."

"When you were like four," I reminded her.

She closed the refrigerator. "How come you don't have any breakfast fruit? You know cantaloupe, blueberries, grapefruit?"

"Because it's my fridge, and I don't eat fruit at breakfast."

She yawned again. "So, where's this hot-shit medal you got?"

"It's at work," I lied. "You look bushed, so why don't you go home and rest? I promise I'll bring it by tonight."

"I might as well, since you don't have anything good for breakfast." She picked up her purse. "But you better promise me."

"Of course."

"Is the coffee ready?" Grace called from the bedroom.

A smile bloomed on Deb's face. "You sly devil, you," she whispered.

"I'll bring it in a minute," I answered, hoping to hell that Grace stayed in the bedroom. I waved my hand for Deb to shoo.

She didn't budge. "Serena did say a girl named Janice would be hard for you to resist." She held her hands out in front of her chest, suggesting that Janice had big tits, which was spot on.

I rolled my eyes. "Can you just give me a little privacy, please?"

My luck ran out when Grace turned the corner.

She startled at the sight of Deb, and the towel she had wrapped around her almost came loose. An instant blush formed.

"You guys?" Deb screeched. "You finally got out of your own way?" She rushed to Grace and gave her a hug. "I've been waiting for this."

Grace fixed her towel when my sister released her. "He's my bodyguard," she said meekly.

"And she's also now my girlfriend," I said proudly. I intended to claim her publicly, and Deb was a good place to start.

"I knew it," Deb squealed. "I knew it."

Grace's eyes bored into me. "Terry." It was not an I'm-glad-you-told-her tone.

"What, Kitten? You're mine. Get used to it."

Deb watched with fascination as Grace huffed out a loud breath. "We could have discussed this first."

I waved at my sister. "What were you going to tell her? That we didn't just—"

"Not another word," Deb said, raising a hand. "Time-out for a second. I don't ever want to hear details, but I'm happier than a pig in shit for the two of you. Grace, you've got the best man I know in your corner now, and you, big brother…" She pointed at me. "Have the classiest, most driven, ass-kicking woman I know to put you in your place when you deserve it. Which we both know is almost all the time."

I grinned, liking her description of the situation.

Grace smiled as well.

Deb shot her a questioning look. "Hold on a second." She raised a hand. "Why do you need a bodyguard?"

"Elliot," I said. "So, I'm staying here until the situation is resolved."

Deb sighed. "That kid needs to grow up. But why are you in trouble?" she asked Grace.

Grace hitched up her towel again. "I have to get to work, but the short version is that Elliot got in trouble with the wrong people, and they think I know where to find him."

Deb cocked her head.

"Or," Grace admitted, "they think taking me will give them leverage over him."

"Which is stupid," I commented. "Because Elliot doesn't care about anybody but himself."

"Duh," Deb concurred.

Grace backed away without contradicting me this time. "I really do have to get ready for work."

My quickie was now off the table. *Table*? That was the answer. The breakfast table would do just fine when the opportunity for a quickie arose—or better yet, the table on the terrace. *Yeah, that would be something.*

Just then, a phone rang in my backpack, and both women looked at me. I pulled out the pair of phones we'd taken from the Russo pair. I'd just been waiting for someone to call one of them.

The one with the pink cover rang again. The name on the screen read *Victor*—no surprise there.

I motioned for Grace. "He's expecting a woman to answer. When I accept the call, just answer it with a *yes*, nothing more."

She nodded.

I pressed a finger to my lips, telling my sister to stay out of this, then I accepted the call on speaker.

"Yes?" Grace said as I held the phone out.

"Where are you?" Victor's angry voice came across the line. "You said you had the girl, and then you don't show. We don't have any time to mess around, Maria."

"Victor, so nice to hear your voice again."

There was a pause. "Who the fuck is this?"

"Maria and the other idiot you sent are busy right now, and they won't be coming back anytime soon." Anger made me grip the phone tighter.

"I want the weasel Elliot," Victor snarled. "Give him to me now, or things are getting very bad for everybody."

"Coming for Grace was a very big mistake, dickhead. Don't make it worse," I growled.

He laughed. "You must be Terry. Last name Goodwin. I looked you up—a fucking LAPD pussy. You give me back my cousin Maria right the fuck now or else."

"Not happening."

"Mr. Policeman, do you have a death wish? You have no idea what my father will do to you when he hears you have Maria."

Hiding behind his father's name told me exactly what kind of wimpy prick I was dealing with.

"I don't give a flying fuck who your father is, asshole. Grace is off-limits, you hear me?"

"I only hear a dead man talking."

Grace paced in a tiny circle.

"Fuck you!" Deb burst into the conversation. "Don't you dare insult my brother."

I mouthed, "*Be quiet*," and pointed an angry finger at Deb, then added a warning glare.

Victor laughed. "Ah, Mr. Policeman, you have a woman to hide behind."

"Screw you, Victor. She's not a part of this either."

"She's got sass. I like that in a woman. I think we should have dinner."

"Fuck off, asshole," Deb spat. She'd never been good at following my orders. "My brother is going to wipe the floor with you, and then I'll cut your balls off for a trophy."

Victor laughed. "I like her. She has spirit."

I grabbed Deb and clamped my hand over her mouth. "You sent Maria and that other idiot after my woman," I snarled. "And that is unfuckingacceptable."

Grace stopped pacing and wrapped her arms around herself.

"Stay quiet," I whispered to my damned sister.

"Fuck you, Mr. Policeman. When I'm done with you and your bitch, you will wish you'd licked my boots when you had the chance. I'm going to enjoy feeding you to the sharks."

"Look, shit for brains, you have no idea who you're fucking with. When you came for Grace after our warning, you crossed a line that your father knows not to go near. Ask him what happened the last time anyone fucked with Lucas Hawk. Good luck explaining to him that you decided to pit your family against us." I chuckled. "And for your information, dickwad—"

"You shut your mouth, Mr. Policeman."

Deb squirmed loose. She was red-faced, but at least she didn't yell into the phone.

"Too bad for you, Victor. I'm not a cop anymore. That means I don't have to play by their rules." I gave that two seconds to sink in. "So when you go out on the street or even near a window, you might want to check the fine print on my resume. I was a Marine Scout Sniper before I joined SWAT. You won't even hear the bullet coming before it splits your head open." I stabbed at the phone and hung up.

Deb was one huge smile. "You told him. I loved that sniper shit. He's probably shittin' himself right now."

Grace hugged herself and shivered. "You were scary."

I shrugged. "That was kind of the point. It's the only language a dickhead like him understands."

"What do we do now?" Grace asked.

"Now we wait and let him stew. Attempting to kidnap you was a very risky play. My bet is that he didn't run it by his papa, and if that's the case, he's got a bigger problem."

Deb nodded.

Grace's eyes narrowed. "And if he did get his father's okay?"

"Get dressed and let me worry about that."

After I kissed her forehead, she did as I asked—this time without argument.

I waited until Grace had closed the bedroom door to turn on Deb. "I told you to not say anything."

Deb snorted. "I'm not going to let some idiot say shit about you."

I sucked in a calming breath. "While I love that you support me, I can take care of myself."

She patted me on the shoulder. "I know you can. But the asshole needed a dose of sister power."

She didn't get it. "This Victor guy is the kind of whack job you don't want to interact with at all."

She spun and walked away. "Right, be quiet and paint my nails or something else female-approved." My pain-in-the-ass sister stopped before she reached the hallway. "Remember, you owe me a look at that medal."

"Right," I said as she rounded the corner to leave.

"Bye, Grace," Deb yelled before she descended the stairs.

"Bye," was Grace's reply.

I dialed Lucas to let him know Victor had made contact.

After a full recounting of my less-than-cordial talk with the younger Russo, Lucas agreed that we needed to wait to hear from Tall Tony himself.

Then he switched topics. "The guy with the neck tattoos is definitely a Marku foot soldier," he told me. "But the driver is a question mark. All we figured out before we had to let them go was that he's Korean—not a talker."

I circled the table. "Prints?"

"I was hoping they'd match someone in the LAPD gang database, but they don't, and they're not in AFIS either, which leaves us with a good possibility and a bad one."

Based on Marku's history, I suspected where Lucas was going with this. "The bad one being North Korea? More missile technology?"

"It's possible, but I don't want to go there yet. The more likely option is that he's a local that Marku brought in for more muscle."

I leaned against the counter. "What makes you think that?"

"Russo is a dirtbag, but not that kind of dirtbag. He doesn't have any way to get his hands on something like missile electronics. These days, the FBI is mostly focused on the Russians. Russo would stay a million miles away from anything that would cause the FBI to shift their focus to him."

I nodded to myself. "Plus, it doesn't make sense that Elliot would be entrusted with something like that."

"Agreed. Jordy will keep digging for chatter. You just keep our girl safe."

"My girl," I corrected him.

A moment of silence followed. "You're going there, huh?"

"I'm already there. She's mine."

"Hmm… Has she bought into that? She's in a pretty vulnerable spot right now."

"She's mine."

"Given your past, isn't that an abrupt change?"

"I said, she's mine."

Lucas pulled in a long deep breath. "Listen to me, Marine." His voice was measured, but insistent. "People under severe stress often compensate by making risky choices that they later regret."

"I don't need—"

His voice entered beast mode. "What part of *listen* didn't you understand, Marine?"

I was yanked back into the corps, and my training kicked in. "Sorry, sir. Go ahead, sir." I'd woken the beast, and it was a damned good thing we weren't in the same room, or I'd have my head handed to me.

"Son…" He dialed back his voice. "Go slow is all I'm suggesting. Don't take any agreement on her part for granted. She needs to actively buy into whatever happens between you two with time to think things through. As the writer Richard Bach said *'If you love someone, set them free; if they come back they're yours, if they don't, they never were.'*"

"You want me to push her away?"

"No. William Shakespeare once wrote, *'Wisely and slowly. They stumble that run fast.'*"

"Yes, sir. Copy that." Once again he was speaking in riddles.

"Don't take this to mean I don't support you, Terry. I do. Have you explained yourself to her? I mean, been totally open?"

I didn't get exactly where this was going. "What do you mean?"

"Don't play dumb with me. I can tell manipulation when I see it. For a long time, your voice has said one thing, while your eyes have said another. You've been pushing her away on purpose."

"We talked." *How could my eyes have given me away?* I'd thought I'd been doing a good job, but Lucas had seen right through me, as he did with pretty much everybody. The man was a damned human lie detector.

"Good. Be honest with her. You've been pretty mean at times."

That hurt. "I will." I'd been trying for annoying. Had I drifted into mean?

"We've all got your back. Catch you later." He clicked off before I had a chance to get an update about Pete. It was hard to wake up each day and wonder if he'd be extracted or if I'd get the bad news that it hadn't been successful.

At least Grace was being spared this daily agony.

CHAPTER 20

GRACE

First thing after Terry's sister left, I raced into the bathroom and threw on clean clothes.

My phone rang less than a minute later.

"Did you forget something?" I answered. It was Deb.

"Tell me what happened," Deb said breathlessly. "I know I won't get anything but a watered-down version from my brother."

I put her on speaker while doing my makeup and gave her a quick rundown on the attacks.

"Elliot must have royally fucked up this time to have the mob after you. Good thing you have Terry by your side now."

I nodded along with that, which was a terrible idea while I was applying mascara. "That's for sure." I grabbed a cleaning wipe to deal with the mascara failure.

"That Victor what's-his-name—"

"Russo," I added.

"—is one sick puppy, but he's also a dumb fuck. My brother and all the guys he works with are lethal with a capital L. If the guy is stupid enough to take on Hawk, he's not long for this world."

I cringed, remembering Terry's sniper bullet comment. Then I reapplied my mascara with my head still this time. "I'm worried they'll bring more men."

"Did I tell you about the time my friend Tina and I thought we were grown-up enough to go to The Broken Spoke?"

This time, I lifted the brush before shaking my head. "The biker bar?"

"That's the one. We were young and wild without a clue, and plenty drunk. Anyway, a pair of guys got real handsy with Tina, and I got scared, so I texted Terry. Luckily, he was nearby. Actually, I think he'd followed us because he was worried about me."

"That sounds like him."

"Anyway, he rolls in, tells the bikers to leave her alone, and this biker the size of a dump truck and his buddy came at him."

I moved to the other eye. "Holy shit."

"After Terry put the big guy down, a bunch more jumped him. My brother laid six of them out cold on the floor, and the whole place went quiet. That's when he dragged us out."

I put my mascara away. "That's some story. I saw something similar when the goons attacked me. It was pow, pow, and the bad guys were down."

"Then he proceeded to yell at us for a half hour for being so reckless."

"Sounds about right," I agreed as I added my necklace. "I gotta go to work. Catch up later?"

"Sure thing. Be careful, and keep Terry close."

"I will." I grabbed my handbag, planning on keeping Terry very, very close.

"We gotta get together," she added. "I want to hear how you reeled in my brother. Should we do Mexican or Italian?"

I changed my mind twice as I walked out toward Terry. "Mexican." Terry had cooked me Italian and might be planning more of the same. Was it weird that I was already looking forward to another of his meals?

"You got it."

"I gotta go," I told her again. It wouldn't do to have Terry hear me planning a girls' night to talk about him. "Bye."

I stashed the phone in my big bag.

"Ready?" Terry asked when I turned the corner.

"As soon as I feed the cats."

"Make it quick."

Once he heard the can open, Clyde bounded in, followed by Bonnie.

I slapped the food in soup bowls and put them down.

"Ready now?" Terry asked.

I nodded and followed him down the stairs, wishing he'd been asking if I was ready for more action. It had to be the biker-bar story Deb had told me, but something had me hot to trot again for this man.

He locked the door behind us and opened the door of the Porsche for me.

"This is Duke's car, right?" I asked after he buckled in and started the engine. "What are you going to do about your car?"

"It was a company car. They'll bring me another one."

"Nice perk."

He shrugged and opened the garage door.

Out on the street, I should have been nervous after the shootout yesterday, but I looked over at Terry and felt at ease. I had the right bodyguard. A biker as big as a Mack truck and a half dozen others? Definitely the right man for the job.

"What?" he asked, catching my stare.

I laid my hand on the center console in invitation.

He took it.

"I can't express how happy…" I was going to say *I am that you're my bodyguard*, but I adjusted. "I am that you're mine."

He chuckled. "You mean that you're mine, Kitten?"

Feeling the warm strength of my man's touch, I agreed. "That too." A second later, I added, "It was a bit of a shock to have your sister walk in on us."

"Agreed. But at least her timing was good."

I cranked my head to look at him. "No way."

"If you'd gotten down to the kitchen earlier, I had plans."

A tingle went straight to my lady parts. "Plans?"

He smiled as he looked straight ahead. "Plans involving you and the table."

My cheeks flamed. On the table in front of the window wasn't exactly public sex, but it was riskier than anything I'd ever done. "In front of the window?"

"Sure. Or maybe the one on the terrace."

"Terrace?" I squeaked. The terrace table sounded so taboo that I got instantly wet. Last week's prim and professional Grace Brennan didn't do danger. What the hell had this man done to me that it excited me today?

"It's going on the list."

The hood of his car and now the terrace table. This was becoming one hell of a list.

∽

After the morning staff meeting, Peyton and Marci followed me to the ladies' room with Terry staying back.

Zane's eyes also followed us, though he seemed focused on Peyton.

Terry stopped at the end of the hall, as if I needed a guard to keep the bad guys from sneaking past Zane and down the hall to abduct me from a bathroom stall.

I shooed him with a wave of my hand, and miraculously, he complied. Nice, but *odd*.

Once inside, the girls were on me. "You lied," Peyton accused. "You're totally banging him."

"Don't deny it," Marci added. "It's so obvious. Terry the lion watches you like you're a gazelle he can't wait to take down."

"And," Peyton added, "when he said you couldn't go out to get coffee, you didn't argue one bit. That's not you."

I sighed and rolled my eyes. "I don't need to add to everybody's stress level by yelling at him."

"Last week, you wanted to cut his penis off," Marci noted. "And this morning it's obvious to anybody watching that you want to lick it instead."

"Did I say that?" I'd actually used the word *dick*, but Marci's vocabulary was more proper than mine.

I blushed.

"And if you don't," Marci said. "Maybe I do."

Over my dead body. I raised my hands. "Hold on... One." I looked at Peyton. "I did not lie. As of yesterday, I had not slept with him."

"I knew it," Marci shrieked. "You are sleeping with him."

"That's still one hell of a turnaround from the way you've always talked about him."

I nodded. "Surprised the hell out of me too, but having a guy save your life a few times can have that effect. I've always known he was a decent guy inside. It's been about the way he talks to me, ya know? But, it turns out he was intentionally trying to keep me away because of Pete." I kept myself in check. I didn't want to sound too slobbery over my man. But he was a lot better than decent in my book.

Peyton rolled her eyes. "The bro code can suck sometimes."

"Yeah," I agreed, "but what can you do? He's a man, and they can be stupid."

"All man, if you ask me." Marci got a dreamy look in her eyes. "He's got so much masculine energy—you know, strong, gruff, and rough around the edges, like he's ready to throw you over his shoulder and carry you off to—"

Peyton grabbed her shoulder. "Hold it right there. Grace has dibs."

Listening to Marci hit me in my core. I hadn't internalized it, but once I got past his cutting comments, I felt the same visceral attraction to Terry. Actually, more so because I'd spent years around him and now knew how strong and principled he was.

Marci nodded. "Yeah, Zane is a close second."

Peyton looked away.

I didn't say anything, but the way Zane had been watching Peyton, I didn't think Marci was in the running.

My bladder yelled at me to get into a stall. "We're a couple. Satisfied?" With these two, Terry and I would be common knowledge in a nanosecond, anyway.

We finished our business, and when I passed Terry on the way back to my office, I whispered, "They know."

He rolled his eyes, then shrugged as he followed me. Closing the office door behind us, he locked it. "Good." He advanced on me.

I put a hand up. "Oh, no you don't. We're not doing anything in the office." I escaped around the desk.

Terry patted the desktop. "I think this will do nicely."

His words sent damp desire straight between my legs. But as tempting as it sounded, my business had to come first. "Not while I'm working and my people are here. It wouldn't be professional."

"You only say that because I haven't explained what I plan to do to you yet."

That only made me hornier. I didn't dare ask him for details. "On a weekend when nobody is here," I proposed, because it sounded so naughty.

"It's going on the list." He backed away and adjusted himself in his pants. "I'll be outside, because if I stay another minute in here with you, I won't be able to control myself."

I settled into my chair after Terry left. I was definitely the gazelle to his lion, and Marci was right. The man was pure masculine energy. With all the havoc Elliot had brought into my life, it seemed the only thing going my way was that I had dibs on that energy.

∽

TERRY

THE MORNING AT SPACEMASTERS HAD BEEN QUIET, AND GRACE AND I WERE now eating lunch in her office.

Remembering what I'd brought in my backpack, I pulled out Clyde's collar. "Fresh battery." I set it on her desk.

She grabbed it and her face lit up. "Thank you. I've been worried about him getting out. I mean, finding him in the marina would be impossible. What if he jumped on a boat?" She put it in her monster purse.

I heard the zipper as she secured it in an inside pocket, while I pulled out my real surprises and slid the first across the desk to her.

She picked up the phone. "What's wrong with the one I have?"

"This is a backup. It has an extended-life battery and it's encrypted. If you need to reach me, I'll always answer it. No matter what you're doing if that one rings, you have to answer it."

"Have to?"

"Yes. Drop anything else you're doing." I slid across the second item still in its plastic bag. "And this."

"I have plenty of pens already"

"Not like this you don't. It's called a Pain Pen, like a mini stun gun."

She shook her head. "I don't know."

"This is important," I emphasized. "You're not going to overpower a man without some help and this is easy to conceal in your pocket."

"So now I have to wear a shirt with a pocket? You know I don't even own a pocket protector?"

I tapped the pen. "Very funny. Carry in your purse if you want, but carry it with you."

Still shaking her head, she picked up the Pain Pen. "I wouldn't know how to operate this."

"Simple. Slide the switch to on, hold the button down, and press the business end with the two little pins into your attacker."

"How long?"

"That depends on the asshole factor."

She laughed, then put down her sandwich and arched a brow. "Were you really a sniper? I didn't know that."

I shrugged, surprised by the change of topic. "I am. Once a sniper, always a sniper." It had once been a source of pride for me, but since leaving the Marines, it wasn't something I talked about. Civilians didn't understand the job and tended to equate the word *sniper* with cold-blooded killer. "My job was to save lives." I had provided overwatch to keep our people safe.

"Where did they send you?"

"I can't talk about my missions. It's all classified." That wasn't strictly true, but this was the kind of talk that could quickly go off the rails with someone as sensitive as Grace. Civilians didn't always understand that combat could come down to a simple question of kill or be killed.

"You had to shoot people?"

"My job was to make sure our soldiers and Marines didn't get shot. I was overwatch, watching their backs. If I saw a threat to one of our guys and I didn't act in time, someone else paid the price. Yes, I had to engage." It had been one of those split-second decisions that kept Lucas alive in Syria and earned me a spot at Hawk.

Grace swallowed and blinked back a tear. "That must have been hard."

I nodded. "You're not human if it's easy. But if one of the enemy was intent on hurting one of my team, it became necessary."

"Did you mean it this morning when you threatened to kill Victor?"

"All that matters is that *he* believes it. Making the other guy scared enough to not start a fight is always the best way to win."

She sniffled once, then got up and closed the distance between us, wrapping her arms around me. "Thank you. I'm so grateful that we have men like you to do the hard jobs so the rest of us can sleep at night."

I held her tight and rubbed her back for a moment. "I'll stop at nothing to keep you safe."

She nodded into my chest. "I know. That call this morning made me so mad."

Apparently, the Victor conversation this morning had affected her more than I realized. I squeezed her tight in response. "Lucas has reached out for a meeting with Victor's father, who's the real guy in charge, and we'll get Victor straightened out. There's no way the old man wants to go to war with Lucas and the rest of us."

She nodded into my chest. "You're all doing so much for me."

I pulled her chin up. "As my woman, you're now one of the family."

She giggled. "Hate to burst your bubble, Rambo, but Lucas already said I was."

"Well, it goes double now."

There was a quick knock on the door, and then it opened.

"Your one o'clock is here," Peyton said before she saw us. "Sorry. Didn't mean to interrupt."

Grace squirmed loose and straightened her blouse. "I'll be right out."

Peyton withdrew and closed the door.

I watched Grace's ass as she walked to her desk, visualizing what was under her skirt, especially the thong.

She picked up a file. "Can I do this one without you hovering in the demo room?" She'd objected twice already this morning to me following her everywhere.

"You remember how that worked out last time?"

"Mrs. Kretchmer is something like eighty years old. I don't think I'll be in danger from her."

"I'll let you go in alone on one condition."

"Name it."

"You let me put a surveillance camera in the corner. Otherwise, I'm joining you."

She shook her head, but a second later gave in. "Okay. That's better than having you lurking in the corner, scaring my clients."

Her lack of argument was refreshing.

"I'll get that installed as soon as possible, then," I told her. I'd call Jordy later to get him on that task.

UNTIL THE CAMERAS WERE IN PLACE, I CONTINUED TO SIT IN THE CORNER OF the demo room, trying hard to act less lurking. Grabbing the nearby clipboard, I rested it in my lap to hide my growing problem. Grace was once again making me hard. This time, it wasn't from watching her incredible ass in that skirt and imagining yanking it up and ripping her thong off.

No, this time, I had one of the VR headsets on and got to watch the process she went through with her customers. The smarts Grace had used to turn this idea of hers into a reality was my turn-on. The process amazed me as much as it did her customer, Mrs. Kretchmer.

"Can we move the shoe rack to the end?" the lady asked.

"Of course," Grace said. Magically, the view of the room shifted. "How's that?"

"I liked it better the other way. But let's try mahogany."

The view from the headset changed again.

Until now, I'd been so busy keeping my distance from Pete's sister that I hadn't paid any attention to her business. My digs at SpaceMasters had been a simple means to annoy her. Only now did I understand how hurtful my comments about her passion project had been.

Luckily, I'd gotten myself back under control by the time the session with Mrs. Kretchmer ended. Following Grace out of the room, I was surprised to find Zane walking our way.

Leaving her to finish with Mrs. Kretchmer, I pulled Zane aside. "What's up?"

He handed me a folder. "The boss wanted you to have the file on the Marku brothers. Fucking slimeballs, if you ask me. Pretty sick stuff."

"I didn't know there was more than one of them?"

He pointed. "It's in there. Aren's older brother, Zavin, is new in town and has quite the Interpol file."

After a quick glance inside, I decided this was not the kind of material I wanted Grace to see. "Gross."

"I'll hang out since the boss also thought it would be good to have two of us on her."

"Right." The last thing I wanted was Zane around my woman, but I wasn't going to argue with Lucas about having more support. "Anything more on the driver from yesterday?"

He shrugged. "You'd have to talk to the boss about that."

"Why don't you park yourself over there on the other side of Peyton?" That was far enough from Grace's door that he wouldn't be listening to us in her office.

CHAPTER 21

Grace

I looked over at my new boyfriend as we drove behind Winston toward Terry's apartment. The square cut of Terry's jaw, the stubble, the wide shoulders and brawny arms filling out the black leather flight jacket. Yes, Marci had been right. Terry was as masculine as they came.

Best of all, he was mine, my boyfriend. I loved giving him that label. If he could claim me, I could claim him. Fair was fair.

Terry felt the shooting had raised the danger level a few notches and decided he needed help guarding me, so Winston had joined us in the afternoon. However, Terry had vetoed the idea of Winston staying in the apartment with us. Instead, he was going to be street-level security tonight. The big ex-FBI agent had merely shrugged, as if staying up all night in a car on the street was a normal assignment.

"Are you hungry?" Terry asked as Winston pulled to the curb ahead of us outside the gym Terry lived above.

"Sure am." I gave my man a knowing smirk, but he wasn't looking my way and probably thought I was talking about food. All afternoon, I'd had something else entirely on my mind. Ever since he'd suggested it, I hadn't been able to get the idea of Terry stripping me naked on my desk out of my head.

Sure, the decision to not attempt it with all my employees just on the other side of the door was a logical one. But that didn't stop me from squirming in my chair all afternoon fantasizing about it.

I used to stay completely focused at work, but Terry had upended everything, and this afternoon, nothing I'd done to put him out of my mind had worked. I had never considered myself a risk taker, but the thought of attempting something so taboo as office sex gave me an unexpected thrill. Twice I almost called Terry in to try out the fantasy.

Inside the garage, Terry parked the Porsche and took my hand after he shut down the engine. "You'll be safe here tonight."

Meeting his eyes, I squeezed his hand. "I know." Why was it that every time we touched, I felt a zing of excitement? Maybe Terry was some kind of a male-pheromone factory. Then I could call my response logical.

He released me and hit the button to close the garage door. We were finally alone.

As I opened my door and got out, safety was the last thing on my mind. "You know what I'm hungry for?"

"Chinese?" he asked as he climbed out and shut his door.

Clueless. I moved to the front of the car and patted the hood. "I think we should start working on that list you've been making."

Hungry eyes devoured me as he strode my way. "I like the way you think, Kitten." A second later, he lifted me and set my butt down on the hood.

I hiked my skirt, spread my legs, and pulled him close. I quickly had second thoughts. "This isn't going to work."

He'd started to attack the buttons of my blouse. "Sure it is. You just lie back and let me do all the work."

"Stop." I pushed at his shoulders. "It's too hot. The engine's too hot." It had taken a few seconds to register the amount of heat coming through the hood of the car.

Laughing, he quickly lifted me off. "I guess we'll save this for later." He grabbed my thighs and lifted me until I was nose to nose with him. "Hot ass is right. I may have to strip you down and check for burns."

"So now you want to play doctor?" It wasn't as funny as it sounded. My backside was on fire. It hadn't helped that my thong didn't give me any insulation back there.

"It will be cooler in an hour or two."

"Are you sure you want to wait that long?" I certainly didn't seal my mouth over his to express myself.

He growled into my mouth as the kiss replicated the last one we'd had.

I came up for air first. "Are we going to stay here all day, or go upstairs and get busy?"

A smile formed on his handsome face as he looked to the side. "I have a better idea."

"The back seat of the Mustang?" I guessed.

"I thought we were going for adventurous here? Everybody has sex in the back seat of a car." He waddled with me clinging to him. "You've got me hard as steel. You know that, right?"

I nodded, having felt the hardness. "And I'm wet as a river for you, too."

He set me down by the motorcycle.

I hadn't had sex on a bike before. Actually, there was a pretty much infinite list of places I hadn't had sex before, including the back seat of a car. "This is one big bike," I said as I hiked up my skirt to pull the thong off. The motor was monstrous.

He undid his belt. "This is a Triumph Rocket 3." He yanked down his zipper. "The engine is twice the size of a Harley and leaves those pussies in the dust." It was just like Terry to have the biggest, baddest ride around. "I remember this one time—"

"Shut up and fuck me already on your rocket." This was too much talking and not enough action for my flaming libido.

"Bossy much?" he asked as he swung his leg over and settled onto the seat.

I started to shuck off my heels.

"Keep 'em on, baby," he commanded. He struggled to shimmy his pants down enough to free his monster cock.

Peyton had been right that I wanted to lick and suck him until he couldn't take it any longer. It would be no different than our other competitions. Even if I were on my knees, I would still be in charge. He would be at my mercy for a change.

He stroked himself and then pulled out a condom. Sucking him off would have to wait. I put one shoe back on.

He rolled the latex down. "Hop on, Kitten, and ride the rocket, if you dare."

I hiked my skirt up, but couldn't figure out how to climb over. So he lifted me like I weighed nothing.

Grabbing his cock to position myself, I giggled. "Rocket. That's his new name."

"I can live with that."

As he settled me down on his enormous cock, a gasp stopped my giggles. He stretched me once again, in that most pleasurable way. Then he started working me up and down. I ground into him with each thrust. This was exactly what I'd craved and denied myself this afternoon.

He attacked my buttons again, and I took over lifting up and driving down as he undid my bra and freed my breasts from their confinement. "You have the greatest breasts, baby." He leaned forward and took one sensitive nipple into his mouth.

Spearing a hand in his hair, I guided him to the other breast between moans of pleasure. "Don't stop." I clawed at his shoulders as I rode him and climbed the mountain toward my climax.

He lavished attention on my breasts before moving up my neck to my ear. "You feel so fucking good, baby," he said between pants. "It's like you were made for me."

I yanked his hair and gave him a quick kiss. "You too, Rambo."

He picked up speed to a point where I worried I couldn't take it anymore. "Come for me, baby."

"I'm gonna—"

He forced a finger between us and rubbed my clit.

That launched me, trembling over the precipice. "Oh my God."

Grabbing my hips, he powered into me two more times and then held deep. With my inner muscles still rippling around him, I felt the throb of his cock as he spilled his release inside me.

A minute later, limply leaning into him, I took a deep breath. "I think we can scratch the motorcycle off the list."

He laughed. "Not so fast. Next time, we do it while we're moving."

I joined his laugh. "You're certifiable."

"And you love it."

I sat back, with Rocket still inside me, and ran my nails down Terry's chest. "Maybe a little."

AFTER DINNER, WE WERE ON THE SECTIONAL TRYING TO CHOOSE A MOVIE WHEN my phone announced a text.

"Leave it," Terry urged.

"It's probably work. I should get it." I pulled away from him, stood, and found the phone in my purse.

He tugged my hand to pull me back to him. "I find your dedication to your company sexy."

I shot him a smile. "Thank you." That was probably the nicest thing anybody had said to me in a long time. "They're my family."

Opening up the phone, the message contained an image.

I expanded it. It was a picture of my neighbor, Millie. She looked scared. This had come from an unknown number.

Two more messages arrived. I read them, and my vision started to blur. Fear froze me. My hand went limp, and the phone fell to the floor.

∼

Terry

I rushed over to Grace when she dropped the phone. "What is it?" I asked frantically as I held her up in case a fainting spell was next.

"Millie," she sobbed as she pointed at the ground. "They have Mille."

After settling Grace back on the sectional, I picked up her phone. My blood boiled with anger.

After two pictures of an older woman I assumed was Millie came the threatening texts.

UNKNOWN: How do you feel about your neighbor?
UNKNOWN: Give me your cousin or she pays the price.

"Who is she?" I demanded.
Grace looked at me blankly. "My neighbor, Mrs. Finn."
I pulled out my own phone, put it on speaker, and dialed Lucas.
"Hawk," he answered after one ring.
"Victor just sent a text to Grace threatening her neighbor lady, Mrs. Finn."
"Shit," I heard Zane say in the background. "Is that the one who has her door open all the time?"
"I've warned her," Grace said with a nod. "But she won't listen. Her name is Millie Finn."
"I'll send Constance right now," Lucas said.
I liked the idea. The former Secret Service agent was well-versed in personal protection.
"I'll go," Zane said firmly.
Lucas didn't overrule him. "What exactly did he write, and how do we know it was Victor?"
I read him the messages Grace had gotten and told him about the photos. "It's an unknown number, which isn't definitive either way, but who else would it be?"
"Probably right," Lucas agreed.
Grace grabbed her phone back, dialed, and juggled it on her shoulder

while slipping into her shoes. "She's not answering her phone," she yelled after a moment, exasperated. "We have to go help her."

"Zane is already on the way," Lucas said.

I grabbed Grace's arm. She wasn't thinking clearly. "We stay here. We can't walk into a trap."

"But—"

"No buts. We stay."

"I agree," Lucas agreed. "Stay put for now. Zane will report as soon as he's on location."

Grace sighed and stomped into the kitchen, dialing the phone again.

Hanging up with Lucas, I followed her.

She was at the counter. "Millie, you gotta call me back right away," she said. "No joke. This is an emergency." After hanging up, she hunched over and cried.

I turned her around and pulled her close. "Zane will keep her safe."

"What if that asshole already has her? She's not answering." She sniffled into my chest.

"If he already had her, he would have said so. Or he would have made her call you, like a hostage-video thing." It wasn't great, but I didn't have a better answer for her. "Zane will be there in no time. And any two-bit hoods Victor would send for her would be no match for a SEAL like Zane. You know that, right?"

She nodded. "Yeah, but I hate that my troubles are putting people, my friends, in danger."

"It's nothing you're doing. You can't blame yourself. This is all on Elliot."

Her phone chimed, and when she checked it, she scrambled away to respond to a text. I swore that one way or another, this would be the last time Elliot victimized Grace.

When she returned, her hand trembled. "My life sucks. I need some wine."

After a few minutes, I got her back to the sectional, where she could lie down comfortably, and I fetched some Advil for her.

She took the tablets without complaint this time and washed them down with her wine.

The agonized look on her face tore me up. "Stay there and rest. That's all we can do until we hear from Zane.

"But what if—"

"Stop," I said, cutting her off. "Negative thoughts don't help anyone. It's going to be a shock to hear that gangsters are threatening her—"

"Because of me," she complained, draining the rest of her glass.

"Because of Elliot. Now, the best thing is for us to be calm and ready to support her after that news. You do want to help her, don't you?"

"Of course."

I rubbed Grace's shoulder. "Then rest up and don't add to her anxiety with your own."

She settled back on the sectional, avoiding putting pressure on her wound. She lifted her arm toward me. "Will you join me? I need to be held."

"Sure, Kitten. But no funny business. I need to be ready for Zane's call."

"I promise."

I situated myself next to her as best I could with an arm over her waist, careful to keep fabric between us and keep my cock under control.

CHAPTER 22

Terry

A LITTLE WHILE LATER, STILL WAITING TO HEAR FROM LUCAS OR ZANE, I extricated myself from Grace on the sectional and opened the folder Zane had given me. I powered up my computer and busied myself with a deep dive on the Marku brothers. Looking over after a few minutes, I caught Grace uncorking another bottle of wine.

She poured a glass and hummed a song to herself. It was cute. However, this being a weekday night, I didn't like how much wine she was consuming. But I likely needed to cut her some slack. At any rate, before I could decide what to do, my phone rang with Lucas's name on the screen. "Goodwin," I answered.

Grace returned from the kitchen, concern written across her pale face. "Millie?"

"Zane is in position, and Grace's neighbor is fine," Lucas said.

I put it on speaker so Grace could hear the good news. "Good to hear she's okay. What's the plan? Will Zane stay with her?"

The color returned to Grace's face as she heaved a breath.

"She's bitching about having a man in her space, but for now, yes. Another thing—Tall Tony has been out of town, and he finally called tonight to yell at me for holding his niece. Man, is she a piece of work. He should pay us for taking her off his hands."

"She's a bitch," Grace noted, slurring slightly. "Let me teach her a lesson."

I ignored Grace. "Boss, did you suggest that?"

"I was damn tempted, but no. We have a meeting scheduled tomorrow to hand her over. I intend to get him to reel in Victor, and I'll make it clear that he is to lay off Grace and everyone associated with her. But he needs a face-saving way to do that."

Grace beamed and rubbed her hands together, wobbling a bit.

"I'd like you to come with me for the meeting," Lucas added.

"Sure. We'll need Winston to take over Grace's protection for a while. Just let me know when and where."

"I will. The timing isn't set yet. I got the impression he's flying back from somewhere. Constance will relieve you in the morning." He didn't need to say any more to remind me that he called the shots. It had been reckless of me to suggest Winston just to keep Zane away from her.

As soon as I ended the call, Grace asked, "Will Zane stay with Millie beyond tonight?"

"We'll see that she's safe," I assured her. "You heard Lucas. Tomorrow, they're getting the message loud and clear. And when Lucas goes into scary mode, people listen."

"But you warned that Victor prick, and the bastard still sent his bitch cousin Maria to threaten me and my people." She moved toward me, and I realized she was notably drunk.

"He put that into motion before we met with him." I took her in my arms when she reached me. "You should get some sleep." I kissed the top of her head and let her go.

"Come on." She took my hand and smiled coyly with a glance at my crotch. "I could make it worth your while."

"You've had quite a bit to drink." With Lucas's reminder that she was in a vulnerable place, on top of Constance's warning, I shouldn't. I would have to wait for sober Grace to reappear. She really had been through a lot. The drinking was evidence enough of that.

When I didn't move, she lurched to the fridge and pulled out the wine again.

"You really should go to bed," I repeated.

"Alone?"

"I have work to do." I wanted to be in bed with her, but researching the Marku brothers had to be done, and it didn't feel right to be with her this drunk. Warnings from two people I respected had finally gotten through to me.

This being noble shit sucks swamp water.

Turning away, I went back to my research.

~

G%%RACE%%

A%%FTER REFILLING MY WINEGLASS%%, I %%OPENED MY PHONE AGAIN%%. R%%EREADING THE%% message made me want to puke.

> MRS. MONTEFINO: I'm coming to L.A. I want to see my daughter.
> ME: Don't bother.

I set down the phone and gulped the liquid memory eraser as if it could also negate the hurt from years ago. I should have written a stronger warning to stay away.

Letting my mother back into my life after the way she'd left was not going to happen—no way.

I leaned on the granite island. I wasn't a heavy drinker, but my life had turned to complete shit, and I needed this glass and more to dull the sensation of helplessness.

"Hey there, Kitten," Terry surprised me from behind.

I turned with my empty wineglass.

"Who's Mrs. Wilcox?"

Fuck. I'd left the phone open to her message on the granite.

"Nobody," I tried.

"Who's her daughter?"

He'd vowed to always be honest with me, and now I felt trapped by his promise. "I am."

His mouth dropped open. He knew she'd left us when we were young, but not the complete story. "Sorry. Do you want to talk about it?"

"No." That was one thing I was certain of.

"I'm here when you're ready."

I had nothing to say to that. He ended the awkward silence. "I'm going out to check on Winston."

"Okay."

Once he disappeared, my mind spiraled. *What if the Russo guys didn't listen to Lucas? What if they kept coming? Who else would get hurt?*

I desperately wanted to snuggle in bed with Terry, but he'd made it clear he wasn't in the mood. *Drunk, my ass. So what if I need to take the edge off after all that's happened?* Finishing my wine, I walked unsteadily back to the sectional.

Opening my phone again, I called the number Elliot had used to call me this morning. It went to voicemail. "Elliot, things are getting bad," I whispered. "You have to call me." I stared at the phone. There wasn't anything else to say, so I hung up.

"Grace?" Terry called. He wanted to ignore me when I needed him, so I could ignore him, couldn't I?

I hadn't meant to drink this much this evening, but the text from my mother had triggered me. And now, I'd been worn down by my troubles spilling over to threaten Millie. Returning to the kitchen, I poured the rest of the bottle into my glass. I should have asked about tequila to begin with. It would have gotten the job done quicker.

Footsteps sounded behind me. "You should get some sleep," Terry's voice came from the doorway. *Talk about repetition.*

I chugged the wine, set down my glass, and opened the fridge. "As soon as I get a refill."

A second later, the glass was lifted from the island. "You've had enough for tonight."

Yup, Terry was back in jailer mode. He could be so exasperating.

"I need another," I complained. I really planned on at least two more.

"Won't a hangover tomorrow make a poor impression with your customers? Go to bed. Now."

"Yes, sir." I saluted and closed the door before stomping off—and I could stomp with the best of them. It wasn't fair for him to use logic against me.

Slamming the guest bedroom door closed, I searched through the things that Constance had helped me unpack. Plenty of shoes, skirts, blouses, bras, and those damned thongs, but nothing to sleep in.

"That's what you get when you have a badass SEAL pack for you," Constance had said.

So, Zane wanted me to sleep naked. Well, screw that. Everyone was trying to force me to do things I didn't want to do. I yanked open the door and yelled down the hall, "Do you have anything I can sleep in?"

"You can sleep in the nude. It's healthier."

"Arg." I slammed the door shut. That's when I spotted the wine bottle I'd brought in earlier.

A minute and two quick swallows from the wine bottle later, a quick knock sounded at the door. "I have a T-shirt, if that will help."

Finally, some compassion from my jailer. I hid the bottle and opened the door. "Thank you."

His eyes held mine for longer than it took to hand me the shirt.

I grabbed the doorjamb to steady myself. "Can you help me put it on?" I tried for seductive.

His lip twitched.

Come on, big guy, give in for once and let me win. I so wanted to cuddle after the day I'd had. The wine had helped, but what I really needed was to be in his strong arms, shielded from the shitstorm around me.

"No. You're drunk, and I have work to do. Sleep well, Kitten," he said before walking away.

"I will," I snapped. Slamming the door didn't make me feel any better. It struck me that I'd gone into the guest bedroom because that's where Constance had helped me hang up all my things.

Terry hadn't said he'd join me. And he hadn't told me to sleep in his bed, asked me, or whatever. Did that mean he didn't want me to—didn't want me? I sniffled, hoping that wasn't it.

I'd never figure him out. *Screw it.* As much as I wanted him here, I wasn't the begging kind.

When the room swam, I decided he was right about one thing—I needed to get in bed while I could still walk.

After brushing my teeth, I tried on the T-shirt. It swamped me, but loose was better than too tight. Clicking off the light, I found the bed in the darkness.

The flashbacks started almost immediately—the two guys slamming me against the car about to abduct me after the party, the Taser and the guy dragging me to the SUV when I met Elliot, the bitch Maria threatening to kill one of my people, the assholes shooting at us, and the message tonight threatening to hurt Millie.

Why had my life become such a shitshow? I couldn't take it and stumbled to the light switch. It blinded me at first, but blinking, I focused on the door handle.

I'd felt safe in his arms earlier, and for a second, I considered finding Terry. But I wasn't drunk enough to ignore reality—it would make me feel ten times worse to be rejected again. I could hear him in my head, *"Don't get hysterical, Grace. Go to bed. You're drunk, and I have work to do."* That would sting.

So screw the hangover, I picked up the wine bottle again. I needed more, a lot more, to get some shut-eye tonight.

TERRY

. . .

At one in the morning, I finally felt I'd gotten everything out of the files that I could, so I turned off the living room lights.

Grace had hit the sack long ago. Was I pervert enough to stop outside the guest room and listen? You bet. But I wasn't perverted enough to open the door and join her when she was, as Lucas had put it, vulnerable. She needed her sleep. Knowing she was safe would have to be enough for me.

I will be strong and leave her alone. I repeated the words in my head several times.

Unfortunately, the devil in me thought of her behind that door in just my T-shirt. That image made me go hard. When I touched my lips, I could feel her and taste her again. Just thinking of her had my brain misfiring.

I am totally fucked. I could tell I was going to have to jerk off if I wanted to get to sleep. *Giving in isn't being weak,* I told myself. *No, it's being expedient.* I needed sleep to face Tony Russo tomorrow and to protect her. It was going to be impossible with my mind constantly picturing our time together earlier.

I found a washcloth before getting into bed, then grabbed my cock and started stroking. I pictured her pussy and stroked harder. Memories of the sounds she made filled my ears. The taste of her felt real. The feel of her soft tits in my hands came back to me.

I increased the pace. My balls pulled up. I tensed at the surprising ache at the base of my spine. Holy, holy, holy shit. With one more rough pull, I blew in record time, almost hitting my chin.

Panting rapidly, I wiped up. My God, I hadn't come that hard in a long, long time, and never that quickly. Memories of Grace packed one hell of a punch. Score one for expediency.

I dropped the washcloth on the floor, too spent to walk it to the hamper, and waited for sleep to come as my breathing slowed.

It didn't come quickly.

∽

The scream jolted me awake.

Grace is in danger.

My training kicked in, and with a finger to the biometric scanner, my gun safe unlocked. In the dark I grabbed my SIG, racked one into the chamber, and moved stealthily to the door.

Another scream followed.

Pulling my night-vision goggles off their hook, I slowly opened the door, ducking low in case they were in the hallway. It was clear.

Gun up, I advanced quickly and silently to Grace's door. How many were there? Victor wasn't stupid enough to send one man alone.

Tortured moans came from inside the room. "No. No."

Taking a deep breath, I flung the door open and buttonhooked in.

There were no attackers.

Grace thrashed under the covers. "No. No."

Making my weapon safe, I left it and my NVG headset on the dresser. I leaned over and gently jostled Grace's shoulder. "Wake up. You're having a—"

Her arm flung out and hit me in the face before I could react. "Get off me."

"It's a nightmare," I said, grabbing the arm she'd flailed. "You're having a nightmare." I grasped her other shoulder. "You're safe, Kitten. I'm here."

"Terry?" One second, she was a banshee in the grips of a nightmare. The next, she clung to me.

Man, she packed a punch. My lip stung from the hit. "Yes, Grace. It's me. You're safe. Nobody's going to get you."

"They were going to shoot…" She sobbed.

"Nobody's shooting anyone." I pulled her up and rubbed her back. "It's okay. You're okay. It was just a nightmare."

The more I talked, the tighter she clung to me. Slowly, her sobs faded.

"I'll let you get back to sleep now," I said, trying to untangle myself from her. I slept naked, and her hands on my skin gave my cock all the wrong ideas.

"Don't go." She tightened her grip.

"I have to." Remembering Lucas's caution, I'd pledged to be the gentleman.

"No, you don't. I won't be able to sleep if you leave."

"I've got to." She was making this fucking difficult.

"I won't be safe alone. I just know it. Don't leave me."

That was a problem, because I couldn't guarantee she'd be safe from me if I stayed.

"Please. I need you to hold me."

With a deep breath, I gave in. "I'll be right back. Let me get something to wear."

"Okay." She let me loose from her octopus-like grasp.

I stood, suddenly conscious of my hard-on, and aware that I didn't own anything strong enough to contain my straining dick, so going to my room and staying there would be the safe thing to do.

"But if you don't come back, I'm coming to your room," she added, as if reading my thoughts.

That eliminated my plan B. "I'll be right back."

After forcing my hard-on into boxer briefs, I knew self-control was going to be a big problem. But I kept my word and returned to her room.

I found her chugging from a bottle of wine. "You're going to regret that."

She set it on the nightstand. "I need it to help me get back to sleep."

After moving the bottle out of her reach, I climbed under the covers to join her. So much for keeping my distance.

She lay on her side and backed up against me, all soft skin and irresistible warmth.

How the hell was I supposed to get to sleep like this? It didn't matter. This was only about allowing her to get some sleep.

"Will you hold me?" A second later, she added, "Please."

When she put it that way, she gave me no alternative. I turned in her direction, which unfortunately put her sweet ass against my hard dick. Tentatively, I laid my arm over her waist. Discomfort gave way to acceptance and then comfort. She felt so right under my arm. Like this was the way we were meant to be.

"Thank you." She shifted against me.

I willed my cock to not notice. It didn't work.

Then I had a terrible thought. I'd told Lucas I'd go slow, and if he found out about this, he might take the assignment away from me and give it to Zane. That would be unfuckingacceptable.

She turned her head. "Do you think—"

I didn't let her finish. "Thinking can wait until tomorrow. Get some sleep. I'm here. You're safe, and you need your sleep for work tomorrow." Being successful with her company had always been her biggest motivator.

"You're right." She shifted against me.

I scooted back a tad. It wasn't enough, as the tip of my cock still rested against her. The movement was not helping. Maybe if I stayed absolutely still, just maybe, I could get my cock to deflate.

Baseball—few things were as boring as baseball. I tried reciting the starting lineup of the Dodgers over and over in my head.

Before long, Grace's breathing fell into the slow rhythm of sleep.

So close and yet so far...This was going to be a long night.

CHAPTER 23

Grace

THE NEXT MORNING, I WOKE SLOWLY, PULLING THE PILLOW TO MY FACE. I rolled, ready to wish a good morning to the man who'd rescued me from my nightmare last night, but he was gone. But the sheets on his side of the bed were still warm. So it hadn't been long.

He'd stayed with me like he promised. Realizing that made me smile through the headache.

Bringing his pillow to my nose, I got the slightest hint of the woodsy scent that was Terry.

I regretted all that wine as I rolled out of bed. This was going to be a hell of a day—one foot in front of the other, and a million Advil in between. After taking care of business in the bathroom, I found the pills in my purse and poured a glass of water. Normally, a shower first thing invigorated me. Today, all I wanted was to curl up under the covers and hope for sleep to rescue me.

The loud voice from behind startled me. "You need to drink these."

Now my ears hurt as well. But as soon as I turned, the view of Terry made it all better. I accepted one of the mugs he held out. It was water. "Two?"

With his free hand he fished into his pocket and produced tablets. "Yes. Aspirin, water, and coffee."

"I already took Advil, thanks."

He pocketed the pills and flipped on the light I'd intentionally left off. Squinting, I tried to keep from having a full-on brain explosion.

"Bad?" he asked softly as he flipped the switch back off.

I nodded. "You warned me." I waited for the cutting attack, the reminder of how stupid I'd been to ignore his advice. It didn't come.

Instead, he leaned into the shower and turned on the water. "I find a shower helps, but first you need to finish these—caffeine and extra hydration to begin with."

I nodded and addressed the elephant in the room. "Did I do something wrong?"

His brows scrunched together. "No. Why?"

"You didn't want to…" I wasn't sure how to ask the question delicately.

A smile grew on his face. "Sleep with you?"

I nodded, having expected a cruder way of putting it. "Do I—"

His chuckle stopped me. "Kitten, you were drunk, and it wouldn't have been right. If you're asking if I'm still attracted to you…"

I hung on his next words like a lifeline.

"The answer is absofuckinglutely. If you had the time, which you don't, and didn't have a hangover, which you do, I'd throw you over my shoulder, lay you out on the hood of my car right now, and fuck you senseless. That would scratch one item off our list."

With that, I had to laugh, even though it hurt. His words, crude as they were, sent sparks of anticipation up my spine.

"Does that answer your question?" he asked.

"Rain check?"

"You need to shower. I will not have you blaming me for being late to work."

"I need to find my…uh, shower things first."

In seconds, he held out a plastic shopping bag. "Zane packed these for you." He leaned against the bathroom counter when I took it.

"A little privacy, please," I said out of habit. It was totally inappropriate now that I'd slept with him, and I'd just imagined him fucking my brains out down in the garage.

He arched a brow. "Aren't we past that, Kitten?"

"Yeah, sorry." My cheeks flushed, and the memory of his face between my legs yesterday hit me full force. It canceled out the headache for a moment.

"I'm staying."

Did he mean to watch me shower? Maybe join me in the shower? In spite of the throbbing headache, the prospect turned me on. Since I was hungover, but no longer drunk, was he now interested in me? If the hood of the car was out, would the wall of the shower be quick enough?

He took in a labored breath, as his eyes traveled the length of me and back up again, lingering on my chest for a moment.

A tingle of excitement shoved the headache aside. Looking down, my body's vote was obvious. My nipples had gone into full headlights-on mode, poking through the T-shirt.

"Go ahead."

With what? Take off the shirt? Was sex a part of his hangover remedy? Sex released endorphins and oxytocin. They relieved pain, right? Would sex mute this headache, or would the headache make sex impossible?

"I'm not leaving until you finish both mugs," he clarified.

Shit. Sex was not a part of his cure. I drank the water first and struggled to gulp down most of the coffee as ordered.

He forced the coffee mug back at me. "All of it." A night of sleeping together, but not *sleeping together*, hadn't smoothed out his bossy streak. Maybe that was the effect of having blue balls if his morning wood was any indication.

"Yes, sir."

After getting the last of it down, I organized my shower kit from the bag.

"Shirt off and turn around."

"Huh?" Now he had me totally confused.

"I don't want you getting the cut wet."

He pulled a roll of tape from his pocket and a piece of plastic.

Obviously, I was the only one with sex on the brain this morning. "On one condition," I demanded.

"Name it."

"You don't boss me around at all today—no arguments and no orders."

"Sure thing, Kitten."

There again was that nickname I associated with nice Terry. "Thank you." I turned and pulled the shirt over my head.

He knelt behind me. "It looks pretty good here."

Did he mean the cut, my ass, or just naked me?

A minute later, he rose after fixing a small piece of plastic to my butt cheek. "Join me in the kitchen when you're done." He disappeared without giving me a chance to tease him and ask if he wanted to join me in the shower.

As the water ran through my hair and down my skin, I was glad he'd insisted on this. It was definitely better than curling up in a ball in bed.

Slowly, I felt almost human again—a human with a monster headache of her own making, but better than earlier.

As I soaped up, I realized how quickly things had shifted for us. Last week, sharing a bed with Terry would have been out of the question. The mere mention of it probably would have made me sick.

But this morning, it felt like...*normal* was probably the best word. A whirlwind of danger had propelled me, had propelled us, into a new dimension, one in which the tyrant was such a gentleman that he refused my bed when I was tipsy—okay, drunk, but it was still so unlike the way I'd seen him before.

A shiver ran through me as that haunting nightmare from last night popped its ugly head up for a second. Recalling Terry spooning with me erased it quickly.

Last night and this morning, he'd obviously been aroused, and probably all night for that matter. Yet he hadn't pushed for anything. How many guys would do that? Holding me to chase the nightmares away had been the ultimate caring gesture. Go figure. Terry was a compassionate, caring jailer.

I smiled, remembering the feel of his hard length against my ass, and hard was the right word. What woman wouldn't feel empowered knowing that she caused that reaction in a man as virile as ex-SWAT, ex-Marine, ex-sniper, Terry Goodwin?

∽

TERRY

GRACE STILL HADN'T APPEARED AFTER HER SHOWER AS I CHOPPED THE BACON I'd fried into little bits. For a second, I considered checking on her, but I decided she might think that was creepy.

I had two pans going at once, waiting for the egg mixture to set up. When they finally cooked through, I sprinkled the bacon in, then grated the cheese over that, before folding the omelets closed and removing them from the heat.

"Breakfast is ready," I called.

No answer came, but I could hear a hair dryer.

Before I could go to Grace, my phone ding-donged. One of my exterior motion detectors had triggered.

Lunging for the phone, I found the perpetrator just as he rang the doorbell. "Zane, what are you doing here?" I asked through the intercom.

"Came to relieve you. The bossman says you're due to join him in rousting that Russo guy, Tony."

"Yeah, Tall Tony Russo."

"That's the one. Can you buzz the door for me?"

"I'll be right down." I'd disconnected the remote unlock mechanism first thing after reading about a case where the system had been hacked and bad guys had unlocked a remote door from outside. The fact that it had been a home invasion with a fatality drove the point home.

Zane rang the doorbell again as I descended the stairs.

"Keep your pants on," I yelled several steps from the bottom. I took a calming breath before opening the door.

He held three Starbucks cups. "Morning. You look like you didn't sleep well." He offered me one of the cups.

"Thanks. You look like shit too." *He didn't.* I ushered him in and relocked the door. "Why are you here instead of Constance?"

"Lucas."

I nodded and followed him up. Upstairs, Grace had finally emerged and was in the kitchen—in nothing but a fucking bathrobe. At least it wasn't my damned T-shirt.

"How are you doing, Grace?" Zane asked. "I mean, with all this excitement?"

She glanced at me and then back to Zane. "Okay, considering."

"Don't hit on my woman," I warned.

Zane raised a brow. "Your woman? I thought—"

"You thought wrong."

When I glanced over, Grace didn't seem pleased by my warning to Zane, or maybe it was the way I'd referred to her as mine.

He nodded with a chuckle. "Copy that, brother."

I moved closer to her. "Maybe you should get dressed," I whispered.

"I brought you this." Zane held out one of the cups.

Instead of acknowledging my suggestion, Grace took the coffee cup with a smile. "Why, thanks."

Zane walked to the stove. "Breakfast smells good."

Grace followed him into the kitchen. "It sure does," she said, checking her watch. "I don't have much time before I'm due at the office."

"Then you should dig in," Zane said as he lifted the remaining coffee cup to his lips. He turned. "Oh, and Lucas said to tell you to hustle to the same meetup point as last time."

"Why didn't he call?"

"He said he sent you a text."

I checked my phone and sure enough, I'd missed the message. He'd wanted me to hurry as soon as Zane relieved me. "Fuck. You be safe," I said pointing at Grace on the way to the door. *No arguments and no orders.* "And lock up when you leave."

"Do I need a key for that?" Zane asked.

I changed direction to the drawer where I kept spare keys and threw one to him.

"Do I need a code to set the alarm?" he asked.

"Don't bother with that. Locking it will be fine until I get back."

"I'll keep her safe," he assured me.

"Terry," Grace called.

I whirled.

"Be careful," she said sweetly.

I nodded. "Always." It killed me to leave her, but I had no choice.

She smiled. "See you at the office."

I would remember that smile and the melody of those words until I saw her again.

∽

Grace

The sight of my car in Terry's garage surprised me as Zane and I descended the stairs a little later that morning. "How did that get here?"

"Constance brought it over this morning. We didn't want it just hanging out on the street downtown."

I pulled my keys out of my handbag.

"Oh, no you don't," Zane cautioned. "I'm driving you. Those are the rules."

"You guys and your rules," I complained, but I put my keys away.

"It's for your safety."

I suppressed an eye roll. That was the same thing that Terry told me every time I complained.

Zane was quiet during the drive until we were almost there. "What do you know about Peyton?" he asked.

Remembering how he'd watched her at the office, the question didn't surprise me. "Peyton, huh?"

"Never mind."

I looked over to catch his jaw working. "She's single, if that's your question."

He didn't answer, just stared straight ahead as he drove.

"She moved here from North Carolina," I added. "She's smart as a whip, but doesn't talk much." Peyton had never offered very much about her background.

Zane remained silent, pulling into the parking lot for our building without another word.

Serena had mentioned that her ex-SEAL, Duke, didn't talk much either. Maybe it was an entrance requirement—good strength, good shooter, good fighter, good runner, good swimmer, but bad talker.

I turned before opening the door. "Would you like me to—"

"No. Stay in the car."

I had meant to offer to talk to Peyton for him, but that was a very curt *no*.

He walked around and opened my door for me. "Now."

I'd misjudged. Apparently, part of the guard-dog ritual was to open my car door and escort me inside. I decided against finishing my Peyton question. Zane was a big boy. He could talk to Peyton on his own, if he wanted to.

CHAPTER 24

Terry

As I drove to meet Lucas, with Grace still on my mind, my phone rang. Lucas's mother's name appeared on the screen.

Shit. I should have called her, but I had forgotten. I pressed accept. "Hi."

"Can you speak?" she asked softly.

"I'm driving and alone, so yes. How can I help you?"

Her voice remained soft. "I need to meet with you this morning."

"Right now, I'm on my way to a meeting with Lucas. I can come over when I finish up, if you like." I'd been to the Hawk house many times.

"No," she said quickly. "Text me, but don't call, and we'll arrange to meet."

Something was up if she wanted to stay away from the house. "I'll be in touch as soon as I can."

She'd already warned me not to talk to anybody about this, and the whole cloak-and-dagger aspect worried me. The remaining miles to the Russo restaurant went by slowly as I wondered what could be up. It couldn't be anything good.

Slowing the Porsche after I rounded the final corner, I found Lucas right where we'd met before.

I passed a guy leaning against a building and smoking, parked behind

Lucas's Porsche, and joined him. "Where are the others?" Last time, we'd gone in as a group.

"Duke and Winston have our two guests three blocks away," he explained. "It's just the two of us going in this time. Tony called the meet, so by his code, we're protected. Last time, we were arriving uninvited, and you never know how they might have felt if we'd interrupted something like him banging his mistress. There's a difference."

"Handguns?" I asked, not knowing these rules.

"As the guest, I can't carry, but as my protection, you can. Just be aware that he will have two guys or more in the room who are fast on the draw, and their sole purpose is to take you down if you even twitch, so keep it holstered unless I yell the code word."

"Which is?"

"Gun, of course." He laughed and slapped me on the back. "Don't worry. Don't flinch, and you'll do fine. One more thing—today I'm introducing you as my brother, so don't object."

I nodded. After Syria, I felt like a part of the Hawk family anyway. They had taken me in as one of their own. But his comment reminded me again that I owed his mother a discreet meeting later.

Lucas looked up and down the block, then started off, pulling a paper and pen from the pocket of his leather jacket. I followed as he wrote a note and then pocketed it.

When we rounded the corner to the restaurant, the same two guards were outside. Once more, they opened the door for us without hesitation. But I reminded myself that this time we'd been invited, while last time they had expected us courtesy of a leak in the LAPD.

I followed Lucas inside, where it was darker than I remembered, and the smells were more pungent, but the same two interior guards greeted us as well.

"Mr. Hawk," the taller one said.

"Tony is expecting me," Lucas announced, lifting his arms to be patted down.

The tall man was thorough. "You too." He pointed at me.

"No." Lucas spun on the guy with a finger inches from his face—a finger I knew could kill the man, but did he know?

He backed away and nodded. "This way."

We followed him into the same back room as before.

The room didn't reek of cigar smoke this time, which was different. The man behind the desk was a match for the photographs of Tall Tony. Behind him were the two guards from yesterday, Baldy and Mustache Guy.

Baldy flinched when he noticed Lucas. His arm probably still hurt from last time.

The surprise was that Victor was also there.

"Have a seat, Lucas," Tony said. "It's been a long time."

Lucas sat, without offering to shake the mobster's hand. "This is my brother, Terry."

I stayed standing.

Tony nodded, before concentrating his glare on Lucas. "You took my niece, Maria. Where is she?" He pounded a fist on the desk. "You said you'd bring her."

I might have flinched, but Lucas didn't. "She's nearby, but first we need to talk. I understand you're looking for Elliot Boyle."

Tony's face didn't give anything away. "We are. Are you interested in helping? Ten grand, no questions asked, if you find him for me."

"And you're looking for a certain metal case."

The twitch of his eye gave him away. He hadn't expected us to know that. "We are, but why would that concern you?"

"Just in case we find it."

Tony's lips curved up in a smile. "It would be a bad idea to open it."

"Understood." Lucas shot me a glance. It was one of the kaboom-type cases.

"You need to stop coming after Grace Brennan." Lucas shot a glance at Victor. "And everyone around her."

"We only requested to talk to her," Tony said in a cool monotone.

"It wasn't a request. You attacked her and threatened her neighbor."

"This is the first I'm hearing of this," Tony said flatly.

"I am unhappy because we made this very clear to your son yesterday in this very room. You don't want me unhappy." There was a chill in Lucas's voice. "Grace Brennan is Terry's woman, and she has no part in this." Lucas pointed a strong finger across the desk. "She is completely off-limits."

Tony shot a look in Victor's direction.

"I'm handling it, Papa," Victor spoke up.

"After we talked with him," Lucas continued coldly, "he sent Maria and a man named Lorenzo to abduct Grace."

Tony spun on Victor, his face no longer impassive. "You sent people to take somebody without my permission?" His face turned redder by the second. "You tried to take a Hawk woman?" His voice reached a crescendo. "You call that handling it? Out of my sight right now."

Victor recoiled, abject fear on his face. "But, Papa—" he spluttered.

"Now," Tony bellowed.

When Victor didn't move fast enough, Tony nodded at Baldy, who yanked Victor's arm and marched him out of the room.

I bit back a chuckle. The little twerp deserved it.

"My apologies, Lucas," Tony said, his poker face returning. "My son overstepped his bounds. I gave no such instruction." He waved at Mustache Guy. "Paulo, leave us."

Mustache Guy looked perplexed for a second. "Are you—"

"Now," Tony commanded. Apparently, leaving the boss alone with guests was uncommon. "You too." He shooed me away with a hand motion.

"She's his woman. He stays," Lucas countermanded. "Terry, hand over your weapon."

Tall Tony nodded at Paulo.

I lifted my weapon, wondering whether Tony knew Lucas could be instantly deadly, even without a weapon.

Mustache Guy took my gun and left us alone with the boss of the Italian Mafia.

Tony didn't speak until the door closed. "Lucas, this Boyle cockroach ripped me off for product worth ten million, and my customer is very fucking unhappy that he didn't get what he ordered. I can't go soft on this."

"She is not a part of it," Lucas said firmly. "Not even close."

"The street says otherwise. You join me in hunting down this weasel, and we will stay away from her for a week."

"Not good enough," Lucas said. "She's not a part of this."

"After the week, you bring her here to answer some questions so I don't have to send people to bring her to talk to me. Questions, nothing more."

"She doesn't know anything," I said, unable to hold back.

Tony shifted his evil glare to me. "You don't know that. She doesn't even know if she knows something important. And, she's the one who knows the most about her cousin. That boy has nobody else. He must have said something that will lead to him."

Tony shifted back to Lucas. "Starting today, you have one week. After that the bounty on Boyle doubles—dead or alive. Nobody rips me off and gets away with it."

"I accept," Lucas said and rose from his chair. "We'll be looking for him as well."

"And my niece?" Tony asked.

Lucas pulled out his phone and dialed. "You can let them go... She what?" He looked at Tony holding the phone away from his ear. "She bit one of my men. Are you sure you want her back?"

Tony laughed. "Let me think about that. She's a spirited one."

"He's not sure," Lucas said into the phone.

We could all hear the shrill shriek on the other end.

Tony gave in to his smile. "Sure, I'll take her."

"You can let them out," Lucas said. Then he pocketed the phone and stood.

I bit back a laugh.

"One week," Tony emphasized as we left.

Outside the office, Mustache Guy had removed the clip from my SIG, and he returned my weapon in two pieces. We left the building, and I slammed home the clip and holstered the weapon as we turned the corner to the side street.

"Why'd you agree to that shit?" I asked as we turned toward our cars.

Lucas looked straight ahead. "Soldier, you're a fuckup." Suddenly he grasped my shoulders. "I told you to keep your mouth shut. You fucked up. Do you hear me, soldier?"

"Yes, sir," I answered. "Sorry, sir."

"As of now, you are to spend one-hundred-and-ten percent of your time on finding Elliot for them." He stabbed me in the chest with that dangerous finger of his. "Do you understand me, soldier?"

"Understood, sir." I even added a salute.

"You better," he said as he bleeped the locks on his Porsche.

I did the same to mine, climbed in, and started the engine as he drove off. Then, I pulled out the paper he'd slipped into my pocket.

Getting chewed out by the boss sucked. After reading the note, I shot Grace a text.

Grace

I stopped at Peyton's desk after we broke from our morning status meeting and I found the message on my phone.

> TYRANT: I have to go into the office. I don't know how long.

She was struggling with her necklace. "I hate this clasp. It keeps getting stuck in my hair."

I set my phone down. "Want some help?"

She nodded. "Thanks."

I tried to untangle the knot.

"Ouch," Peyton complained when I pulled on the wrong end of a single hair.

"Sorry." I leaned over and squinted at the problem. It wasn't a simple task with my nails as long as they were.

"Let me try." Zane appeared next to me.

Catching Peyton's smile, I moved aside. "Sure. Just be gentle with her. I can't afford the time to train a new assistant."

For such a big man, his fingers were surprisingly nimble as he worked the problem and freed her hair from the clasp. "All done." He swept her hair around her neck and over her shoulder.

"Thank you."

"Who's Tyrant?" he asked, glancing at my phone screen.

I picked it up quickly.

Peyton grinned, but obeyed the glare I sent her way and kept her mouth shut.

I escaped to my office without answering his question. Through the glass I might have noticed an admiring gaze my assistant aimed at the big man as he walked back to his post.

Then I did something completely out of character and sent the tyrant a text.

ME: Thinking about you.

That was a mistake, because I felt less good when a minute later a reply hadn't come. *What was I thinking?*

∼

TERRY

BEFORE DRIVING OFF, I REREAD THE PIECE OF PAPER LUCAS HAD PASSED ME.

> When I call play along. Start toward Grace and then U-turn
> to the office when I tell you.

185

I hadn't seen anybody watching us, but Lucas's code that we could be overheard had been clear. He, of all people, knew never to call an ex-Marine like me a soldier. Marines were called Marines and nothing else.

The meaning of the note was clear. He thought one or both of our cars had been bugged, and they may have been listening on the street as well. All it would take was a parabolic mic from a window or rooftop. Since he wanted me to make a U-turn, he was also concerned about being followed or them having a tracker on my car.

I stashed the note and pulled away from the curb, turning right at the light on the way to Grace's building.

Lucas's call arrived less than two blocks later.

"Are you going to fly straight, soldier?" he said as soon as I answered.

"Yes, sir." If I said anything else, he would assume I hadn't gotten the note.

"That was one hell of a meeting. Tony is a scary motherfucker."

"Yes, sir."

"Like I said, we need to put every effort into finding this Elliot asswipe. Do you have any leads on him from your girl?"

I guessed that playing along meant *no*. "Sorry, sir. No."

"Then you better develop some pronto because I want that ten grand he's offering."

Now we were clearly in deception mode because Lucas had made it quite clear that he would never work for any of the criminal organizations in town.

"Yes, sir."

"Okay, then. I'll see you back at the office. Don't dawdle."

"I have an errand to run first, but I'll be in as soon as I can. I'll text when I'm on the way."

"Roger that." He disconnected.

This meant leaving Grace's safety in someone else's hands for now.

I hit the steering wheel, hard. *I should be with her.* Deciding I should be an adult about the situation, I pulled into the next gas station and parked to compose a text to Grace. I didn't dare put down how I felt, so I made it simple.

> ME: I have to go into the office. I don't know how long. Zane will stay with you until I can get there.

Then I texted Carol.

> ME: Done with my meeting.

Her response was quick.

> CAROL: Longwave Park 30 min?
> ME: I'll be there

Carol Hawk needed my help, and it couldn't be good if she wanted to keep it from her sons.

CHAPTER 25

Terry

Reaching the park, I shut down the engine and checked my phone.

> WILDCAT: Thinking of you.

What was I supposed to do with that? It scared the shit out of me that I felt like sending the same thing back to her. Texting sentimental shit wasn't the kind of thing I'd ever done. The women I'd seen before hadn't expected it.

> ME: Thinking of you too.

My finger hovered over the send icon, but instead, I deleted the line and started again.

> ME: How are you feeling?

I sent that more manly message and pocketed the phone before getting out of the car.

The park was warm, with a light breeze off the ocean. Grace would like it here. *Fuck me.* That wasn't it—*I'd* like it if Grace was here with me.

Feeling guilty, I leaned against the car, pulled out my phone, and typed again. She was my woman and needed to feel it.

ME: I haven't stopped thinking about you.

Satisfied, I sent it.

As I approached, Carol Hawk stood from a bench at the center of the large, nearly deserted park. Come lunchtime, with weather like this, it wouldn't stay deserted for long.

Habit had me scanning the area for anyone who might be able to listen in, but I didn't detect anything.

She'd chosen a good location for confidentiality.

"Thank you for coming, Terry." She gave me the same hug she did every time we met, the same way she hugged Lucas and each of her children.

That thought warmed me. The Hawks had become the family I hadn't had in a very long time. "How can I help you?"

I followed her lead and sat on the bench.

She handed me a folder, keeping another back.

I opened it to find a power of attorney. "What's this?"

"This is very difficult for me. I want you to handle a delicate matter," she said. "But first, you must agree to not tell anyone about this unless I release you, not even the family. Not ever."

I was in too deep to back out now. "Of course." This had better not be a marital issue between her and Henry. I closed the folder and set it down.

She handed me the second folder. "I've been doing genealogy research, going back into our family trees. Henry and I used one of those send-in-your-DNA sample kits. I thought it would be interesting to see our backgrounds, like where our ancestors originated. Henry remembers being told that his family had roots in Scandinavia."

I took in a relieved breath that this wasn't a marital issue.

"I got a surprise result," she continued. "A family member had also used the service, and requested to be notified if any family matches were found." She tapped the folder I held.

I opened the folder. It contained a contact request from a male, thirty-eight years old with a family match to a sample number. "Who is this?"

Carol swallowed hard. "I don't know. The company wants my approval before they will release information to either of us."

I took her hand in both of mine. I didn't know the structure of the extended family, but something about this was obviously difficult for her. "How can I help?"

"I've read of scams where people steal DNA—like off straws from strangers—and then submit them to these services, claiming to be a long-lost family member."

I hadn't read that, but it certainly sounded like a possibility. "Is this what you're afraid of?"

She took in a long breath. "There is another possibility. I had a sister, Wilma. She was wild."

Neither Lucas nor any of his brothers had ever mentioned having an Aunt Wilma.

"Our father was a pastor, strict as could be, and threw Wilma out of the house very young. She moved away, and we were never in touch after that. Father said she went to prison, and I was to never ask about her again. I was an only child, as far as he was concerned. She was dead to us. She never existed. I'm ashamed to admit I never mentioned her to Henry or any of my children."

I waited for her to go on as she tried to put the words together.

"It's possible that I do have a relative out there, who I never met or even knew about. I'd like you to look into this person and figure out if this is one of those scams, or if he's possibly a nephew of mine. And if he is, what does he want from me, from us? Is he even the kind of person we want to know?"

I squeezed her hand.

"Can you do this for me? Please?"

"I think it would be better if you asked Lucas." Getting invited to dinner was one thing, but I wasn't a blood relative.

She shook her head rapidly. "No. If this is person is really related, then I'll get Lucas involved. I'll have to admit to Henry that I've lied to him all these years. It will be hard, but I'll do it for the sake of the family, for the sake of this nephew. But..." She hesitated. "If he isn't real, if this is one of those scams, I don't want Henry, Lucas, any of the children to know. Can you understand that?"

"Of course." She was scared. This was how a simple lie told once could live on to haunt a person for years. "If that's the case, I'll keep your secret."

We said our goodbyes, and I left with the two folders of paperwork.

∽

GRACE

. . .

I was rummaging through my purse in search of the aspirin when Peyton walked into my office. She closed the door with a wicked grin on her face. "I know why you look like crap this morning—no sleep."

I'd sworn to myself that I wouldn't bring my personal drama into the office. "I drank more than I should have last night."

She ignored my comment. "Tell me it's because he's a tyrant in bed, too, isn't he? Banging your brains out all night long?"

I wish I'd spent last night that way. "I wouldn't know. For your information, I didn't sleep with him last night." I had slept with him, but not in the sleep-with-him way that she meant. "I look like shit because I feel like shit, because I have a shitty hangover from drinking way, way too much shitty wine last night." That was absolutely true.

"And?" she prompted.

"And that's it."

She stood there, arms crossed.

"Don't you have work to do?" I asked.

"What are you not telling me?"

"Perhaps we should talk about Zane?"

She huffed and left, closing the door behind her.

Her response solidified that I was on to something. Finding my aspirin bottle, I chased two more tablets with the remainder of my coffee.

I'd just had three customer calls in a row when Zane was polite enough to knock before he opened the door.

He smiled. "I have to take a call with the boss. I promise I won't be long."

I nodded. "Knock yourself out." I noticed Peyton behind him, checking out his ass.

"Stay here with your door locked until I get back, okay?"

"Paranoid much?"

"It's the job," he said before closing the door.

I saluted him through the glass.

~

TERRY

I drove up to Hawk Central, as I liked to call it, and hit the button to open the gate to our garage. Lucas had bought the building and moved us into it last year after upgrading it to his specifications.

I parked in the garage, next to my car with its bullet holes from the run-in with the Marku crew.

Joe, our mechanic, talked with Lucas, shaking his head and gesturing at the car. Joe treated our cars like his children. He had all the tools he needed to modify and keep our vehicles in top shape, including a car lift, and he hated seeing us bring one back banged up.

Lucas glanced at me, putting a finger to his lips as if I had to be reminded not to say anything a bug could pick up. Then pointed at me to stay in the car and wait for Jordy.

I'd been through this bug-search routine twice before with Lucas and Jordy, and both times the car had been clean.

"Aw, fuck. Where did that damned thing go?" I said, in case I was bugged and they wondered why I hadn't shut off the engine yet.

Jordy appeared from the hallway that led to our guest accommodations for the dirtbags we occasionally had to detain.

We also had a full gym on this floor, and an indoor shooting range. Upstairs, we had room to grow with abundant office space and proper apartments for visiting clients of specialists from out of town.

Jordy joined Lucas, and they motioned for me to shut down.

After I killed the engine, Jordy timed his opening of the passenger-side door with me opening my door. He held his little sniffer that he claimed could detect any transmissions.

Lucas leaned over to watch.

Jordy smiled and pointed. The dial of his sniffer responded as he waved it under the dash on his side of the car.

Lucas pointed upward, and I followed him past our guest accommodations.

A janitor was disinfecting suite number two.

"The guy last night puked up his dinner when Duke questioned him," Lucas deadpanned. "They just don't make bad guys like they used to."

I chuckled. Duke could make threats that would have a grown man's balls shrink to the size of canary eggs. It was one of his superpowers.

Lucas turned as we reached the second floor. "We'll keep that car on ice in case we want to send them a message later. Get a new one from Joe when you go out."

"Sure." It made sense to keep a misinformation channel open to the Russo gang in case we needed it.

"Review in my office in five," he said as we neared his doorway. "Tell the others."

"Roger." I turned left.

"Hey, lover," Constance chided as I walked by her on the way to my office.

I ignored the jibe. "Lucas wants a review in his office in five."

"Good. I've got something."

"What?"

"You'll see."

I made the rounds to tell Duke, Jordy, and Winston about the meeting and had enough time to make myself a cup of coffee before we got started. I made it to the conference room just in time to beat Jordy and not be the last one in.

Lucas swiveled to address the squawk box. "You there, Zane?"

"Yup," came the response over the speaker.

"Hold fast," the boss said. "We're waiting on Jordy."

"How are you sleeping?" Duke asked.

"Better," was Zane's response.

Winston lifted a brow. He also thought there was a story there.

"I'm not late," Jordy grumbled as he closed the door behind him.

Lucas checked his watch and shrugged. "Close enough. Terry summarize the attack last night for us."

I did, including that Zane had been sent to guard Grace's neighbor.

"If we're doing that again tonight," Zane said. "I nominate Constance. That old lady complained the entire time about not wanting a man in her space."

The group chuckled.

"That won't be necessary," Lucas said. "Terry and I visited with Tall Tony this morning, and Tony agreed to back off. The interesting part is that the attacks on Grace were run by his son Victor—"

"A real piece of shit," I interjected.

Lucas nodded. "He didn't run them by his dad, and that fuckup got him sent back to Italy." He pointed at Jordy. "And…"

"I confirmed that Junior is already in the air to JFK, connecting to Rome."

"Wow," Winston said. "Daddy doesn't mess around."

"I didn't know early enough to affect the current flight, but I reseated him for his second leg," Jordy noted. "Middle seat in the last row of the plane, right by the lavatories." He threw a jelly bean in the air and caught it in his mouth like a fucking seal.

More laughter, and Winston fist-bumped Jordy.

Lucas pointed. "Constance, you have something?"

She nodded. "My Secret Service contacts are buzzing about a new round of counterfeit hundreds popping up in town. One guy that was caught on camera passing the bills is a runner for the Russo family."

"That doesn't mean Russo is printing them," Duke pointed out. "He could be buying them, though."

"That's a risky play for them," Lucas said. "Their entire strategy is to avoid federal entanglements, and counterfeiting is a federal case."

"They could be the middleman," I suggested. "It's the final distributors passing the bills to merchants who end up getting caught."

"Could that much bogus money be what's in the case?" Zane asked.

Duke shrugged. "It makes more sense than drugs."

"No way," Constance said. "One million in bills is a forty-three-inch stack. Ten mill is about thirty-five feet. That much doesn't fit in a case, and that's before you factor in the discount, which means the case would have to hold something like forty million in bogus bills to have a street value of ten million."

Everybody nodded after Constance's lesson.

"But," she added, "it might not be the whole delivery. The buyer typically gets a sample before buying in bulk. What if Victor's number is the worth of the total transaction at stake? Do we trust Victor that what was in the case was worth ten mill?"

Lucas shook his head. "In a word, *no*." He looked around the room. "One more thing. Based on Tony's response this morning, the missing case is one of the ones rigged with explosives."

Winston shook his head. "I hate that shit."

"I told Tony we'd help him find Elliot," Lucas said. "We have one week."

Duke raised a hand. "Do we think Elliot stole it and still has the case?"

I kept quiet.

"Most likely," Lucas said. "The bombs in the cases were started when one of the couriers was caught stealing. They have enough C-4 in them to level a few houses. If he'd tried to open it, there would be a smoking hole in the ground somewhere and whatever was inside would be worthless. So, best guess, he's trying to open it without damaging the contents or killing himself."

"If Victor is on his way to Italy, and Papa Russo has backed off Grace, why are we spending so much time on this?" Jordy asked.

Lucas leveled his brother with a glare. "Because she's Terry's woman and one of us, that's why. This isn't over because Marku is in the mix."

Jordy's head jerked to me. "Your—"

"My woman," I said emphatically enough to settle that for everybody.

Duke high-fived me. "About fuckin' time."

"Yours?" Zane asked.

"Isn't that what the fuck I just said?" I wanted it crystal clear to him.

Constance turned a grimace on Lucas. "If he's involved with the protectee, that could be a problem."

Lucas raised a hand. "Not here it isn't."

Winston shook his head at her from across the table.

Constance clamped her mouth shut.

"Any luck finding where Elliot is hiding?" Lucas asked Jordy.

"I have him on camera several times down near the pier. I'm getting closer. Maybe by tomorrow."

"Great. Anything else?" Lucas asked.

When nobody spoke up, he stood, and the meeting was over.

Outside the conference room, Constance pulled me aside. "What is it I don't know? Why is it okay for you to be protecting the woman you just told us all you are involved with? That's a clear violation of proper protocol."

I waited until nobody else was within earshot. "Lucas has different rules. He married a woman he was protecting."

Her mouth dropped open like I'd just proclaimed that the Earth revolved around the moon. "I never—"

I stopped her. "We don't talk about it…about her. It's just too painful."

"What happened?"

"It's not my story to tell. And for Lucas's sake, don't ask."

With that, I left her before I got myself in trouble.

CHAPTER 26

Grace

"Who's my next demo?" I asked Peyton. "I'd like you to check demo one and refresh the water and drinks."

She sat back down and checked her computer. "Mr. and Mrs. Lim at one. And Mrs. Garcia wants us to look at her house before the demo and advise her on knocking out a wall or two, which will redefine the space she has to work with."

"Let Marci handle that. Then she and I can do the demo with and without the optional room extension."

She frowned. "She said she saw the magazine article and wants you. She was adamant."

"Fine, but who is Mrs. Garcia? I don't recall the name."

"New customer. She's in the small conference room right now with Marci. She read the article about us and has a rush job."

The article in the Sunday paper a while back had been a turning point in our business, but these rich ladies could be a pain to work with. So I made sure the prices we charged made the effort worthwhile, especially if they were in a hurry. "Fine."

"Do you want to poke your head in and say hi?" she asked.

"Not the way I feel today. I'll meet her tomorrow."

"Good choice. You look like crap."

I rolled my eyes. "Thanks. You already said that."

"An excellent assistant," she argued, "keeps her boss grounded."

I nodded. "Keep it up and you might even get a raise one day."

"There's no time like today."

Usually I appreciated the banter with Peyton, but not while dealing with a headache. "You don't want to be pushing this right after forgetting that I asked you to check on the status of demo one."

"It's fine. I checked first thing this morning."

"And refresh the water."

She sighed and stood. "I like you better without the hangover."

"Me too," I answered as she marched off.

Later, my phone rang with an unknown number. "Hello?" I answered wearily, hoping for a new client, but ready for it to be another spam marketing call.

"Gracie?" Elliot's voice was hoarse.

"Elliot, where are you?" I looked out the glass of my office, but didn't see Zane.

"I need money to get out of town. If I stay here, they're going to kill me." He sounded frantic.

"You need to come to me, so Terry and the guys can keep you safe."

"No way. He'd just as soon shoot me himself. You can't tell him. You can't tell any of them. I hear they're working with my boss. I'll end up dead."

Elliot blew everything out of proportion, like he always did.

"He's not like that," I argued. "I promise you." I knew in my heart that Terry was a good man we could both trust.

"Money. Money to get out of town. That's the only way this works."

Typical Elliot drama. It was all about him.

"No. You come in and let Lucas Hawk talk to Russo. He knows them. By staying out there, you're putting me in danger."

"You're safe. Captain America won't let anything happen to you."

I shook my head at his stupidity. "Elliot, they've tried to kidnap me more than once, and yesterday they shot at us. You hear me? I almost died because of you. You call that being safe?"

"You gotta give me money. Or do you want them to kill me? Is that it? That's what happens if I don't get out of town. Maybe you'd like that."

"Of course not," I insisted, horrified that he'd even say such a thing,

"If you don't give me the money to get out of town, you're signing my death warrant."

"Don't be ridiculous. I'm telling you to come in and have the best security firm in town protect you."

"Nobody can protect me. Not from him. But that's what you want, isn't it? Me out of your life once and for all."

Guilt ate a hole in my stomach. If I didn't give him money, and he did get hurt or killed, how would I ever live with myself, knowing I could have stopped it? "Okay, but I don't have much."

"Remember, you can't tell Captain America about this."

I rolled my eyes. Typical Elliot. Not even a *thank you, cousin. I'm so grateful, cousin. You saved me, cousin.* "You have to tell me everything that's going on, and I mean everything."

"Right. When you get me the money."

"I mean it, Elliot. Everything."

"Sure."

"I'll have to go to the bank to get it."

"Text me when you do. I'll give you the meet. Oh, and you gotta ditch Captain America for that too. I'll get another phone and call back later."

Ending the call, I dropped the phone in my purse.

Peyton looked up when I opened my door.

"Is Zane still on his call?" I asked her.

"He took it in demo two." She stood. "Do you need him?"

"It can wait until he finishes."

Zane appeared a few minutes later. "Good news. Jordy has narrowed down where Elliot is, and thinks he's only a day away from nailing him. This is almost over."

"That would be nice," I said without feeling the conviction I tried to add to my voice.

Zane stepped out, and as he closed my office door, Elliot's words came back to me. *"I hear they're working with my boss."*

Leaning back in my chair, I felt trapped. How could I know if Elliot was telling the truth about the Hawk people working with his boss? Zane had said that as well…

I did the one thing I knew was right.

"Kitten, glad you called," Terry said when he answered.

He deserved my trust. "I have a problem," I told him.

His voice lowered. "Go ahead."

"Zane said you and Hawk are looking for Elliot to turn him over to his boss."

He paused a second. "You know we're looking for him, but to find the case and settle this, not to turn him over."

"Zane said—"

"Screw what Zane said. He's new. Lucas and I are clear on this."

I let out a long, relieved breath. "Elliot called me."

"What did he say?"

"He wants money to get out of town."

"Of course he does."

I recounted the entire conversation for him.

"Then we pick him up when you meet," Terry suggested, as I'd known he would.

"That won't work. I told him I wouldn't give him the money unless he told me everything. I'm the only one he'll open up to. You need to give me five minutes alone with him to get the story. He won't tell you."

"Okay. I'll get you the time alone with him. Find Zane. I'll call back in three minutes with a plan."

Opening my door, I waved Zane over.

Peyton looked at me quizzically, but I didn't entertain the question.

I closed the door to my office and told him Elliot had called, as well as the gist of the conversation. Then we waited for Terry to call back.

Zane angled his chair so that he could look toward the offices and my pretty assistant instead of out the window.

I laughed. "Why don't you just ask her?"

"Huh?" he asked just as my phone rang. *Saved by the bell.*

I put it on speaker as I answered. "I have Zane with me."

"The plan is simple," Terry said. "Keep your phone with you so we can track you. Zane will escort you to the bank. From there, take an Uber to the meet. Duke and I will tail you from the bank and give you the five minutes before we close on Elliot. Zane, after the bank, the boss wants you back here."

Zane spoke up. "Copy that, but I have a suggestion. If this Elliot twit is as paranoid as it sounds like, he could be watching the building to see if she leaves alone or with one of us."

"Good idea," Terry commented. "Then Grace takes an Uber from the building as well, and you tail her to the bank. We still need to be aware that Marku is out there somewhere."

After agreeing on the plan, I noticed that my hand wasn't shaking this time—progress.

Down on the street, I climbed into the Uber I'd called.

"You all right?" the woman driving asked after the third time I craned my neck around to see if Zane was following.

"My ex," I croaked, figuring it was a believable cover story.

"Mine is a piece of shit too. I'll keep an eye out," she said as she sped up.

I typed a message to Elliot.

>ME: On the way to the bank. Where do we meet?
>UNKNOWN: Behind the dentinator

CHAPTER 27

GRACE

I HUDDLED BEHIND AN SUV IN THE PARKING LOT BEHIND OUR OLD DENTIST, which Elliot had nicknamed the dentinator. With five thousand in hundreds in a giant wad in my purse, I felt much more vulnerable than I should have. I mean, how could a robber look at me and know that I carried that kind of cash?

He couldn't, right?

Still, I kept an eagle eye out for bad-looking dudes because logic wasn't working for me today.

Elliot must have parked down the street, because he appeared on foot, coming from the west. He had on the same clothes as the other day, only dirtier.

I stood up and waved when he looked my direction.

He shifted toward me, and I ducked down again.

He rounded the SUV and looked around. "You come alone?"

"You see anybody else?"

He hunched down to my level. "You got the money?"

"First, you tell me the whole story. What's going on?"

He checked around again. "I told you, a shipment got messed up."

"The whole story," I repeated. "All of it."

"Uh...I got ripped off."

"Somebody stole the case from you? Who?"

"Rudi."

"Your roommate, Rudi?"

He nodded.

"Hey there." It was Duke's voice.

Elliot spun. "You promised you'd come alone."

I stood, and there was Duke, large as life, blocking Elliot's way out.

"She kept her promise," Terry said from behind me. "We invited ourselves."

Elliot tried to run by Duke. He failed.

Elliot squirmed, but it was no use against Duke's strength. "You're coming with us."

"We're all going to get this sorted out," I assured Elliot.

"It can't be sorted out. They're killers," he whined.

"And what the fuck do you think we are?" Duke sneered. "We eat pussies like that for breakfast."

Terry wrapped an arm around me. "Elliot, you're coming with us. We're going to fix this so nobody gets killed."

I walked with Terry. "He doesn't have the case anymore."

A couple came around the corner and stopped, staring at Elliot, still struggling against Duke.

Terry noticed them too. "The car's this way."

"Hey," Elliot squealed when Duke muscled him to follow.

Terry whispered into my ear as we reached the Cayenne. "He doesn't deserve it, but we'll keep him in one piece." He opened the door for me. "For you."

∽

TERRY

DUKE DROVE WITH GRACE UP FRONT, WHILE I KEPT ELLIOT COMPANY IN THE back seat.

"You missed the turn," Grace complained. "Go right up here. I have to get back to work. Then you guys can go do your thing."

Duke wasn't moved. "We're taking him to Hawk for a little chat."

"No," Grace insisted. "You're taking me back to work first. I have a customer meeting I can't miss." Her determination when it came to her company hadn't diminished one bit.

She was my woman, all right. I smiled, finding her determination endearing. "Duke, she's right. We go to her building first."

Duke grumbled, but made the turn at the next intersection. He then decided against waiting until we had Elliot back at Hawk Central and started the interrogation. "Who's got the case?"

Elliot shrank. "I dunno."

"His roommate Rudi took it," Grace countered.

"Strike one," I said, as I grabbed Elliot's scrawny arm and squeezed hard.

"That hurts," he whined.

I increased the pressure. "Listen to me very carefully, you little weasel. One more wrong answer, and we drive you straight to Russo and collect the reward."

"You can't," Grace screeched.

She'd already forgotten what I'd whispered to her. Lucky for me, she was in the front seat and couldn't interfere. "I can, and I will. This little creep put you in danger, and that is utterly and completely unfuckingacceptable."

Elliot cowered at my yell.

"Do you hear me?" I asked, calming my voice.

The twerp nodded vigorously.

I upped the volume. "Do you hear me?"

"Yes, sir. Yes, sir."

"Keep in mind, this is not fucking baseball. You do not get three strikes. Now, one more time," I intoned slowly. "And if you lie to me, I'll cut off one of your balls."

"Make it two," Duke said.

"Okay. Both balls."

Elliot blanched.

"Think carefully. Who has the case?" I asked slowly.

"Rudi."

"What's Rudi's last name?"

"Sanchez."

I let up on my grip. "Now that wasn't so hard, was it?"

His eyes remained wide with fear. "But he skipped out."

In the rearview mirror, I saw Duke's brows rise. "Skipped out on you?"

The weasel nodded. "Yeah."

I couldn't believe how short of functioning brain cells this little idiot was. "You planned on stealing from Tony Russo? You're a moron."

Grace swiveled in her seat. "You mean this entire shitshow is because you decided to rip off the mob?"

"It's ten million in cash," he said, like that was a reason to risk his life—

and Grace's as well. "Rudi has this place down on the beach in Colombia. We were gonna—"

Duke cut him off. "You know the cases are rigged to blow if you open them, right?"

Elliot's eyes darted back and forth. "Yeah, I saw inside one once." He fidgeted. "But Rudi did the math and said we could try out all the combinations in a little over two weeks, and that way we wouldn't get blowed up—cuz that would ruin the money and ten million would go a long way in Colombia."

I didn't bother telling him that ten million in cash wouldn't possibly fit in the little metal briefcase or that it was probably counterfeit. "So where is he…Rudi? While he tries to open this case without getting his ass blown to smithereens?"

I squeezed his arm harder when he didn't answer.

"I dunno," he squeaked.

"You're pathetic," I told him and let go. "And you have shit for brains." Looking at Grace, I could tell she was furious as well.

As we neared Grace's building, the twerp spoke up again. "I gotta pee."

"You pee in my car," Duke said ominously, "and I'll make you lick it up. Then I'll wring your scrawny neck."

Elliot shrank toward the door, looking like shitting his pants was a real possibility.

"He can come inside," Grace said, "and use our facilities before you take him off to the dungeon or whatever."

As soon as Duke parked, I exited the Porsche and dragged Elliot with me.

Grace opened her door and climbed out on my side as well.

"Hurry back," Duke said as he shut down the motor. "I'll wait here."

Then two shots rang out.

The glass of the neighboring car shattered.

Duke threw his door open.

I let go of Elliot and took Grace to the ground.

Another shot, and glass shards rained down on top of us.

CHAPTER 28

GRACE

TERRY PUSHED ME HARD, TACKLING ME TO THE GROUND. HIS HAND BEHIND MY head was the only thing that protected my skull from breaking open. The force of his weight knocked the wind out of me.

I closed my eyes against the sounds of gunfire, breaking glass, and bullets hitting metal. This couldn't be happening again.

Terry lay on top of me, a huge weight pinning me to the ground. I couldn't move. I could barely breathe. The sound of another shot hitting the glass above us made me scream with what little breath I had left.

Terry's hand covered my mouth. "Quiet." He lifted a slight bit of his weight off me. "Duke?"

"They've got us pinned," Duke responded. "Three shooters across the street. Keep Grace there. Too much open ground between here and the building."

"We're gonna die," Elliot whimpered. "I just know it."

"Shut up and stay flat on the ground," Duke barked. "If you say another word, I'll shoot you myself."

Turning my head, I saw Duke's foot and knee from under the car. He rose, fired three shots, and crouched again.

The other gunmen, whoever they were, peppered our car and the neighboring ones with more bullets.

Terry took his hand off my mouth. "Don't move and keep your eyes closed."

Right. There could be blood. I nodded, but didn't follow his order. With his safety on the line and my heart about to explode out of my chest, I tensed instead. There was no way in hell I was taking my eyes off my boyfriend, my protector.

Terry crawled off me and squirmed across the ground to the back of the car with his gun in hand.

"Don't leave me," Elliot moaned.

I twisted toward him. "Shut up and grow a pair."

I'd seen enough TV to know that if Terry took a bullet, someone had to apply pressure to the wound to control the bleeding. That had to be me, blood and all. I fucking refused to let my boyfriend die because I had a crap-ass nervous system that shut down at the sight of blood. If my boyfriend needed a nurse, I was determined to be there for him.

Boyfriend, that word echoed in my head as I watched him. The attacks had crystallized how I felt for my ex-Marine. If I survived this, I was going to tell him exactly how hard I'd fallen for my onetime tormentor.

Terry extended his arm alongside the tire and squinted. He fired, the sound surprisingly loud this close to me. A second later he fired again. "One down," he announced to Duke.

Duke laughed. "If Marine scout snipers are so good, why'd it take you two shots to hit the guy?" He popped up and let loose another volley of shots.

More bullets peppered our car.

"Fuck you." Terry's tone was joking. "At least I didn't empty half a clip without hitting anything like some washed-up SEAL."

"It's called drawing their fire to save your ass and giving you a target to aim at," Duke argued with a laugh.

Their humor helped me relax a tiny bit. Maybe it was the badass key to handling the stress of such a deadly situation.

Terry stretched out and squinted again. "I'm ready."

Duke shot twice more before ducking.

More return fire hit around us.

I could barely breathe. I was safely behind the car, but Terry had to be exposed to shoot. With the sound of each bullet hitting nearby, I feared the next one would strike him. That I'd lose him. We couldn't end like this before we even got started. I couldn't lose him, not now.

Bang. Terry fired once more. "Winged one."

"Aren't snipers supposed to go for headshots?" Duke joked.

"Bite me, sailor boy. A case of beer says I take you at the range, even lefthanded."

"You're on."

Several more seconds went by with an eerie silence.

Duke popped up at the sound of squealing tires, and back down again. "They're bugging out."

"Don't move," Terry told me before he stood and gave a silent hand signal to Duke. The two split up, moving in different directions before crossing the street.

Now that the gunfire had ceased, I could hear the groaning coming from a distance.

Whoever our attackers were, they'd left one guy behind, presumably the first one Terry had hit.

Sirens became noticeable in the distance just before screams of pain came from behind a car across the street.

I struggled to my feet as people started pouring out of our building.

Another scream. Since the asshole had shot at us, I didn't care what pressure Terry or Duke used to get information from the guy. *Magnanimous* was not in my vocabulary today. If I wasn't scared of the blood, I'd have been the first one over there demanding to know who was targeting us.

Marci was the first to find me. "My God, I didn't know you were in this much trouble. I can't believe people were shooting at you."

Peyton and several others from my company joined us.

"Me either," I said.

Paul pushed into the circle. "I called 9-1-1."

"Good. Now let's all get back inside and let the professionals take care of this." That's when I saw Elliot running down the street.

A police car roared up and screeched to a stop.

Duke waved them over to the other side of the street.

Peyton walked toward our building. "You heard the boss. The excitement's over. Back to work."

After a few grumbles, the group of my employees followed her back inside.

I got the side-eye from Albert Sakman, whose high-end financial consulting company occupied the floor below us. I would have loved a chance to sell to some of his clients.

Terry ran toward me. "Grace." His hands were bloody.

This time I followed my training, and tensed immediately, leaned against the nearby car closed my eyes and slid down to a seated position. *It is not his blood. It is not his blood.* I kept repeating the words to myself, tensing hard between breaths.

"Are you okay?" I felt Terry's hand on my shoulder and heard the worry in his voice.

I kept my eyes closed. "Thanks to you. I'm just being careful." The backs of my eyelids remained pink from the sunshine. The darkness I feared didn't come. I'd conquered my broken nervous system this time. It could be done. "You have blood on you."

"Shit." He pulled his hand away.

If it wasn't for the blood and the possibility of making a fool of myself by fainting again, I'd be tackling him right this second. He'd put his body between me and those mad gunmen. He'd taken one of them out and wounded another. My man was a certified hot-as-fuck badass.

A few seconds later, he announced, "All cleaned up."

When I opened my eyes, he was marvelously shirtless, with just a slight red tinge to his hands, and the shirt he'd used to wipe off the blood lay in a clump yards away.

He pulled me to my feet and into a wonderfully tight hug.

"You are one hot badass," I told him, admitting how watching him in action was the turn-on that kept my fear in check.

"Elliot?" he asked.

"He took off."

"You scared my people," Sakman complained. "You're a menace, Brennan. I'm going to talk to the landlord about having you removed."

Talking to him had never been a pleasure. The man grumbled about everything. "I was scared myself, but everything's okay now."

"You call shooting a man on a busy street okay?"

Terry stepped between us. "I do."

"Did you shoot that poor man?" Sakman demanded.

Terry advanced on him. "He attacked my woman and my friend, so yes, I shot back. I protect the people close to me against anyone who threatens them—anyone. I only regret that I didn't get him between the eyes and now he's going to take up a hospital bed that should go to somebody who matters."

"You're a menace too. I'm definitely getting her thrown out of this building."

Terry advanced, forcing the older man to back away. "It sounds to me like you're threatening my woman."

"No. No. Of course not," Sakman spluttered. "I would never."

"Good. Because Grace has put a lot of effort into her business. It's important to her, and she's important to me." Terry forced him back farther. "If you do anything that hurts her, I will be back to see you, and you do not want me to come looking for you. Do you understand?"

Even though Terry's words were aimed at Sakman, his lethal tone scared the shit out of me.

"Yes, sir." A wet spot appeared on Sakman's pants.

Terry backed away and lowered his voice. "What's your name?"

"Sakman. Uh, Albert Sakman."

"Albert... I like that. It sounds like an honest name. What do you do, Albert?"

Sakman partially regained his composure. "Financial... financial consulting."

"Rich clients?"

"The upper tier of the one percent," Sakman said, puffing up and putting on his sales voice.

"Albert." Terry put his arm around me. "Grace and I got shot at today because she went out of her way to help her cousin. I happen to think that helping family is pretty damned admirable, don't you?"

Sakman nodded vigorously. "Uh-huh."

"Maybe she's the kind of high-integrity person you'd refer your upper-tier-of-the-one-percent clients to?"

Sakman did a bobble-head imitation. "Absolutely."

"I like that. It's good to know that you'll have Grace's back in the future."

Sakman was still nodding.

"It's been nice to meet you, Albert, but we have to go now." He pulled me against his side. "Kitten, let's get you inside."

Could this man be any more perfect? I blinked back a tear of joy at the way he'd gone out of his way to turn a complete shitshow into something positive for me. "We need to get you something to wear." I liked his chest and his ink, but I didn't like the idea of all my employees ogling him.

"I left a windbreaker in your office." He waited until we were alone in the elevator to add. "Or, we could go into your office, pull the blinds, and I could rip your shirt off so we're even."

I slapped his shoulder. "Stop that. This is my place of work, Goodwin."

His thumb teased my breast. "You know what they say about all work and no play?"

His words sent a rush of heat between my legs. I pulled the red emergency stop button.

As soon as the alarm bell started ringing, I grabbed him for a kiss. He fought me, but I took control, plundering his mouth. The noise of the alarm only heightened the experience for me, and I was breathless when we broke the kiss. "I had to say thank you for being there for me."

He touched his nose to mine. "You know, they're probably calling the fire department right now." He had to speak loudly over the blaring alarm.

I nodded, gave him one last peck on the lips, and released him. "When we get home, I plan to show you how thankful I can be."

He reset the emergency stop, and the elevator started back up silently. "We don't have to wait." He grinned mischievously, cradling my waist. "Your office is closer."

I pushed at his shoulder. "As fun as the office sounds, I have a client demo to do."

"I figured you'd say that."

"Were you really going to punch Mr. Sakman for me?"

The ding sounded, and the door opened on our floor.

"What happened?" It was Marci among a gaggle at the elevator.

"Some kind of glitch," Terry answered. "You might want to call maintenance and take the stairs down when you leave."

A few heads nodded as the women ogled my bare-chested hero.

I folded my arms over my chest. "Doesn't anyone here have work to do?"

Grumbling, the group left.

"He threatened you. I will not let that stand," Terry said, answering my previous question.

It was as much of an answer as I was going to get. Although I wasn't a fan of violence, it was a thrill to think I was that important to Terry. I pulled him to a stop when he started to leave. "Hold on. I need to say something…"

"Yes?"

Peyton rushed up before I could get the words out.

Telling him how I felt was going to have to wait. I wasn't doing this in front of an audience. Maybe her interruption was a good thing, because I wasn't even sure of the right words, and rehearsing might be a good idea.

"Mr. and Mrs. Lim are waiting in demo one." Peyton didn't hide her admiration for my boyfriend's physique. There was that word again, *boyfriend*.

"I left a windbreaker in your office. I'll join you in a sec," Terry told me.

"Right."

We followed Peyton through the space, and so many eyes tracked Terry.

I grabbed his hand, staking my claim for all to see. Several steps later, I decided that wasn't enough and pulled him to a stop.

"What?"

I answered by slipping my hand behind his neck and lifting up to kiss him, making it public in front of my employees. He said he'd claimed me, and now I'd claimed him as well.

The only sounds in the room were gasps.

When we broke apart, he nuzzled my ear. "I thought you were against PDA."

"It's a woman's prerogative to change her mind." My words would have to wait.

CHAPTER 29

Terry

Grace's kiss in front of all her employees surprised the hell out of me—not that I was complaining.

Breaking off to stop by her office and get my windbreaker, I got a chance to watch my woman's ass as she and Peyton continued to the demo room. I joined them as soon as I was presentable.

Inside the demo room with Grace, Paul, and their customers, I had trouble staying still. Adrenaline still surged through me. Outside, I'd been wound much tighter than in any previous firefight.

Overseas, I'd been in dozens, but none with the same stakes as today. Today, I'd experienced fear that I might lose Grace if I wasn't good enough, strong enough, accurate enough.

Today, if I'd missed, it could have cost Grace her life, and that was not happening. I clenched and unclenched my fists, doing my best to concentrate on the meeting, but the voices were a jumble as I played back the firefight in my head. I'd seen the face of the leader. That fucker was going down.

As soon as we figured out whether Russo or Marku was behind this, I was sure Lucas would organize a takedown.

Instead of aiming at the leader, I'd taken the easier shot at the guy next to him, because my hand wasn't as steady as it should have been.

"Never mind him," Grace said.

I looked up to see her shift her gaze to me for a second.

"He's new and observing how this is done."

Her words woke me from my trance. I had a job to do, and that required concentration. *Get it together, Goodwin.* Focus, stay in the here and now. After-action review was just what it said. It was for after the action was completed, and the day wasn't over yet.

"If you put on your headsets," Grace told them, "we can get started."

I grabbed the headset from the chair next to me and put it on. I was inside a huge walk-in closet with four avatars.

"We can change the stain on the oak," Grace said, as the wood in the virtual room shifted tones.

I gave myself a mental slap.

It was amazing to see Grace and Paul work as a team with the husband and wife customers wanting to improve their "cottage," which from the pictures looked like what any of us would call a mansion.

Even after what she'd just been through, Grace seemed totally focused and at ease. Most civilians took an entire day or more to recover from a live shooting incident.

As I sat in the corner, I swelled with pride at how accomplished she was. Grace was mine, and looking back, I could kick myself for not having seen this earlier.

I'd already texted Jordy and Lucas with the details about Elliot and his harebrained scheme to rip off the Russo family. Most importantly, I was waiting to hear what Jordy could dig up on Elliot's roommate, Rudi Sanchez.

Sanchez was the key to wrapping this up. Regardless of the outcome for Elliot, getting the case back would ensure Grace's safety.

Without a knock, the door to the demo room opened. Lieutenant Wellbourne appeared.

"I tried to get him to wait," Peyton explained from behind him.

He pointed an accusing finger at me. "You shoot up the neighborhood like you're still overseas and then leave the scene without giving a statement? I should lock you up, Goodwin."

I pressed a finger to my lips as I stood. "Quiet. They're working here." I headed to the door.

Grace whipped off her headset. "Who are you?"

"LAPD," Wellbourne said, flashing the badge on his belt.

"Do you have a warrant, Officer?"

I smirked and stayed quiet. Wellbourne didn't know who he was up against.

"It's Lieutenant Wellbourne, and I don't need a warrant in active pursuit of a suspect." He pointed at me.

"How can it be a pursuit if he's been sitting here quietly waiting for you? I heard him tell Duke Hawk he'd be waiting upstairs when you were ready."

I hadn't had to say those words to Duke, and it was super smart of Grace to think of them.

Wellbourne turned red. "I'm sorry, ma'am. Mr. Hawk failed to mention that to me."

"It's my customers you should be apologizing to," Grace stated.

Wellbourne backed toward the door. "I'm very sorry to have interrupted your meeting."

I looked at Wellbourne and cocked my head toward the door. "We can talk in her office."

I followed him out and closed the door. "Sorry, Lieutenant, she's my protectee. I couldn't allow her to stay exposed on the street in case there was more shooting, and I couldn't leave her alone and unprotected, either. That's the job." I ushered him to Grace's office.

"You guys are a pain in my ass," Wellbourne complained.

Duke was at a nearby desk, providing extra support in case those idiots decided to take another run at us. He waved discreetly, and I nodded back.

"Duke claimed battle amnesia," Wellbourne said, "about what happened beyond the fact that the one guy you hit and two more who escaped began firing at everything in sight, and you two didn't do anything to provoke them, which I highly doubt. Were they unhappy clients shooting at you and Duke, or was it the girl?"

Since he didn't know about Elliot, I wasn't bringing him up, but Wellbourne's question was a good one.

Before this, they had wanted Grace alive as leverage to get to Elliot, so shooting at her didn't make sense. If Elliot had stolen the case, how did killing him advance their cause? That didn't make sense either.

"Tell me what's going on," the lieutenant prodded. "Why does that girl need Hawk-level protection in the first place? Who's after her?"

"Her name is Grace Brennan, Pete Brennan's sister. Pete and Lucas served together."

I didn't need to say more than that for him to understand why she was getting Hawk protection, and invoking Lucas's name would shorten this discussion. Lieutenant Wellbourne owed Lucas more than he could ever repay, which came in handy in situations like today. Duke and I had both discharged our weapons, but neither of us would be getting more than an interview.

Wellbourne nodded. "I knew Pete—good guy."

"He was," I agreed, keeping it in the past tense. "Did you ID the guy on the street yet?" I asked.

"We'll get to that. Who shot him?"

"Who does he work for? Did you figure that out?"

He didn't give in. "How did this start?"

Keeping the Russo and Marku names out of this would make our lives easier. "Well, Duke..." I pointed to the demo room door. "...Grace and I drove into the parking lot, and the guys across the street started shooting as soon as we exited the vehicle. Duke and I returned fire. That's the whole story. There were three shooters in total. I hit that guy down on the street and winged another who drove off with the third. The escape vehicle was a black Suburban. It left southbound."

"Plate?"

"Too far for me to see, and we were busy ducking a lot of lead." I tried again. "Who's the guy and who does he work for?"

With a sigh, he gave in. "He's part of a contract hit team in from Houston."

I nodded as if I expected that answer when I really expected a Russo or Marku connection. "How did you figure out the Houston angle so quickly?"

"We got lucky with a traffic cam down the street. The black SUV was a rental picked up at the airport this morning, and the fake ID used to rent it was in the pocket of the guy you laid out on the street. He was traveling with two men."

"That tracks. They emptied several clips at us."

"The crime scene guys picked up thirty-seven casings from that side of the street so far. It's like it was fucking Beirut down there. You guys can't go shooting up the city like this."

"Trust me, it's different in Beirut. There, the tangos also carry RPGs. And we didn't start this. We only returned fire."

"I'm going to need your gun. How many clips did you expend?"

I pulled out my weapon, released the clip, cleared the chamber, and set the lot down on the desk for him. "I fired three shots total."

"You're kidding. Two hits out of three shots at that distance with a pistol?"

"Snipers don't kid," I deadpanned. "We practice."

He shook his head, then nodded toward the demo room. "So what's she mixed up in?"

"She is not 'mixed up'..." I added air quotes. "...in anything. She felt threatened, and we are providing protection."

"It's pretty heavy-duty to get a get contract hit team sent after her. Who has threatened her and how?"

"What makes you assume she was the target?"

"Are you saying you guys were the target?"

"You know better than to ask that a second time. I'd be interested to hear what that guy on the street has to say."

"We both would, but he's lawyered up already. His fingerprints ID him as Jerold Needling, formerly employed by Blackwater. Like I said, the FBI field office in Houston suspects he's part of a contract kill squad of ex-mercenaries, but they haven't been able to nail down enough evidence yet."

"Maybe now you have it."

After needling me a few more times for more information that I couldn't tell him, he gave up.

I stayed in the office, watching him through the glass as he left. Peyton wandered back to her desk.

Wellbourne was right about one thing. Involving out-of-town hitters moved this up several notches on the danger scale. Elliot had gotten himself into a pretty deep pile of shit.

Before rejoining Grace, I called Lucas to relay Wellbourne's information.

∽

GRACE

I HIT THE POWER BUTTON ON THE VR SYSTEM AFTER WE ALL TOOK OFF OUR headsets. "What do you think?"

Mr. Lim nodded at his wife.

"We love it," she said. "I can't wait to get started on the remodel." They had chosen the design that only needed one wall moved in their house instead of two.

"This is quite the setup you have," Mr. Lim said, pointing at my demo equipment. "Very innovative."

"Thank you."

"I'd like to have lunch next week to discuss investing in your company."

Like a deer in headlights, I was frozen by his suggestion.

"She's busy," Terry spoke up. "She can't make it."

I nodded in agreement, not knowing how to handle this development.

More money in the account would be great, but taking on an investor might mean giving up some control of my baby.

"The week after next, then," Mr. Lim suggested.

"She's busy then, too," Terry said firmly.

"He's right," I said as calmly as I could. "I'm very busy right now. I do appreciate the offer, Mr. Lim, and I want to think it over. I'll be in touch when I have some time available to give it my full attention."

Lim stood, an unreadable expression on his face. His wife followed suit.

My belly churned, afraid that Terry's interruption had derailed the sale.

They were cordial as they departed, but less than enthusiastic. When I shook hands with them, I sensed we'd lost the sale because of Terry. I handed them off to Peyton to see them out.

Serena and Duke stood quietly by my office door, no doubt here because of the shooting outside, but that would come second.

Stifling my rage, I waved to my best friend and her man before shoving Terry back into the demo room and closing the door.

"What?" he asked, as if we had been in different meetings.

"I only let you in here," I yelled, "because you agreed to be quiet, sit in the corner, and not be disruptive. How dare you interrupt and speak for me? I run this business, and I can make my own decisions about investors." I flailed my arms in frustration. "You doing that gorilla imitation may have cost me that investment."

Terry was unfazed, standing in front of me with his brawny arms crossed and a hint of a smirk.

Damn him. "You think this is funny? SpaceMasters is my baby. I built it up from nothing."

"No. I don't think any of this is funny. I admire your passion for the business."

That was almost nice.

"But," he raised his voice, "weren't you just downstairs when we were getting shot at?" He advanced on me and pointed a finger. "Do you think that's funny? Like it or not, your safety comes first, last, and everything in between. You will not go out in public. There will be no business dinners, business lunches, or any of that shit until this crap that Elliot has brought down on you is finished."

I backed away. "You don't need to yell at me." Of course I ignored that I'd started the yelling.

He backed me against the wall. "I will not apologize for giving a shit about you." He put his hands against the wall, caging me in. "You follow my instructions when it comes to your safety. That is not up for debate. I will not apologize for being passionate when your safety is on the line." Fiery eyes held mine with an intensity that matched the volume of his voice.

Heat bloomed in my chest. We may have gone back to arguing with each other, but that was actually a really sweet sentiment. "Are you done?" I breathed in a lowered voice.

"Not quite." His breath was warm on my face.

I licked my lips, awaiting his.

The door opened. "Hey, guys," Serena said. "This room isn't as sound-proof as you think."

∼

Terry

Serena had the worst damned timing. I pulled back, releasing Grace from the wall.

"Oops," Serena said as her eyes shifted to us.

Grace's cheeks were flushed as she moved away from the wall. "I think we're done with our discussion."

"Totally," I agreed.

Duke walked in behind Serena. "Sorry, man, I couldn't stop her."

I nodded. Serena could be an unstoppable force.

Jordy, Constance, and Zane followed Duke in.

Serena punched Duke in the shoulder. "I needed to make sure my girl was all right."

Duke rubbed his shoulder, although I doubted Serena could possibly hit hard enough to hurt him. "She's his girl first."

I couldn't hold back the smile. "Damned straight." I gathered Grace against me, and she didn't resist.

Jordy held out his hand. "Hey, I need the keys to your place."

"Why?"

"Because of what Thomas Edison once said." Lucas's ice-cold voice announced his presence before he appeared. "What's that, Duke?" It was his turn to get quizzed.

Duke hesitated only a second. "'Good fortune is what happens when opportunity meets with planning.'"

Lucas nodded.

"Which is?" I questioned.

Constance spoke up. "To be ready for them. Your name will be in the police report regarding the shooting downstairs, and your place could become a target. Jordy is going to link your security system into Hawk."

"And video's of the shooting have already gone viral on the internet," Jordy said. "I think the best one is this clip." He pointed his phone toward us. "Of you and the rest of Grace's team facing off against this other dude." It was me putting Sakman in his place, with most of Grace's employees in the background.

Lucas stepped forward. "Sending an out-of-town hit team after Grace is a serious escalation. We're going to be prepared if they decide to come back at you tonight, and once we figure out which group hired them, we'll go after them. I will not allow this to stand."

"I think it's Elliot they were after," Grace mumbled.

Lucas looked first to me and then Duke.

"I can't say one way or the other," Duke responded.

"When this whole thing started," I said, "their plan was to get Grace in order to lure out Elliot. I think Grace is right. It's more likely that Elliot was the target. Shooting her doesn't advance their agenda."

Grace cringed.

Lucas nodded. "That takes a bit of the pressure off, but we're still not going to let our guard down tonight. Duke, Zane, and Constance are providing backup at your place. Winston and I are on call if you need us. Jordy, you need to locate Amir Marku. One way or another, he's going to hear from me." He pivoted to Grace. "Any idea where Elliot would slink off to?"

She shook her head. "The warehouse was my only idea."

Serena moved next to Grace and took her hand. "I'll be with you too."

Grace smiled and nodded. "Thanks."

"Let's get to it," Lucas announced.

CHAPTER 30

Grace

With Constance and Zane keeping watch outside, and Terry, Duke, and Jordy messing with the security system and adding cameras, Serena and I were free to hang out.

"Do you have any wine?" my best friend asked. "I feel like a glass to take the edge off."

I nodded in agreement and went to check the fridge. "Dammit, Clyde." My cat almost tripped me. "Over here he's always underfoot like I'm going to leave him. He so wants to get back home to my apartment."

"I think this is a pretty nice place." She shrugged. "At least you can find him."

"It is nice, but it's not mine. The cats need us to be home."

Terry's place was much bigger than mine, and the tracker collar had been invaluable this morning in finding Bonnie. "The other cat will only show herself if I open a can of tuna."

Serena cocked her head. "*They* need it, huh?"

I nodded. "I'm only here until the danger is over. They're not happy."

"The cats? What about you?"

"What about me?"

"Why wouldn't you want to stay?"

Her question was nonsensical. I stared at her until the refrigerator beeped at me for keeping the door open too long. I closed and opened it again. "Because a week ago, I hated him and he hated me."

Serena shook her head. "Earth to Grace—he never hated you."

Remembering Terry's words, I gave in. "Maybe so, but he treated me like crap."

"And now?"

I couldn't hide it from my best friend. "He's been great, and I think…"

She waited patiently.

The fridge beeped again.

"I know it's too fast, but I think I've fallen for him, the Terry I see now."

"Trust me." A dreamy look came over her face. "When it's right, there's no such thing as too fast. It was the same with me and Duke."

I considered that… *When it's right, it's right.*

"Now where's that wine?" Serena asked.

I looked back inside the fridge. Terry had two choices. "Pinot grigio or Chardonnay?"

"Either."

"Life is about making choices." I reminded her of her own words.

She giggled. "The pinot."

I brought over the bottle and glasses and flopped down.

"You look tired."

I twisted the corkscrew in. "I think all afternoon I was running on adrenaline from the shooting, and now that it's worn off, it's catching up with me." With a pop, the cork came out, I poured for both of us. I'd thrown myself into work all afternoon as an escape from the dread.

Serena took her glass and sipped. "Watching you this afternoon, I was surprised at how little this morning seemed to affect you. If they'd been shooting guns at me, I would've wet myself and hidden in a closet for the rest of the day."

I rolled my eyes. "Give me a break. You're the strongest woman I know. You survived a car bomb."

She nodded slowly. "That was a bad day."

"I was at work today. For my people, I have to be the adult. I can't show fear. When we lost the Archer Brothers account last year, I had to be the one to tell them it was no big deal and shelter them from the truth that it cost us almost two hundred thousand in custom materials. I almost didn't make payroll the next month." I sipped from my glass. It went down cold.

"You don't have to take all the responsibility on yourself."

I stared into my glass for a second, looking for an answer other than the one I knew. None appeared. "Yes, I do. They depend on me. Their families need the paychecks I write."

"They're adults. You should tell them what's happening. Be honest with them. They could be a support to you as well."

"But I don't know what the truth is. I don't know when this is going to end."

"Terry and the guys will find your cousin and this Rudi character and put an end to this madness," she assured me.

"Hey, ladies," Duke said as he arrived with Terry just behind him. "Solving the world's problems?"

Serena lifted her glass. "Just waiting for our men to stop playing."

He came up behind her and leaned over to nuzzle her ear. "Playing? This is serious stuff—camera angles, encrypted connections, and shit."

She turned and rose up to give the big guy a seriously wet kiss. "I bet two teenagers from Best Buy could have finished it quicker."

He pulled back with a smirk, but didn't break contact with her, keeping a hand on her hip. "No way. It's technical as hell the way Jordy links this stuff together."

I noticed that crinkle at the edge of Serena's eye. She was toying with him.

He looked around the kitchen, sliding his hand up her side and pulling her close. "We put you in charge of cooking dinner, and I don't see much progress."

"We outsourced," she told him. "Pizza will be here any minute."

I looked away. Their dynamic was cute as hell. Would Terry and I be this comfortable around each other soon?

"Did I hear pizza?" Jordy said, rounding the corner. "Hey, get a room."

AN HOUR LATER, MOST OF THE PIZZA HAD BEEN DEVOURED.

Serena and I were cleaning up while Jordy, Duke, Terry, Constance, and Zane all worked on laptops.

Jordy had parceled out territories to each of them to comb through CCTV footage that had been triggered by the search for Rudi Sanchez. He said there were so many hits to check because they didn't have a clean photo of him for facial recognition to work with.

"Got another possible," Constance announced.

Jordy got up to check it out. "I'll put it on the list."

Dying of boredom, I caught Terry's eye. "What's the plan for tomorrow?" What I really wanted was to go to bed with my man and pretend we could ignore the killers we knew were out there.

Terry left his seat on the other side of the table to sit next to me.

As soon as his big hand took mine, it made a huge difference.

"Tonight the four of us take watch shifts," he said. "Tomorrow you go to work and do your normal thing. Two of us will be with you. Everybody else will be locating this Rudi turd. Lucas is even bringing on some contract help. Then when we catch him, you can put this entire episode behind you."

I grasped his arm and leaned my head on his shoulder. "Promise?"

"I promise." He kissed the top of my head. "Why don't you go and get some sleep?"

I straightened up. "What about you?" With the awful premonition that tomorrow would be even more dangerous than today, the last thing I wanted was to sleep in an empty bed.

"I'll join you when I can."

~

Terry

WE'D FLIPPED COINS FOR WATCH ASSIGNMENTS, AND I ENDED UP OUTSIDE, IN the car. Constance drew the roaming slot outside with me.

Duke made the mistake of offering to swap with her.

She almost bit his head off. *Lady* was not a term that applied to her when she got riled. She was tough as nails and refused any accommodation.

A half hour in, a light from the doorway surprised me. Zane walked out, waved, and started my way.

I lowered the window. "Out for a stroll?"

"I thought I'd relieve you."

I checked my watch. "You're not on for hours. You should be catching some shut-eye."

"I'm a SEAL. We don't need no fucking sleep, so why don't you go inside and get some, jarhead?"

"Marines pull their own weight, sailor boy."

He put his hands up. "Didn't mean any disrespect. It's just that you've got a woman inside who needs you, and...I don't."

As tempting as the offer was, it wouldn't be fair. "I'll stand my shift, but thanks."

"Lucas said you'd say that."

That surprised me.

"He also said to tell you it was an order."

My cock insisted that I stop arguing. Lucas was the boss, after all. I opened the door and climbed out, slapping Zane on the back. "In that case, thanks, man."

"I got your back. You know that."

I nodded. "Thanks again."

Once inside, I waved to Jordy and slipped silently into my bedroom. With the sliver of moonlight that came in through the curtains, I was able to see as I shucked my clothes and sat on the side of the bed.

"I've been waiting for you," a sleepy Grace said. She pulled back the covers.

I slid in next to my warm woman.

CHAPTER 31

Terry

The next day, as we drove toward the third house Lucas wanted us to check out, Jordy's voice came through the car's speakers. "I'm conferencing in Constance. She has something she wants to pass along."

She and Zane were assigned to watch Grace today, while Duke searched for Elliot.

I braced for the complaint that Grace wasn't following our security protocols.

"Guys," Constance said, "one of my contacts passed along an update. The Secret Service now believes the plates being used to print the local funny money are being sold."

"Are you saying you think it's printing plates in the case?" Winston asked. "Not cash?"

"It fits the facts," she confirmed. "Plates would be worth that much or more, and they're small enough to fit in one of those cases."

"That makes more sense than any of the other scenarios," Jordy agreed.

I nodded along. "Thanks, Constance. We're getting close, so I'm going off speaker."

"Good hunting," Constance said.

I switched over to the earbud. "Sound check."

"Five by five," Jordy replied.

Winston drove us around the block in a quiet neighborhood in Santa Monica. This was the third house Jordy had sent us to check out.

"Park in front of the gray house, ten forty-one," Jordy told me.

"Roger, gray house, ten forty-one," I repeated as I pointed.

Winston pulled to the curb at that location.

Jordy had a drone high in the air above us. "That's good right there," he said. "The target is the gray-blue house directly behind the house you're parked at. You can approach now."

We started around the block on foot, and would use the opposite sides when we reached the target street.

"Slow down," Jordy said in my ear. "Dog walker about to turn the corner."

I slowed. "Man and dog," I whispered.

Winston matched my pace. "I think the Dodgers need a new shortstop."

"I'm with ya on that," I agreed. Two guys talking sports were invisible in this town.

We yakked it up until the man walking his Pomeranian turned the corner.

"Did you see that little thing?" Winston commented when the dog and owner were out of sight. "The guy should have some self-respect."

"Not the dog for you?"

"Hell no. I'd get a real man's dog, like a shepherd or a Doberman, not a freaking purse dog."

I laughed. "I know what you're getting for Christmas."

"Don't you fucking dare."

We casually crossed the street. You never knew who might notice movements that didn't fit the neighborhood.

I went up to the door, and Winston stopped short and turned to watch the street. "Clear."

Crouching, I worked the lock picks on the door.

We'd already determined the house didn't have any cameras, and Jordy's drone hadn't picked up any heat signatures inside. We knew we wouldn't catch Rudi here, but we hoped to find evidence that this was his hideout.

"Car," Winston said.

I left the door and ducked behind a bush while he pretended to study his phone on the sidewalk. Letting ourselves into a house was problematic, to say the least, but with Grace's life on the line, I was all in.

The car passed, and Winston checked both directions. "Clear."

I started again with the tools and got a slight click. The locking cylinder turned. I pocketed my tools and turned the knob. "We're in."

Winston followed me in and closed the door. "This place stinks."

There were discarded pizza boxes, empty burger wrappers and other trash strewn around.

Winston and I pulled out our tactical flashlights and began scanning the front room and the kitchen.

"Somebody's definitely been squatting." Winston coughed as he searched through the trash. "You see any yet?"

We were looking for a specific snack food that Elliot had told us Rudi liked.

"Yup. Pig ears located." I held up two empty bags of smoked pig ears. Elliot said Rudi liked to chew on these damned dog treats while he worked. I sniffed a bag. "Not for me."

"Fucking disgusting," Winston agreed. "But this might not be him. Could just be a guy with a dog."

"Anything else?" Jordy asked.

"Nothing else in the common space unless you want moldy pizza," I reported. "Moving to the bedrooms."

"Copy that," Jordy said.

I moved down the hall and into the first bedroom. "Bingo," I announced.

"What do you have?" Jordy asked in my ear.

"Laptop and what looks like tracking sheets." The pad of paper next to the computer had a series of numbers crossed out.

Winston joined me and flipped over several pages. "Yeah, man. He's been tracking his combo attempts." The sheets showed a set of numbers increasing by hundreds, each one crossed out. Rudi had definitely been here.

A check of the nightstand, dresser, and under the bed came up with zilch. "No case in the first bedroom."

My earbud came alive. "Lucas says to finish quickly and vacate before the target returns.

"Fast search and boogie," I repeated for Winston.

"Tell Lucas I want to stay and wait for the target," Winston said.

"Winston wants to stay for the target's return," I told Jordy.

"Negative," came the reply. "Lucas doesn't want to risk an uncontrolled situation with explosives in play. When you're done, vacate and leave it the way you found it. We'll surveil and bag him when he's a safe distance from the case."

"Roger."

Winston checked the closet. "If it was me, I wouldn't leave ten mil lying around when I left the house. I'd backpack it with me." He stopped, then pointed to some dirt on the carpet at the edge of the closet and motioned for me to keep the conversation going. Seems he'd found something that made him suspect we were being overheard.

"That makes sense." I moved closer to get a look.

Winston leaned over and outlined a rectangular crease in the carpeting, then pointed down. It was a cutout to access the subfloor. He thought there was a chance Rudi was underneath us.

I pointed at the floor and spoke loudly. "Orders are to leave."

"Copy that," Winston huffed out, unhappily.

We walked to the front door, where Winston stopped and held up a closed fist.

I stopped.

He put his finger to his lips, opened the door, counted to five on his fingers, and then closed it loudly.

We turned toward the hallway and silently crept closer, stopping at the end of the hall.

Winston tapped his watch and held up five fingers.

"What's the holdup?" Jordy asked in my ear. With a drone in the air, he knew we hadn't exited.

I tapped the earbud three times without saying anything.

Jordy got the message. "Copy that. Standing by."

My heart rate hadn't slowed since Winston pointed out the subfloor access. We could be standing over a very nervous guy with an explosive case that could blow this whole house sky high.

It only took two minutes before we heard the sound of the floor panel being displaced around the corner.

Winston positioned himself against the wall on one side of the hallway entrance, and I hugged the wall on the opposite side.

After more scuffing sounds and some huffing and a cough, we finally heard the sound of shoes approaching on the hardwood of the hall.

When he reached us, Winston snatched the case, quick as a snake.

I wrenched Rudi's arm behind him and slammed him against the wall. "We've been looking for you."

"Don't hurt me," he squealed. "I have two more days before the deadline, and I'm getting close."

"Shut up," I hissed as I patted him down for weapons. He wasn't armed, but I pocketed the phone and wallet I found.

He whimpered. "Who are you guys?"

"Shut up," I told him again. A deadline was news. "We'll talk later." It was never a good idea to speak to a suspect right away, as we might give away how little we knew. "Both packages are secure," I told Jordy.

"Copy that," Lucas said. "Good job. Now get them back here for a debrief. And be careful with that case."

"Roger that, sir." It felt good to get a verbal pat on the back from Lucas. He wasn't effusive with praise. "Back to Hawk," I told Winston.

"What's Hawk?" Rudi asked. "Marku didn't send you?"

"No talking." I twisted his arm higher, and he yelped. "Any more noise from you, and I break it. Nod if you understand."

He nodded vigorously, and I released his arm. "I changed my mind. If you make a sound, I'll just shoot you. It's easier."

He went pale and nodded again.

"And then I'll shoot you," Winston added.

"The three of us are walking out the front door and strolling around the block, easy as can be."

I led the way with Rudi, and Winston followed. But we hadn't made it to the door before I halted. "Hear that?"

Winston nodded. "Fucking A." It was police sirens approaching and not far away.

"Jordy, we hear sirens," I said.

Jordy's voice lost its cool tone. "Hold fast one—shit. You're blown. Cops incoming, three blocks out."

I swallowed hard. That wasn't enough time to get out the door and around the corner.

Grace

Constance was in my office with me today, and Zane was outside. Lucas had assigned them to be my bodyguards at work. Terry and the others were on the hunt for the case that everybody wanted, which meant finding Rudi Sanchez, if Elliot could be believed.

For purely selfish reasons, I'd wanted Terry to be with me, but Lucas had insisted that Terry knew the city better than Zane, and that was the end of that discussion.

"You really have it bad, don't you?" Constance asked after I finished my sales spiel over the phone to a new potential client.

"Pardon?" I wasn't following.

She moved from across the room to the chair in front of my desk. "Your feelings for Terry." She pointed at the compass I had my finger on. I'd played with the tiny thing all during my customer call. It had been a present from Terry this morning.

I sighed. "Surprising, I know. If you'd told me last week how I'd be feeling about him now, I would have laughed my head off."

"*Keep this with you,*" Terry had said when he'd placed the compass in my hand. "*It'll help when it comes time to make a decision about Elliot. Always knowing which way was north helped me when I was deployed.*"

He'd been referring to the difficult decisions he'd faced as a sniper about if and when to shoot. Elliot had dug himself one hell of a hole, and I didn't see a way out of it for him.

Constance nodded. "I'm happy for you. He's one hell of a good man."

"That he is." Smiling, I remembered exactly how good he'd been to me last night and this morning.

"I have to admit," she continued, "I wasn't originally in favor of this thing between you two."

As the woman on the team, I would have thought she'd be supportive. "And now?"

She leaned forward to place a comforting hand on mine. "I'm happy for both of you. My training dictated that we needed to keep emotional distance from our protectees to be objective about risks."

I nodded.

"But now that he's not the only one on the case, and I see how happy you've made him, I'm rooting for you both."

"Thank you." It was more than a blush the way her words warmed me. To hear that she thought I made him happy was a gift.

TERRY

"Shit," Jordy exclaimed. "We're blown. Some neighbor must have seen you. Cops inbound. Exfil back fence."

"Roger, exfil back fence." I turned and pointed to the back of the property. "Cops on the way."

Winston double-timed to the back door with the case.

I pushed Rudi ahead of me. "We're going out the back."

"But there's a fence," he complained.

"Simple, we go over it." The sirens were getting closer.

Winston reached the fence first. "There better not be a dog." He handed me the case and was over in an instant.

I heard the rip of fabric as he landed, but no barking. I handed the case over the fence to him before hefting Rudi up. "Over you go." Lucky for both of us, he was on the scrawny side.

"I got ya," Winston said, as Rudi went over the top.

"Expedite. Cops at the front door," Jordy announced.

"Roger," I repeated as I climbed over and hand signaled to the street.

We casually walked to the Porsche. I kept a firm grip on Rudi's arm, but otherwise we were just three buddies out for a stroll.

With no cops in sight, I climbed in back with Rudi, and Winston took the wheel.

"So who are you guys?" Rudi asked after Winston's door closed.

"We're the good guys. Now, no more talking until we get where we're going."

After we buckled in, Winston started the car and slowly drove off. Jordy's instruction came two blocks later. "Looks like you're clear."

Lucas added, "Back to the nest. I want to talk to Sanchez."

Talk didn't imply he would be gentle about it.

"Roger that," I answered.

I hung up the call. "Back to Hawk. He says we're clear."

Winston nodded and turned left. "I hate nosy neighbors. This was a good pair of pants." The suit pants he'd worn today had a nasty rip in them.

"It could have been worse," I reminded him. "We could have gone out the front door and had that nosy neighbor following us around the block to our ride."

He shook his head. "Fuck, yeah."

I tapped the silver case and looked over at a terrified Rudi. "But it all worked out."

"Copy that," Winston said.

"Are you guys military?"

Shook my head; Rudi didn't get it. I punched him hard in the shoulder. "What did I say about talking?"

He cowered against the door.

Today I hated nosy neighbors, too. Combat was one kind of stress, but at least you could shoot back. Being cornered by the cops without a good excuse for being in that house was a different animal.

CHAPTER 32

Terry

Lucas was waiting, arms folded over his chest, as Winston parked us in the garage under Hawk. The boss's expression was as cold as I'd ever seen.

Joe had the hood up on Lucas's Cayenne.

I exited the car with Rudi in tow and handed him over to Lucas.

"Mr. Sanchez," Lucas said. "You and I are going to have a very honest talk.

"But I don't know nuthin'," Rudi protested.

"In that case…" Lucas pulled out his phone. "I'm going to call Tony Russo and claim the reward for finding the man who stole from him."

Rudi went white as a sheet. "Hold on. That wasn't me."

Lucas shrugged. "Tell it to him. I hear he takes special guests out on his boat to swim in the ocean."

We'd all read the story in the *Times* about when one of Tony's rivals' shoes had turned up in a shark's stomach. *Horrible.* I'd faced bullets, but there was something about being eaten by an animal that elicited a primal fear.

"No. You can't."

Lucas grabbed Rudi. "I can and I will if I think you're holding a single thing back."

"I'll tell you everything. You just gotta let me go."

"Right," Lucas agreed. He looked at Winston. "Which of the rooms is ready to use?"

I'd seen this skit make more than one tough guy pee himself.

"Number one," Winston answered. "They're still trying to get all the brain matter off the walls of number two."

Rudi looked ready to barf.

"Let's go," Lucas said as he towed Rudi off. "If you pee on my carpet, I'm going to be very upset."

Winston pulled the silver case from the car. "What do we do with this briefcase bomb in the meantime?"

"Get that thing outta here," Joe yelled. "How dare you bring a fuckin' bomb into my garage?"

Lucas looked back. "The terrace is probably the safest place for it."

That made sense—a blast on the terrace would do a lot less damage than one under the building.

"My money's on Lucas getting the truth out of him," I said after the pair turned the corner.

Winston shook his head. "No way am I taking that bet."

"Hey," Joe yelled. "Will you guys stop jabberin' and get that fuckin' bomb outta my garage?"

I let Winston carry it. I'd seen the effects of too many IEDs to want to be anywhere near explosives.

I felt better once the case was headed for the terrace, but something still didn't feel right, so I strode to holding room one and opened the door without knocking. "Boss, I should be doing this. He put my woman in danger."

The boss turned, and his dark eyes drilled into mine. "You think so?"

No man had ever scared me until I met Lucas Hawk. Anyone who wasn't scared of him had shit for brains. "Yes, sir," I answered without hesitation. The responsibility should be mine. "He put my woman in danger. I should get revenge."

Rudi shrank in his seat.

Lucas scooted his chair back and stood. "I see your point. Keep in mind, if he barfs, it had better be in the bucket, or the cleanup is on you."

"Copy that," I said, taking the chair he'd vacated.

Rudi glanced down at the plastic bucket by his feet. "I swear," he started, even before the door closed after Lucas.

"Shut up." I let him stew for a few seconds.

Rudi squinted at me. "So you're the good cop?"

I laughed. "You've been watching too much TV. This is the real world.

I'm the bad cop." I took out my knife and unfolded it. "He's the worse cop."

Rudi swallowed. "What do you want to know?"

I leaned forward. "Put your hand on the table." It was an old oak piece I'd fashioned with numerous gouges and dark stains.

"What?"

"You heard me. Hand on the table."

He complied. "Why?"

"Because a wrong answer is going to cost you a finger."

He threw up into the bucket, right on cue.

While he did that, I refolded the knife and put it away. I'd made my point. "Now, start from the beginning and take it slow. How did this go down?"

Rudi wiped his mouth on his sleeve. "Elliot and I had been talking a while about getting together enough money to go down to this place my family has in Colombia."

I nodded. That part at least matched Elliot's story.

"Elliot heard there was a big courier gig coming up."

I got up and grabbed a pad of paper from the corner table. "How big?"

"Ten million?"

That matched what Russo had said he'd told everybody, although he'd admitted to Lucas and me that the real number was twenty million. "Go on."

"Elliot said this was our chance."

I returned to the table and wrote the ten-mil number down. "It was Elliot's idea?"

"Of course. Except it was really Paulo's idea to do it. But Elliot got the case and decided to do Paulo's idea himself."

"Who's Paulo?"

"The dude who was assigned to make the delivery. At least that's what I heard. He was the one who thought of it."

"And you just went along for the ride?"

"Uh, yeah."

The hesitation in his voice prompted me to bring out my knife again.

Rudi's eyes went wide. "Okay, okay. I mean, I agreed that it sounded like a good idea—a lot of fucking money."

I put the knife down, still closed. "How did a fuckup like Elliot end up doing such a big delivery?"

Rudi smirked. "He and Paulo went out the night before. The morning of the job, Paulo calls in sick with food poisoning." He snickered. "Pretty unlucky for Paulo, huh?"

I nodded. "Meaning Elliot took his place to get his hands on the case?"
He nodded.

"You willingly participated?"

"For that much, sure."

"How did you figure to get into the case?"

His face lit up. "That was the easy part. Elliot brought one of them home with him one night. It had been opened, so I took a look at how it was wired. They did a good job of gluing a mass of crossed trip wires on the inside so you couldn't cut into it. Cut one of them and—" His hands went up in the air. "Kaboom."

"You said it was easy."

"Okay. They had the left-hand lock rigged so the right combination deactivated the circuit. But if you tried the clasp without the right combination…" He cocked his head. "Not good."

"Kaboom," I suggested.

"Uh-huh. But…" He raised a finger. "They left the right-hand one alone, which meant I could try all the combinations on that side, and only try the left one when I had figured out the combination." He smiled broadly. "I was almost there when you guys came along."

"What if they set the two sides to different combinations?"

His face dropped. "Oh…"

He hadn't thought of that.

"What were you going to do with the merchandise? Pawn it?"

"That's the cool part. Elliot went to the buyer and offered to sell it to him for half."

"Five million?" I wrote the number down.

"See? It's perfect. Marku gets whatever it is for half price, and we get paid five mil for snatching it for him."

Rudi had no idea what was really inside and didn't care.

"Marku already paid Russo half the money," I pointed out.

"He'd get his money back, and we'd be long gone to Colombia."

He was a moron if he thought it was that simple.

"Where's Elliot?"

"I don't know. I was supposed to stay hidden where even Elliot didn't know where I was. I'm supposed to call him when I get it open, and he'll take it to Mr. Marku."

Calling the gangster Mr. Marku made him sound like a simple businessman who would uphold his end of a deal, which I doubted.

"What's to keep Marku from killing you two and getting it for free?"

Rudi's mouth dropped open.

I shook my head. He wasn't cut out for dealing with mobsters.

Retrieving his phone from my pocket, I opened it. It was a burner without even a PIN code, and the only contact was E. I closed the device and stood.

"I can go now?" Rudi asked hopefully.

"No."

"But—"

"I'm the bad cop, remember?"

I locked the room on my way out. Upstairs, I joined Lucas in his office. Winston followed me in, and I gave them both the story Rudi had spun for me.

"Hey, Jordy?" Lucas called after I finished.

"Yeah?" came his voice from around the corner.

"Call Duke back in. We have a line on Elliot."

"How does this tie into the hit squad yesterday?" Winston asked.

Lucas steepled his hands. "I don't know. Maybe Russo got tired of waiting and went after Elliot as a warning to his other couriers. Since I can't prove he hired that crew, he can claim he didn't violate our agreement."

It sounded tenuous to me, but possible. "It still could have been Marku. And those guys are still out there."

Lucas nodded. "At least we now have the case and can get our hands on Elliot, which is all we need to get Grace off Russo's radar."

I spoke up. "The toad might deserve it, but I don't think Grace will want us to hand over Elliot."

"That's one way to go," Lucas commented. "Or we could send Elliot back to Russo with the case and it's up to him to convince Tony that he got ripped off by his roommate, and it took a few days to track him down and get it back."

"Send the roommate down to Colombia, and that has a chance of working."

I pushed again in Grace's interest. "He is a pretty accomplished liar, but I don't like the odds."

"Unless you have a better idea, I'll call Marku and Russo to tell them we found the case, and I'll hand it over to Russo tomorrow," Lucas said. "That should at least take the Houston team off the board for now."

"Sounds good." I very much liked the idea of not having a professional hit squad around.

~

Grace

. . .

Constance sat in the corner of my office, much less intrusive than Terry had ever managed.

Peyton knocked once and poked her head in. "Don't forget, after lunch you're due at the Garcias' for their measurements, and the four-oh-five is backed up."

Constance stood. "She's not going anywhere." The ex-Secret Service agent might be short, but when she wanted to be authoritative, she had the in-charge voice down pat.

"But we talked about this yesterday." Peyton pointed her argument at me. "She insisted on having you involved, remember?"

I did remember, but after the shootout on the street outside our building yesterday, I was done arguing with my bodyguards. This time I allowed my business to take a back-seat to my personal desires. "Sorry, it looks like I'm grounded."

"Okay," Peyton said, drawing out the word. "I'll cancel it."

I shook my head. "Don't cancel. Send Marci with Paul. I'll apologize later." If we lost this sale, so be it.

"You got it," Peyton said and left.

When the door closed, Constance retook her seat. "I know our rules can feel stifling, but it's necessary. Terry and the guys are working the search hard. You'll be done with us soon enough."

"I hope so. These people and their families depend on me." Then I asked a question I'd always avoided with Constance. "What was it like protecting the First Lady?"

She sat back in her chair. "Boring when she was at the White House, which was most of the time, and very long days when she took a trip."

"Do you miss it?"

"Not for a minute. Lucas is the best boss anyone could want in this kind of business, and the guys are great."

I checked my watch and tapped it. "It's time for me to make a few customer calls, if you don't mind."

She rose. "I'll be right outside with Zane."

Before I could start my first call, my phone rang. My heart sped up when I saw that it was Terry. "Hi. I miss you, Rambo." It was a silly thing to say, but it was the truest I could be.

"Kitten, I miss you too. Look, we found Rudi and the shipment that Elliot lost."

"Really?" I squeaked. "That's great, right?" Finally, a light at the end of this terrible tunnel. "And Elliot?"

"We haven't caught him yet, but having the case to give back to Russo means this is almost over for you."

I took in a huge breath. "So I can go out?" Warmth flowed over me as I envisioned myself walking to Starbucks in the sunshine without a bodyguard.

"Not so fast, Tiger. Not until Lucas gets agreements from the bad guys that everything is settled. Kitten, I gotta go now. Stay safe."

It wasn't as good a sendoff as *love you*, but I mirrored his words. "You stay safe too." With the craziness behind us, we'd soon have a moment to talk.

∼

AFTER LUNCH, I HAD JUST FINISHED A CUSTOMER FOLLOW-UP WHEN MY cellphone rang. The screen read *unknown number*, but Mrs. Fletcher had said her husband was going to call me. "Hello?" I answered cheerily.

"Don't move," the cold male voice said. "I can see you. Your pretty little assistant, Marci, will die if you try to alert that short lady or your other guard dog." His voice was pure evil.

A chill ran down my spine as I heard sobbing in the background. Quickly, I swiveled my chair to look out the window. The asshole had to be in one of the taller buildings around us, if he could see into my office.

"I see you looking for me. That's good. Stay facing the window." Mr. Evil added a sinister laugh. "I have a knife to pretty Marci's face. Say hi, girl."

My heart lodged in my throat when I heard Marci whimper in the background, "Please don't hurt me."

"If you phone anyone, I slit her throat. I can see into your office. If you try to write a note or send a message, I slit her throat. Nod if you understand."

I nodded. "Please don't hurt her." Marci's innocent face was all I could think of.

"Follow my instructions exactly, and she'll be just fine. Otherwise I'll cut her again and again so you can hear her scream as she bleeds out." Mr. Evil laughed.

Sadistic fuck. I shifted the phone to my non-trembling hand and whispered, "What do you want?"

"Put your phone on silent—we don't want any noise calling attention to you—and do exactly as I say."

CHAPTER 33

GRACE

THE TREMORS IN MY HAND GOT WORSE AS I WAITED FOR HIS INSTRUCTIONS, still facing the window.

Marci sobbed in the background. "Shut the fuck up," Mr. Evil said. "You're going to leave the building and walk south to the bus stop," he told me. "Sit down, and I'll call you there with further instructions. Nod if you understand."

Gripping the phone angrily, I nodded. I didn't know how, but this fucker was going down for threatening one of my people. Terry's threat about a bullet sounded a lot better right now. There was a special place in hell for someone who would threaten to murder a sweet girl like Marci.

"You're going to leave the building now without anybody following you, and without letting any of those guards know you're gone. You understand me?"

"How?"

"You figure it out. Sweet Marci is depending on you. If I see anyone following you, she dies…painfully. If you're late—"

"I get it, asshole. I'll get there." Maybe that wasn't the smartest thing to say, since I had no idea how to do that yet, but I refused to cower. I'd find a way for Marci. I had to. Then I'd let Terry loose on him.

Marci cried uncontrollably.

"Shut up, bitch," he said angrily. "Or I'll tape your mouth shut."

"You can't do that," I told him. "She has asthma."

"Another reason for you to hurry." He laughed. "No funny business—"

"You have to let her go if I come to you."

"Of course." He laughed that evil laugh again. "I can't wait to get rid of her. You have five minutes. Remember, I'm watching you. Warn your guards, and she dies. Tick-tock, tick-tock." The line went dead.

It was decision time. I stayed facing the window. But there weren't any alternatives, so there wasn't a decision to be made.

I clasped the tiny compass Terry had given me, and my choice was clear. Sneaking out without notifying Constance or Zane was the only way to free Marci. Knowing the Hawk people, if I let them know about the call, they'd either prevent me from going or follow me and put Marci in danger.

When it had only been about me and Elliot, calling Terry had been the smart thing to do, but calling now, or letting Constance or Zane know, would doom Marci. It might even lead the monster to attack another of my employees.

As the phone went into my big handbag, I noticed my keyring, and a plan formed. I had a key to disarm the alarm bar on the emergency exit by the bathrooms at the back of our offices. I only needed to avoid having Zane or Constance see me slipping out that way.

Noticing the Pain Pen Terry had forced on me, I shifted it to the bottom of the bag. Then I remembered the phone he'd given me. I didn't dare risk calling him, or having the phone ring when I met Mr. Evil, so I powered it off and hid it in one of the inside pockets that zipped shut. With any luck, I might get to use it later.

The tremor in my hand had stilled. Fear had turned to anger. It was time for this momma bear to take care of her people, and I would gladly Taser this guy's ass into next week. Nobody, but nobody, got to hurt my family.

Hefting the bag, I strode out of my office and looked right.

Zane looked up. Constance was nowhere to be seen.

"Where's Constance?" I couldn't risk running into her during my escape.

Zane stood. "She's on a Starbucks run."

"Bathroom," I said and turned toward the ladies' room.

Zane jogged over.

"You going to listen to me tinkle?" I chided to get him to back off.

He fell into step next to me. "Terry said to not let you out of my sight."

I stopped at the entrance to the short hallway with the restrooms.

"Maybe you could give me a little privacy and guard the hallway from here? Or do you need to come in and help me with my tampon?"

His nose wrinkled, and he pulled out his phone. "Here is good."

Success. The more masculine the man, the more the T-word affected him.

I pushed open the door to the ladies' room and looked back. Zane stood at the end of the hallway, with his back to me, scrolling on his phone.

I let the door close and tiptoed down the hall and around the corner to the emergency fire escape. Careful to keep quiet, I retrieved my keyring and located the odd key for the alarm bar. Which way did it go?

The key slipped in my sweaty hand. I tried both directions, but it didn't budge.

"Hey, man. Can I use the bathroom?" It was Paul.

"Sure," Zane replied.

In this location around the corner from Zane, but directly opposite the door to the men's room, I was out of time. Pulling out my phone, I sent a quick text to Paul.

ME: Come

Not a great message, but it was all I had time for. With my blood rushing loudly in my ears, I almost didn't make out the sound of Paul's phone chime.

His footsteps stopped, then started again, but going away rather than coming toward me.

I let out a breath. That had been close. With a very short time before Paul found my office empty, I pulled out and re-inserted the key. This time, it turned.

But had I properly disarmed it? My heart was in my throat as I pushed on the bar.

A whoosh of incoming air from the stairwell greeted me as the door opened. Quickly, I slid through and gently closed it behind me. My nerves were shot, and the sound of the door latching again might as well have been a gunshot, as loud as it sounded to me.

The clock was ticking for Marci as I hurried down the stairs and out into the alley on the side of the building. When I rushed to the street, Constance was returning with her haul from Starbucks, so I slipped back into the alley. *Tick-tock, tick-tock.* I waited until I heard the door to our building open and close.

A careful glance around the corner showed the coast was clear, and I hurried down the street to the bus stop, guessing I wouldn't have to go far if the monster could see me through my office window. My phone rang as soon as I sat on the bench.

"Good girl," Mr. Evil said. "You're going to need to hurry, because I'm getting tired of this whiny bitch here."

Marci sobbed in the background. "Please don't hurt me."

I had to get to her.

"You hear what I have to put up with?" He was a true monster. "A phone and a small box are taped under the bench to your right. Pull them out and take them with you. A Yellow Cab will arrive in a moment."

"What?"

"You heard what I said. Get the phone and box and be ready for the cab. You've seen them—Yellow Cab, like the color. Do not hang up on me."

I located the items under the bench and yanked them loose from the tape right before the Yellow Cab pulled up.

The cabbie lowered his window. "Grace Brennan?"

"That's me." As I climbed into the back of the taxi, my hand started trembling again.

"For such a long fare, I'm going to need a credit card in advance," the driver said. "You understand."

"Sure." I pulled out my Visa and inserted it into the reader he held over the seat back. Paying a fare to be abducted was a new twist.

When the taxi left the curb, the driver looked in the rearview mirror. "Settle in. It'll take a while."

"Tell him yes," Mr. Evil demanded.

"That's right."

As soon as we started off, a phone started ringing in my purse.

"Answer it," my tormentor demanded.

It was the phone I'd just gotten from the bus stop bench. "Hello?"

"Now end the call on your cellphone and slide it under the seat in front of you."

I hit the end button as requested. This was my one chance to contact Terry, and I took it.

ME: He has Marci

Then I added.

ME: Find me

If this was a movie, the cabbie would be working for Mr. Evil, so I slid the phone under the seat as instructed.

Terry

Jordy's fingers flew over the keys as multiple windows opened on the various screens on his desk and walls. His room looked like the pictures of a NASA space control room.

"Anything?" Winston asked.

"Patience." Jordy snorted. "Even greatness takes time."

Winston rolled his eyes, but we both knew the value of Jordy's talent and had long ago stopped kidding him.

Jordy was an odd bird—a nerd who also hit the gym and the dojo.

Cables ran between the laptop Winston and I had secured from Rudi's hideout and one of Jordy's large computers. Far be it for Jordy to be satisfied with one computer. He had five operating around the room, plus one opened up on a side workbench.

I knew my way around normal computer stuff, but Jordy was in a completely different league than the rest of us humans.

"How much longer?" Winston asked.

"Give my brother space to do his thing."

I hadn't heard Lucas come up behind us.

Winston backed away. "Yes, boss. I'm just eager to get this guy."

"We all are," Lucas responded.

My phone vibrated in my pocket, and I pulled it out.

> WILDCAT: He has Marci
> WILDCAT: Find me

I left Jordy's room and immediately called Grace. My heart sped up when it went to voicemail. I dialed Zane.

"Hey," he answered.

"Get Grace on the phone," I demanded.

"She's in the bathroom."

"Get her."

"She's busy doin' a woman thing."

"Get her on the fucking phone."

After a few-seconds delay, I could hear Zane's voice in the background.

"Grace, Terry wants to talk to you. Grace… Grace?" A door slammed. "Fuck. I'm sorry, man. She's not in here."

"What do you mean she's not in there?"

"I don't know. I was at the end of the hall the entire time."

I heard him running.

"Fuck, the emergency exit has been disarmed. She must have gone down the stairwell."

"You had one fucking job to do—"

Lucas spun me around. "What's going on?"

"Don't just stand there. You and Constance go find her," I said into the phone before answering Lucas. "Grace is gone." I swiped to the messages she'd sent me to show him and then admitted the bad news. "She skipped out."

Lucas shook his head. "She should have contacted you before she ran off… Jordy, we need a twenty on Grace, now."

Lucas and I joined Jordy and Winston in the office.

"She's northbound on Lucchese Boulevard, moving fast enough that it has to be a car."

She was moving away from Zane and Constance and toward us.

"Jordy, she doesn't have a car, so do your rideshare thing and find out where she's going." I pulled out my key fob. "And keep feeding me her position."

"I'm coming along," Winston called as I ran for the door.

We peeled out of the garage like a cat with its tail on fire.

Winston punched up the call on the screen as I drove.

"We've also got Zane and Constance on," Jordy told us when he answered. "I've got her phone. She's turned east on Warmwood Drive. It looks like she might be headed for the freeway."

I took the next right at speed and let the twin-turbo V8 loose. "Hold on."

Winston braced. He was no wilting violet, but I was pressing pretty hard to catch up to Grace.

"Jordy, what's her destination?"

"I don't see a ride booked under her name," he said.

That sucked. Now catching up to her was the only option.

Winston hit the mute button. "Why is she doing this?"

"Whoever it is took one of her people, and they're like family to her. She'll sacrifice herself for them." Saying it out loud made the stakes all the more real, because I was certain Grace would take any risk to help one of her people.

"She's now northbound on the four-oh-five," Jordy announced.

I unmuted the phone line. "Copy that. We're only about a minute from the freeway entrance."

"Grace planned to visit a customer's residence today for measurements," Constance said. "But I vetoed that, and she sent Marci and Paul instead."

"So where is Paul?" Winston asked.

"On it," Constance replied.

It took ten minutes of weaving through freeway traffic to get near Grace.

"You're very close to her signal," Jordy said.

"She went old school." Winston pointed. "See that Yellow Cab up there?"

I saw the taxi ahead, and a half mile later, I pulled up alongside when he moved to the center lane to pass a slower car.

"You're right on top of her," Jordy confirmed.

I didn't see her, but she could have been lying down on the backseat. I honked.

Winston held his credentials up to the window when the driver looked over, and pointed to the side of the road. When the driver didn't move over or slow, Winston pulled his weapon and tapped the window again.

This time the cabbie got the memo and quickly pulled over to the shoulder.

I parked us behind the taxi. "Jordy, it's Yellow Cab number triple three seven."

Winston beat me out of the car. "She's not here," he yelled over the traffic noise.

When I reached him, the driver rolled down his window and put his hands up. "I don't carry cash."

I holstered my SIG. "You can put your hands down. We're only looking for a woman we thought was in your cab."

"Grace Brennan?"

"That's the one. Where is she?"

Winston pulled open the back door on his side.

The driver held up a small box. "She was my fare, going all the way up to Magic Mountain, a sweet ride. But then she got out back in town and told me to take this box up to Magic Mountain."

"Found it." Winston held up Grace's phone. It was her personal phone, not the encrypted one I'd given her.

"Where in town?"

"Whippleson Drive," the cabbie said.

I held out my hand. "I need that box."

He pulled it away. "I can't. My job is to deliver it."

Opening my wallet, I pulled out three Benjamins and offered them. "Now you're being paid to deliver it to me."

He snatched the bills and handed over the box.

I shook it, then opened the box. It was empty.

We let him go and piled back into the Porsche.

The phone line to Jordy was still open. "She ditched the cab back in Santa Monica," Winston told them.

I accelerated back into traffic. "The driver said Whippleson Drive. See if you have any cameras in the vicinity."

"You got it."

"Also, Jordy, you were tracking her personal phone, right?"

"Of course."

"I also gave her one of our encrypted ones. Number seventeen, I think."

"Hold on," Jordy said.

Grace had complained about the phone and Taser when I'd given them to her. I hoped she hadn't left them behind.

"It's off," Jordy reported. "It was last active at her building. I'm going to switch to traffic cameras."

Shit. Grace didn't have the time that would take.

CHAPTER 34

GRACE

I WAS AT AN INTERSECTION, WAITING FOR THE PEDESTRIAN LIGHT TO COME ON. Mr. Evil had demanded that I get out of the taxi, and so far he'd had me walk three blocks without telling me where I was going.

"Now what?" I asked him as the light turned and I started across the intersection.

"Turn right. Go to the third building. Tell me when you reach the door in back labeled Montgomery Automotive."

The third building was a creepy abandoned warehouse with fading paint and no windows at ground level—a movie-perfect bad guy's lair.

As I walked by the second building, my stomach turned sour and my mouth went dry. This was it. Looking up, I didn't see anybody hanging over the edge, so when I reached the side of the third building, I didn't think he would be able to see me—or so I hoped.

Hugging the building wall as I walked, I pulled out the Pain Pen Terry had forced on me and checked the feel of the switches as I recalled Terry's instructions on how to use it—turn on, jam into attacker, and press button. If it hurt half as much as the Taser barbs I'd gotten, this would do nicely.

A crow cawed at me from above. Was that a good omen or bad? I had no idea.

Feeling familiar with the weapon, I stuck it, along with a real pen, in my shirt pocket. It made me look dorky, but my vengeance would be handy when I met the sick fuck who'd taken Marci.

The knot in my stomach tightened when I reached the door. "I'm at the door," I said into the phone

"Come on in." Mr. Evil made it sound like a simple invitation.

I took in a deep breath before pulling on the handle of the large metal door.

It didn't budge.

I pulled harder, and it creaked open. Inside was a dark hallway, with light spilling from a doorway near the end.

The door closed behind me with an ominous clank. Then, strong arms closed around me. "I got her," a male voice said. His breath stank of anchovies.

"Then bring her here already." Mr. Evil's voice came from down the hall.

I struggled, but it was useless as the goon lifted me off my feet and pinned my arms against my sides to carry me down the dank hallway. I kicked and got his shin. It was the best I could do.

"Bitch." He slammed my head against the wall as he walked.

Lucky for me, the wall was plasterboard and not cinder block. But I saw stars for a moment, then felt intense pain. This asshole was going to pay. It was now a toss-up which of these guys was going to get my Taser treatment first, but for now, struggling wasn't going to help me or Marci.

Anchovy Breath carried me around the corner into the brighter space that was definitely a warehouse. There were a few rooms to the left and shelves on the right all the way to the end of the building with a ton of car parts on them, everything from motors and transmissions to seats and doors.

"Goron, put her down," Mr. Evil said. "I want to see what I'm getting." The man fit the name I'd given him—partially balding, with one droopy eyelid and a scar down the other cheek.

Goron yanked my purse away.

Marci sobbed in a chair behind him. Two other thugs stood behind her.

Mr. Evil turned around. "I told you to shut up."

I stood tall. "I'm here. Now you have to let her go."

He shook his head. "I don't have to do anything. And she's been making me mad."

Goron rummaged through my purse, located the encrypted cell phone Terry had given me, and held it up. "She has another phone. It's off."

"Fix it," Mr. Evil barked.

Goron dropped the phone and stomped on it with a sickening crunch. "Fixed." He laughed.

Mr. Evil advanced on me. "I should kill her. I told you to leave your phone in the taxi."

"You told me to leave my phone. I did. That's my boyfriend's phone. He wanted me to get a new battery for it."

"Give me your watch."

I tossed it toward him, not wanting to get close enough to hand it over.

He caught it and threw the watch to Goron, who happily crunched it under his boot.

Mr. Evil's grin turned wicked. "I like this one."

"Enough talk, Marku." A slim Asian man I hadn't noticed stepped forward into the light. He wasn't a smiler. "We need the plates. Make the call."

"Hold on, Mr. Kim. You'll get your merchandise soon enough."

"You and your partner said that days ago." *Kim* labeled the Asian man as most likely Korean, and now I knew Mr. Evil was Marku, the Albanian gangster Elliot was supposed to deliver the case to.

My priority had to be Marci. "If you let her go, she won't annoy you anymore."

"I'm a businessman," he countered. "And a pretty young thing like her is worth too much to just let slip through my fingers."

"You're no businessman." Marku was a human trafficker, the worst kind of filth. I'd told Terry I didn't like guns, but in this moment I couldn't think of anything more appropriate than shooting this sick bastard between the eyes.

Marci looked horrified.

"I'll buy her freedom then," I blurted.

"You couldn't afford her." His grin said he was toying with me and enjoying it. "Besides, I already have a buyer who is interested in her."

Marci slumped in the chair. This was becoming too much for her.

Marku lifted his chin toward me. "Turn her around."

"Hands off." I slapped at Goron when he tried to manhandle me and turned completely around for Mr. Evil under my own power.

"Oh, yes," he said. "Pretty and spirited. A very good combination. You'll fetch quite the price."

Price? His words sent a shiver through me, but I refused to give him the satisfaction of seeing me afraid. "My boyfriend is going to make you wish we'd never met."

"You Americans all think you are tough, but you are weak. How you Americans say? Bring it on." He raised his arms high. "Chechens try to kill me. I spit on their graves. Russians try to kill me, yet I live. I ate the livers of the Spetsnaz men they sent for me."

"You're wasting time," Kim said. "Make the call. My boat leaves tomorrow."

Marku pulled out a phone.

He did it without argument. *Interesting.*

TERRY

"HEY, TERRY, YOU WANT TO CHECK THIS OUT AND TELL ME IF YOU THINK IT'S her?"

I rushed over.

Winston and I were back at the Hawk offices, waiting for Jordy to give us something useful from his traffic camera search. He didn't have coverage at the intersection mentioned by the cabbie, so the area to be scanned was large.

I leaned closer and squinted at the screen. "Can you sharpen it any?" The still image he had was incredibly grainy.

"This is the real world, not the make-believe shit that happens on TV. This shot is from a block away, and I can't just press a button and create detail where none exists. If the pixels aren't there, they aren't there. Try this." He ran the video forward and back a few times. "What do you think?" We were looking for Grace getting into another car, taxi, or anything to track her movements further.

"Not her." The clothing was close, but there was a problem. "This woman is opening the door with her left hand. Grace isn't a lefty."

My phone rang.

It was Constance. "I found Paul. The measuring visit was a setup. They were jumped right inside the door. They took Marci and left him tied up. And before you ask, no, he can't describe them."

"Why not?"

"They pepper-sprayed him. I'm washing out his eyes now."

"Okay, thanks." At least pepper-sprayed was a lot better than being shot.

"Jordy?" Lucas called. "Get a location on the call that just came in on my line?"

I rushed to the boss's office, with Winston directly behind me.

"Marku just called. He has her and wants to trade her for Elliot and the case, plus fifty grand."

"But we don't have Elliot," I pointed out. The fifty grand I could swing.

"He doesn't know that."

"So what did you tell him?" Winston asked.

"That it would take some time to get the money together. Have they located Marku yet?"

We'd heard from LAPD that the Marku gang had left their previous location, and nobody knew where the new hideout was yet.

"Not as of yesterday, but I'll double-check," Winston answered as he left the room, phone in hand.

"We could try the exchange without Elliot," I suggested.

Lucas stood and shook his head. "Not a good play. We need their location to arrive unannounced and catch them unprepared. At an exchange, they'll have all their soldiers and be on alert."

"The phone is a burner," Jordy yelled from his office. "Can't get a location on it."

"Fuck." I felt like slamming my fist into something. The situation couldn't get much worse. My woman was being held by a sicko. We only had one half of the ransom he wanted, and we had no way of knowing where she was being held.

"Lock that down, Marine," Lucas scolded. "We'll get her back."

Grace's last message haunted me—*find me*.

Winston reappeared. "LAPD doesn't have a twenty on them yet."

Failure was not an option. We had to find my woman. I marched back into Jordy's lair—checking more video was all we had left.

"It's quite a distance, but here's another one," Jordy said as he put another video up on the screen.

"Not her," I said dejectedly. She wasn't even close.

Less than a minute later, Jordy broke out laughing.

"What?"

"Check this out." He put up a video showing a woman walking down the street with a baby in a front pack. "Ten to one it gets away and she loses it?"

"What are you talking about?"

He zoomed in. "The cat. Who the hell takes a cat on a walk?"

As he zoomed, I saw it—it wasn't a baby in the carrier, but a fur baby, an orange tabby, a fucking cat.

Then, it hit me. "The cat tracker."

Jordy spun around. "What?"

"I changed the battery on one of Grace's cat trackers and put it in her purse. If she didn't take it out—"

"What brand is it?"

I wracked my brain. "It was tacky. Kitty something, I think."

His fingers flew across the keyboard. "HereKittyKitty, maybe?"

"It sounds right, but I can't be sure."

"I don't suppose you know what the serial number is?"

"Not a clue."

"Never mind. I'll hack in and get it from her customer profile, but it'll take some time."

"She doesn't have time," I shot back.

"Hey, man, I get it. I'm going as fast as I can."

Lucas's voice came from behind me. "Terry, let him do his thing. You bellyaching will only slow him down."

It sucked, but I left Jordy's office, feeling completely helpless. I'd always hated the wait for a mission to start, but this was the most excruciating of all, because the stakes had never been higher. Grace needed me, and I was stuck sitting on my damned hands.

CHAPTER 35

Grace

Marku returned with a grin on his face. "They'll make the trade, but first I make them wait by demanding money."

"Why wait?" Kim asked. "You and your partner are already late delivering what I ordered."

Partner?

He strode to me and lifted a few strands of my hair. "Waiting makes them more frantic to make the trade. I make them wonder what is happening to their woman."

I tried to swat his hand away, but Goron's grip was too strong.

Marku smirked. "They value you, and I can see why."

"Fuck you." I spat and got him on the chin.

He backed away, laughing. "I bet I could make you like being fucked by a real man."

Yuck. If he got anywhere near me, I'd yank his balls off and swallow them. I spat again, but it didn't reach him.

Quicker than a snake, he stepped forward and slapped me.

My head snapped to the side, my face stung, and I tasted blood. When I opened my eyes again, focusing on him was a struggle.

"Once was interesting, but any more…" He pulled a knife. "And I make your face not so pretty."

I sneered at him. "You are messing with the wrong people."

253

"Enough," Kim shouted. "I want what I paid for."

Marku wheeled on him. "Quiet. Without us, you would have nothing." The anger pumping off Kim was palpable.

"Nobody else in our business would work with you. You know that. Only we had the contacts you needed. You'll get the delivery, and nobody will ever know what it was."

"I will not tolerate failure." Kim stabbed with an angry finger before stomping off. "You will both pay."

"Put them in the room," Marku ordered with a wave of his hand.

Goron shoved me to the wall. "Stay." He whipped out a knife and cut Marci free. Then he grabbed us both and pushed us toward a doorway with a padlock on it.

Marci walked with a severe limp.

After they forced us into the room, I heard the lock snap shut. The good news was the lock meant we'd have a warning before Marku or one of his thugs came in. The bad news was there was no way to reach the lock and attempt to pick it.

"Did you hear what he said?" Marci sobbed.

I pulled her into an embrace and rubbed her back. "He's a blowhard. We're not letting anything happen to you."

"We?"

"Terry and the guys are looking for us right now. When they arrive, that bastard is going to learn a very difficult lesson."

"Zane too?" Her Zane interest hadn't diminished one bit.

"Zane too," I assured her. Recalling Terry's advice that anything could be a useful weapon, I added, "I'm going to see what we have here."

Reluctantly, she let me go.

A mattress with dubious stains lay in the corner. Above it, a set of handcuffs attached by a chain to an eyebolt in the wall was a haunting reminder of the fate that befell the women Marku captured. Two ratty chairs were farther in the room, and a metal cabinet.

"You're hurt?"

"I tried to run, and I twisted my ankle."

From the look of the swelling, she'd probably sprained it.

I examined the chairs. They were metal, but I couldn't see a way I could get a piece loose to use as a bat, and the chairs were too heavy for me to swing as a weapon.

Terry could probably heave one across the room and take a bad guy out, but no way was I capable of something like that.

The cabinet contained piles of shop towels. Then, behind one pile, I found a spray canister of carburetor cleaner. In the movies, the underdog could use a can of hairspray and a lighter to make a flamethrower. This was close, but we didn't have a way of making a flame. Still, I took the canister and closed the cabinet.

"We should sit." It was time for a frank talk.

She sat in one chair.

I settled into the other and took her hand. This was going to be hard. "If I get a chance, I'm going to attack and make a run for it."

"Do you think we can make it outside?"

"You need to stay put." With her ankle the way it was, she couldn't possibly keep up.

"But—"

I squeezed her hand. "I'll come back for you. You know that, right?"

She nodded with tears in her eyes.

"Trust me. It'll be safer for you this way. Their anger will be directed at me." The truth was that in their minds, they needed me to get their hands on the stupid case the Korean wanted. If I ran, they had to catch me.

Marci fidgeted. If she stayed put, she had value to them. If she ran, she was expendable, and they wouldn't hesitate to shoot.

Looking down at my footwear, I was damned glad I'd chosen these heeled boots instead of the cute stilettos that had called to me. These weren't as good as my Nikes, but I could run without breaking an ankle.

Marci bounced her knees. "What now?"

"We sit and wait." Sitting in the chair gave me the best chance of hiding the canister from view until it was time. I moved the writing pen from my pocket to the chair and sat on it. That way I wouldn't grab the wrong one from my shirt pocket when he was close enough to attack.

TERRY

I WAITED IN MY OFFICE, GIVING JORDY THE SPACE I HAD BEEN ORDERED TO GIVE him. I finished another lap around my desk and sat down to reread the news article on the computer screen for the millionth time.

"Don't worry," Duke said from across the hall.

I ignored him. I didn't do waiting very well. I didn't do waiting at even a first-grade level.

He was back from his morning bodyguard gig for some Hollywood starlet—or wannabe-starlet, it wasn't clear to me which—and he'd told me to *not worry* at least ten times. It wasn't helping.

I got to the end of the story with the picture of four cute little balls of white fur and stood for another lap around my desk. What the hell was the big deal about a polar bear giving birth to quadruplets?

Standing, I started another lap. Every circuit of my desk and reread of the article took up another minute and twenty seconds of the time I had to wait before I could rescue my woman.

"Jordy will find her," Duke said. "And we'll get her back." He'd been through something similar when Serena was taken, and he wouldn't admit it now, but the not-knowing had torn him up the same as it was doing to me.

"I've got it," Jordy yelled from down the hall.

I raced down to his room, even beating Lucas there. It was go time.

He zoomed the screen in on a large building not far from where she'd left the taxi. "We were wrong. She never switched rides. She walked." He'd superimposed a dotted line that ran down the street the taxi had taken and then to this building.

"Jordy," Lucas said. "Get a drone in the air and brief us on the way. Let's gear up, guys." He caught Constance's glare. "And ladies."

We all double-timed to the armory.

"Light kit today, no long, quiet," Lucas said as he opened his locker. "We don't know how many soldiers Marku has with him, and like the late, great John Wooden said, *'Failing to prepare is preparing to fail.'*"

No long meant handguns, no rifles. I grabbed two extra mags for my SIG Sauer. *Quiet* meant adding my Sabre stun gun, zip ties, and duct tape to my loadout. The stun gun and hand-to-hand attacks would make it a silent takedown rather than going in kinetic. Our handguns would be a last resort.

Constance nodded my way and pocketed her Sabre as well.

Light kit meant we'd go in with light Kevlar vests hidden under jackets instead of full body armor, and no helmets. The less-military look made it easier to sneak up on the bad guys, and also made it less likely we would scare a civilian who would get anxious and call the cops.

A minute later, we were all assembled in the garage.

Lucas laid a hand on my shoulder. "Don't worry. We'll get her back." He turned to the group. "Constance, you're with Terry. Duke, you're with me, and Zane, you're with Winston."

Constance quickly popped the trunk of my Cayenne and threw her kit in the back. I added mine.

We completed a comms check and drove out with Lucas in the lead.

"Guess what's in the building?" Jordy asked once we were underway.

"Dammit, Jordy," Lucas complained. "I don't want to fucking guess."

"Okay already, Mr. Grumpy," Jordy said. Being Lucas's brother, he got away with that shit. "It's a Marku-owned automotive used-parts warehouse taking the output of their wrecking yards, and the website says they're shut down this week and next, so no customers will be there. I'm sending you what we have for the layout."

"The drone?" Lucas asked.

"Overhead soon," Jordy responded.

Constance looked over at me. "Don't worry. We'll get them both out."

I shook my head. Everyone was telling me to not worry, but it wasn't helping.

CHAPTER 36

GRACE

I'D LOST TRACK OF TIME WHEN MARCI JERKED UPRIGHT AT THE SOUND OF someone working the lock outside the door.

I locked eyes with her. "Be calm, and it'll be all right."

"Sweep the perimeter, inside and out, all of you." It was Marku just outside. He swung the door fully open and scanned the room before entering. He wouldn't fall for a person hiding behind the door to knock him on the head when he opened it.

Terry's words came back to me. *"To get them close enough, look defenseless right up until you attack."* I slumped and lowered my eyes. Marku expected fear, so fear was what I projected.

He stepped closer and held up his phone. "My buyer wants to see what's being offered. Stand up and take off your shirts."

Marci's mouth dropped open as she looked to me.

Staying strong for her was what mattered most. I nodded and started to unbutton mine. I needed him distracted for when I made my move. "Do it," I told her. My movements stayed slow and jittery, giving him exactly what he expected. At least he hadn't told us to strip completely.

His eyes stayed glued on me as he inched closer. *Yeah, keep coming, you pervert.* He wasn't close enough yet.

I hunched my shoulders after slipping the shirt off. I'd chosen a lacy bra and panty set for Terry today and now regretted it.

"All the way," Marku yelled at Marci.

She was on the edge of losing it, but slipped her shirt off and held it in her hand as I did mine.

"I have." I waved my shirt to draw his attention away from Marci.

"Drop it," he commanded.

Not having my electrocution device handy put me at a disadvantage, but I folded my shirt with the pocket on top and dropped it into the chair behind me.

His smile was sickening as he shot pictures of both of us. Marci's chest was bigger than mine, and from the attention he paid her, that clearly appealed to him.

I was going to wipe that smile off him any second now.

He moved closer, taking many more pictures than he would need to show anyone.

As he approached, I shifted closer to her to keep the spray canister behind me.

"Take it off." He pointed at poor Marci.

Tentatively, she reached behind her back.

"You sit down," he growled at me.

He looked away as I leaned down to move my shirt and sit.

My heart raced. It was now or never. His order gave me the cover I needed. Just as Marci reached behind her, I snatched the canister in one hand and the Pain Pen in the other. I sprayed him square in the face.

He dropped the phone and backed away, screaming and clawing at his face.

I pursued him, giving him another full stream in the face.

Covering his face against the spray and in obvious pain, he tripped backwards onto the dirty mattress.

That's when I flipped on the Pen, pressed the button, and jammed it into his neck. He moaned and jerked uncontrollably as the electric shocks overwhelmed his body. He tried to yell, but it came out as a weak, hoarse moan.

I dropped the Pen and grabbed for the handcuffs. In a quick motion, I snapped one on his wrist. "Asshole." I kicked him for good measure before turning to Marci.

Her jaw was slack. She hadn't moved.

Running for the door, I called back to her. "Remember what I said."

Leaving her tore at my conscience, but I knew it was the best way to keep her safe. Expecting one or more of the goons to be guarding the door I'd come in, I sprinted down the first aisle toward the other end of the building. At the very least, there had to be emergency fire exits somewhere.

Things were going better than expected when I reached the end of the aisle without bumping into any of Marku's goons or hearing any yelling from Mr. Evil. But that didn't last long.

"The girl got away," Goron yelled. "Find her."

That sent my heart into overdrive. When I didn't see a door in either direction, I chose right. It now looked like I could make it outside, and all that remained was finding a phone to call Terry and the guys.

"Find the bitch and bring her to me," Marku's angry voice reverberated through the building. The Pain Pen had worn off.

At the corner, I turned and took in a deep breath when I saw the emergency exit sign halfway down the wall. I hated backtracking closer to where Marku was, but I didn't have a choice.

Just then, one of his thugs appeared near the exit. He saw me and yelled, "Over here."

I ducked into the first aisle I came to, then decided I needed to change aisles. I wouldn't make it down to the end before he reached this aisle, and then he'd have eyes on me. No way was I winning a footrace.

Finding a gap between what looked like a dashboard and the hood of a car, I slipped between them to get to the next aisle.

Shit. I scraped my arm on a piece of metal protruding from a dashboard. It hurt like hell, and when I squeezed it to lessen the pain, my hand came back red.

My vision narrowed. I stopped, tensed, and looked away. After wiping my hand on my hip, I settled my hands on my knees and leaned forward. Fainting now was not an option—absolutely not. Watching the end of the row, I saw the guy overshoot this aisle to go down the one I'd left.

With renewed energy, I sprinted to the end and turned the corner. The exit was just ahead.

Pushing out the door, I was temporarily blinded by the intense sunlight. As soon as my eyes acclimated, I located the street I'd walked in on to the right and ran that way.

I was free. I'd saved myself. But to save Marci, I needed to find someone with a phone. I probably looked like a lunatic running through the city in only my bra, but I needed to call Terry.

My legs pumped.

My lungs burned.

My mind focused.

Find a phone.

Call Terry.
The street was only a few strides away.

CHAPTER 37

Grace

I raced around the corner of the building and ran right into a hard chest.

"I've got you now." It was Goron.

Before I could react, he lifted me for the second time, this time shirtless.

He carried me back inside and down the same corridor, and once again, none of my struggling made any difference.

"Throw her back in the room," Marku commanded. He pointed a finger at me. "I'd gut you right now if I didn't need you."

I spat in his direction, telling him just what I thought of him.

He looked at his feet. I'd only managed to nail his shoe. "I was going to spare you this, but I changed my mind."

Goron shoved me back into the room with Marci, and I heard the lock snap shut. That was bad. I grabbed my shirt and slipped it on. Then, through the door, I heard something even worse. "Tell the men they each get ten minutes with her."

Marci gasped.

"I go first," Goron said.

"No," Marku corrected. "I go first. You can start with the quiet one. But no marks."

Goron's laugh was creepy.

The room felt twenty degrees colder.

Marci moved to the corner, cowering.

I searched, but the Pain Pen had been removed. There was nothing to do but wait. I still had fingernails and the element of surprise. Marku didn't know that Pete had given me some self-defense lessons—lessons I wished I'd practiced more.

∽

TERRY

I'D PARKED A BLOCK NORTH OF THE BUILDING, LUCAS AND WINSTON A BLOCK south.

Constance was fastening her vest when Jordy came on the line again. "You're clear to advance. They don't have anybody on the roof, but they have three pairs guarding each of the entries to the building. Image coming your way."

When it arrived, the drone image showed two men by the door we were closest to. I showed the image to Constance.

"Silence is golden here," Lucas said over comms. "Don't let them report to whoever is inside."

"Copy that," Constance said before I could.

We hurried to the corner nearest the men.

"Two down." Lucas's voice came in my ear before we even reached our guys. Of course the ex-Omega operative would be the first to get his guys down.

Constance glanced around the corner.

I followed. There was no cover at all in the alley—no way to sneak up on them.

Constance already had a coin out when I looked back. "Heads, drunk lovers. Tails, marital spat."

I hoped for tails since the last time we'd done drunk lovers, I'd been in character and copped a feel, grabbing her boob. Totally out of character, she'd kneed me in the groin. It wasn't an experience I wanted to repeat.

"Tails," she called after catching the coin.

We both hid our weapons behind us before I dragged her around the corner.

"I'm never going to a wedding again with any of your family," she yelled at me as we started toward the pair.

"Maybe they served a little too much champagne," I conceded.

"I'll slap you senseless if I catch you kissing your sister again."

"She's my half-sister," I argued as we got closer to the pair.

"Are you still sleeping with her?"

"Uh… No." I didn't sound convincing. "I was only consoling her. She lost her pet turtle."

"That's no reason to put your tongue down her throat and grab her boob."

"I lost my balance."

"You disgust me."

"You're just jealous that her tits are real."

We were getting close.

"I have no idea why I married you with that tiny dick of yours."

"I'm not that small," I argued. "Not after the surgery."

We were almost there.

She pushed me away. "I used to think it was cute that your wedding ring fit on it."

The second guard joined his friend in laughter as we passed.

I spun and jabbed my stun gun into the guard's neck. After a very short burst of crackling electricity, he slumped to the ground.

Constance had gotten her guy as well and threw me a pair of zip ties.

"Two down here as well," I said into comms. I held them down while Constance sedated each of them.

The door was unlocked, and after duct-taping their mouths, we dragged them inside and finished securing them with more zip ties.

A few seconds later, Winston's voice came over comms. "Last two secure."

"Jordy, update?" Lucas asked.

"No change," he responded. "But five more went into the building on the south side before you arrived."

"Copy. We've got the office along the south wall," Lucas said. "Winston, you and Zane sweep the interior space. Terry, you and Constance take the rooms along the north wall. Execute in three, two, one, execute."

I took the lead, and Constance followed as we hugged the wall, moving in the direction of the rooms on the plans Jordy had sent.

"No," a woman screamed.

I froze in place for a second and listened.

"Fuck you." The voice was heavy with an Eastern-European accent. "You want to play, do you?"

Constance tapped my shoulder and motioned that she would go right. She slid between the crap on the lower shelf.

"Contact," Lucas whispered over comms. "Found two of the extra five."

I crept quickly and quietly up to the corner, where I stopped and chanced a quick look.

A huge monster the size of Godzilla had Marci cornered. Two other goons looked on, laughing.

She waved a piece of wood in front of her. "Stay back."

"Three tangos at the south rooms," I whispered into comms. "Preparing to engage."

"Just one more row," Constance whispered in my earpiece.

"On the way," Zane said.

"Go slow," Lucas instructed. "We don't want to miss any in the interior."

"Roger," Winston said.

Waiting like this was torture when Marci could be hurt any second.

"Ready," Constance whispered. "You distract, and I'll take him down."

It should have been me, not tiny Constance, taking on Godzilla, but we didn't have time to argue. I stepped out. "Hey, asshole."

When Godzilla turned around, Constance leaped on his back and got him in a headlock. She was tiny, but fearless.

Godzilla gurgled and swung around wildly.

I ran forward with my SIG trained on the two others before either could get his gun out. I fired a round above their heads. "Feel lucky?"

Godzilla spun again and with his eyes bulging out, rammed Constance against a rack.

She lost her grip enough that I heard Godzilla get a breath.

I motioned to the ground with my weapon. "Drop 'em."

Constance almost got thrown when he spun again.

I aimed at one of the guys' heads, and they both threw their guns away.

Once more Godzilla rammed Constance against a rack.

Just when I thought I'd have to get involved, Marci swung her bat and caught Godzilla in the crotch.

He stiffened and fell to his knees before Constance's choke hold finally dropped him.

"Move." I waved my weapon to motivate the two I had on my right. "Where's Grace?" I yelled at Marci.

She pointed at a door. "He's got her."

I saw red, but I couldn't take my eye off these other two until Constance finished with Godzilla.

She had her zip ties out, but he was struggling.

Zane burst into the open room and trained his weapon on the two I had disarmed.

A shot came from inside the closed room. I turned, ran, and kicked the door Marci had pointed to. It didn't budge.

I drew my SIG and kicked harder.

CHAPTER 38

Grace

"Don't disturb me until I tell you," Marku barked. He stood near the door.

I gulped and stepped back.

"Don't take too long. I want my chance." Goron laughed from outside.

I heard the lock snap shut, which meant getting around Marku and making a run for it was out.

Marku just watched me.

"Get away." Marci's scream pulled my eyes to the door.

Faster than I expected, Marku leaped forward and grabbed the front of my shirt.

When I spun away, it ripped open, but at least he didn't have his hands on me. I was prepared to give him one hell of a fight.

Marci screamed again.

I had to help her. I had to find a way.

It seemed Marku could read that on my face.

"You want to help your friend?" he asked. "If you make this easy, you might have time for that."

That was a choice I didn't expect.

"What will it be? Do you want to help your friend? Submit, and I will tell Goron to stop." He shook his head. "On second thought, maybe I enjoy the fight."

"Okay." Relaxing my stance, I started to unbutton what was left of my shirt. Saving Marci was the only choice available.

"Good choice." He pulled his own shirt over his head.

With a sigh, I slid my shirt off my shoulders and dropped it to the side. His lecherous eyes stayed glued to me.

Bile rose in my throat. My skirt was next. After lowering the zipper, I slipped it down my legs, stepped out of it, and kicked it away. I was down to my lacy bra, black thong, and boots. "Hurry up and call him off."

I could hear Marci sobbing now.

I controlled the reflex to vomit and refused to show him the fear I was sure he craved. *He is going down.*

He released his belt and unzipped his pants, laughing to himself. "I bet you fuck as good as you look."

Sickened, I reached behind me to grip the clasp on my bra.

He lowered his pants.

I launched myself at him. Terry had said to never go quietly, to fight with whatever I had at hand. I knew in my gut that with sick fucks like this, submitting wouldn't save either of us.

With his pants down around his ankles, he couldn't avoid my kick.

His scream of pain when my boot connected with his groin was music to my ears. I'd put all my strength into it, and my aim had been true.

Marku doubled over in agony.

Quickly, I jumped behind him and got him in the choke hold Pete had drilled into me.

"Hey, asshole." I heard Terry's voice outside. He'd come for me.

My eyes went damp with emotion. Straining to hold Marku, I couldn't pull a breath into my lungs, and my call to Terry came out a weak squeak. "In here."

Marku clawed at my arms, trying to break my grip.

"Feel lucky?" More words from my man outside, followed by the sounds of a struggle.

My muscles burned as I gripped the monster with all my strength. What if Goron had surprised Terry?

More indistinct words came through the door.

Marku's nails tore skin from my arm.

I closed my eyes and pulled with all my strength, concentrating on the form Pete had taught me. It shouldn't be taking this long.

"Where's Grace?" I heard Terry yell.

Marku let go of my arm, pulled at his pant leg, and out of nowhere, he had a gun in his hand. He fumbled with it, then pointed it back at me.

It was let him go or die.

Bang.

The shot was incredibly loud, but it missed my forehead as I fell back against the floor.

The door shuddered under some kind of assault.

Coughing, Marku yanked me up by my hair.

I cried out, my scalp burning from the assault as I tried to elbow and kick him. It was no use.

He jammed the gun against my ear. "Stay still, or I'll shoot." He struggled to his feet and yanked me up between him and the door.

With a loud crunch, the door gave way.

Terry stepped in, looking madder than I'd ever seen him. His gun was raised. "Let her go." His voice boomed in the small space.

Marku pressed the gun barrel harder against me. "Drop it, or I kill her." I heard the click as Marku cocked the hammer. "You have ten seconds to drop your gun and let me walk out of here, or she dies."

Terry raised his gun to point at the ceiling. "Settle down."

"Nine… eight… seven," Marku counted down.

"Don't," I warned Terry. If he put his gun down, I was sure Marku would shoot him. I couldn't let that happen. I couldn't let Terry sacrifice himself. "Don't do it."

"Six… five," Marku continued.

"I have to. I don't have a clear shot," Terry said.

What I had to do was clear—fight with whatever I had, give him space to shoot, and save my man.

Terry's words made Marku lose count. "Five… four." He had me by the hair instead of an arm around my throat. "Three, two."

I raised my right foot and slammed the heel of my boot against his foot just as I lifted the left foot and became a dead weight he couldn't hold up.

Bang, bang.

Something wet splattered my cheek as Terry's bullets slammed into Marku. As I fell to the floor, my scalp felt like I'd lost half my hair.

TERRY

WITH WIDE EYES, GRACE LOOKED AT ME AND SMILED AS I KEPT MY SIG trained on the asshole, in case he needed another round. It was a smile that warmed my soul. My woman was safe.

The asshole moaned, cradling his useless arm. "You shot me," he whined.

"Don't move." Zane came in just behind me and kicked the asshole's weapon to the side.

Just then, Grace looked down at the bloody mess that used to be his arm.

Dropping my weapon, I rushed forward, grabbing her just before she went limp. And this time kept her from hitting her head.

"I need a doctor," the asshole whined.

"You need to shut up." Zane kicked him. "Did she get clipped?"

"She fainted. It's the blood." I cradled Grace to me. "I got you, Kitten."

Cradling her head in my lap, I whipped my jacket off, placing it over Grace. Marci followed Constance into the room. Her hands went to her face. "Oh my God."

"She's all right," Zane assured her. "She fainted."

Constance pulled her weapon and trained it on the blubbering asshole. "I got him."

Zane quickly toed off the running shoes he wore, removed his pants, pulled off Grace's boots, and tugged the pants up her legs.

I nodded. "Thanks."

Constance laughed. "Puppies? Really?"

Zane's boxers had cute little puppies on them. "Give me a break. They were a joke gift from my cousin."

She pulled out her phone.

"Don't you dare," Zane warned.

She took the picture anyway.

Zane rushed her.

She stuffed the phone down her shirt and got in a fighting stance.

Zane backed off. "I'm going to get you for this."

Constance smirked.

"Call me an ambulance," the asshole complained.

Constance kicked his leg. "You pointed a gun at my friend. One more word out of your useless mouth and I'll be calling the morgue instead of an ambulance."

Asshole only whimpered.

Lucas finally arrived with Duke. "The other five are down." He shook his head at the sight. "Marku, you're a piece of shit." He nodded at Constance. "I got him." He looked back at me. "And Grace?"

"She fainted," Zane explained.

"He had a gun to Grace's head," I explained. "I didn't have a choice."

"I was right behind him," Zane said. "It was a righteous shot."

Lucas nodded, then noticed Zane's attire. "What? Are you six?"

Zane was smart enough to not answer.

Lucas glanced at my gun on the floor. "Is that yours?"

I nodded.

"Leave it right where it is for Wellbourne."

Duke tended to Marku's wounds while Zane called for an ambulance and Lucas called Lieutenant Wellbourne.

I adjusted my position and tried to make Grace comfortable. I had my woman in my arms. She was safe, and the nightmare was over. This Marku asshole and his goons were going down for kidnapping at a minimum.

"Ambulance is on the way, but he's losing a lot of blood," Zane said. "I need better light. Help me get him on the table in the other room."

Zane, Duke, and Lucas hefted Marku out the door, while Zane kept pressure on his shoulder wound.

Grace shifted in my arms. "Marci?" Her eyes struggled open.

"She's okay," Constance told her.

Grace moved to sit up. "I need to get to her."

I held her back. "In a minute. How do you feel?"

"Like shit, but that's normal. This isn't my first time, you know."

"How many have there been?"

"I don't know."

"This is no way to live. The doctor said you could do training to keep this from happening again, and you're going to start on that today."

Constance cocked a brow.

"Aren't you bossy?" Grace complained. "I need to check on Marci."

"Someone has to make you deal with this. You insist on looking after others, but refuse to take care of yourself. That stops today."

"You're wrong," she scoffed. "I'm fine."

Constance knelt beside us and touched Grace's shoulder. "What if you'd fainted today when Marci needed you?"

I closed my eyes. Those were the words I should have been smart enough to use.

Grace stopped resisting as her eyes flicked from me to Constance and back again. Then her drive to take care of her people overpowered her independent streak. "We don't even know if it will work, but okay. I'll try the training. Now, will you let me up to see Marci?"

I stood and pulled her to her feet. "There's blood out there."

"I'll close my eyes until you tell me it's okay." She took two steps and then had to hitch up her pants. "What is this?"

"Zane thought it would help preserve your modesty, so he donated his pants," Constance explained.

"That was nice of him." Then she too caught sight of Zane. "Aren't you cute?"

"Don't you dare tell anyone."

I was pretty sure he was only referring to one particular employee of Grace's.

Sirens sounded in the distance.

I took Grace's hand before we reached the door. "Close your eyes." I guided her out. In the far corner, Winston had his arm protectively around Marci. We walked around the bloody table where a pantsless Zane was still working on keeping the moaning Marku alive.

"What the hell is in that case that's so valuable?" Duke asked.

"My money is still on missile tech," Winston said.

"I like diamonds," Duke answered.

"He—" Grace threw a thumb in Marku's direction. "—promised the buyer that nobody would ever know."

Lucas turned quickly. "Who's the buyer?"

Grace didn't turn around. "His name was Kim. That's all I heard."

Two quick shots rang out to our right.

Grace gasped as her head swiveled toward the noise.

Without my weapon, all I could do was pull her down into a crouch with me.

An Asian man disappeared down an aisle of junk. He'd shot at Marku and Zane.

"I got him," Constance yelled as she sprinted to follow the guy.

"No," Lucas yelled. "Not alone."

Constance stopped, looking unhappy with Lucas's order.

Marku made a gurgling sound and then went silent.

Zane stood back from the table. "He's gone. Why the hell did that dude shoot him?"

I guided Grace to Marci and told her she could open her eyes. The two women hugged.

"I was sure we restrained all of his soldiers on the way in," Duke said.

"That was Kim," Marci said, without turning to face the group gathered around Marku. "The buyer."

"Police!" The yell came down the hallway that led in from outside.

We all raised our hands and stood still. You never knew when a nervous rookie cop would be the first on scene.

With a dead body, I resigned myself to a long interrogation. But my woman was safe, and nothing else mattered.

CHAPTER 39

GRACE

I SQUINTED ONE GROGGY EYELID OPEN AGAINST THE LIGHT AS SOMETHING tickled my nose.

Bonnie's tail swished across my face as two angry eyes watched me.

"What do you want?" I knew the answer without asking. Bonnie only ever wanted one thing—food.

Swish, swish.

When I levered up on my elbow, Bonnie finally moved.

"Meow." Clyde was also here, at my feet.

But as I remembered last night with Terry, and then falling asleep cradled in his arms, the bed still felt empty.

Turning, I slid my hand under the sheets next to me. The bed was cold. "Terry?"

Silence.

Swish.

I reached out to stroke Bonnie and was rewarded with a loud purr. In the right mood, she had the loudest motor. "I've been ignoring you, and I'm sorry."

Not to be left out, Clyde bounded up and forced his head under my hand for his share of love.

"Yeah, I missed you too," I told them as they competed for my attention.

A rap of knuckles sounded at the open door. "Grace?"

I looked up. "Constance?"

It came back to me. Terry had asked Constance and Winston to come home with us last night. "Have you been here all night?"

From the doorway, she nodded, smiling as if keeping watch over me was a normal part of life. "Good morning. I hope you slept well."

"Uh-huh." Heat rose in my cheeks because she'd probably heard the fact that we hadn't spent the entire night sleeping. "Where…" I stopped, feeling suddenly insecure, asking about Terry.

"Terry didn't want to wake you. Rudi gave us some clues about where to find Elliot, and he's out chasing them down." She raised her phone. "If you're ready to get up, Winston is down on the street and bugging me about making breakfast."

Holding the sheet against me, I sat up. "Nonsense. You don't need to wait on me. I should be making food for you guys."

"I promised Terry I'd treat you to my famous French toast."

Guessing that Constance had that I-keep-all-my-promises gene, I gave in. "That sounds great. I'll be out as soon as I shower." I didn't need to do my hair this morning, but after a sweaty evening under the sheets with Terry, a rinse was on the agenda.

As the warm water sluiced over me, Clyde stood staring through the glass. *Meow… Meow.*

"I know. I miss him too." In just a few days, Clyde had taken to Terry, often rubbing up against him to get an under-the-chin scratch.

∼

A LITTLE WHILE LATER, I WALKED INTO THE KITCHEN TO FIND WINSTON AT THE table pouring juice.

He paused. "You're going to love this."

Constance looked up. "You're just in time. Hot off the griddle." She laid a heaping plate of French toast slices on the table. "Grab some quick, before Bigfoot eats them all."

The aroma was scrumptious. After sitting, I chose a piece and topped it with a light drizzle of maple syrup.

The first bite didn't disappoint. "This is terrific," I said as I cut another bite of Constance's creation.

"She does a good job on this." Winston put down his orange juice. "I have it every week. Too bad it's the only thing she can cook."

Constance sent him a glare. "It is not, and how would you know, anyway?"

Winston turned to me. "We were undercover as a married couple for a week at this mountain retreat. I learned all about her." He added a wink.

I giggled.

"It was a surveillance job." Constance felt the need to clarify. "Undercover. Not under the covers."

"Of course not," Winston agreed, still smiling. "She's too good for me."

"Thank you." Color rose in Constance's cheeks.

"But honestly, name one other thing you cooked that week without using the microwave," Winston pressed.

She huffed. "I can cook. I just don't like to."

"Go ahead. Name one thing."

"The burritos."

Winston lifted another forkful of French toast to his mouth. "Now this breakfast is truly good. I mean it. You can cook this for me any day, but frying a store-bought burrito instead of nuking it does not constitute cooking." He chuckled playfully before popping the food into his mouth.

Constance was not amused. "At least I don't fart in my sleep."

"You're the one who chose bean burritos."

Constance scowled.

I added fuel to the fire. "They say that being uninhibited enough to fart in front of someone is a sign of closeness in a relationship."

"We're not in a relationship," Winston noted swiftly.

"Definitely not," Constance agreed, narrowing her eyes at the big man. "We bring him along when we need some muscle."

Winston nodded. "And we bring her along for someone who can get into small spaces."

Constance brandished her fork.

He slid back in his chair. "And when we need someone smart," he added. "Everybody knows that."

I couldn't help it, and a laugh escaped. I tapped my fork on the plate. "Constance, this is delicious, and in my book, it counts as real cooking." I loved seeing a side of these two beyond stern looks and guns at their hips.

"It is," Winston admitted with a smile. "And I'll go undercover with you again anytime, dear."

Constance made a show of rolling her eyes, but I caught the smile she tried to hide and guessed that she agreed.

"You have breakfast together regularly?" I asked, going back to Winston's original comment.

"Pretty much every week," Winston mumbled with food in his mouth.

Constance picked up her glass. "Yeah, he's like one of those sad-looking puppies you just have to feed."

A pang of guilt shot through me—or maybe not guilt, but a realization of something I'd missed out on. I'd spent years building my business, and not until this week had I spent a single morning eating breakfast across from someone.

Clyde rubbed up against my leg and meowed.

I looked down and gave him the bad news. "It's not meat, so no, you can't have any." Breakfast with two cats was not the same.

Clyde repeated his meow.

Picking up my phone, I tried Terry's number again. It went straight to voicemail. "Just calling to say good morning," I told the recording. I needed to talk to him.

"It's not you," Constance assured me. "While he's in the field, he keeps it on do-not-disturb."

The sound of the garage door opening came up the stairs, and my heart accelerated.

Constance stood. "Speak of the devil. It looks like I'll need to make a little more."

I ran to Terry when he reached the door and jumped into his arms.

"Whoa, Tiger. I haven't been gone that long."

"I still get to miss you."

"I missed you too." He set me down and stroked my hair. "I got your messages."

Not what I wanted to hear, since he hadn't called me back.

"After Russo bugged my car, I didn't want to say anything over the phone."

"Hey, big guy," Constance called. "Get your hungry ass to the table before Bigfoot here eats everything I cooked."

I was busting to know what he couldn't talk about in the car, but I waited until he'd loaded his plate and taken a bite.

"Constance, I should hire you as my cook."

Winston laughed.

Then curiosity got the better of me. "What's the news?"

Terry finished chewing before answering. "Jordy and I checked out a place Rudi gave us. Elliot had definitely been there. Jordy set up surveillance, and we'll nab him when he returns."

"And then what? He said he needs money to get away and disappear."

Terry turned to me and took my hand. "Remember how this started? The Russo family came after you to get to Elliot. This never ends until he faces them. If he runs now, you'll never be safe."

I shivered. "But they'll kill him—"

Winston stopped eating.

Constance sighed. "They might not. Lucas has some leverage with them."

My tears erupted. "We can't just let him die."

Terry stood and pulled me up with him. "Let's go outside for a minute."

Winston and Constance started clearing the plates as a very obvious way to give us some space.

I walked with Terry out onto the terrace. "What do you think will happen to him?"

He closed the door and held me tight in the morning sun.

When he pulled my chin up, I braced for the bad news.

"I know he's your cousin, but he's brought this on himself."

That's what Terry always said about Elliot. "You mean you don't think he's worth saving."

"No. What I mean is, he's a grown-up who has to make his own way in the world. He's not a child you can protect completely." He stroked my hair behind my ear. "But for you, I'd save him if there was any way I could."

I sniffled a half smile.

"There's no way to know," Terry said, "how Tony will come down on this. I think it depends on what kind of story Elliot weaves. It's going to be up to him to tell a story that doesn't have Tony losing face."

"That's not good enough. I can't throw him to the wolves and wait to see what happens. There has to be something you can do. What about Lucas?"

"We're outsiders. I'll talk to Lucas and see what influence he has."

I nodded. I didn't see anything else to hope for.

He took my shoulders and locked eyes with me. "For you, I'll do everything I can."

Nodding, I rested my head against his chest. I believed my man. "I really, really like you." The words I'd been looking for the right time to say just wouldn't come out. It had only been a week, and I felt it, but couldn't use the L-word.

He squeezed me tighter and whispered in my ear, "I really like you too, Kitten."

Sobbing into his chest, I admitted, "I think I'll keep you."

He rubbed my back with that soothing touch he had. "Then you admit you've been wrong about me for years?"

I laughed. "That's not what I said. I only hated you because you've been a jerk to me forever."

"Hated?"

"Okay. Disliked."

It felt like the right thing and the wrong thing to be admitting my feelings for him with Elliot's life hanging in the balance. How would I ever explain it if asked when we first exchanged our I love yous?

CHAPTER 40

Terry

(Three days later)

For the third time, we walked up to the restaurant doors to meet with the Russo family.

"Are you sure you want to take the lead on this?" Lucas asked. It was just the two of us today.

"Absolutely. Grace's safety is my responsibility, and it's her cousin who made this mess." A vision of Grace from this morning, stretched out lazily on my bed, came to mind. I could not fail her today.

The entrance routine was just as it had been before, except this time Lucas kept his weapon as my backup, and I was unarmed.

I walked into the room with my back straight and my head high.

Lucas followed with the roller suitcase.

Today, Tall Tony was flanked by Baldy and Mustache Man as before, but also another four goons, all of them obviously armed.

I was a sniper without his rifle, and felt as naked as the day I was born. I wasn't bringing Tony good news, but hopefully he wouldn't feel the need to take out his frustration on us.

Tony eyed the suitcase skeptically and steepled his hands. "You told me you'd find that little Elliot fucker. Tell me you brought me his head."

"Better than that."

Tony's face lit up. "His head and his balls?"

I took the suitcase from Lucas. "Would you like to see?"

"Damned straight. Up here." Tony stood and slapped his desk. "Hold on. It isn't going to leak or anything?"

I shook my head. "No." It was an honest answer.

Even though Lucas knew what was coming, he didn't even smile.

Lifting the suitcase onto the desk, I slowly unzipped it.

Seven sets of gangster eyeballs watched as I opened it. A burned smell filled the office.

"What the fuck is this?" Tony bellowed.

Baldy pulled his gun, waving it back and forth between me and Lucas.

"You said you wanted the case back," I answered. "This is what's left of it. Elliot Boyle, the little idiot, thought he could open it and died trying." The suitcase was filled with a thousand little pieces of the case Elliot had been tasked with delivering, and the two engraved counterfeiting plates that had been the cargo. We had scratched them enough that they were now worthless.

"I don't see no head here."

I shook my head. "Have you ever seen what two pounds of C-4 does to a body?"

Tony didn't answer.

"Well, I deployed to Syria, and I can tell you what you get is mostly a red mist from this much explosive. Maybe a few little pieces."

"I want those fucking pieces to mount on my fucking wall as a lesson to people that you don't fucking cross Tony Russo."

Typical. I'd expected as much. "An explosion of this size catches the attention of the cops, and they got there before we did. We greased a few palms to get this stuff, but the body parts had already gone to the coroner. Since the manner of death was pretty obvious, what was left of him was released to cremation." I shrugged. "But I'm claiming the five-hundred-grand reward for the return of the case."

"For this pile of junk?"

"Are you saying that's not the case?"

"Hold on." Tony motioned for Baldy to put his piece away, and he did. "Without a body, how do you know it was Elliot what blew himself up?"

I pulled out the pieces of the chain and spider pendant Elliot had always worn and threw them on the desk. "There's blood on there. Check the DNA, if you want. We already did."

"That's Spider's all right," Mr. Mustache said.

I held out my hand. "My reward for the case?"

"Fuck that," Tony spat. "I meant for the case in one piece."

"Tony," Lucas said ominously. "If you welch on this with my brother, you disrespect me. Do you really want to treat my brother that way?"

Tony gritted his teeth. Nobody threatened more effectively than Lucas Hawk. "Okay, already." He nodded to Baldy. "Get him his fucking money."

Baldy moved to a painting on the wall. He pulled it to the side, revealing a safe.

"One more thing," I said. "It goes without saying that you will leave my woman, Grace Brennan, alone and forget you ever knew her name."

"Yeah, yeah, sure," Tony said as he picked up one of the printing plates and examined it. "Shit, these are fucked."

"We have one more thing to discuss," Lucas said.

Tony looked up.

"In private," Lucas added.

Tony tossed the block back into the suitcase. "I think I've heard enough today."

"Not quite enough," Lucas pressed. This wasn't something we wanted the lower levels of his organization to hear.

Tony stared at Lucas for a moment.

Lucas didn't flinch. "Fine, but don't blame me when it blows up on you."

Tony couldn't let that pass. He nodded to Baldy. "Out."

Just as before, Lucas handed his weapon to Baldy as the entire group of them filed out.

Tony waited until the door closed. "What?"

I started. "The heist of the case was planned by Marku and a member of your organization as a way to get that merchandise for free. Marku figured he'd get his deposit back from you when it wasn't delivered."

"I don't believe it," Tony said.

Lucas had warned me that would be the tough guy's first reaction.

"I've seen this a million times. You try to weaken me by getting me to turn on my own."

"We're not your competitor," I challenged.

He scoffed. "A million times, I tell ya."

"Okay. If you're sure it couldn't be true, then we're done here."

He hesitated. "How do you know this?"

There it was. The crack we'd expected—he didn't trust all his people.

I pulled out a single sheet of paper and offered it. "Electronic communications like this email."

He read it slowly. The email which laid out the basics of the plan had been written by Paulo, but Tony wouldn't be able to tell that from the Gmail address it had been sent from.

Tony's face turned redder the farther down the page he got. "Who is this fucker?" He pounded a fist on the table. "Who?"

"Paulo."

"I don't believe it. He doesn't have the brains for something like this, or the balls to cross me."

"Paulo recruited Elliot, but he was not the brains behind it."

Tony shook his head. "I told you, I seen this a million times."

I could tell I was losing him. "Paulo got paid a quarter mill the day after the case disappeared."

"How do I know you ain't jerking my chain? You have any proof?"

"Check his bank records and ask him where the money for his new Bentley came from," I suggested. "Do you pay him enough to buy a Bentley?"

Tony perked up. "You're saying Marku paid my guy a quarter mil?"

Lucas spoke up. "The money came from Victor."

Tony's jaw dropped, and he slumped back into his chair. "My Victor? No fuckin' way."

I pulled out the bank account records. "We didn't want to say this in front of your men, in case Victor has a good explanation for it."

He took the paper and studied it, blood draining from his face. "Get out of here." He waved us dismissively from the room.

We were happy to comply.

It felt great when a plan came together. We'd left the meeting alive, Grace was safe, and I had five-hundred K stuffed in my pockets.

"You should call her," Lucas suggested as we rounded the corner to our cars.

Leaning against the Cayenne, I dialed. Her voice was the sweet balm I needed right now.

CHAPTER 41

Grace

"I only see one," Deb said. "I thought you had two cats."

She, Serena, and Constance were upstairs at Terry's place with me, holding a vigil while we waited to find out if Terry's plan to save me was going to work.

Zane was out on the street, backing up Constance as my second guard.

Terry had said he thought he could get Russo to back off and I'd be able to go back to my normal life. I was looking forward to that, though I was still recovering from the news that Elliot had blown himself up in the process. I'd cried for a few hours after getting that report.

Terry was always saying to stay clear of Elliot because he was a walking disaster, and his end had proved Terry right on that score.

"Where is the other one?" Deb prodded.

"Bonnie is still scared of this place and hides pretty much all day." I shifted in my seat, looking for her. The tingle between my legs reminded me of the strong man who'd said he'd do anything to keep me safe.

"Cats can be stubborn," Serena commented. "But she'll adapt."

"I don't know." I hadn't seen any evidence of that yet. "I'm afraid for her mental health. I need to get her back to my place, actually both of them. Being away from home has been stressful for them."

Uninterested in my cats, Constance studied her phone. "The call should come anytime now."

A confused look came over Serena's face. "Say that again?"

"As soon as the danger is over, I'm going back to my apartment," I explained. "I'm only supposed to be here until the danger is over." I thought I'd made that clear to her before. Plus, that's what Terry had told me the first day he brought me here. "And, I need underwear."

"I know Terry has a washer and dryer," Deb noted. "Just do some laundry."

Constance laughed. "That first day, she couldn't go to the apartment, so Zane packed for her, and he only packed thongs."

Serena laughed. "It figures. But you can just pick up what you need and come back."

I shook my head. I'd stick to the original plan.

Constance cocked her head. "Didn't you say Terry had claimed you?"

"That's just caveman talk for he likes me," I argued. Though as I again twisted in my seat, the renewed tingle in my lady parts reminded me how much I enjoyed my caveman.

Serena rolled her eyes.

"What?" I demanded.

Deb laughed. "You obviously don't know my brother well enough. He'll have something to say about that."

"It's not his choice." *I am my own woman.*

"I remember thinking the same thing," Serena said wryly. "When Duke first claimed me."

What was I supposed to do with that comment?

"Is leaving here what you want?" Deb asked.

"I don't know. Two weeks ago we were at each other's throats. It feels like we should date a while before I move in with him."

"Grace, you're dealing with a Marine," Constance interjected. "Honor is everything to them. He wouldn't have claimed you if he didn't mean it."

"Those aren't the kind of words I was hoping for."

"What words did you use?" Serena asked. "When you told him how you feel?"

I shrank down in my chair. This was not going the way I wanted.

"Grace?" Serena wasn't going to give up.

I concentrated on a small scratch on the table. "I've been meaning to."

Deb shook her head and threw up her arms. "I expected my brother to be the emotionally stunted one, but you're both dumber than rocks."

My phone rang, and TYRANT showed up on the screen.

Deb giggled. "Cute nickname."

Constance craned her neck and laughed.

I really did need to change it. I answered tentatively. "I'm afraid to ask."

Terry's voice was jubilant, or as jubilant as he got. "It went fine. You're a free woman now."

"Really? They're done coming after me?" I squealed.

"Really."

The girls around me celebrated with their own little squeals of joy.

"I don't know how I can ever repay you."

He whispered. "Maybe by the time I get home, you'll think of something."

"I'll see what I can do." I was willing to bet his idea was a year of sexual favors. Which didn't sound too bad.

"I've got to go," he told me.

"When will you be home?" God, as soon as I said it I realized how clingy I sounded, and I was not clingy.

"Soon as I can, Kitten."

I could listen to him call me Kitten all day long.

"Oh, and I have a surprise for you."

"What kind of surprise?"

"You'll just have to wait."

I sighed. "You're mean."

"The meanest."

Deb made hand motions at me, but I couldn't bring myself to sign off with my first love-you. "See you soon."

"Count on it."

I hung up, feeling like I might float away—finally free of the danger Elliot had put me in.

"You're dumb as a rock," Deb said.

The other two nodded.

"I'm just looking out for myself, like I always have." Things had been both crazy bad and crazy good this last week. I needed some time to let things settle.

Deb shook her head.

Constance rolled her eyes and picked up her phone. "He's my teammate. I have to."

"Have to what?"

Serena patted my arm. "Having a man in your life means not being alone. It means being a team. It means you're not the only one looking out for you."

"Hey, Terry. Just a heads-up, Grace wants to move back to her apartment," Constance said into her phone. A second later she held it away from her ear, and we all heard the yelling. "I'll tell her," she called as she hung up. "He's not happy."

"How could you?" I demanded.

Deb and Serena had smug smiles.

Constance put her phone down. "I told you. He's my teammate, and I have to have his back."

I seethed and looked over at the group. "I thought you guys would have my back."

Deb shook her head. "Don't look at me. He's my brother."

Serena backed her chair away. "He's my man's teammate too, and besides, in my book you're making a big mistake."

I blew out a big breath and stood. "Thanks for nothing."

Leaving the table, I wondered how much time I had to pack before Hurricane Terry rolled in.

∼

TERRY

CONSTANCE'S WORDS HAD SLICED INTO ME LIKE A RUSTY KNIFE AND TORN OUT my heart. How could Grace be about to leave?

"Fuck that," I cursed as I pulled into the Hawk garage.

I was stuck between what I wanted to do and what I had to do.

CHAPTER 42

Grace

I QUICKLY PACKED WHAT LITTLE ZANE HAD BROUGHT OVER.

Serena helped.

Deb kept saying I was making a mistake.

Constance only said, "I don't think you know enough to make a clear decision just yet. You should wait and talk to Terry first. He might have something to say that changes your outlook on this."

Deb also thought I was being too rash, too abrupt.

But if I knew anything, I knew following that advice was wrong for me.

Terry would come barging in, and we would argue—if *argue* was even the right word, in his house, on his terms. That was not for me.

I'd leave and change the status quo. Sure, he'd come over to my place, but at least then the conversation would be about me moving in with him, which was a completely different frame than talking about me moving out.

"Are you sure?" Serena asked. "I'm with Deb. This is like creating a fight where there doesn't have to be one."

Sighing, I stopped folding. "I've been independent my entire life, on my own. First it was just Pete and me, and then…" My voice threatened to crack. "And then, alone. I allow one high-testosterone male to claim me…" I added air quotes. "..and he starts dictating terms I have to live by. I'm not breaking up with him. I'm just not ready to be told I have to live with him."

"Have you thought about how he'll feel when he gets home and finds you gone the moment you don't need protection from Russo?"

That did bother me, because I didn't want to hurt Terry. In fact, I cared for him so much, it hurt me to do this.

∾

TERRY

SERENA: She is afraid you're going to demand she live with you.

THE TEXT HAD COME IN AFTER I'D FOUND MY HOUSE EMPTY, AND WHILE I WAS ON the way to Grace's place. It was a word of caution that I considered as I parked.

My heart hammered in my chest as I reached the door of her apartment and held up my hand to knock.

True to form, the door was open at her neighbor Millie's.

"Is she in?" I asked.

"Sure is. First time in a while."

I knocked hard. When I heard only muffled sounds inside, I knocked again.

"What's the password?" It was Serena's voice.

"I'm not in the mood, Serena."

"What's the password?" she repeated.

I looked toward Millie. "Password?"

"Please is the best one I know," she answered.

"Please," I repeated.

Thankfully, the deadbolt clicked open, and I didn't have to break the door down. My woman stood in the middle of the room, arms crossed, ready to do battle.

"I just remembered I have some laundry to attend to," Serena said as she slipped by me and out the door.

"Hi," I offered. I suddenly realized that it would be manipulative to give her the good news first.

She stood her ground. "Thank you again for working things out with those Russo people."

"Anything for my woman. Now, tell me why you're doing this."

She fidgeted. Her ringing phone saved her from answering. When she picked it up off the counter, her face went both pale and slack.

I charged over, worried that she might have another fainting spell.

The name on the screen read, MRS. MONTEFINO.

"God," she complained.

"Who is it?"

"My mother. I don't want to talk to her," Grace said with a trembling voice.

At first, Pete had told me their mother had died when they were young, but later he'd admitted that the woman had left them at a hotel and run off after a man.

Their mother had left them like spare change on the dresser and just checked out—no goodbye, no hugs, no crying, no note, no nothing. Pete had said it had hurt Grace even more than him. After the initial barrage of questions, they'd decided to deal with it by telling people that their mother had died in a car accident.

They'd lived with a remote uncle until Pete was old enough to take Grace with him and leave. That uncle had been no peach either.

I grabbed for the phone. "Let me handle this."

Reluctantly, she let go.

I accepted the call and put it on speaker. "Grace Brennan's line."

"Who is this?" the woman demanded.

I put my finger to my lips for Grace to be quiet. "Who may I say is calling?"

With a haughty tone, she answered, "Contessa Alexandria Montefino. The count and I wish to invite her to dinner."

Grace shook her head violently.

"No," I said.

"What do you mean?" she asked.

"No means no. Do you have a language other than English you'd like me to use?"

"I demand you let me speak with my daughter. I'm entitled to speak with my daughter, you... you peasant."

"No."

"You are extremely rude." Off to the side, she said. "Stephano, she doesn't have time to dine with us."

"Here's the thing, Alex—"

"It's Alexandria." She huffed. "And who are you?"

"I'm her boyfriend, someone who actually cares about her."

"Well, I'm her mother."

I laughed at her until I could hear exasperated sounds from the other end. "Her mother died a long time ago."

"That's a lie. I'm her mother."

"Tell me, lady, and I use the term loosely, are you are on marriage number four or number five?"

"I'm a Contessa, and you can't talk to me that way," she snarled.

"Somebody should you old hag. Now, how many?"

"I'm her mother. Put her on the phone right this instant. I demand it. I'm her mother."

Grace smiled and held up five fingers.

"Let me tell you, Alex, when you skip out on your kids to marry some South African businessman you lose the right to call yourself a mother."

"I couldn't take them with me. It wouldn't have worked with Peter."

"Did you even call them on their birthdays?" I knew the answer to that one.

"I couldn't. My schedule was…"

Unbelievable. In her mind, it was all about her. And from what Pete told me, marriage number two had only lasted four years.

"Being a mother is being there for birthdays, for school plays, for soccer games—"

"How dare you talk to me like that?" she complained.

Since Grace was smiling, I continued. "Being there for her first date and her first kiss. You didn't stick around for any of those things, so you never earned the title of mother, Alex."

"It's Contessa to you. I always knew Grace would end up with a heathen. You're rude."

"I may be rude, but I can learn to be better. You're just a bitch."

The woman spluttered, unable to get out a coherent word.

"Bad news for you, Alex. Being a bitch is something you can't change." I stabbed the end call button.

The biggest smile in the world filled Grace's face.

"Your mother is a bitch."

She nodded and laughed. "And you told her that to her face."

"If the truth hurts, that's her problem, not mine. I'm glad it's not an inherited trait."

Grace blushed bright red. "Thank you, kind sir."

Having now virtually met her mother, Grace's devotion to her employees crystallized for me. They were her family, and she treated them as her children in an attempt to be the good mother she'd never had. Her laser focus on her company was her attempt to provide stability she'd never known.

I sensed that pity for her plight was the last thing she wanted, so it was time to pivot to the real issue. "Anyway," I began. "What are you doing here?"

The smile I'd put on her face dropped away. "I'm doing what you said when you forced me to move to your place. It was only for as long as I was in danger."

"That was then. Haven't I since then made it clear that you're my woman and I want you to stay?"

"Your woman? You don't own me." Her fierce independent streak had surfaced. "I get a say. I decide what's right for me. Not you, not anybody else."

Take it slow. I took in a deep breath. "Try it this way. I have committed myself to you, and you alone. We're in a relationship, so why would you want to move out?"

"Relationship?" she squeaked. "After a week? It doesn't work like that."

Hold it together, Marine. "It hasn't been a week." I took her hands. "I've wanted you for years."

Tears formed in her eyes. "I'm scared. This is going too fast. We haven't really gotten to know each other."

"Maybe I've tried to hide the real me by being mean to you, but I've known you for years, the real you." I slid my hands up to her shoulders. "I know the woman you are, and you're the one for me."

"We don't know each other like a normal couple gets to know each other because we haven't dated. I don't even know your favorite flavor of ice cream."

Finally, some steps I could take. "Rocky Road, and we can do a dinner date tonight."

"It's not a set of boxes to check off."

"Fine, no dinner date." I backed off a step. Stupid me. I knew she always reacted to pressure by pushing back. It was her default fighting response, which had enabled me to keep her at a distance for years. It also meant I couldn't give her the good news I wanted to, knowing she'd take it as coercion.

"Look, I'm scared that maybe we're not compatible. My business is on the edge and needs all my time," she said. "I'm afraid that as fast as you've decided you want me, maybe you'll let me go just as fast when I can't give you the time you want. And that we don't enjoy the same things, that we don't want to do the same things."

Those were separate concerns that I clearly couldn't address all at once. She wanted to be in charge, so it was time to retreat and regroup. Remembering Lucas's quote, *"Set her free,"* I pulled out my keys, removed the one for the house, and set it on the counter.

She stared at it wordlessly.

Noticing a Sharpie nearby, I pulled off the cap and drew on the head of the key.

"Christmas. The alarm code is Christmas, one-two-two-five. You can come over if and when you want."

"But—"

I cut her off. "I've told you how I feel. It's time for you to decide how you feel." With that, I cradled her face in my hands and gently kissed her goodbye.

In Syria, facing a crazed terrorist, I'd once been completely helpless when my ammo ran dry. When the dude had changed mags, I'd charged him with only my knife. That had been the scariest day of my life.

But closing the door behind me now was a new level of scary.

I'd just let go of the most important person in my life. I'd invited her to leave me. What if she never used the key?

Then she'd never really been mine, according to the quote.

∼

Grace

The door closed, and I walked to the couch and slumped into it.

He was gone. What was I doing? What was he doing?

"Clyde?" I called for my cats. "Bonnie, you can come out now. It's safe."

No cats. Not even a meow in response.

"Traitors, where are you? I came back here so you'd be happy."

Nothing. The room was as empty as my heart. That's when I noticed that this room had none of the sunshine that permeated Terry's place.

Knuckles rapped on my door, and my heart leaped into my throat.

He's back.

Rushing to the door, I was about to fling it open when I remembered to check the peephole like Terry had always warned me to do.

Happy to see Serena, I opened the door.

She breezed in. "I saw Terry leaving downstairs. What happened? Did you guys get things settled?"

I walked toward the kitchen. "Want a drink? I think I have some margarita mix in the fridge."

She hurried to get in front of me. "I don't want a margarita. What happened?"

I went around her. "Nothing. I might have some wine then." I couldn't remember what I had in the fridge. Pulling open the door, I realized it was a good thing she didn't want a margarita because the bottle of mix was almost empty. "It looks like hard cider is the best I can offer."

"Fine."

I retrieved two bottles and handed one to her, laughing when I couldn't find a bottle opener in the drawer.

"What's so funny?"

"I can't find an opener."

"It's okay. I didn't want one, anyway."

"Me either." My laughter fell away, and my eyes went wet. "You know, he once accused me of thinking he opened bottles with his teeth?"

"Ouch."

I smiled. "It was a joke."

She reached out and took my hand. "Are you going to tell me what happened?" She led me to the couch.

This was hard—really hard. "He left."

She sat next to me and leaned close, brows scrunched up. "What do you mean?"

"I fucked up. I pushed him away so hard he left."

"Tell me."

I explained what I remembered about the conversation.

"But he gave you a key?"

I pointed to the counter.

She picked it up and studied it. "This is so cute."

"What?" It was a simple key. It didn't even have any color to it.

She turned it toward me and held it up to my face. "I think it's romantic."

The head of the key had the word MY written on it, with a drawing of a heart underneath.

I blinked back a tear. "I'm scared. We've fought for years until this last week. What if it doesn't work?" I sniffled.

"Are you kidding? The key to his heart? Of course it'll work."

"No, I mean us. When I told you at the party that I didn't have time for a man, I wasn't kidding. My business is hanging on by a thread. My people need all my time."

"When Duke claimed me, I was scared shitless too. These military men are intense with a capital I. But what Duke and I have now is amazing."

"I always thought you were fearless."

She shook her head. "Not as fearless as Duke. Look, talk to Terry about your fears."

"But—"

"Stop that negative shit. No buts. If you'll let him, he can probably help you in more ways than you can imagine. Life with him will be a lot to handle, but I've never looked back, and I bet it will be the same for you."

"I don't know."

She stood. "None of us does until we try. It's not my job to tell you what to do. It's your path to choose. Stay here with Bonnie and Clyde, for all I care. Become an old cat lady. I'll think you're crazy, but you'll always be my friend."

I rose and followed her to the door.

With her hand on the handle, she stopped. "Or, take a risk with something you've never tried before. Choosing a SEAL worked out for me, but if you don't want to be claimed by a real man and enjoy a full-throttle life, that's your choice. Just be prepared for Deb to accuse you of being dumber than a sack of rocks."

I turned the deadbolt after she left.

"And she'd be right," Serena yelled through the door.

I waited before calling for my roommates. "Bonnie? Clyde?"

Neither came to comfort me.

CHAPTER 43

GRACE

WITH APPREHENSION, I TURNED THE KEY. THE LOCK RELEASED, BUT THE ALARM panel didn't start beeping when I opened the door the way it had when Terry had brought me in. What did that mean?

Walking through the garage and past the big motorcycle, I recalled the time Terry had fucked me on it, and then Serena's words, *"full-throttle life."* It had been a full-throttle experience for sure.

With my heart in my throat, I climbed the stairs.

At the top, the rest of the clothes I hadn't taken sat folded in a neat pile.

Terry rounded the corner from the kitchen. "Hi." His greeting was tentative.

Holding up my hand, I announced, "I used the key." I hoped I hadn't waited too long. It had been three hours since Terry left my place.

"I see that." He didn't move closer. "The rest of your things are right there."

Since it was up to me to make the move, I strode his way. "We need to talk."

"Okay." He waited with a pained expression.

"I want to try."

He opened his arms.

I jumped up and into them, wrapping my legs around him and initiating the kiss. It started rough. He tasted like coffee and sin as our tongues danced. The room melted away, and my pulse thundered in my ears. I couldn't get enough of this man. Panting, I let him break the kiss after a while.

"Welcome home. Did you bring the cats?"

I looked down at his chest. "You need to understand what you're getting into."

He tucked my hair behind my ear. "I'm a big boy. I know what I'm getting into."

I looked up at him. "Seriously, I need to explain that with my business the way it is, I need to spend a lot of time at work, and I don't want you to think it's because I don't want to be with you, because I do."

He stroked my back. "Kitten, let me help with that."

It was just like Serena had said.

"Terry, I'm scared. I'm worried that you'll get tired of me being bitchy and always busy."

He laughed, really laughed. "That's one thing you don't need to worry about."

"Are you sure?"

"Kitten, I've never been more sure of anything in my life."

I sighed and hugged him as tightly as I could. "I wanted to say it earlier, but I couldn't get up the nerve."

He pulled my chin up. "I know. I love you too."

My gasp was unintentional. "I was going to say I was falling for you," I admitted.

"The L-word scares you?"

"Everything about this scares me."

"I'll wait. Now I have something to tell you."

"Talking can wait." I wasn't spending one more minute waiting for my full-throttle life to begin. "I want to ride the rocket."

He lifted me up. "I like the way your mind works." He carried me toward the bedroom.

"Not that rocket," I objected. "The one downstairs. Will you take me for a ride?"

The disappointment on his face was clear. "Woman, you have the oddest set of priorities."

"I've never been on a bike before."

"Okay." He smiled. "With the wind in your face, it's a sense of freedom like nothing else."

We went down to the garage where he outfitted me with a leather jacket a dozen sizes too big and handed me a helmet. "We can talk to each other over Bluetooth with these."

I climbed on behind him, wrapped my arms around him, and was surprised at how quiet the bike was when he started the engine.

"Hold on." He twisted the throttle and the acceleration pulled me backward—*hold on* was right.

I grabbed him tighter.

He took us through the city streets, toward Malibu. "I have some news," he began.

"Later. Don't you dare ruin this." I concentrated on the lean into each turn, and the sprint to the next intersection.

Eventually he got us on the Pacific Coast Highway. "Hold on," he repeated when an open section of road appeared. We zoomed even faster.

"I love it," I screamed. "When can I drive?"

"Never."

I didn't like that answer.

"Elliot is alive," he added.

I had trouble swallowing. "What did you say?"

"I couldn't tell you before, but Elliot is alive."

I squeezed him tighter. "You're not joking?"

"I gave him and Rudi some money and put them on a plane today. Elliot has a new identity, and if he stays out of the country, he should be safe."

I teared up. "Really? How? I thought he blew himself up."

"That's what everybody is supposed to think."

I knew Terry hated Elliot's guts. "Why?"

"I did it for you, Kitten. Because you asked me to find a way. But you can never mention this to anyone, not ever."

Serena had been right. Life with this wonderful man was already a lot to handle, and he'd just saved Elliot. "Wow." It was a lot to take in.

"One other thing. I have four hundred and fifty thousand dollars for you to invest in SpaceMasters."

"You're kidding." I wished I wasn't on the back of this bike. I couldn't see his face to know if he was joking or not. He had to be joking.

"It's the reward money for finding the case. You earned it. It's yours to put into your business."

"Stop right now."

"No."

He had me hostage, and there was nothing I could do about it. "You can't be serious."

"I wouldn't lie to you," he said. "You got shot at, kidnapped, and gave us the clue to find Rudi. You earned it. All I ask is that you learn to delegate a little to give yourself more free time."

God, this man had made my life so much better than it had been. "Can I say I love you?"

He laughed. "As often as you want, baby."

I had been trying to avoid the truth for too long. I did love him. "Turn this bike around. I want to go home and ride the other rocket."

The strength of the brakes threw me forward against him. Then, once he found a break in the traffic, we were hurtling down PCH back toward home, *our home*. Those two words had a nice ring to them.

After a motorcycle ride I'd never forget, I got a ride on the other rocket —and we checked the hood of his car off the list.

EPILOGUE

IF YOU LOVE SOMEONE, SET THEM FREE. IF THEY COME BACK, THEY'RE YOURS; IF THEY DON'T, THEY NEVER WERE – RICHARD BACH

GRACE
(Ten days later)

GROGGILY, I BLINKED AN EYE OPEN. TERRY HAD CONVERTED ME TO SLEEPING IN the nude, and nothing could be better than waking up in this bed with his arm over my waist, and his morning wood up against me.

Then that stupid bird started chirping again. Okay, there was a way it could be better—if Terry didn't insist on leaving the window cracked open at night. That damned bird was way too cheerful, way too early in the morning. At least when winter came, he wouldn't be waking me so early.

Terry shifted. "Morning, kitten."

"You're awake?" Normally, I could tell when he woke by the change in his breathing.

"Yeah." His hand slid up to cup my breast. "I wish that damn bird would shut up."

Yes, waking up next to Terry was a hell of a lot better than sleeping alone. "I agree. If we shut the window, at least it would be quieter in here."

"Fresh air is good for the soul." It was the same line he'd used the last three times I'd suggested we close the window.

"If you know anybody who is a Marine Corps scout sniper, maybe we can fix the problem another way." I'd asked everybody what to do about the bird, without any usable suggestions.

His thumb lazily circled my nipple. "I only shoot dirtbags who deserve it." Yes, my Marine was a good man.

I twisted to face him. "How about a milder solution, like a slingshot?"

The move elicited a groan because he really liked to reach around me to handle my boobs. "Adopt a cat and put it in the tree."

I moved on to the big problem. "Do we have to do the party tonight? My birthday's not for another week." I'd been fighting the idea of having my birthday party this weekend since Terry sprung it on me two days ago.

"Baby, you know I have an out-of-town assignment, and I don't know how long I'll be gone. So, yes, it has to be this afternoon. I'm not missing your birthday party, and we're not doing it late either."

I reached down and wrapped my fingers around his cock. "Are you sure I can't persuade you?"

"No, but I'd love for you to try." He smiled when I pushed him over on his back and straddled him.

It might not change his mind, but I intended to personally thank my man, my protector, my lover anyway. Sliding my wet folds along his length, I raked my nails over his chest. "How about we see if we can make it an even better morning?"

"I like how you think," he said, as he twisted to reach the nightstand.

I pulled on his arm.

He gaze swung to me. "What?"

I couldn't believe that after less than a month with this man I was about to take a step I never had before, but with Terry it felt right. "Can we skip... I mean if you want?"

He pulled his arm back. "You want to take me bare?"

"I'm healthy, and I have a contraceptive shot. I've never... I mean I want to... with you."

"You've never done this before have you?"

I shook my head.

The emotion in his eyes shown through. "Me either. I'm clean if you're sure you want to."

I nodded. Looking into the eyes of the man who'd sworn to always keep me safe, I'd never been more sure of anything in my life. If I couldn't trust him, who could I trust?

His grin grew as he cupped both my breasts. "Bring it on, baby."

Rising up, I positioned him at my entrance, and got to work making it *an even better morning* for us both. I relished the times I got to be in charge and started slow, but quickly ramped up my pace. My moans matched his.

He lavished my breasts with his hands and mouth, occasionally tweaking my nipples as I rode him. Each downstroke filled the room with the slap of flesh on flesh. "Take what you want, baby. I love how slick you are. That's it, baby. You're so fucking beautiful."

My pleasure amped up and up, tingles radiating throughout my body. I ground down hard on him again and again, watching the cords of his neck strain as he fought to hold back. I loved how he filled me, but I'd be damned if I didn't make him lose control first.

He seemed to give in and began thrusting up into me with guttural grunts.

Close to the edge, I slowed down to hold back the white-hot release building within me—a climax that would destroy me. All I needed was a little longer to win by losing the race.

"That's it, baby," he grunted. "I can tell you're close." He wasn't wrong. "Come for me." He brought his thumb to my clit and strummed.

Without warning, I was in free fall over that edge and into the shudders of my release. My pussy fluttered around his cock as the waves flowed over me.

A second later, he pulled me down hard on him. He was a magnificent sight as muscles strained, a roar escaped, and he pulsed inside me. I dug my nails into his ass, urging him deeper.

I settled forward onto him, chest to chest with Rocket still inside me. "I love you, Marine."

He ran his hand over my back. "Love you back, Kitten. Are you looking forward to your party?"

I listened to the beat of his heart, the heart I'd somehow won. "You know the answer to that, but for you, I'll grin and bear it."

"I think it'll be much better than you think."

I lifted up on my elbows. "Wait. You're up to something." I saw the very slight lift of the lips that gave him away. "What is it?"

He tweaked my nipple. "Just a good time."

I knew that badgering him wouldn't get me the answer, so I'd have to resort to other means. Duke probably knew, which meant Serena knew.

He pulled me down onto him for a nice hug. "I think you'll have a good time. Dinner with people supporting you, what could be better?"

"Not having a party for the sole purpose of reminding me I'm getting older would be better."

"You're only getting better, and think of it as a celebration of having survived shootings and kidnappings."

What was I supposed to say to a line like that?

~

WHEN DINNERTIME ARRIVED, I ZIPPED UP THE LEATHER MOTORCYCLE JACKET
Terry had bought me. "You know, I think this jacket is a good enough birthday present."

Terry grunted as he slid into his. "I think you deserve more special things." He was taking this birthday thing way more seriously than I wanted.

I cringed, realizing that *things* was the first solid clue I'd managed to get out of him. "Are you going to tell me now where it is?"

"You'll see when we get there," he answered in my helmet.

Serena had told me to expect Terry's Hawk friends, but even she had clammed up when I asked her for more details.

Terry lifted his leg over the big bike and flipped up the kickstand.

I grabbed his arm as he helped me up and onto the tiny sliver of cushion behind him. Without a backrest, I would be dumped off the bike in an instant if I didn't wrap myself tightly around him.

Terry started the beast and raised the garage door. We left the building sedately for once. Maybe that was one of my birthday presents.

Three blocks later, we stopped when the light ahead turned red. We were in the center of three lanes when a big bearded, heavily tatted biker pulled alongside on a louder-than-shit Harley.

The woman behind him on the bike sneered at me.

Big Beard revved his engine several times, looking over at Terry.

"The idiot wants to race," Terry said inside my helmet. "Should we embarrass him in front of his old lady?"

The other woman stuck her tongue out at me.

That was that. "Shit ya.'

"Hold on tight."

Big Beard revved his motor several more times.

When the light flashed green, we launched forward. A few seconds later, Terry let off the throttle.

When I looked back, we were way ahead of the Harley and I waved.

I lost track of the route, but recognized the restaurant we parked near. It was Cardinelli's, the place where I'd been attacked that first night, the place where everything between us had changed. We were coming full circle.

Constance and Winston greeted us out front, and we were escorted to one of the private rooms off the side.

"There's the birthday girl," Duke's voice boomed in the space as Serena rushed to hug me followed by her bear of a man and Terry's sister, Deb.

"I tried to keep it from being all Hawk people, so I invited Marci,

Peyton, and Paul from your work," Serena said. "But Paul and Marci both had family things going on." She shrugged her shoulders. "I tried."

"No problem." I hadn't considered inviting anyone from work, thinking it seemed odd for a party with gifts.

Lucas, Jordy, and Hawk's mechanic, Joe, arrived in a group, each granting me hugs and happy birthday wishes,

Jordy offered a jelly bean.

Nervous as all hell, I took and started to chew. The hell with tooth decay.

Peyton arrived at about the same time as Zane, not surprisingly, and Paul a short time later.

I was surprised when Terry introduced me a little later to Lieutenant Marcus Wellbourne of the LAPD.

"Sorry to hear about your cousin," the cop said.

"Thank you," I answered. "He finally found trouble he couldn't out run." It was an answer I could deliver without giving anything away.

Terry's face was deadpan. At least he didn't make a sick joke about him.

"Does she know?" Jordy asked Constance.

Winston quickly punched him in the shoulder.

Jordy rubbed it.

I moved closer to Constance. "Know what?"

Constance's eyes darted to Winston. "What you're having for dinner, I think?"

Something was definitely going on. I pivoted to Serena. "Know what?"

"How good the fettuccini is here," she said like a practiced liar.

After trying Winston and getting an equally stupid answer, I gave up.

Dinner was fantastic, with great food, and good company. Although the table with the presents on it haunted me during the meal. I'd never been a good gift receiver.

We were almost done when the lieutenant leaned over to Lucas. "I thought you should know that the organized crime unit has news."

Lucas looked up from his fish. "Okay?"

"Tony Russo died two days ago," the cop said.

Conversation around us stopped.

Lucas was now laser-focused on Wellbourne. "How?"

"We don't have an autopsy yet, but the doctor at the hospital said it looked like a poisoning."

Lucas nodded. "Sometimes it can be dangerous to be the king. Any idea who is in line to take over after he sent his son back to Italy?"

"The son, Victor Russo, came back to our fair city two days before the old man croaked and yesterday, he installed himself as the head of the family."

"Convenient timing," Winston said with a huff.

"I just thought you'd want to know," Wellbourne added.

Lucas shook his head, his countenance darkening. "Thanks."

Terry joined the headshakers.

"That's not good," Duke said.

I leaned into Terry. "Why?"

"Because it was a complaint from us that got Victor punished by the old man. These guys can have a long memory."

Lucas obviously heard Terry's comments. "At least for a while, he'll have his hands full getting control of the organization."

To me, that didn't sound very reassuring. "Do you think Victor killed his father?" I asked Wellbourne.

The cop twisted his water glass. "Nobody's talking. Even if the autopsy indicates poisoning, there's no way we'll get any information out of them to prosecute anybody in either the organization or the household."

After dessert and coffee, I was ready for a nap. "Can we lie on the beach for a bit while I digest all this food?"

"You're the birthday girl, you get whatever you want."

"Really?" I whispered into his ear exactly the naughty thing I wanted when we got back home.

An honest to God blush came over my man as he smiled.

"Happy birthday to you..." Serena started the birthday song, with everyone joining in as a server carried a large chocolate cake to my place with a lit candle on top.

"You have to make a wish," Serena reminded me after the song finished.

I blew the candle out with a quick puff. After the last few days, my wish, of course, was for some peace and quiet.

The cake was delicious, and I ate as slowly as I could to put off the inevitable.

"Come on," Serena urged me. As soon as my fork hit the table, she took over, bringing me the first two presents to open. Of course they were from Duke and her.

I opened Serena's first. "Wow." I hugged her for the set of silk pajamas that I'd have to wait until Terry's out-of-town assignment to have a chance to wear.

"So cool," I exclaimed when I opened Duke's to find tickets for two to Disneyland. "I've never been."

"A little birdie mentioned that," Duke said.

It continued with me opening present after present.

Constance got me a spa day certificate.

Cool candlesticks with a base of a cat jumping for a ball came from Peyton.

"Yes, I'll go with you," Terry assured me when Winston's present was shooting lessons.

Lucas was very uncomfortable accepting my hug when I opened his and found a certificate for a week in Hawaii, of all things. "You're part of the family," was his explanation.

Old Joe's box was the biggest and contained a cat tree. Clyde would probably love it.

It seemed everybody knew of my fondness for cats. Lieutenant Wellbourne's box contained a set of cat coffee mugs.

Peyton gave Zane the side-eye when the envelope from him contained a gift certificate for Victoria's Secret.

"What?" he complained. "Every girl should pamper herself with nice lingerie."

I wasn't complaining, but Peyton rolled her eyes.

"How are we doing on timing?" Terry asked Lucas.

The boss man checked his phone. "Right on schedule."

I put the gift certificate in my pile. "What?"

Terry ignored me, and Serena put another box in front of me.

This one was from Jordy. I rattled it.

"I heard you had a sleep problem," Jordy said as I pulled the wrapping off. "Keep it upright and open it from the top," he added, pulling out his phone.

"Probably a pillow," Winston guessed.

"Or sleep socks," Duke tried.

"Definitely bigger," Joe argued. "Probably like a comforter or something."

I jumped back when I opened the top and a shrill squawk came from the box.

"It's alive," Serena squealed.

"Quick, shoot it," Lucas ordered.

Everybody laughed, obviously in on whatever the joke was.

Cautiously, I approached the box again and pulled back the crumpled paper on top. Beady eyes looked back at me when it squawked again. This time, I caught Jordy fingering his phone. It looked so real.

"The battery should be good for a few months," the tech guru said. "It's a red-tail."

I pulled the big hawk model from the box. It was covered in feathers.

The head rotated left and right, and the beak opened when it squawked again.

Jordy held up his phone. "You can control it from your phone, and it's guaranteed to scare the shit out of any songbirds in the area."

I rushed to hug the nerd. "This is so cool."

"Now you can fix the problem," Terry said. "And we can still have fresh air."

I hugged Jordy a second time. "I can't thank you enough."

"It was Lucas's idea," he told me. How many people knew about our sleeping issues?

"And I saved the best for last," Serena announced as she plopped the last box in front of me. The card said it was from Terry. Of course, I'd only seen him put a card on the table of presents when we came in.

Impatiently, I tore the paper off and opened the box. Inside was another box. "Like nested Russian dolls?" I asked.

Terry shrugged.

Inside the second box, I found a third, and then a fourth, which was now small. "How many more to go?"

Terry shrugged again. "Close your eyes while you open it." That was ominous.

I sent him a grimace. He was probably out to embarrass me.

"I'll help," Serena offered. "Close your eyes. She took the box when I closed my eyes.

"Holy shit," I exclaimed when I opened my eyes.

Terry was next to me instead of Serena, holding a small velvet box, and worst of all, he was on one knee.

"Grace, I know you've hated me much longer than liked me."

I swallowed hard, looking through my tears of joy at the diamond ring and the man who loved me.

"But," he continued. "I can't see any future for me that doesn't include you in my life. I can't breathe without thinking of you."

I sniffled, feeling the same way.

"If you think it's too soon, you can say so, and I'll understand. But know that you'll only be putting off the inevitable. I may not be the smartest man alive, but I know that you were meant for me, and I for you. I promise to forever—"

"Stop already," I sobbed out.

His face fell.

"How can I answer if you don't ask me the damned question?"

His smile returned. "Grace Erin Brennan, will you marry me?"

"Sure as shit yes." I offered him my hand.

Applause erupted as he slipped the diamond solitaire on my finger. What followed were dozens of smiles, hugs, and congratulations.

Terry whispered in my ear. "You'll be a wonderful mother."

It should have scared me, but for some reason, picturing my belly swollen with Terry's and my child warmed my heart.

The money Terry got for the reward had stabilized my business. My life had been completely turned around. In the last few weeks, I survived car chases, gun battles, kidnappings, and found a happiness with Terry that I hadn't known existed. As I stood hand in hand with my love, I couldn't imagine anything better.

Lucas tapped his watch.

Terry leaned over. "You have one more present."

I hugged his arm. "You've given me enough already."

"No," he insisted. "The best one yet is coming soon." He pointed at the door.

A few people nearby turned.

I swung my eyes that way. "What?"

Terry moved behind me, putting his hands over my eyes. "Patience, woman. It's supposed to be a surprise."

"I'm not twelve."

He gripped me tighter when I fidgeted.

"Very soon," Lucas said.

None of this made sense.

I heard gasps, a few "holy shits", and clapping before Terry let me look. The sight took my breath away. It wasn't possible.

Pete walked in. It was a miracle. He was alive—much thinner than he had been, and he had a scar on his cheek, but my brother was alive.

Hoping I wasn't hallucinating, I ran to him with happy tears in my eyes. I crashed into him and gave him the strongest hug I could manage. My heart was beating so fast I could barely get the words out. "They told me you died." I wiped at my tears.

"Omega got me out."

Terry was right. This was the best present anyone could ever hope for.

∞

TERRY

TWO DAYS AGO, LUCAS HAD PASSED ALONG THE GOOD NEWS THAT AN OMEGA team had rescued my best friend, and now soon-to-be brother-in-law, Pete.

Lucas was one of the few people who could call the secretary of defense to get a delay in the normal debrief scheduled after a hostage was released or rescued. SECDEF even sent his own plane to give Petet a ride back here from Ramstein after his medical eval.

Seeing Pete walk in and the joy on Grace's face was now the second-best moment of my entire life, just after the moment tonight that Grace had agreed to become my wife.

Grace's tears were still flowing when she finally let Pete loose to be welcomed back by the crowd.

I held back to give the others a chance to hug it out with him.

He'd survived what were certainly unbelievably horrible conditions in Syria.

The important thing was that Grace had her brother back—alive. Today rocked.

Grace made her way back to me. "Why didn't you tell me?" she half screamed in my face.

I'd rehearsed this one and it was the honest truth. "After seeing how it tore you up to hear he was KIA, I couldn't put you through that a second time if I told you he might be extracted and then didn't make it."

"But you should have—"

I shut her up with a kiss.

She speared her fingers into my hair, wrapped her legs around me, and gave herself over to the kiss and then some.

I finally let her lips loose after a wolf whistle from someone. "Forgive me?"

She nodded as loving eyes held mine. "I guess. The ring is nice, and beating you up is probably a bad way to start our engagement."

Letting her down, I stroked the loose hair behind her ear. "I love you, Kitten." She was special.

"Love ya back, big guy."

Suddenly, someone yanked me back. A hard fist struck me in the kidney. Staggering forward, the attacker kicked the back of my leg, sending me down to my knees. Then strong arms wrapped me up in a headlock. "You asshole." It was Pete.

I scratched and pulled at the arm around my neck to no effect. This guy knew his stuff.

"You promised to keep her safe."

"Let him go," Grace screeched.

I couldn't breathe, and swinging an elbow didn't get me anywhere.

"Lucas told me she'd been attacked. And you thought you'd move in on my little sister when she was vulnerable? I should end you right here, right now." He tightened the hold and my vision blurred.

On my knees and unarmed, I was helpless with no leverage.

"Let him go," Grace screamed. "I'm marrying him."

Her words made Pete loosen up enough that I didn't black out. "What?"

"I love him," Serena said more calmly now. "And I'm marrying him whether you like it or not."

Coughing, I fell forward when Pete released me. I stood as soon as I could and spun to face the angry bull.

Pete pointed an angry finger my way. "You… you promised—"

Grace got between us and faced off with her brother. "You apologize right the fuck now. I'd be dead if it wasn't for Terry."

Lucas stepped forward. "It's true."

Pete's gaze swung from Grace to Lucas and back again. "You can't marry him."

"You don't get a freaking vote." My wonderful woman let him have it with both barrels. She shoved the ring at him. "I'm marrying him and if you don't apologize this minute, you're not invited to the wedding."

Pete took a long, labored breath.

"And I'll never talk to you again," she threatened. Her tone was icy.

Pete straightened then walked around her to me, extending his hand. "Sorry."

"Like you mean it," Grace snarled.

I shook with him. "I'll take care of her."

Pete grimaced. "You fucking better."

She cuddled up next to me. We'd both survived—her, the Russo and Marku attacks, and me, her brother's rage.

"Hey, guys?"

We turned to find Serena standing on a chair. "It's time for pool and darts at Tito's."

"Eight ball in the corner pocket," Lucas announced.

He had challenged me to another round of pool at Tito's after the mechanical bull riding competition that Duke and Serena had won. We'd been here a while, and after several beers, I wasn't lining up my shots as cleanly as I should be.

"I'm going to meet with this Sinclair guy tomorrow. Are you sure he's real?"

"Positive." I couldn't get a read on whether Lucas was happy to learn he had a cousin that none of the family had known about or not.

Yates Sinclair was the man Lucas's mother, Carol, had asked me to check out. The one she'd been contacted about as a familial DNA match. I'd met with Sinclair and confirmed enough details to satisfy me that he was the son of Carol's lost sister, Wilma.

"You better be right," he said as he sank the ball. Of course, Lucas made the remaining shots and beat me. Smiling, he collected my twenty bucks. "A rematch?"

"No thanks." I was a decent player when I hadn't been drinking, but I knew when to quit.

"You sure?"

I knew better than to fall for that. "Maybe you should try darts against my fiancée."

Lucas laughed. "Hard pass. I know my limitations."

When Grace peeled herself away from Serena, her eyes connected with mine. The jolt her smile sent through me was as strong as it ever had been. I joined her in a dozen determined steps. "I missed you."

"You're the one who accepted Lucas's challenge."

"True." I swept her up for a steamy kiss.

"I missed you too," she said breathlessly when I set her down. She then cocked her head in the direction of Zane and whispered in my ear. "Have you noticed?"

I nodded and answered equally softly. "You mean Peyton?"

"Yeah."

Just to be safe, I wanted to keep someone at Grace's work last week while I was on assignment. Zane had jumped at the opportunity, and it became pretty obvious that the pretty Peyton was the reason.

"Do you want me to tell him to back off?" I asked.

"Of course not. She's a big girl. She can make up her own mind if he ever makes a move."

Their chemistry had been obvious to all this evening.

It was only about ten minutes later that Peyton wandered over. "I've got to call it a night." She took Grace's hand. "I'm so happy for you guys."

"Thanks for coming," Grace answered, hugging her. "And thank you for the lovely candlesticks."

She continued her goodbyes and left.

I didn't say anything when I noticed Zane exit shortly after she did.

The shout came from the door a few minutes later. "Call an ambulance." It was Zane, and he was carrying a limp Peyton in.

"You call," I told Grace as I rushed to the door.

Lucas beat me there. "What happened?"

"She got mugged," Zane said as he set her gently down.

Peyton moaned. "Let me go."

"Where?" I demanded.

"At the bank machine across the street."

With plenty of people huddled around the pair, I bolted for the door. Outside, I scanned the street, but couldn't see anybody in either direction. The asshole or assholes had gotten away, so I went back inside.

"No," Peyton complained. She was sitting up now. "I'll be fine."

"I called the cops," Serena said.

"No cops," Peyton said louder than I thought necessary. She stood up. "It was only forty bucks."

"And your watch," Zane argued. He was animated as well.

Her wrist was missing the Rolex she normally wore.

"It was a knockoff." Peyton pulled her arm loose. "I'm going home."

Zane followed her. "You should go to the hospital and get checked."

She threw up a middle finger and stomped to the door.

"Look after her," Lucas ordered.

Zane followed her out of the bar.

My woman wrapped an arm around my waist. "Maybe you should help. I'm worried about her."

"Zane's worried enough for both of us."

"Something's wrong," Grace said. "That watch wasn't a knockoff." She'd noticed it too.

With the commotion over, the bar quickly went back to its rowdy self. I tensed when Pete started our way.

His demeanor had softened. "Hey, man. I'm sorry about before." He looked down and took in a labored breath. "She's my baby sister. I just lost it."

"Forget it." I'd expected him to have a hard time accepting anybody being with his little sister and I damned sure wasn't going to tell him she wasn't a baby anymore.

"No, I mean it. Lucas and Duke filled me in, and I can't thank you enough for what you did to keep her safe."

I nodded. "She's special."

He waved a finger at me. "Don't you dare hurt her."

"Not a chance, brother. She's it for me." I expected the warning. We were friends, but she was his blood. "You look pretty good for what you've been through."

He had a scar on his face and wasn't as buff as when he'd left, but he wasn't as emaciated as the average rescued hostage. "They were negotiating to trade me for Al-Hamadi and joked that a skinny goat doesn't bring a good price."

Al-Hamadi was a leader of the terrorist cell that the US captured last year.

"Want to hit the range next week and see how badly you can lose to me?"

When he accepted, I knew I had my friend back.

Grace waved me over.

"Anyway," Pete said. "I gotta say I'm glad she chose somebody honorable. Semper Fi, man." He gave me a one-armed hug.

I bro-hugged him back. "Semper Fi." As Marines, we knew honor came above all else. Most important, I had my best friend back in one piece.

Grace arrived to pull us apart. "Give me back my man."

Duke called out Pete's name for a game of pool and he left.

She rose up on her toes to whisper in my ear, which probably wasn't necessary with all the noise in the bar. "I think it's time you took me home."

"Not before I beat you at a game of darts."

"Dream on, big guy."

Printed in Great Britain
by Amazon